PEARL'S PROGRESS

PEARL'S PROGRESS

James Kaplan

ALFRED A. KNOPF   NEW YORK

1989

THIS IS A BORZOI BOOK
PUBLISHED BY ALFRED A. KNOPF, INC.

Copyright © 1989 by James Kaplan
All rights reserved under International and Pan-American Copy-
right Conventions. Published in the United States by Alfred A.
Knopf, Inc., New York, and simultaneously in Canada by Random
House of Canada Limited, Toronto. Distributed by Random
House, Inc., New York.

Owing to limitations of space, all acknowledgments for permission to reprint previously published material may be found on
page 307.

Library of Congress Cataloging-in-Publication Data
Kaplan, James.
Pearl's progress.
I. Title.
PS3561.A559P44   1989   813'.54   88-45440
ISBN 0-394-50093-8

Manufactured in the United States of America
First Edition

*This is a work of fiction. All names, characters, and
events, except for certain incidental references, are
products of my imagination and do not refer to or portray
any actual persons or events. Likewise, the geography
herein is imaginary. A few of the places referred to may
be found in the actual state of Mississippi, but for the most
part the cities, towns, streets, and roads depicted exist—
apart from coincidences—only in the novel. There really
is a U.S. Highway 88 in Mississippi, for example,
but it does not go where mine goes.*
—J.K.

FOR KAREN AND JACOB

The great interests of man: air and light, the joy of having a body, the voluptuousness of looking.
—Mario Rossi

And you may find yourself
living in a shotgun shack,
And you may find yourself
in another part of the world,
And you may find yourself
behind the wheel of a large automobile . . .
And you may ask yourself,
"Well, how did I get here?"
—David Byrne, *Once in a Lifetime*

The heart is half a prophet.
—Yiddish proverb

BOOK I

I

Within one hour of arriving in Pickett, Philip Pearl almost broke
his neck. That, he later thought, would have been rich. He had
spent the day as he had spent the day before—driving, driving,
driving, pointing the overloaded old battleship-gray Volvo south
and west through state after state into which he had never before
set foot: Maryland, West Virginia, Tennessee, Alabama. It was
like losing your virginity over and over, this continual crossing
of fresh borderlines.

Alabama was huge, like a country itself. And it was here
that Pearl, slow learner that he was, first sensed something was
Up. Nothing special happened; he simply walked into a Burger
King and ordered a burger and a cup of coffee—a stop like so
many of the other stops he had made. He sat down with his
food, his head still thrumming from the road, and looked around.
The place was nearly empty. A boy in a red-and-white Burger
King outfit and a white paper hat mopped the floor. Two women,
one carrying a baby, walked in and sat in the booth next to
Pearl's. He stared at them, first unseeing, then seeing: something
in his brain clicked and shifted. What was it about them? Their

hair piled up in a certain way, the thinness of their arms, paleness of their skin, their high cheekbones, their teeth, their voices. Those voices! What was the origin of all this? Pearl thought for a moment. Scotch-English-Irish. The slow transformation, over time and the ocean, of accents. The music of the talk, the cheekbones and teeth, the pallid eyes persisted. Who could say that these two women were not the very image of some Liverpool sea captain's wife and sister-in-law, two centuries dead? Oh, but those voices. Pearl's ears pricked at the new music. The women lit cigarettes. The mother gave her baby a sip of Coke. And, just like that, Pearl realized he had left his orbit, was in fact far, far beyond it.

Twenty miles later, in Birmingham, the temperature on the electric bank signs read a hundred and two. Gigantic thunderheads reared up in the hazy sky. It was late August. The highway went through instead of around the city; there were at least fifteen traffic lights, and Pearl caught every one. He would throw the ancient Volvo into neutral and gun the engine, but the temperature needle would creep to the right, into the red, and the car would buck and shudder as if in sexual transport. Later Pearl would discover that his engine had been badly in need of a tuning, the oil, gas, and air filters completely gummed up. And what if he had known? He was all but flat broke, down to his last forty-three dollars. He was heading south toward his first paycheck in more than a year. The car stalled three times, and three times, magical number, Pearl was able to revive it, though honking lines formed behind him, though his burgundy Lacoste shirt soaked through, wine-dark. "Come on, baby, oh come on, oh fuck you, *come* on," Pearl growled through clenched teeth, and somehow his car shook back to life. This was at noon. He wanted to reach Pickett by nightfall, had even, as an act of faith, made a reservation at the Holiday Inn.

Once the superhighway picked up again the Volvo was fine, and the ferociously hot air, rocketing through the windows at sixty miles an hour, felt almost temperate. Pearl sang, loud, every song he could think of. For company, he had, on the seat next to him, his stereo turntable and piles of shirts and sweaters. In the passenger's footwell sat a stack of records and two potted spider plants. The back seat was so full that it was impossible to see out the rear window. He changed lanes with his fingers crossed. The car was like a space capsule, completely packed except for Pearl. It was a little lonely traveling this way, but the pain was somehow pleasant. He was embarked on a great adventure. He sang until he got hoarse. *Que sera, sera!*

Western Alabama, though, was difficult. The superhighway vanished once again, and Pearl traveled on old two-lane blacktop, the colossal disk of the setting sun directly in his eyes. He drove more by touch than by sight: oncoming trucks made him stiffen with fear. The miles went slowly. He was passing through ancient tiny impoverished towns, flat, red-clayey, piney country, which in the orange light made him ache with an almost unbearable nostalgia. He was eleven years old again, at Scout camp, home unimaginably far away. His eyes smarted. But there was more to it than homesickness: the hot sweet dusk air shooting in the windows seemed redolent of a lost age, a time and place that Pearl, Manhattanite, had never known yet seemed to know deeply. The shotgun shacks and rusting soda signs, palmettos, slow dogs. This was a past that he recognized from the movies— but an actual breath of it, a *revenant*. The gaps in the otherwise seamless interstate highway system could still, at this late date, refute the system itself and hint at something lost and magnificent. The country had had character once. It had had size. Pearl actually seemed to remember this. Where had it gone?

Then the sun was down, the orange light gone, and Pearl was left with only the narrow road itself, the hurtling oncoming trucks with their too-high headlights and concussive air pockets. But soon, miraculously, just like that, the road jogged right, jogged left, and hooked up once more with the present. The fact was heralded by a big green sign, that universal American-highway-sign green, emeraldy, lovely, as lulling as TV. One can take only so much character, Pearl thought. It was exhausting to wonder again and again whether the next tractor-trailer had your number on it.

Pearl realized he'd been dead silent for the past hour—partly out of awe at the anachronistic landscape and partly because his voice was shot. He considered singing again, but this seemed too much like whistling in the dark. The air had cooled dramatically. He bent his neck down and peered up through the top of the windshield. There were stars out. Stars over Alabama. Just then, however, another big green sign loomed into his headlights and told Pearl that he was entering Mississippi.

He had somehow, crazily, identified his destination with the state itself. It hit Pearl now that he still had quite a way to drive—he didn't even want to think how far. His estimated time of arrival, plotted optimistically that morning on the Exxon map, was already long past. He had, he realized with horror, something like the distance between New York and Boston—almost the entire length of the state—to go before he could sleep. He yawned, passionately, helplessly. When would he ever learn?

The Volvo plunged on through the night, now heading due south. Pearl squinted out the window, trying to get a fix on the countryside he was passing through, but it was too dark to see. There were no lights, no billboards, no gas stations—nothing. There weren't even any other cars on the road. He seemed suddenly to have passed into Nowhere. Didn't the interstate guarantee service stations at regular intervals? Pearl glanced nervously at his gas gauge: half a tank. How long could that last? He eased off the pedal—in his fear, he had accelerated up to seventy. Now he held at fifty-five. It felt like a crawl. The choice appeared to be between getting nowhere fast and driving all night. The tenth-miles on the odometer moved mesmerizingly slowly.

Pearl turned on the radio. He half expected hillbilly music and twanging voices, but on FM there was dead silence. Across the entire band, as a matter of fact, he could raise nothing but one easy-listening station. AM was crowded and noisy, but most of the noise was static, and the few voices he heard were without character. He found a news show and listened to it for ten minutes, needing badly, for some reason, to know exactly where it was coming from. The announcer's voice was accentless. Pearl heard national and local news, commercials with street names—even, finally, call letters—but no town was mentioned. He twiddled the dial nervously. The profusion of signals spoke of a nighttime land that was provincial and cozy, with everything in its place but Pearl. He felt as if he were drifting through deep space, exiled, far from earth, picking up faint terrestrial static, imagining the smell of grass. Perversely, he tuned the radio to 770 AM. If he really had left his orbit, he wanted proof. This was the spot on the dial that his deepest consciousness, his metropolitan race-memory, thought of as 77 WABC: fast music, fast-talking announcers in echo chambers, pimple commercials. The lodestone, the North Star, the ground tone of the universe. Pearl had never liked the station much, but it had always *been* there. Its huge signal was rumored to have been picked up in Canada, and even, on nights when odd meteorological conditions were in effect along the Eastern seaboard, in Florida. Within fifty miles of Manhattan, you had to turn down the volume when you tuned anywhere near it. But this was *thirteen hundred* miles from New York, for God's sake. He had *left*. You couldn't shoot into the city for the weekend from here. All at once Pearl felt desperate.

Of course 770 AM was as empty-full as the rest of the band, a little cacophonous district of bleeps and static and drifting disembodied voices. Nevertheless, Pearl bent over the dial, fiddling, searching. Why not? Nobody else was on the highway: he barely had to watch the road. He heard familiar music!—lost it, tuned back through and past it, then into it once more. The signal just held, wavily. Pearl recognized the song: the moronic thing had been number one all summer. Too depressed to change the station, he had awakened to this song practically every morning in the caretaker's cottage where he had lived in upstate New York. "Blooer than *bloo*, sadder than *sad . . .*" the singer crooned. It had seemed apt, and wretched, enough. Hearing it now, however, Pearl felt an unexpected start of nostalgia. Perhaps it wasn't such a bad song after all. Before he could consider the matter further, there was a chime, and a fast, skillful, insinuating voice, the very voice of civilization, of all he had left behind. "Ronnn Lundy!" a little chorus sang. Pearl had gooseflesh, his neck hair stood on end in primitive defense. *This wasn't physically possible.* Was it? His mind raced, searching for explanations. What about what's-his-name, he thought—the one who'd sailed the Atlantic alone. Chichester. He had had extremely realistic hallucinations—sprites leaning against the mast, making sensible and entertaining conversation. Or was it diabolic conversation that they had made? Pearl bent even closer to the speaker, one eye on the yellow cone of his headlights. Lundy gabbled on for a few seconds, mentioning a time and temperature (one hour later, ten degrees cooler) appropriate enough to the lost world, saying precisely what he would have said had Pearl tuned him in somewhere outside of Hackensack—until a rising wave of white noise drowned the signal for good, and no twiddling of the dial could restore it.

It was past midnight when Pearl pulled into the front drive of the Pickett Holiday Inn. He had been on the road since seven that morning, in the middle of Virginia. He left the Volvo running, lest it refuse ever to start again, and ran into the lobby.

The desk clerk, a gangly, oddly pious-looking young man, stood with his hands spread on the counter—as if it were a pulpit, Pearl thought.

"Can I hep you, sir?" he asked.

Pearl told him his name and mentioned that he had a reservation. The clerk smiled unreassuringly and began to pull cards from a rack on the wall. He stared at one for a moment, frowned, replaced it. He began to leaf through a ledger.

"That's Pearl," Pearl said. "P-E-A-R-L. Philip."

"Yessir? I'm sorry, sir, but I'm not findin' it."

"But I put down a deposit. Last night, in Newcastle, Virginia."

The clerk shook his head wide-eyed at the unimaginable remove.

"Wait," Pearl said. "Wait. One second." He pushed back out through the two sets of glass doors, into the tropical night. His heart gave a surprised little jump at the sight of his car, its headlights and grille facelike and friendly, waiting faithfully at the curb. Panting. There was a pile of papers in the receptacle between the front seats: orderly Pearl had thrown away nothing. He shuffled through the papers with thick fingers. Yellow. Yellow. He had it.

"Here," he told the clerk triumphantly.

The young man read it for what seemed like a full minute. "Yessir," he said. "We'll be glad to refund your deposit for you."

"A room," Pearl said. "I just want a room."

"I'll check awn that for you," the clerk said brightly.

Lost as he was to exhaustion, to irritation, Pearl now flared his nostrils. He detected an odor, something strange and acrid just above the standard-issue Holiday Inn bouquet. It smelled like creosote, or burning rubber.

"Yessir," the clerk said. "We do have a room, but it isn't poosod."

"Pardon?"

"Poosod should be openin' up tomorrow, though."

"Poosod?"

"Yessir? By the poo?"

"But you do have a room?"

"Yessir?"

"May I have the key?"

"Yessir?"

The Volvo's throbbing engine now seemed to have developed a cough. Alarmed, Pearl saw that the temperature gauge was well into the red. "Easy, sweetie," he told the car, which was beginning to buck. Pearl pulled around to the back of the motel, where, with one last fitful sputter, his car gave up the ghost. In eerie silence, Pearl glided, on momentum alone, into a parking space.

He stood in a dimly mercury vapor–lit rear parking lot bordered behind by strange, black, spiky vegetation. The night was silent but for the low roar of motel air conditioners and the loud ratchet of jungle bugs. Pearl's ears hummed. He glanced at his key: his room was upstairs, on the balcony. What if instead of taking the easy, familiar route to the wide, soft bed, air conditioner, Bible, shower, color TV on a stand—what if instead he were to claw his way into those strange black bushes and collapse on the ground, taking his chances with whatever lurked there? He had been alone with his thoughts too long, he realized; his own temperature gauge was in the red. He badly needed sleep, if his body would let him have it.

Then he had an inspiration. First he would go for a swim. Never had anybody deserved one more. The thought made him smile as he opened the Volvo's dented trunk. But which bag was his bathing suit in? The unwanted complication brought tears to his eyes. He had packed in another lifetime. The suitcase on top felt as though it were filled with lead, with thousands of those little lead fishing weights. Pearl wrestled it up the concrete steps and down the balcony to his curtained cubicle.

The key worked. Why did this seem miraculous? The air that emerged was stale and slightly rank, as if lichens were growing within. Pearl reached behind the drapes for the light switch and hit it on the button. No surprises. Hadn't that once been their slogan? The beds looked like fields of lilies. He refrained, however, from hurling himself down. He turned on the air conditioner, high, slung the huge suitcase onto the nearer bed and clicked it open. His swimsuit sat right on top. Like a fair omen of things to come. Pearl changed where he stood, dropping his travel clothes in a moist pile around his feet. Then he took a stiff folded towel from the clip over the sink, grabbed his key, and padded barefoot down the cool concrete steps, through a breezeway, past a soda machine—a soda machine oddly humanoid in its proportions, not at all unkind in aspect; a soda machine with which one might conceivably hold a civilized discourse—and emerged in the central courtyard.

Although it was well past midnight, several small children were playing in and around the pool. Their corresponding adults lay nearby in chaises, chatting. The pool, lit underwater, glowed like a rare gem—like turquoise, like tourmaline. Pearl saw the pool through a kind of haze. He would fall in, he imagined, the way he had once, in an old movie, seen Frankenstein's monster fall—stiff, arms at his sides, as if ossified. He eagerly anticipated the coolness of the water on his limbs. Even at twelve thirty, it must have been eighty degrees, with humidity correspondingly high. The air felt like a shroud.

Pearl carefully placed his towel and eyeglasses on a chaise. He had certain rules for avoiding low comedy: one must never put one's glasses anyplace that might conceivably be used for sitting. But this was a night for breaking rules. The children, laughing and splashing and jumping, drove the precious green-blue water into choppy little waves that gaily refracted the pool lights. Now that his glasses were off, these dancing lights looked magical. A white cord separated the pool into halves, and the children were making a game of racing back and forth under it. Pearl waited patiently till they were out of the way, then dove.

His head and right shoulder hit the floor of the pool the instant after the instant he entered the water, a quick one-two count. He lay on the bottom for a moment. I'm dead, he thought in the green silence. Then realized that he was thinking it. He stood up into air and sound (the children were shouting with laughter—at something else?) in water that came only as high as his waist. Pearl climbed out and put his glasses on with shaking hands.

The adults lay in their chaises, chatting as though nothing had happened; the children swam back and forth. Exactly as it had been before he'd arrived. As if he had never existed. Had he, perhaps, really died? If this were a movie, Pearl thought, he would now see his own lifeless body on the bottom of the pool; the children would scream; the adults would scurry. He shook his head. His right temple and shoulder ached. He felt for blood. There was none. He began to shiver. He was alive—more alive, strangely enough, than he had felt for some time. As if he had just awakened from a long sleep. Shivering quite violently now, he wrapped the stiff towel around his shoulders and walked back to his room.

II

The number rang four, five, six times. Squeaky clean from his morning shower, Pearl sat on the edge of the bed, phone receiver in hand, lips compressed with disappointment. He had been bursting with his news; now it would have to wait.

But then there was a click. A deep voice: "Yellow."

"Walter?"

"Yup."

"Walter, this is Phil Pearl. I'm here."

Here! He was barely able to keep from shouting it. The word was spoken as much for his own sake as for Wunsch's—there was even a sense, Pearl thought, in which he hadn't *been* here until this moment. Here and now, he thought happily. It had never been his forte, here-and-now. Suddenly he could think of nothing else. At the same time he was aware of a strong need to please. *Reporting for duty*, he all but said to Wunsch.

"What"—there followed a longish pause—"time is it."

"Shit. I woke you."

"Thass all right, Philly. Perfly O.K."

"Why don't I just call back in a couple of—"

"Philly?"

"Walter?"

"Talk to me a minute. Tell me how you're doin'."

"I'm fine. As a matter of fact, I—" Pearl stopped himself. He had been about to tell Wunsch what had happened at the pool last night, had been on the verge of relating it as an amusing anecdote. What was so amusing about it? He tended, he knew, to tell people too much. But something else, too, stopped him. "I'm fine," he repeated.

Silence at the other end.

"I just thought you might like to have some lunch later on, or something," Pearl said.

"Lunch?" rumbled Wunsch. As if it were an exotic new concept.

"I thought maybe we could go out someplace and grab a bite."

"Out someplace. Where would we go?"

The line of conversation suddenly felt all too familiar to Pearl: as if a curtain or heavy drape had fallen on the proceedings. "Oh, you know," he said. "A restaurant? Something like that?"

Wunsch let out a hoarse cavernous laugh that ended in a spasm of smoker's cough. " 'Scuse me," he croaked, and began to laugh again. After a while, he said, "Phil?"

"Walter?"

"Why don't you just mosey on over to my place 'round twelve or so. 'Kay?"

Pearl was silent for a moment, his mind elsewhere.

"Phil?"

"Yeah."

"You there?"

Strange, Pearl was thinking, to find the all-too-familiar in a brand-new place.

Almost brand-new. For he had been here once before.

*   *   *

It had been three weeks earlier, when the school had flown him in for his interview. The trip had begun as a lark—Mississippi?! Pearl liked going places for free. But sometime after he'd changed planes in Atlanta, he had found his heart inexplicably in his throat. *Why so nervous?* he kept asking himself. And then, there was his answer, as plain as the nose on his face (very plain): as usual, he was fooling himself. If he didn't take (if he didn't *get*) this job—the only job he had applied for, just to make matters thoroughly idiotic—what was he going to do? Spend another winter alone in Delbertsville? It was simply out of the question. And what was the Pickett State University English department doing interviewing for a fall opening in August? It was probably better not to think about it. Pearl sat miserably in his window seat on the little Southern Air 727, twirling the ice in his plastic glass, staring at the pure high-altitude light on his sandwich tray, trying to imagine ways to slow his heart. There didn't appear to be any. The problem intensified as the plane landed, and by the time Pearl stood in the tiny terminal, suitcase at his side, looking for someone looking for him, he wondered if he would be able to speak—if he would even be able to make sounds come out—when Walter Wunsch showed up.

Wunsch, until this point, had been a disembodied telephone voice. Albeit a remarkable one. Even in his misery, Pearl felt curious to see what the owner of such a voice might look like. Over the phone, Wunsch spoke in tones as low as the crypt and in monosyllables, a peculiar halting diction reminiscent of David Brinkley. When he had first called to try to interest Pearl in the job (assistant professor of English, fourteen thousand per), Pearl had been a bit put off. Wunsch had sounded aloof, forbidding, disengaged. But as they talked (and talked) over the next few weeks, Pearl came to see that the man's phone manner went beyond arrogance or even shyness—it was a style. A telephone aesthetic. Besides, Wunsch was always the one to place the calls. At first, when Pearl was wavering about whether to consider the position (Mississippi?!), Wunsch would phone every day. The fainthearted double ring on the black dial phone in Pearl's caretaker's cottage, deep in the cow country of Washington County, would sound at any and all hours, and Wunsch (calling from Mississippi!) would come on the wire with deep-toned advice, inducements, small talk. Pearl understood that he was being wooed, and he was flattered. But there was also something strange about these calls. Having spent the last year in hermitage, a self-exile from Manhattan, on a farm in upstate New York (its owner, a West End Avenue psychoanalyst, was teaching in England); having known, at times, a solitude so dense it could practically be cut, like a Stilton or a cheddar—Pearl had developed a fine appreciation for the various tints and gradations, the marbling textures, of loneliness: a nose for it. And, despite Wunsch's self-assured rumble, he thought he caught a whiff of it here. He was being thrown a lifeline—but did the line come from the dock or from another dinghy?

The flattery was what lingered, however—the flattery, first, of being called at all, not to mention being called by Walter Wunsch, whose name Pearl recognized from the little magazines. (He knew the name, but, try as he might, he still—even now, as he stood fidgeting in the airport waiting room—couldn't summon up the work. It was minimalist, somehow; very up-to-date. Was it poetry? Fiction? Criticism? All three, he thought, fuzzily; he couldn't make any one piece of it come into focus. Would Wunsch ask him about it? he wondered. Surely he should have looked up some of Wunsch's work?)

Ready or not: one of life's little mottoes. For there could be no mistaking—among the double-knit grandmas, chamber-of-commerce types, and teenaged servicemen—the bearded figure in blue jeans, cowboy boots, pressed white shirt, and thin black tie now

lumbering toward him. But, miracle of miracles, something
about the man put Pearl immediately at ease. Wunsch was singular-looking, for one thing—as singular-looking as he was -sound-
ing. The man approaching him was large and balding, with a
trimmed red beard and pale blue eyes that seemed by quick turns
amazed, amused, and deeply bored. Pearl shook Wunsch's hand;
Wunsch rumbled something. The pale eyes searched his for a startling second. These were eyes, Pearl saw at once, that had nothing
to do with the standard American male principle of challenging or
deflecting. Instead, they admitted one—but to what, one scarcely
knew. *To what had he been admitted?*

The two men went outside. It was like walking into a wall.
This was midsummer, southern-Mississippi heat—heat such as
Pearl had never felt before. It was suffocating, nauseating. One's
vision was affected. But the interior of Wunsch's black Alfa
Romeo sedan was icy (he had left the engine running), and, as
they whisked out the drive of the little airport, the bearded man's
small talk was as crisp as his Brooks Brothers shirt. Pearl was
vastly grateful for all this. His heart slowed. He had not landed
on the moon. He was riding to town in a well-maintained foreign
car with a civilized man. What was more, the man seemed to
like him. For as Pearl stared out the window at the continuous
blue-black palisade of pines flanking the highway—almost like
Maine, he thought happily, feeling calmer every second (almost
like Maine except for the strange black helmetlike corpses that
gleamed now and again in the melting tar by the roadside:
armadillos, Pearl the explorer thought with wonderment)—as
Pearl stared and stared, Wunsch kept saying, in that sea-deep
voice, embodied at last, "Ah, Philly. You're good as gold. Good
as gold."

Gold was not precisely what Pearl felt like, however, as he
sat a while later in the book-lined office of the university's as-

sistant dean, a courtly, quiet man with a plantation owner's white goatee. It was beginning to dawn on Pearl that he had every reason, his lack of alternatives aside, to be nervous. He had never taught anything. He had no graduate degree. His sole qualifications were the single slim book he had published, and the few (very few) poems he had written since. The magazines his work had appeared in were mostly obscure or expired or both. He had sold two poems to *The New Yorker*—not two of his best, in Pearl's opinion. (One, in galleys for almost a year and a half, had yet to appear.) Both works, oddly enough, had been about snow. ". . . the way of man is/To ask, and the way of the world/Is to answer: snow," went "Interrogative." Pearl had tried to play these two poems down, when Wunsch had first phoned, but Wunsch continued to insist on making a big deal of them— whether he'd read them or not. (Pearl had tried to draw him out on this, over the phone, but ductility was clearly not one of Wunsch's virtues.) These two snow poems were, according to Wunsch, Pearl's ace in the hole, a large part of the reason he stood a good chance of getting the job. Two poems! Two lousy poems about snow, written almost two years ago (Pearl had written next to nothing since, nothing at all for the past six months). Still—*The New Yorker*! People were stunned, rendered insensate, by these three little words.

But the assistant dean was less than stunned. Worse. The man seemed mildly incredulous that someone like Pearl, with his painfully obvious lack of academic grounding (B.A. in Comp Lit from Columbia, period, nine years ago) should even be considered as a possible teacher at Pickett State. Wunsch sat in on this supposedly informal interview, at Pearl's back, which, despite the extreme, overcompensatory chill of the assistant dean's office, was soaked with sweat. As the interview began, Pearl's heart rose to his throat once more: he was barely able to croak out answers to the dean's polite but pointed questions. Finally, finally, the subject of publications came up.

"It says here, Mr. Pearl," the assistant dean said blandly, "that you have published a *book*."

"Yes, sir."

"Titled—uh"—the man held Pearl's résumé a little farther from his half-glasses, as if it were an entomological specimen—"*Oedipus at Secaucus?*" He said *ee*-dipus at *see*-caucus.

"Yes, sir."

The assistant dean cleared his throat. There was a long silence. The interview was over.

Wunsch escorted Pearl out of the building, back into the unbelievable heat, along a diagonal sidewalk that crossed a broad quadrangle. They seemed to be shuffling crabwise through this heat, heat that felt like a fifth element, something beyond earth, water, fire, or air—or perhaps a hybrid of all four. The sky was oatmeal-colored. Pearl's vision was unfocused, his throat cottony. All he could think was *gone, gone, gone.* What would he do? Where would he go?

"Well," he was eventually able to say to Wunsch. "That's that."

"Easy now, Phil," Wunsch said. "You did great."

"Great? You're kidding. He hated me."

"Nah, he loved ya. He's always that way. 'Sides, he don't matter anyway—he's small fish." Wunsch talked in a deep-South accent, though Pearl's vague memory was that he was from someplace in the North.

"So where are we going now?" Pearl asked. "The big shark?" For, horribly enough, it seemed that they were now on their way to another interview.

Wunsch punched him on the shoulder. "Relax," he said. "Larry's a snap."

The office of the vice-president of the university was large, cool, full of light. By some trick, the light in the office was not the light of Mississippi but of somewhere else—Trinity College in Cambridge, perhaps? One long wall, floor to ceiling, was entirely books: well-used Oxford dictionaries; faded volumes of Livy, Pliny, Plautus, Tacitus, Terence. The vice-president, a chunky, white-haired, apple-cheeked leprechaun of a man, stood in white short sleeves, putting golf balls across the thick green carpet.

"Do you read Latin, Mr. Pearl?" he asked, waggling the putter and scowling with concentration.

"Caesar, Virgil. Not much more. I hunt and peck in the *Metamorphoses.*"

"New Testament?"

"But that's Greek."

"Well, now"—the putt rolled up the side of the aluminum cup and then glanced off at a right angle, caroming off the leg of a chair—"good. Good! *Here* is an educated man." The vice-president looked up at Wunsch and winked. "Sounds just fine to me, Walter."

"Will that be all, Larry?"

" 'Less you can think of something else I ought to ask the boy."

So—like that—Pearl was in. All the way back to the motel in Wunsch's car, and then as he lay on the bed in his room, Pearl felt dizzy, motion-sick: as though he had been lifted bodily by some force and moved, as a boulder is moved by a bulldozer. *He hadn't planned for this.* His life, it seemed, was now going to change. Oddly, all he could think of at first was the money— fourteen thousand for eight months' work, an immense, a fabulous sum. The thought of it all, rolling in week after week, unstoppable, like the sands in an hourglass, was intoxicating.

Only after he had lain on his bed a long time (Wunsch wasn't due back to pick him up for dinner for three hours; and the thick heat had finally given way to rain, so there was little else for Pearl to do but stay in his room and consider his situation) did it occur to him, in a rather startling way, that in return for this money, he was going to have to *be* here. To be in Mississippi.

It didn't quite compute. In fact, the thought jarred him so that he got up and opened the door of his room. What was he getting into? Pearl looked out across the motel parking lot for an answer. Instead he saw: two curving approaches to the interstate, median grass, a mall across the highway, rain. The sky brown-green. Cars with strange license plates sizzling by. The scene was at once overpoweringly mundane and otherworldly. Could he live here? He was barely able to take the thought in—the idea of a quotidian existence, *here*—but something in him began at that moment to feel profoundly depressed. He had made a horrible mistake. Had he? Had he committed himself? Well, he had signed no contract. There was nothing to prevent him from getting on the next plane and never coming back. But Wunsch putting his arm around his shoulder, all that winking business with Larry—they certainly seemed to expect him. *And it was good to be expected.* A year in the woods had brought Pearl to the point where the most minor affirmative human contact could give him gooseflesh. Still, did that contact have to be here? What were his other options? He shut the door, lay back down on the bed, and stared at the ceiling.

Wunsch's shiny black car, beaded with rainwater, reappeared under the porte-cochere of the Vagabond Inn precisely at six.

"Where to?" Wunsch asked as Pearl got in.

"I thought we were going to dinner."

"Yeah?" *So what,* Wunsch's tone said.

"It's on the school, right?"

"Right."

Pearl all but rubbed his hands. He had made his decision. (He had accepted his decision's having made him.) Now he was elated. His hunger went far beyond the need for dinner: he had decided to reingest the world. He was famished. "Let's go someplace good, then," he told Wunsch. "Let's go to the best damn place in town."

Wunsch stared at him, almost puzzled. "Phil?" he said. "What?"

"Ain't any best place. Ain't even any good place."

"Come on. Aren't there restaurants? I saw restaurants."

"Oh yeah. There's restaurants. About a hundred thirty of 'em."

"And none of them's any better than the rest?"

"Phil, you have any idea where you *are*?"

Pearl felt slightly irritated at this. He got Wunsch's drift. Why did he have to rain on Pearl's parade?

The place where they ended up, Hezekiah's—low light, Tiffany lampshades, diagonal paneling, hanging plants—seemed cloned but not half bad. Pearl's Snapper Pontchartrain was, if microwaved, pretty good. And their waitress was nice—tall, comely, funny, with long curly hair of an odd, red-brown shade. She had an anachronistic look: hourglass-shaped, along the lines of a Gibson Girl. Her name tag read JEWEL. Not precisely Pearl's cup of tea, but not uninteresting. She flirted with Wunsch and Pearl, looked at Pearl puzzledly and a little overlong, as though they might have met before. A professional trick? If so, Pearl was susceptible.

But Wunsch, for some reason, seemed disconsolate. He picked at his steak, drank Coke after Coke, said next to nothing. Pearl was drinking beer—free beer!—and, despite Wunsch, feeling quite good. He was taking Rilke's advice: he was changing his life, in one broad sweep. What was Wunsch's problem? He was obviously oppressed by the place. He had been here too long. He, too, had been isolated—it took one, Pearl thought, to know one. Maybe he could help Wunsch out of it. Surely things couldn't be *that* bad.

III

Pearl hung up the phone, threw on his clothes, and went downstairs. The day, at nine a.m., was already too hot. Three weeks ago he had been too scared to notice anything; now he walked across the Holiday Inn courtyard, eyes and nostrils wide open, like a dog in a new neighborhood. *Terra nova*, he thought excitedly. *Terra incognita*. Something about this place—something he hadn't picked up in the rushed gray day of his interview—really was different. What? The sun! The angle of light had changed, not subtly. This, of course (thought Pearl the geographer), was due simply to the difference in latitude. But even as he realized this, he thrilled: he had shifted on the planet. If such a physical shift was possible, why not an inner one as well? His career as hermit, depressive, pauper, could—would—end here. If, in upstate New York, he had come to the end of his rope, why not (as in a rope trick) simply leave the rope behind?

Then the thought of the coming Wednesday morning tumbled into his consciousness. This was the bargain. His heart began to bump. Next came the rebuke, then the reargument. Pearl's stomach growled. To quiet it all down, he sniffed the air. Nothing exotic, no orchids or jasmine, merely cut grass and exhaust fumes—the interstate was a hundred yards away—but at the edge of it was something else, the tinge of a strange reek. Pearl remembered the creosote odor he had detected in the lobby last night. I really should have been a dog, he thought. He filed the thought away, like a bone. Someday he would write again. The odor was faint, unattachable—maybe someone was burning garbage?

He had three hours to kill before he could show up at Wunsch's. Easy. He would eat breakfast and read the Sunday *Times* by the pool. He would do the crossword! The sheer normality of the idea calmed him. He inhaled deeply. By God, he would flirt with the waitress.

But she was sixty and sullen. Pearl had expected, at least, a little Southern blarney, some Sugar and Honey with his overpriced motel meal. Instead she merely dropped the specked menu and then brought the food—runny eggs, tiny desiccated sausages, miniature slices of white toast. Yet there was one unfamiliar detail, grits, that he rather liked. A good sign. The dining room was almost empty. By the window wall that faced out on the driveway sat the requisite leisure-suited late-middle-aged couple, getting an early start on the road, no doubt. Their eyes, behind spectacles, were flinty—they were guarding their money, this look said. The world was trying to take it from them. The breakfast was too expensive. They huddled over their free second cups of coffee, not speaking, not quite facing each other.

Then Pearl sighted an anomaly. Far over to his left—his chair was angled so that he couldn't quite see without twisting his neck—sat a boy in a fringed buckskin jacket, jeans, boots up to his knees. His hair, bright red, was tied into a long, frizzy ponytail. Pearl puzzled over this. The old couple he could understand, but this kid? Here? Pearl stared, his eyes strained to their maximum leftmost limit, as a waitress brought the boy— surely this wasn't possible—what appeared to be an American

Express card. The boy signed, stood, stretched, strutted across the room, vanished. Presently he reappeared outside the picture windows, opening the door of a camper with Florida plates. Pearl sighed. *That* was the life. (Anything but teaching Wednesday morning was the life.) The kid hopped into his van—not a care in the world. Drugs or music, or both, were no doubt in the picture. And American Express to boot. Pearl himself had been turned down for Visa, no mean trick. He always felt he had missed something when he saw people like this. Inwardly he cheered them. Yet at the same time, he realized, he despised them. What did that say about himself? Who was he to cast such judgments? Who was he, period? A poet—at one time. *Jeune homme moyen sensuel*, he thought, smiling wryly. *Jeune homme à la chemise Lacoste*, spoke another, less satisfying, voice within him. And not so *jeune* anymore, either. Who was he? The truth was, at thirty-one he hadn't a clue. Perhaps it didn't pay to question too closely: you might, in answer, simply get a seashell sound, the roar of your own blood.

Yet this kid seemed somehow ahead of the game. In a flash, Pearl saw himself running out to the parking lot, handing the musician a pile of bills, and trading places completely—clothes, car, everything. Like the prince and the pauper. Driving off to Florida to a life of chromosome damage. Ha ha, thought Pearl mirthlessly. What bills? Who was the prince and who the pauper? After he paid for his breakfast, he would have thirty-four dollars and change left until his first payday. Whenever that was.

The only paper available in the lobby dispensers was the Pickett *Post*, with—tackiness of tackinesses—a color photograph on the front page. Could they have run out of the *Times* so early? But there was no dispenser for it, even. Surely he could pick one up somewhere in town; perhaps at the airport? He would inquire at the desk. He was halfway there when it began to sink in on him: this was just his foolishness, hanging on for dear life. He who explores must take the consequences. He put two quarters in the machine and took his paper outside.

The pool was deserted this morning except for what was patently a honeymoon couple. They were very fat and gloriously happy. The husband lay on the cement, panting and dripping and smiling, while his wife sidestroked up and down, never taking her eyes off him. Their eyes locked, every once in a while they would simply burst into laughter. They never said a word. The meridian rope had been removed from the pool: by daylight, the contrast between the pallid blue shallow water and the inky deep was painfully apparent. Not to mention the diving board. How could Pearl have been such an idiot? It had been dark. He had been exhausted. He hadn't been wearing his glasses. Still. It was funny, even hilarious, in a sick way, to think of driving thirteen hundred miles to die in a motel swimming pool in Mississippi. Odder, more perversely disastrous things had happened to people. But not to him, Pearl thought. He didn't intend to die young. He wore his seat belt at all times. Pearl thought again of the rock musician in his van. *He* didn't wear no fuckin' seat belt. And yet—where would he be in ten years? The best he could be was dead. Not Pearl. Pearl was in it for the long haul, belted in by moderation in all things. The Moderate Poet. This, of course, was part of the problem.

The fat bride was now getting out of the pool. Her thighs, seen from behind, were large yet remarkably white and smooth: at their top, at the bottom inner edge of her bathing suit, was a fine haze of wandering pubic hair. She hooked a quick finger around—woman's third eye—and pulled the edge down.

Was that really what he wanted, Pearl wondered—immoderateness? Scenes, drunks, all-nighters? And even if he did, was he constitutionally able? He was already getting to the age where he should have worked such things out of his system. He had worked nothing out of his system. What was in his system to start with?

This, here, Pickett, was his act of daring. Standing in front of a class—his chest once more constricted at the thought. It wasn't just Wednesday morning that was getting to him. It was the whole venture, his hubris. In Pearl's mind thoughts of daring brought, by reflex, thoughts of death. Could he die here? This was, after all, Mississippi; he was, after all, a Jew. He thought of Schwerner, Goodman, and Chaney; he thought of Leo Frank. Of course he was being ridiculous. Melodramatic. He was no activist; he kept his nose clean (all too clean). Anyway, those things had happened years ago, in the newspapers. This was now, here, real life: Holiday Inn, drone of the interstate, smell of the grass. Sunday morning. Complacencies of the peignoir. His belly was full. The sun warmed his face and arms. How could he ever die? A psychic (Pearl, the sensible poet, had gone on a self-dare, to beef up his irrationality quotient) had once told him that his death would come after many years, in a hot, dry place. This had a pleasingly biblical sound to Pearl, although he knew it might well have meant Palm Springs. In truth, the thought of dying, of his own actual death, had never actually occurred to him.

He picked up the paper. The headline over the color picture read: PSU TO START CLASSES WEDNESDAY. The picture was of an immense blond football player, in black-and-gold uniform, with a cheerleader standing on his enormous padded shoulders. The caption read: "Panther co-captain Brett Edwards and Pussycat Doreen Pitts are rarin' to go for PSU's first home game, against Flower State on Sept. 3." Pearl smiled—then frowned. He was unable to take his eyes off this photograph. Were they serious? Was this what he had lived through the sixties for? He immediately tried to muster every counteractive thought he could: 116th and Broadway on a slushy day; the droning voice of a

militant lesbian on WBAI; the fusty aisles of his beloved Gotham
Book Mart. Nothing worked. It was like trying to summon
anaphrodisiac images while sliding into ecstasy. (At which, fur-
thermore, Pearl was considerably out of practice.)

The new Southern sun drenched everything, Pearl and his
paper alike, making the tawdry rotogravure colors leap from the
page. He was in a new land. The rules were new rules. It was
not an abstract or intellectual horror Pearl felt now, but a visceral
one: up to this point, in the back of his mind, at the root of all
thought about his Adventure, he had vaguely (but, yes, em-
phatically) seen himself as a special import into this wilderness,
an exotic quantity, like Beluga caviar. His value would, of course,
be seen and appreciated. The possibility now occurred to him
that he might simply be an oddball. If Brett Edwards was the
sexual paragon here—and surely he must be—then what chance
did short, slight Pearl, with his brown kinky hair and dark
(penetrating, he hoped) eyes, his rather prominent nose, his
circular brass-rimmed glasses and khaki pants and shirts with
alligators, stand? He looked anxiously at Doreen Pitts. Her full
cheeks dimpled, as did the downy knees of her strong and comely
legs, which were turned slightly out. (Pearl imagined, with an
inward groan, the corresponding pelvic flexions and openings.)
He wondered if Brett had had the presence of mind to glance
upwards as the picture was being snapped. The question was
moot, precisely what made the grinning faces so infuriating.
Actors in pornographic movies smiled this way; so did pastors'
families on group tours of the Holy Land. There was a smugness,
an implicit exclusivity, whatever the habits of Brett and Doreen.
Pussycat indeed! Pearl had been told that his own smile, at
moments of great amusement or warmth, resembled nothing so
much as a smirk. *Manhattanisch.* If he wasn't lynched, he was
bound, at the very least, to be misunderstood.

* * *

When lunch was over, Walter and Margo Wunsch drove
Pearl around town. This, Pearl thought, was very nice of them.
He liked going for rides. He sat in the back seat of the cool Alfa
Romeo, a little hunched but happy. Wunsch was driving; Margo,
part sideways in the passenger's seat, smiled sociably. She was
large, like her husband, but by no means fat: she was a handsome
woman. Had the dimensions of her face resolved themselves a
shade more predictably, she would have been conventionally
pretty, but as it was something odd had happened: she looked
more like a cat than any woman Pearl had ever seen. It was not
an exact resemblance, of course, but the impression was strong.
Her face was rather flat, the eyebrows arched, the nose small and
a good distance above the upper lip. Her mouth, quite wide and
thin, protruded slightly, almost like a muzzle. Perhaps Pearl was
scrutinizing too closely. She did have a sweet smile, one that
seemed, oddly, largely without irony. This was strange; but then,
Pearl thought, weren't couples usually strange?

Margo actually *said* very little; she just turned around from
time to time and smiled her cat's smile at Pearl. Who dismissed
the idea of flirtation immediately. Not that Margo intended any;
but Pearl knew he was apt to take any kindness by a woman
sexually. Both out of vanity and because You Never Knew. You
really didn't. It was one of Pearl's great rules of life. He understood it to be jejune and unrefined but also to contain strong
currents of truth. In years past girlfriends had told Pearl that he
was attractive. But this was perhaps because they were girlfriends:
as much for their sake as his. In the cold light of reason, Pearl
knew he wasn't bad-looking; he even suspected himself of having,
from time to time and in certain lights, a couple of good angles.
But nothing really outstanding. An unformed face; roundish,
pleasant. Jewish. A good-camper face. Even now in his thirties.
People—nice, well-meaning people: storekeepers, his parents'
friends—were always asking him about "school." As if he had
just come from the malt shop. He was almost ten years out of

college, yet there were times when he suspected they meant high school. Sometimes Pearl felt he must embody the Platonic ideal of Student. Still—did it matter? You never knew what women responded to. They stared at your hair. They spoke of the fullness of your lips. Strange creatures. Exotic Margo smiled at him lynxily. Pearl smiled back in his sunniest manner. He hadn't the least intention of trying to cuckold Wunsch. He was after what was in season. And, if the truth be known, he was not so interested in Margo.

Pickett confused him utterly. Nice as it was of the Wunsches to drive him around, how could he be expected to absorb anything on what was essentially his first day here? He preferred to discover for himself, at leisure. For the moment, all he saw was a homely, sleepy, spread-out Southern town, bleached by the ferocious late-August sun into a dazzling whiteness that made it easier to focus on the interior of Wunsch's car.

He vaguely took in the strip, with its mallmotelgasstation-fastfood jumble, and the gridded quiet back streets with low white houses, many of them on platforms instead of foundations (something to do with the water table, he guessed). Spiky grass, pine trees, palmettos. Churches. There seemed to be a lot of churches. Now they were driving over a double railroad track, which divided the town not in the conventional way, but still somehow significantly, according to Walter's terse deep-toned narration. Actually, Wunsch seemed to become a little more voluble around Margo—she brought him out. But sitting in the back, Pearl didn't quite follow. It was partly just that he couldn't hear very well. People in the front seats of cars seldom understood this simple acoustic fact.

It was an ugly enough burg. True, he hadn't come for the scenery. (What had he come for?) But he hadn't quite been prepared for a place that so resembled—on the strip, anyway—everyplace else. The neighborhoods, with their odd vegetation, their stilted houses, were identifiably Southern, at least. Of Mississippi, though, he had expected something more—what? Dark, mysterious, deeply poor. Faulknerian. It was shameful, he knew, but the tourist in Pearl had expected black children playing in mud puddles in dirt streets. (This was to come. He would see these things.) As they passed yet another row of tire stores, car dealerships, rug outlets, Pearl was struck by the similarity of parts of Pickett to, say, New Jersey. He was musing on the increasing, depressing homogeneity of America, and on some of the countervailing factors—the persistence of dialect; the growth of museums, ballets, symphonies, in smaller cities—when he noticed that they were slowing down. They had entered a residential neighborhood. Wunsch turned his large head around.

"O.K., Philly. Ready for this?" he said. "Big moment."

"Walter," said Margo, showing Pearl the left side of an expression not meant for him.

"Don't you think Philly ought to meet Francesca? Fall in love? Get married? Have babies?" Margo was now staring at Wunsch, and he at her—they were face to face, like those ambiguous figures, in the psychological illustration, that also form a loving cup. Wunsch shot Pearl a glance with his right eye, arching the brow suggestively.

They had stopped across the street from a large yellow stucco house with a swing on the front porch. In the driveway, Pearl noticed, sat a low, astonishingly sleek silver car—its roof could have been no more than four feet off the ground.

Margo turned to Pearl. "Walter's in love with one of his students," she said, with a quick, practical, dismissive smile.

"Nice car," Pearl said.

"That's Giuseppe's," said Walter. "Francesca's pa*pa*. Car's hot."

Margo protested. "Walter, that's not—"

"All right, all right. Warm," said Wunsch.

"So, who's this Francesca?" Pearl asked, grinning, his chest and the base of his throat buoyant with what he already knew was a foolish feeling. *Foolish*, he told himself, yet the buoyancy only grew.

Wunsch turned around and looked at Pearl, his pale eyes wide and strange. *Admitting to what?* Then he laughed his barrel-bottom laugh. "We must *see*," he said, in movie-French, "if we can ar-*rahnge* an introduction."

IV

"I hear you say something about tennis?" The speaker was an extremely thin man, cadaverous almost, balding at the temples, black-mustached, deeply tanned. A large hooked pipe rested in the corner of his mouth. Young-old—around forty-five, Pearl guessed. Wearing a purple T-shirt, pale pleated trousers with a stretch band at the waist and a bicycle clip on one leg. Sandals. Something slightly mad about the dark eyes: he stared at Pearl as if searching for a True Believer.

"That's right," Darla said, a little apprehensive. "Dr. Juniper."

Pearl had been making small talk with the department secretary, fishing around desperately for ideas about a place to live. Darla, he had seen at once, would not be much help. Dewy-cheeked, big-eyed, long-lashed, slow-talking and shy, she reminded him of nothing so much as a Disney character—one of Bambi's friends. The conversation had begun to feel like a molasses bath, and Pearl, who was down to his last fifteen dollars, with no prospects of an apartment, thought wildly of his belongings, which sat locked in his car, baking under the incredible

Southern sun out in a wide asphalt lot someplace on campus, he was no longer sure if he remembered where. His Deutsche Grammophon Telemann would be licorice by now. Unable to extricate himself from Darla, Pearl had brought up tennis, asking in passing if any of the other teachers played. And this man had spoken up.

"Name's Ted Juniper," he said, taking the pipe out of his mouth with his left hand and offering his right. "You must be the new boy."

"Philip Pearl." They shook hands.

"Well, I'm mighty pleased to meet you, Phil. You any good? None of these fat ole fogeys around here can play a lick."

"I'm all right." Pearl was actually rather vain about his tennis game—*a good Central Park game*, he thought.

"Yeah." Juniper squinted appraisingly at Pearl's torso and arms. "You look good." Pearl felt a kind of animal danger signal, an extra thrum of blood in his palms. *Calm down*, he told himself.

"Damn," the man said. "*Damn!* This is *good* news. When you want to play? How 'bout this afternoon." He stressed the first syllable in the last word.

"Sure." This was nice, Pearl thought. A game with a colleague. *A colleague.* The sound of it amazed him. Maybe he, too, would smoke a pipe. Then he thought of the laden Volvo. "Listen," he said to Juniper. "I just remembered. I can't. I have to find a place to live." Pearl shrugged, smiled apologetically. Just a little quirk we Northern boys have.

Juniper's eyes narrowed. "Where you stayin' now?"

"I've been at the Holiday Inn. But I have to get out. Too expensive."

"Shee-it. Why don't you stay at my place?"

Pearl felt the palm-thrum once more. Was this merely his hermit self, and his city self, joining to make one distrustful whole? Why could he take nothing at face value? "Really?" he said. Without much conviction.

"*Shoot* yeah. I got a whole houseful of space. My wife and I—well, I think we're in the process of gettin' divorced, though I can't be too sure about that." He winked at Darla. "I got nothin' but space and time, too damn much of both."

"That's really very nice of you. I mean, I—" Pearl tried to think of an excuse, an out, just in case. He was lousy at this. What in case? What were his other options?

Juniper squinted at him. "Where you *from*, boy?"

"New York."

"Uh-oh, Darla. We got us a carpetbagger here."

Darla looked up sleepily. "Yessir."

"Well, you're welcome anyway, Phil. Where's all your stuff? At the motel?" Emphasis on the first syllable.

"My car."

Juniper shook his head at the thought. "Damn," he said, comprehensively. "Well, you just truck it all over to my house whenever you feel like it. Door's open."

Five cars sat in the front yard of the house on Caddie Street: not in the driveway—there was none to speak of—but in the yard itself, on a patch of dirt only a little more sparsely grassed than the area around it. The only shade in the yard came from a single bedraggled pine by the curb; a tire swing dangled from a lower branch. Under the tree lay two toppled garbage pails, and next to one of them reclined a very large tan dog, chewing thoughtfully on a chicken carcass. The dog made a noise low in its throat as Pearl approached.

"Easy, boy." Pearl held up a hand. He didn't like dogs. Especially big ones. "That's all right." The dog watched closely as Pearl edged toward the house; finally, bored, it looked away, and with a leap of faith Pearl turned his back and continued across the yard.

Music was blasting from the house—it sounded Mexican.

What did you expect, Mozart? Pearl thought. He didn't like any of this. Maybe he should go back. But where? Manhattan? Delbertsville? The Holiday Inn? He looked once more at the dog, then opened the door of the screen porch. Pearl saw frayed director's chairs, an aluminum chaise, many open Budweiser cans. A guitar on the floor. An open book, spine up, on a tin TV tray: *Arabia Deserta*, by Doughty. Interesting. A chicken bone lay on the book's cover. Pearl called out, but he could barely hear himself through the music.

> *Wastin' away again in Margaritaville,*
> *Searchin' for my lost shaker of salt*

the singer sang, in a gravelly, morning-after voice.

> *Some people claim there's a woman to blame,*
> *But I know*
> *It's my own damn fault.*

It probably is your fault, Pearl thought. He hated this twangy stuff. Inside the front door, which was wide open, the sound from the stereo speakers felt like wind on his skin. The hall was dark but hot, the odor of spicy food lingering amid the disturbed air particles. Feeling that his ears were in danger, Pearl squatted and turned the volume knob sharply to the left. In the new silence, he listened. There was a secondary sound, above the ringing of his ears: an electronic whine. A hair dryer. Suddenly the whine stopped, a door clicked. "Hey!" called a deep voice. "Hoozat?"

Before Pearl could think of an appropriate response, he found himself facing—facing up to—a very large person, bearded, bare-chested, and wet-haired, with a blue bath towel knotted around his waist.

"Shit you give me a scare," he said. "I thought I'd blown the fucker out again."

"Uh—Ted said I could bring some of my stuff over here?"

"Oh. Sure." He looked Pearl up and down. "You a student a Ted's?"

"I'm a colleague of Ted's."

He stared openmouthed. "You're shittin' me."

"No."

"God damn. You look too young to be a teacher," he said. "Thass O.K. I look too old to be a student. *Am* too old." He grinned, showing a chipped front tooth, and extended a large hand. "Leon's my name. Whaddya teach?"

"Poetry. And literature and composition."

Leon squinted at him. "You ain't a poet?"

Pearl nodded.

"Boy, you don't look like one—no offense. Hell, what do I know."

Pearl smiled politely.

"Matter of fack, I write a little poetry myself," Leon said.

"Oh?"

"Yup. I ain't much good, though. Ted's been showin' me a coupla things. Gave me a book by this dude Roth, Reth—?"

Pearl stared. "Roethke?"

"That's the one. Shee-it! That dude was *crazy*! I hear he had some bad trouble with women and drinkin', too."

"So they say."

Leon shook his head and smiled. "Damn."

"Well," Pearl said. "I—"

Leon popped his fingers loudly, startling Pearl. "That's right. You wanted to bring your shit in."

"I, uh. Just don't know how much to bring, or where to put it."

"Well now, I ain't exactly sure what to tell you about that. What time you got?"

"One fifteen."

"Shit. I got to start keepin' me some regular hours." He winked at Pearl. "Ted'll be back any minute, then he can tell you. He never misses his show."

"Show?"

"You can go sit in the den if you want." Leon pointed to a pair of French doors. "Tastefully air-conditioned. I gotta go finish dryin' my curly goddamn locks."

The den was dark and deeply, deliciously cold. Venetian blinds were drawn against the overpowering sun, and an air conditioner was blowing full blast. Maybe, Pearl prayed, Juniper would let him sleep in here? He flipped on the overhead light and saw a pair of beat-up but comfortable-looking red velvet couches and a large old-fashioned television with foil-festooned rabbit ears on top. At the other end of the room was a wall of books. Dropping down onto one of the couches was Pearl's first impulse, but now the books drew him irresistibly.

It was, he saw at once, not a bad collection. Keats (letters and poems), Stevens (ditto), Harold Bloom, Sir James Frazier, Jessie Weston, Eliade, Bergson, Lévi-Strauss, Kierkegaard. The mainstreams, tributaries, even rivulets of Juniper's thought seemed not so different from his own. Strange, the oases you found in the desert. Then Pearl thought of the sandals and the stretch-waist pants, the purple T-shirt. He pulled out *The Necessary Angel*, to see if it had been read. It had been. And underlined, and copiously annotated—though the notes, in a tiny, crabbed hand, were for the most part illegible. Pearl could make out an "and" and a "the" here and there, and one word that looked like "heifer." The rest, just lines and squiggles, might as well have been Arabic.

"Phil, m'boy. How you makin' out."

Pearl spun around, his heart knocking as if he had been caught stealing. Juniper—dripping with sweat, guitar in hand—plopped down on a sofa and mopped his forehead with a bandanna. "Damn," he said. "Whoever invented the damn air conditioner ought to get a No-*bel* Prize. See anythin' you like?"

"I, uh—"

"Borrow whatever you want." Juniper strummed a sour chord, winced, turned a tuning peg. "You get your stuff in all right?"

"Actually, I wasn't sure where to put it."

"Shit. And I didn't tell you, either, did I. Fine host I am. Come on, boy. Back out to the tropics."

They crossed the front hall to a tiny, stifling room with walls that were painted a nauseous, vibrating purple.

"This is Dawn's studio," Juniper said wistfully. "Was, I mean. There's some of her paintin' stuff over in the corner. I don't think it'll be in your way any." Several smeary-looking canvases leaned against the wall. "You can stay long as you like," he said. "Unless she comes back. I mean until." At this he allowed himself a half-smile. His tanned, gaunt, black-mustached face was almost wicked, except for the nose, which was small and surprisingly delicate. The nostrils faced you as he talked. Pearl was reminded, for a disquieting moment, of a death's-head.

"Here's a closet," he continued. "Just push the dresses over to one side. What else? Oh yeah. This here canvas thing? It's a foldin' cot. You know how to operate one of these? I got it at the army surplus."

Pearl felt gratitude rising in his chest—the reaction he always had to sheer altruism. For what else could it be? "But, Ted," he said. "This is really too good of you."

"You got any towels? We're kinda low on them. Why don't you steal a few from the mo-tel."

"Hey, Ted." Leon loomed in the doorway, in jeans and a cowboy shirt opened to reveal a wide expanse of hairy chest.

"Hey, bro. You meet the new boarder?"

Leon nodded affably at Pearl. "Sure did. Ain't you watchin' your show?"

"Damn! What time is it?"

"Almost twenty of."

"Damn! O.K." He turned to Pearl. "Why don't you just start bringin' your stuff in while I park my ass in front of 'Guidin' Light' for twenty minutes. I'd help you now, Phil, but first things is first. Leon, my man. You off?"

"Off to the wars."

"Poonic Wars, eh?"

Leon laughed. "Ain't it the truth. Perfesser"—he winked at Pearl—"pleased to meet you."

And Pearl was alone in the purple room. Now he walked back and forth between the Volvo and Dawn's studio, carrying everything he owned—suitcases, boxes, sports jackets on hangers. The heat was unbelievable. As was the amount of stuff he'd brought. Whatever had possessed him to think he would need his Brooks Brothers trenchcoat here? He gritted his teeth and cursed as he balanced boxes under his chin. He passionately hated moving. Why couldn't he just have stayed put? His shirt and pants were soaked through, a lost cause. The Margaritaville song played over and over again in his head, unbidden, idiotically, as he tripped up Juniper's porch steps.

But soon he was bearing in the last few things—a few ties, a bottle of Scotch. (He never wore ties; he never drank Scotch.) In a square of sunlight on the porch, he suddenly stopped short. He stared at this square of light. Hadn't he dreamed up Juniper's house once, long ago, in a night of indigestion? The conviction seemed both undeniable and unbelievable. It then gave way to a wave of intense homesickness, combined somehow with a memory of those shacks along the road in Alabama. Whatever it was, the sensation kept flowing through him, a sweet sharp pain in the center of his chest. He would, he knew, remember this instant forever, in minutest detail: the webwork of cracks in the gray paint on the floor, the broken screen, the bobbing wasp, the smell of hot pines, the dots of white sunlight diffracting in the slowly waving branches, the sough of wind. Time was a trifle, a joke. He felt close to tears. Perhaps he was overtired. Somewhere, a car horn honked—a car horn here and now. Wednesday morning was approaching at the speed of light.

Juniper removed his shirt and put on his sweatbands. It was five o'clock, and the day's ferocious heat was beginning— just beginning—to moderate. Pearl's colleague's bandido look was somehow emphasized by the white terry bands he wore on each wrist and around his head: they reminded Pearl of cartridge belts. They also made Juniper look just a shade goofy. His torso was darkly tanned and painfully thin—scrawny, even. Still, there was something stubborn and sinewy about the arms and shoulders, as if he had tried hard to build them up but failed. Just beneath the rib cage on his left side was what appeared at first glance to be a large jagged horizontal scar, smooth with age, not quite as tan as the rest of the skin. Pearl registered it with a blink, quickly looked aside, then glanced at it once more. It existed. It didn't look neat enough, either, to be a surgical scar. Now he noticed that despite Juniper's thinness, there was a slight thickening or settling at the hips, oddly womanly. It was nothing but age, he realized—gravity doing its inevitable work. Pearl kept his shirt on. He bounced a ball while Juniper unscrewed his racket—an old wooden Wilson—from its bulky press.

"Let's hit a little while," Juniper said. "I need all the pre-parin' I can get before I play a young fella like you." He peered at Pearl intently, smiled crookedly. His close-set black eyes looked, as usual, slightly crazed: Pearl had no idea whether his colleague was trying some sort of psych-out or simply being friendly. He smiled back, nervously. Would he ever relax?

They walked to their respective ends and Pearl hit a ball to Juniper. The ball came back cross-court to Pearl's forehand, drastically sliced: mis-hit. Pearl hit the ball back, and it returned the same way. And again. Juniper had a funny forehand, his elbow flying out like Red Skelton's seagull imitation. His backhand was an act of desperation, his whole body corkscrewing into a corner of the court, the racket arm suddenly lurching out as if fending off an enemy. But the balls Pearl hit all came back, all with that funny diving spin. Juniper dug for every shot, no matter how hard or radically angled, as though his life depended on it. Yet at the same time there was something lifeless about him—zombielike. It worried Pearl.

They began a set. After a while, growing exhausted from chasing down the balls that Juniper was chasing down, Pearl forgot the score and called the question across the court. Juniper had no idea. At all. Of the point score, the game score, anything. Pearl (to his horror, he was working hard to stay even) could have claimed he was ahead 5–0, forty–love, and Juniper wouldn't have blinked. But Pearl was honest—or tried to be. It was his great flaw. He held the score in his head, Juniper sliced the balls back, and the set kept going—and going.

Now the sun was setting, and the mercury vapor lights around the courts were flickering on. Dried sweat stung Pearl's eyes; his legs were rubbery. The score of the first set stood at 24–24. Pearl wanted to win; he also wanted to go home. It felt sad out on the courts, with a slight chill rising from the ground, out here between the empty football practice field and the empty parking lot and the almost empty interstate. He felt a pang of intense longing, for something. Something in the base of his throat ached. He had played on through dinnertime. So? Who was expecting him? He could, if he wanted, play till ten. Still, something in him wanted deeply to be somewhere else. His sweat was getting cold. The chartreuse tennis balls hopped around strobe-fashion in the white lunar vapor light. *Where?* he wondered. Outside the chain-link fence the world was darkening: the funky brown of the dusky trees, the streak of orange at the horizon, and above, deep pure blue—indigo. The sky was vir-

ginal, unmarked by clouds or jet trails. Did anyplace that nothing
flew over exist anymore? Apparently it did. This was it. Beyond
the fence, the practice field, black-green in the rising dusk, gave
off a powerful, loamy tang, the smell of an ancient, greater world.

And Pearl thought: *here?*

It was black night outside the fence, bats and bugs circling
and circling in the mercury light, Juniper running back and
forth, and Pearl holding on to the score, in his head, for dear
life: his ad in the fifty-fourth game. He was one point from
winning, but this no longer seemed to matter. His arm was
swinging like something not himself; he could barely feel his
legs at all. Now a rally began that wouldn't stop. Pearl would
stagger toward the ball, touch it with his racket, somehow bloop-
ing it back; Juniper would do the same. The ball hopped and
skidded in the flickering white light, the bats and bugs circled.
Drawn wide to his right, Pearl hit a cross-court forehand so weak
it grazed the net tape. Juniper's return, as Pearl struggled back
to the middle of his baseline, seemed about to go down Pearl's
backhand line, a clear winner—but it too hit the net and hopped
up weakly, a yard into the center of the court.

Pearl, his body feeling loosely assembled, lurched toward
the net as if in a dream. Something seemed to snap in his shoulder
as he lunged toward the ball, which was about to come down
for the second time. At the last instant he trapped it, Ping-Pong
fashion, and scooped it feebly to Juniper's forehand.

Juniper seemed to smile, the first change of expression on
his face in more than three hours. He pulled back his racket and
hit the ball straight up. Pearl stood at the net, paralyzed. The
ball rose and rose into the white shimmering light. It rose some
more. As it reached the top of its arc, a bat dived at it, describing
a trail like a French curve that lingered in the air. Then the ball
began to come down. Pearl knew it would be good. He started

to limp back to his baseline, shaking his head. Deuce again. He would concede, he thought. Nothing mattered this much. His shoulder was beginning to throb. The ball descended through the black air, gathering speed, then touched the concrete, an inch long.

"Well, son, you whipped me," Juniper said.

"It was close, Ted." They were standing at the drinking fountain outside the courts. Juniper bent over the arcing stream; the water dripping from his Mexican mustache mixed with the sweat rolling off his nose. He hadn't put his shirt back on, though the air was shivering cold. He was demented, Pearl had decided.

"Damn," Juniper said, standing up and wiping his mouth with the back of his hand. "Thought I had you there a couple of times."

Pearl bent over the fountain and drank. The water was warm and slightly rusty. It was even faintly nauseating. However, taste didn't seem to matter. Pearl counted his swallows, then stopped counting. A car went by, its windows open, its radio on loud.

After you've gone
I'll stay out all night long if I feel like it

the singer sang.

Juniper was gazing out at the practice field, the cold glow of the mercury lights picking up his chip-nosed profile. His mouth was ajar.

"Ted?"

"Yeah," he said flatly, turning to Pearl, his heavy eyelids half-lowered.

"It's only a game, Ted. You'll win next time."

A corner of his mouth went up a fraction. "Thanks, amigo."

"Are you O.K., Ted?"

Juniper stared out at the field.

"Ted?"

"Yeah."

"What is it?"

"I just can't understand why she keeps callin' me up if she's still livin' with this gent."

"Dawn?"

Juniper stared.

"What gent?" Pearl asked.

"This rock musician dude. Drummer."

An associative light went on. Could the ponytailed boy he had seen in the Holiday Inn have stolen Juniper's wife? Things were never this neat. "She calls you from his house?"

"Two, three times a week."

"What does she want?"

"She doesn't even like the dude—she says. Says she just has to be away from me for a while. What I want to know is, why in hell can't she be away *alone?*"

Pearl had no idea what to say.

"Maybe 'cause she's so damn much younger than me. Still, she swears that's got nothin' to do with it."

Pearl looked into the dark listless eyes. Was Juniper depressed enough to try and harm himself? It would somehow be on Pearl's head if he did—Pearl, who had accepted his hospitality; Pearl, who had beaten him in tennis. What were you supposed to do in such circumstances?

"You want to go get a beer or something, Ted?"

"Think I'll just go on home."

"You sure? Because—"

"Thanks anyway, amigo. I'll just go strum my gee-tar a little, howl at the moon." He smiled, snaggle-toothed.

Pearl sighed, relieved. He was glad Ted felt better; also, the offer of a beer had been genuine, even if, in some basic way, not Pearl's style. "Good. Good," he said.

"You know, maybe I ought to be takin' out some other women?"

Pearl punched him on the shoulder. "Now, that's a great idea."

"Damn! Why has it taken me this long to think of that?"

"Maybe you just needed the time, Ted."

"Yeah. Maybe I did."

"Sometimes it takes a while to get your bearings when you've been—when you've had a loss."

"Just like ol' Davy Crockett: 'I've never been lost, but I have been a mite bewildered a few times.' "

Roethke and Doughty and Davy Crockett—goofy Juniper! All at once, to Pearl's surprise, he felt a surge of affection for the man. "Exactly."

Juniper pumped Pearl's hand. "Amigo, talkin' with you has done me a world of good. Let's play again *real* soon."

V

The night had given no relief from the day's heat, and in the terrible, portentous early light, Pearl was sweating already, yesterday's sweat and today's all mixed, the past unpurged. His sheets lay in damp knots around his legs. His dreams had been epical, perhaps in tribute to the *Iliad*, the first two hundred lines of which he had spent the previous evening carefully annotating. He had started awake several times in the night, each time positive he had overslept; and each time his eyes closed again the epic continued, loud, complex, bellicose. Finally, sometime after four, Pearl was able to slide back into a calmer state, the grand nightmare blessedly shifting into an erotic scherzo—extrapolated memories of an affair he had never quite brought off, but which, by dream-justice, now bloomed and swelled.

It was from this refuge that Juniper's windup alarm (sitting on top of Pearl's own clock-radio; he had not failed to include a power failure in his catalog of fears) jolted him, painfully priapic and marooned, marooned—God knew where.

As Pearl stood before Juniper's toilet, thumbing with his left hand through the Roethke anthology that sat on the window ledge (how booming, how orotund the poems seemed in the delicate morning), his heart was galloping. In the past, the first day of school had never failed to excite him. Also, Pearl's birthday was in September, and the first cool mornings at the end of August seemed to betoken not approaching death but rebirth: the quickening, after summer's suffocation, of the life of the mind—not to mention the issuing of fresh pads, pencils, books!

But on this morning, with even theoretical autumn almost a full month away, and the temperature at six thirty a.m. something like eighty-five (the trees in upstate New York would just be starting to turn, Pearl thought sinkingly; the mornings would be apple-crisp), his mind felt anything but quickened: it was numb with terror. What kind of place was this, where they started school in August? A place where he was trapped. Where there was no way out, other than just getting in his car and driving off without a word—and could Pearl ever do such a thing? Could he? On the way to the kitchen, he passed Juniper's bedroom. The door was wide open. Juniper—half out of the covers, on what had been his conjugal bed, bare-chested, his sunken-cheeked bandido's head looking for all the world like the death photograph of Che Guevara—snored loudly through dilated nostrils.

In the kitchen—dark, reeking of chili—the Pickett phone book lay where Pearl had left it the night before, still opened to the Yellow Pages: he had spent the previous day in a fruitless frantic search for a place to live. The town was booked solid. He had visited every one of the five apartments listed in the classified section of the Pickett *Post*, and had realized that he was seeing the dregs—dank, dark, deeply dirty places, homes for unimaginable lizards and insects. They were also not cheap. With school starting, it was clearly a seller's market; Pearl had simply not come to town in time. Every bunny was in its hutch. Phoning realtors had been Pearl's sensible, Northern idea. The people he talked to were pleasant enough at first, but they all but laughed when they heard what he wanted, even though he used his most official voice and continually dropped the phrase "teaching at the university." It cut no ice with them. Was he interested in buying a house?

Juniper had insisted Pearl could stay as long as he liked, rent-free—all he had to do was kick in some groceries. And Juniper was just nutty and nice enough (and this was the South enough) so that the offer was not merely polite. Which was exactly the trouble. Pearl had one overpowering emotion, these waning days of August: he wanted a place of his own. He could feel it in his teeth. His own air conditioner (was it too much to hope for?); his own refrigerator (he could never open Juniper's without a stab of guilt, despite having contributed thirty dollars' worth of groceries, despite his fastidious avoidance of any food specifically not his—despite the fact that Juniper would never, in a thousand years, have noticed or cared if Pearl had totally cleared the refrigerator out); his own bathroom, somewhere he wouldn't have to run into Juniper's and Leon's jockstraps, hanging chummily side by side on the shower-curtain rod. Pearl just wanted a place where he could walk in the front door and be alone. (He had spent the entire past year alone. Why did he still care so much about being alone?) His suitcases and boxes sat assembled by the cot in the purple room, packed and ready, awaiting marching orders. His books had just arrived, fourth class; the sealed cartons were stacked in his cubicle at the English department. His mind was everywhere, and nowhere, at once. Was this any way to live?

He wouldn't need coffee this morning. Pearl held the refrigerator open for a long time, wondering why he was even bothering to think about eating, yet full of superstitious dread at the thought of going without. Ordinarily he loved breakfast, and today he desperately wanted to feel ordinary. He tried (as he looked with rising gorge at the orange juice, milk, eggs) to imagine that moment of grace, ninety minutes hence, when

World Masterpieces 101 would be over, when his lungs would function properly again—and he couldn't: it was like trying to imagine life on another planet.

He started to close the refrigerator door, but stopped just short. The red-white-and-blue cans, sixteen-ouncers, stood on the bottom shelf. He smiled at his idea, as if at someone else's pleasantry—the habit he had developed in solitude. He was no longer in solitude. The rules were all changed, changing, changeable: Pearl, who was no drinker, took a beer and popped the top and drank his breakfast where he stood.

There was a crush at the doors to Culpepper Hall. Clots of boys in designer jeans and football shirts and baseball caps, and girls in pastel summer dresses (dresses! and every girl, seemingly, with the same coif: straight hair center-parted, scrolled back from the corners of the forehead and the cheeks) took their last breaths of unserious air. A few black students, their faces impassive, slipped through the doors. They had other places to gather and grin. Pearl pushed his way through the crowd, making so bold as to glance into a few faces. The girls smiled at him; the boys gave a curt nod or a wink, as if he were a frat brother whose name had just slipped their mind. Which was a matter of some wonderment to Pearl. He had worn his lucky outfit: seersucker suit, white shirt, even a black-knit tie—he was Brooksed to the eyeballs. And he was not only palpably a Northerner and a Jew, he was—he was trying to be—a teacher. Yet despite all this, despite his circular brown-metal glasses, despite his kinky hair, he wasn't taken aside and questioned; he wasn't looked at askance. He was actually passing. For what, he had no idea.

The hallway inside the front doors was cool and dark and echoing. Pearl felt a deep, familiar pang in his stomach, and realized that this same brown linoleum and tan tile had once lined the halls of P.S. 163, holding much the same terrors and promises. *School*. The crowds streamed down the hall, and Pearl moved along with them—then stopped and stared in astonishment.

Among the white plastic letters fit snugly in the furrows of a ridged black-felt board,

ASST. PROF. P. PEARL

leaped out. He stood a long time taking this in, his mouth a little open, as the crowd pushed by.

You stood dry-mouthed at the head of the room, arranging, then rearranging, your books on the table. They gawked at you as they entered, finally, unbelievingly, granting you what hadn't at first seemed possible to them. They glanced at each other for confirmation and smirked, or they sat alone, eyes blank. The room filled. It was a big room, much deeper than it was wide, and there were a lot of them. You cleared your throat and looked at the faces. You were supposed to imagine them undressed, you remembered; this was supposed to help. It didn't help. Nothing did. You cleared your throat again. You walked down the middle aisle to the back of the room, the heads turning to follow you, and you closed the rear door; then you walked back up to the front and closed the door there—you didn't want whatever it was you were going to say to be heard out in the hall. What were *you going to say? You cleared your throat again. "I need your registration cards," you announced, startled at the sound of your own voice.*

You collected the pink cards, walking among the desks, trying to smile at the kinder faces, a fraction of the tension broken. What struck you then, weirdly, as they looked up at you from their chairs, was how completely they were yours. You could lecture them, harangue them, tell a story. You could make up anything you wanted. They would sit and watch and even perhaps listen. It gave you a strange, exalted feeling— cutting, to your surprise, through the terror. You took the cards back to your table, and made some business for a long moment out of stacking

*them because suddenly you had lost the nerve to look out there. Then you
took a deep breath and looked out. The silence was like a tremendous
transparent balloon, bellying out at the pale-green walls. You looked
at the notes you had carefully made the night before. Suddenly it hit
you: they were just notes. How would you expand them into sentences
and string these sentences into a lecture that would fill the next forty
minutes?*

*To cover the sound of your heart, you simply began talking. You
told them who Homer was, or wasn't. You told them what the* Iliad
*was. You told them about oral poetry, epithets. Most of this you said
without quite looking at them, as if you were somehow ashamed of it.
A voice from the back of the room asked you to speak louder. A little
annoyed, you stared at them and repeated what you had just said,
speaking out, the words coming more easily now. The faces were dull or
incredulous, but they were awake, and no one was looking out the
window. You told them about Helen and Paris and Agamemnon, and
about fabulous Troy, astonished as you spoke that they were very probably
hearing this for the first time. From you. Now you paced as you talked,
pausing occasionally to sit on the table. If you moved, you found, their
eyes followed you. If you talked loudly and paced and seemed as though
you might be about to get angry, you found they stayed with you. You
said everything you could think of, the sentences less than miraculous
and joined by too many "and"s, your tongue a little thick; but the fact
that you were speaking at all, and that they were listening to you, ran
through you like liquor.* I could even like this, *you thought, wildly;*
they might even learn something. *It struck you for the first time.*

*Then, as abruptly as you had started, you stopped. You glanced
down at the notebook as if it would help you: someone coughed. There
was nothing left to say. You couldn't look up. Your face began to burn.
You thought desperately for a moment, as they began to stir. Wasn't
there some way to bring it all, roundly, to an end? You glanced out.
They were raising their eyebrows, beginning to rustle papers, stack books:
you had riveted yourself, you saw, but you had held them only provi-
sionally. You held them no longer. That they belonged to you was an*

illusion. You smiled, confused, as they stood and began to move toward the doors, talking and laughing, as if you had never existed. But then, as the doors opened, you remembered, as in a dream, the magic word. The spell that would hold them. Wait, you said, and they stopped, silent, as you told them what they must do if they were to come back the day after tomorrow. And they groaned, with displeasure and pleasure, and they were, they were, yours.

"You meet her yet, Philly?"

Pearl was sitting in his cubicle, at his gray metal desk, shuffling papers—the fruit of the first essay he had ever assigned. "What's that, Walter?"

"Oho, you heard me. C'mon now. Tell Uncle Walt. You meet her?"

"Meet who?"

"C'mon, Phil. Fron-*chess*-ca."

"No, Walter. How would I have met her? Why *should* I meet her?"

"Oh, Philly." Wunsch, just outside the doorway, shook his big head. "You gawn fall in love. Get married. Make babies. Live happily ever after."

Pearl clenched his teeth to restrain a smile. Part of him warmed to Wunsch's speech. It was like a spell, or a bedtime story to which a child listens raptly. Moreover, he liked Wunsch. He was a grand sensitive stranded in an improbable outpost. Pearl believed he knew the feeling. On a week's acquaintance, he felt a deep aesthetic sympathy with the man. But something was wrong. Friendship did not seem in the cards. For even as Pearl listened to Wunsch spinning out his future, he noticed something uncanny: he was accustomed to classifying utterances as sincere, or ironic, or ambivalent. Here was an ambivalence— or was it an irony?—so rich and strange that Pearl found himself unable to fathom it. The mere tip of it, all that showed, was in

Wunsch's pale glowing eyes, which seemed to convey, among a myriad of other things, a precognitive pain.

"Why don't you introduce me, Walter?"

Out at her desk, Darla looked up from her paperwork. Wunsch blinked. His innocent expression turned, for a second, almost horrified. This violated his sense of subtlety. Then he smiled slyly.

"Uh-uh, Philly," he said. "Uh-uh. That wouldn't be right."

"Right? What the hell are you talking about, Walter?"

Wunsch, a great one for poses, stood frozen in the middle of the office.

Pearl shook his head and looked back at the papers on his desk.

"You ain't mad at me, Philly?"

Pearl opened his grade book.

"Oh ho," Wunsch announced. "Philly's mad at me." And then he walked into his own office and shut the door with a neat click.

A man in a powder-green leisure suit was leaning in Pearl's doorway, lighting a pipe.

"You shouldn't let Wunsch get your goat," he said in a dry gravelly voice, shaking the match out, tracing a pretzel of smoke in the air. "He gives everyone a pain in the butt. Trick is to try and ignore him." The man smiled lopsidedly and puffed on his pipe. He was Shmoo-shaped: there was a sizable paunch beneath the leisure coat. He had a large blondish walrus mustache under a little beak of a nose, and small, wary eyes that seemed, even as he lounged in the doorway, to be aware of the space behind him. Under his Adam's apple bobbed a big yellow bow tie.

"I'm Tommy Havens," he said. "Your next-door neighbor. That's all right, don't get up. Save your energy. This place'll kick it out of you soon enough." His eyes fixed meaningfully on

Pearl's, he shifted the pipe to the other corner of his mouth. He looked, this bow tie and leisure suit, to be fiftyish. "Understand you've had poems in *The New Yorker*."

"One. One on deck."

"Well, you're way out of my league. Like to see some of your work, though, sometime." He took out the pipe and pushed at the tobacco with a match. "Ever teach before?"

Pearl shook his head.

"And ol' Wunsch is on your case right away, huh? Boy oh boy." He sniffed. "You must scare the shit out of him."

"Scare him?"

Havens relit the pipe, puffing clouds of fragrant smoke. A tentative voice came from behind him. "Dr. Hivens?"

"Yes?" he said, turning to reveal a tiny girl with a round, flushed face and two long braids. "Ah, Sueleen. My grade book awaits." He turned back to Pearl. "Teacher time," he said. "Anyhoo. I'm next door. Don't be a stranger. Oh—" He smiled with half his mouth. "Good luck."

" 'Course," Perry Armbruster was saying, "ol' Mr. Bill did like his whiskey."

Pearl and Perry were standing just outside the English department, next to the vending machines, near the second-floor landing. Faulkner was the Bill Perry was referring to, his large brown eyes wide and reverent behind brown-rimmed horn glasses. In fact, everything about Perry—eyes, glasses, hair, three-piece suit; the Mr. Pibb root beer in his hand—seemed brown. Faulkner was being wheeled out like a statue on a wagon, and Pearl stood nodding and smiling, half his attention on the milling crowd on the stairs. It was eleven: classes were changing. Faces, hair, clothes: everyone seemed healthy and Southern and placid and blank—cookie-cutter people. Faces like cookies! Like Pecan Sandies. In the week since he had arrived in Pickett, Pearl had once more become achingly aware that he was overneedy of beauty of any kind. In the past, in dry places, he had been able to distill it from unlikely sources. It was fast becoming apparent that this place was very dry indeed.

"Hello, Perry. Young Master Pearl," said a big, pale man in a tan short-sleeve shirt and gray patterned tie. "Discussing the Abstract Entities?"

This was the department chairman, Edwin Marshak. Marshak, who was built like a linebacker gone to seed, held a manila folder of papers under his large forearm as if it were a football. He put the folder to his temple.

"No, wait. I've got it," Marshak said. "The Bard of Oxford, Miss. Ol' Count No 'Count."

Perry smiled, his thin mouth making a little U.

"Sorry I can't add to the discussion," Marshak said. "My subscription to *Faulkner Studies* just ran out."

"Ha ha," Perry said, as Marshak backed away.

"Keep your ears open, Philip," Marshak said. "Never too early to specialize." He disappeared into the department.

As Pearl turned back to Perry, his attention shifted, as if guided by some homing device, to one figure among the many on the stairs—a girl, slim, dark-haired, long-legged, in designer jeans and a boy's beige shirt. She turned at the landing, walked down the hall, disappeared into a classroom on the right. All in fifteen seconds or less. And Pearl, at that moment, actually felt his tear ducts sting, as if he'd been slapped. He wasn't ready for this.

"Phil?" Pearl's eyes flicked back to Perry's baby face. Perry looked concerned, his forehead was wrinkled.

"I'm sorry, Perry. I thought I saw someone I knew."

"Well, I must say you Northern boys work fast. Here just a week, and you've already made social contacts."

Pearl smiled the briefest of social smiles back. Was Perry speaking in some kind of code? Over the past days Pearl had felt, obscurely, as though he were being watched. By whom? Surely

he was being oversensitive. Perry's brown eyes seemed to contain
not a trace of guile or gloat. He smiled sunnily at Pearl and went
back into his talk.

Pearl could not yet have described her well: he had caught
only a flash of profile, an intimation of milky skin, thick dark
eyebrows. But he knew. Our senses, he thought as Perry talked
on, were overrefined, redundant in many cases: we were lavishly
provided for. The blind, too, fell in love. Were they deluded?
Who was to say? He should be writing all this down, he thought.
Then he remembered her skin once more.

What was writing next to that skin? A shadow-play, a
simulacrum. Suddenly all the random particles of the whole
senseless world had magnetized into a dizzy dance; everything
made sense—the right and the wrong kinds of sense. This was
dangerous territory, Pearl knew. He recognized the symptoms,
dreaded them as he thrilled to them.

For the girl who had just walked by had been not merely
pretty but finally, piercingly, beautiful. No wonder poor Wunsch
was acting strangely. His highly refined sensibilities had been
deranged by this girl, thrown out of kilter. Now he wanted Pearl
to share the trouble.

Which, despite all his aesthetic hankerings, Pearl was profoundly unequipped to do. Pretty had always been hard enough;
beautiful was quite out of his depth. When push came to shove,
the real thing, the undiluted article, intimidated him. Among
all his misgivings, however, he seemed willing to try. More than
willing. *Stop*, a small voice within him said. The voice grew
smaller. For a moment he envied the blind. What a terrible thing
sight was! he thought, uneasily remembering the one last
strangely disturbing, strangely *unnecessary* bit of visual infor-
mation: the tick-tock—no, that wasn't quite it, there was a
syncope, a slight stutter; the *t-tick-t-tock*—of her exquisitely
shaped, tightly jeaned behind as she walked down the hall and
turned into the doorway, again and again and again.

VI

Pickett was white-hot under its flat blue sky. Every sane person in town was indoors—everyone, Pearl thought, except for himself, a loose nut in a hot car, searching, no longer very hopefully, for a place to live. As if to mock him, the rock singer on the radio (there was nothing on the air but rock, religion, and country; Pearl had chosen the least of the three evils) was chanting, hoarse-voiced, over and over:

takin' it to the streets

Pearl had been at Juniper's for a week now, and the canvas of the army cot was beginning to feel like the fabric of his existence. He wanted out in the worst way, yet Pickett didn't seem ready to oblige. This afternoon he had given up on the classifieds and realtors and simply gone on a random drive. But the endless grid of back streets was totally claimed, utterly settled: perhaps, he thought, fate simply hadn't meant for him to fit in. To make matters worse, he was no longer certain just where he was. He had entered a neighborhood south of the main drag, Jackson Street, and had proceeded practically enough by a series of right-angle jogs. Most of the town was laid out lattice-fashion. But then Pearl had turned onto the aptly named Lawn View, a district of hypertrophied ranch houses and their eponymous expanses of thick smug sward, and the street had begun to curve and curve, until at last Pearl felt like an upside-down figure in a Chagall. He looked with discomfort at the big, low houses. Their air conditioners hummed cozily. Not an occupant was in sight. In his hopelessly sensible and optimistic way, Pearl had somehow expected to be granted a place to live as a matter of course. Sensibleness, he was beginning to see, was a Puritan virture, painfully irrelevant here among the spiky vegetation and strange license plates (lipstick-red letters and numerals on a white background, with a faintly limned, almost subliminal, tooth-paste-green magnolia blossom in the center, over which was printed "the Hospitality State").

At last, Pearl came to an intersection—34th Avenue. 34th Avenue! To the Manhattanite in him, it connoted such a remove from the real, coherent, twelve-avenue world that it made his brain ache. *Where was he?* He turned right. And suddenly 34th Avenue was ending, and he found himself—alley-oop—at the main drag again. Spat back out, like a foreign body. The cars whizzed by. Still, at least he knew where he was now. If he turned right he could go home to Juniper's. This knowledge, though smacking of defeat, gave him an odd shiver of pleasure: in a strange, unwilled way, he was beginning to know his way around. *Right is home.*

Yesterday he had ascended the new science tower, at ten stories the highest building, by far, on campus—the highest in the county. From the top floor (there was a constant, faint, eerie whistling up there, like something in a movie about ancient Egypt) Pearl had observed that he was smack in the center of a vast plain of pines. Pickett, someone had told him, was the population center, the commercial hub, of the county. Elsewhere, all was trees. The blue-green expanse extended in every direction, modulating, at vision's limits, into an all-blue haze. Not a hill of any sort in sight. The campus sat at the crossing of the interstate and Jackson, which met in the center of the circle of his purview like the crosshairs of a bomb sight, or an X and Y axis. X would be the interstate, with its motels and big malls. Y was Jackson Street, with its convenience stores and gas stations. Where was Z? Of course it would be vertical. Vertical? Yes. Z would represent transcendence of some kind, or at least the possibility of getting up high enough to glimpse familiar ground.

But familiar ground was thirteen hundred miles away. And unless you went to the top of the science tower (and something about that Egyptian whistling and the painted cinder block and gleaming linoleum and locked blond-wood doors with wire-glass panes gave Pearl the creeps, made him want to *get back down*), you never saw a horizon. A fact Pearl found fundamentally disturbing. You just walked around down there among the grinning cookie faces, a point on the Cartesian plane.

Back in upstate New York, there had been hills to climb! If little else. He remembered, with a pang (pain mixed with regret, tincture of nostalgia) the vastnesses of Washington County: the ten-mile roads between somethings in the middle of nowhere, with only the black-and-white Holsteins, standing munching on their steep hillsides, for company. Pellagra country. Child abuse, alcoholism, welfare, out among the gorgeous green hills. A few stolid working farmers. Social contacts had been infrequent. But in his bleakest moments in Delbertsville, Pearl could always walk up one of the steep sheepy knobs that surrounded the farm, and dream. Never before had he felt so ground-bound as he did this late-summer afternoon, sitting in his car at the intersection of 34th and Jackson. The sky above—it had been the exact same bright-blue each and every single day since his arrival—seemed mortuary somehow: not an ether but a lid.

Jackson Street was divided by a grassy median, so the only

turn Pearl could make here was a right—back, through already covered territory, to the army cot. He sighed, and turned. But then, on an impulse, at the next gap in the median, he hung a U and headed west.

He had never been out this way before—the opposite direction from everything, downtown and the highway and school. The street was less built-up here, was still lined with tall pines, first growth. Up ahead, on the left, was the Little Big Mall: the westernmost edge of town, the county line. Beyond, the trees. Pearl felt a superstitious dread at the sight of the mall, an explorer's fear—as if he were approaching the edge of the earth. Pearl the city dweller couldn't quite get used to the emptiness of much of the country. There was something scary about it— it made him understand the urge to conquer and pave. In medieval Europe, reports had filtered back from Africa that men's heads, down there, grew under their necks. After a week in Pickett, Pearl understood how something like that could get started. He wondered who lived out there in the trees. Nervous, he took a quick left into the Little Big Mall's parking lot.

Here, at the outskirts of the asphalt expanse, was a small white concrete cube with a roof overhanging a driveway, a drive-in branch of First Mississippi Trust. Under the blasting sun, the short overhang gave the only shade for acres. Pearl drove underneath.

Behind the green glass sat a girl. She was pretty-plain, her purplish mouth wide and thin-lipped, her skin so white it must have been powdered, her dark hair lank. She looked big-boned— a girl capable of handling herself.

She sat up straight and smiled, as if she had been expecting him. Pearl smiled, too.

"Hi," he said into the microphone.

"Hey." Her husky voice, issuing from the speaker, seemed ever so slightly out of sync with the movement of her lips.

"I, uh—" What? "I wanted to ask about opening an account," Pearl improvised. "Not right away. I mean, I don't get p—I wanted to wait a week or so."

She leaned her chin on her hand and goggled at him.

"Would that be possible here?" he asked.

She blinked.

"Or would there be a better branch?" he asked. "The main one or something? Maybe downtown."

Now she squinted at him a moment, as if trying to get him into focus.

"Hello?" Pearl said.

"I am *sorry*," she said, "but I am just *dyin'* of curiosity? I mean I—" She shook her head vigorously, almost vehemently. Her gestures themselves seemed big-boned—too big for the confines of the little booth. "Never mind," she said.

"What?"

"Never mind, never mind, never *mind*. Oh"—she closed her eyes and put a hand to her face—"I am makin' a *fool* out of myself? Never mind."

Pearl caught a flicker of movement at the edge of his vision. He glanced into his rearview mirror and saw a white car behind him, part in and part out of shadow. The driver was invisible behind the stunning white light reflected off the windshield. "I think I'd better move," he said.

The voice coming from the speaker was suddenly tiny, breathless. "You're not from New *York*?"

He stared at her, then slowly nodded.

"I *knew* it?" she whooped. "Now how did I know that?"

A large red hand plopped onto the Volvo's windowsill. Pearl looked up the thick arm and saw a blistery red face, under black sunglasses, over a white short-sleeved shirt. " 'Scuse me, son," the man said to Pearl, with a blistery wince of a smile. He turned to the green pane. "Young lady, you open for bidness?"

The girl sat up very straight. "No sir?" she said. "I mean. It's just now three o'clock?"

"Well now. That light was green when I drove up."

"No sir?"

"*Young* lady—"

"No sir, it was green, I mean red? I mean—maybe it was the strong sunlight makin' you see it the other way? 'Cause I know that happens with me sometimes."

The man looked at her and then down at Pearl. He shook his head and went back to his car.

She grinned behind her glass. "My name's Tammy?" she said.

They walked with their Cokes across the heatstruck parking lot. The white cube and the gray Volvo were shimmering dots in the distance. Tammy was talking.

"Wow, that must be so excitin'? To teach and all? What subject? Now, don't tell me. Science."

"English."

"It was just a guess. I take real lucky guesses sometimes— it runs in my mother's side of the family? I look lots more like my daddy, though. Huh, English. Now, that figures, doesn't it. I bet you're real good at it, too. English, I mean?"

Pearl cleared his throat. "I, uh—"

"That's right, that's right, that's right. You were lookin' for apartments." She squinched up her forehead. "Now, have you tried the Deauville? That's a real nice place."

"Full."

"How 'bout the Versailles?"

"Also."

"Stratford Arms?"

Pearl shook his head.

"Alpine Village? Fountain Bleau? Forrest Royale?"

"Nothing."

"Colonial Oaks? El Madrid?"

He sighed.

"Now, I guess you already tried Camelot? Because I know this girl Jewel that lives there, and she likes it a *whole* bunch? Of course she lives right by the pool, but she hasn't always lived by the p—"

"Camelot?"

A left on North 36th brought Pearl into a pine grove, sparsely populated, with only the odd dented trailer or dusty shack peeking out from between the tall trunks. This was exurban Pickett: tracts here were marked with stakes and twine. New fire hydrants, visible down to the pipe connections, stuck out from the orange clayey soil.

He had been driving for a half hour, and the park and the golf course Tammy had mentioned were nowhere in evidence. The shadows were beginning to lengthen. Pearl's stomach churned: he suddenly remembered he had eaten no lunch. Now the street came to a dead end. This was a nightmare. His temples felt as though they were in a vise. He thought of Juniper's, and suddenly felt a sweet rush of longing. *Home.* He turned right—onto Morningside Drive. He stared at the street sign. Good luck? After four blocks the street came to a halt. Pearl took a right, turned right again; turned left, then left again and again. And again. There were tears in his eyes. He took a deep breath: *calm down.* He would ask for help. Why must he always insist on his sense of direction? He slowed, looking for anyone on foot, and then saw the sign, reading, in armorial print: CAMELOT.

The complex was a low brown mock-Tudor sprawl, its design some triply removed parody of Anne Hathaway's cottage, the resulting module replicated and stacked all over the place. It didn't appear to be quite finished, however. Bare-chested men were pushing around wheelbarrows full of dirt, and the narrow strips of ground between and in front of buildings were checker-boarded with fresh sod and earth.

Jewel by the pool, Pearl kept thinking, as he climbed the concrete steps to the balcony above Camelot's central courtyard, with its smallish but—now that he thought of it—very jewellike pool. It was a very big deal down here, being by the pool. In the heat of the afternoon, Pearl began to understand. He started to wonder, anxiously, if he could be one of the pool-elect. If there was even a vacancy. He shook his head. He was dreaming again.

He rang the bell, which appeared to be out of order. He tapped on the brick-red steel door. Nobody home. He sighed. *Jewel not by the pool*, he thought, as he started back down the balcony. Wrong turns, dead ends—when would he connect?

On the patio by the diving board, he squatted down for a second and sloshed a finger in the water. Not too warm, not too cool. Just right. He half-considered stripping off where he stood and jumping right in. They wouldn't like that. Strangers in underwear. Unwelcome.

He trudged back toward his car. The men with their barrows looked busy, purposeful. What if . . . why not?

"Excuse me," Pearl called to one of the workmen. "Can you tell me where to find the manager?"

The man, flabby and pale-chested, with a wispy mustache and narrow eyes, one of them crossed, grinned and put down his load of sod. He clapped the dirt off his hands, spat, and nodded. "I'm it," he said.

"How long has the place been open, Mr. Stubbs?" Pearl asked. They were standing in the central courtyard, where the manager had stopped so that Pearl might—once more—admire the swimming pool. A Styrofoam coffee cup, one of the workmen's, no doubt, had blown or fallen into the water. Pearl watched it bobbing on the surface for a few moments. The windows of the surrounding apartments gazed down, blank and impassive.

"No Mister. Just Stubbs," Stubbs said. He scratched his belly thoughtfully. "Two weeks, about." He jerked his chin toward the water. "Nice?"

Pearl nodded. Nice. But this was not their final destination. This was just to show Pearl what he had missed. Stubbs glanced around and sighed. "Poolside was snatched right up," he explained, grinning regret. Now he led Pearl through to another set of buildings. They walked on a newly poured concrete path that twisted and turned around the freshly sodded property like something in a child's board game. The path passed a huge forest-green dumpster, crossed a small plot of cedar chips, and came out on another street. They turned past a stumpy palm tree, climbed a flight of concrete-and-steel steps, walked down a balcony, and stopped in front of another red-brown steel door. The door, and its doorbell, were identical to Jewel's, but oh so far from the pool. Pearl looked around. The view here was of the dumpster, the stumpy palm, and another, much uglier apartment complex across the street. Stubbs, his white chest and belly heaving from the climb, pulled a gigantic ring of keys from his jeans pocket and opened the door.

A draft of overpoweringly stuffy air emerged. Pearl saw a brown-carpeted room littered with cartons and clothes. "What's all this?" he asked.

"Oh, I'm havin' to evict the present tenant."

"What for?"

"Nonpayment of rent." Stubbs grinned, screwy-eyed, as if he had just told a terrific joke. "She'll be out by tomorrow mornin', though," he said. "I'll have it cleaned right up for you."

Pearl walked through the first room into the next, numb. He stared at the brown shag carpet, scattered pathetically with the evictee's belongings. A bright-green Afro comb lay at his feet. Was this, after all, where he was ending up? Now that he could have it, he wasn't at all sure he wanted it. *But there was nothing else.* He saw himself in the maze of his housing quest, driving the streets of Pickett, turning right, bumping a wall, turning left, bumping another wall, turning, turning, ending up here. Surely free will was a joke.

Stubbs, pungent, stood behind him in the bedroom doorway (the only exit), his plump arms folded expectantly. Pearl could, of course, simply say no and walk out. He looked unhopefully at the white walls and up at the white impastoed ceiling, its stiff swirls like petrified frosting or aerial photos of Arctic wastes. The place seemed as compact and sterile as a space capsule. It also had a sweet new space-smell, something compounded of carpeting and wiring and wall material. The one eccentricity was a huge walk-in closet off the bedroom, almost a room itself. Pearl walked in. For some reason he had always liked closets. They reminded him of hide-and-seek. He remembered the almost sexual pleasure of hiding, standing in the dark among clothes that exuded parental aromas. In hide-and-seek he had invariably chosen the closet, had invariably been found first. Something glorious about being *found* . . .

Pearl lingered in the closet, meditating, pretending to size up the water heater and fuse box. Behind him, Stubbs was actually tapping his foot. Pearl was wasting the man's time. Why couldn't he come to a decision? Something about the place spooked him. There seemed to be no room for the imagination. He found himself once more thinking longingly of Juniper's hound-dog house, with its redolent expanses: cars and animals in the yard, Leon in the attic, chili on the stove, twangy stuff on the stereo. It wasn't so bad. He could, he knew, stay on in the purple room until Dawn came back—he could stay forever. He must, he knew, get out. And this place was clean, modern, available. *Available.* There had to be something wrong if it was available. His mind chugged uphill like the Little Engine That Could, and now Stubbs, in the closet doorway, was clearing his throat. Loudly. The engine reached the Now. "I'll take it," Pearl said.

Stubbs glowed like a light bulb. "Well, fine!"

"I can move in tomorrow?"

A wink. "How 'bout today?"

"I have a class at two. Maybe around four o'clock?"

"You the boss, Big Chief."

"You'll need a security deposit? A month's rent in advance?" Was he saying the man's lines for him?

"Nah. You teach over to the college, right? I can always just put a lien on your salary." Stubbs giggled.

Pearl's first official act as a householder, once he had dropped his boxes and suitcases on the brown carpet, was to drive downtown and buy a queen-sized mattress. (Juniper had lent him a hundred—flip flip flip flip flip, five twenties, no questions asked.) Two boys tied it on top of the Volvo ("What kinda *cor* is this?"), and Pearl drove home—*home!*—at fifteen miles an hour, his left arm hooked out the window over his huge, weirdly light cargo. The brown-paper-wrapped mattress flapped perilously in the wind, threatening to take flight at any moment. This, Pearl felt, was a picture for eternity: himself as a young man, driving through the slanting orange light of a Mississippi late afternoon, his hopeful burden (twin-sized had been only twelve dollars less) atop his faithful car. The knight embarking on his quest. Like Rembrandt's Polish Rider at the Frick. He hugged the gigantic unwieldy package up the concrete stairs and down the balcony and into his apartment by main force, by sheer dint of will; once inside, he heaved the mattress to the floor and stood panting and sweating. *Home.* He ripped off the brown paper, and the mattress lay revealed on his floor, pale-blue, expectant, beautiful. He said a silent, godless benediction over it.

Later that evening he bought sixty dollars' worth of groceries and kitchen supplies at Winn Dixie. The next morning he had a phone installed. A red telephone. His own number. There was fire in his cave.

And soon he was playing with it. The moment he got home from class that evening, he opened his crisp new directory (on the cover was a photograph of a stream rushing through a forest of deciduous trees—where was this stream? Pearl wondered) precisely to the R's, and saw, immediately before his eyes, as if fate had placed it there, "Raffi Giuseppe 42 Sparks." He put his books down on his new Formica counter (beige, lightly flecked with silver) and stood for a moment, his head bowed in thought. During this brief meditation, Pearl considered what still lingered of his adolescence. Much of it lingered, apparently. He wasn't actually going to go through with this? Evidently he was. He remembered, with full force, what it felt like to be eighteen— the painful hesitations and imaginings. . . . Eighteen! He could almost laugh at himself. He was thirty-one years old.

And alone.

And this was foolish.

He remembered the milky skin. He extrapolated.

And he was out of his depth. He thought of the crystalline pool. He looked at the rushing stream.

A woman's voice—light, not quite ageable—answered. She?

Pearl asked for her by her full name, savoring for the first time *Francesca Raffi* on his tongue.

"She's not in right now. May I ask who's calling, please?"

There were a thousand ways this line could have been delivered, most of them falling somewhere between the Guarded and the Forbidding—but something, something, about this woman's voice made Pearl melt. It was her mother, then. There was something liquid and intelligent about the voice, songlike.

Moreover, the accent was Northern. It made Pearl, stranger in a strange land, want to confess, to tell this woman his secrets, his life story.

But what could he *say?*

He cleared his throat. This was absurd. He had come too far to falter. "Is this Mrs. Raffi?"

"Yes?"

"Mrs. Raffi, my name is Philip Pearl. I teach in the English department?" He paused. *Idiot,* he thought. So what? What else? *I want to marry your daughter. When can I meet her?*

"Yes, Mr. Pearl! Are you new here in Pickett?"

"Yes, I am. Please—call me Philip."

"But Philip—we haven't even met! What do you think of our burg? You sound like you're from out of state."

"Oh, it's very nice."

"Well, aren't *you* nice and polite. Chesca's off at an Honors picnic right now. Shall I have her call you back?"

An Honors picnic. She was at an Honors picnic. The images raced through his mind: nymphs and satyrs in mortarboards. Crinoline. *Déjeuner sur l'herbe. Speak.* "Oh, no, no," Pearl said. "No. I mean, I should—I should be the one who calls, I think. I guess." He blushed. Audibly, he was sure. This was absurd.

"Well, why don't I just give her the message and leave it up to her."

"Thank you."

Incredibly, however, the woman didn't seem quite ready to get off the phone. "Have you met Joe?" she asked.

"Joe?"

"Giuseppe. My husband. He teaches in the music department—I thought that must be why you called."

Pearl winced. "No. No, I haven't."

"Oh well, you will. Joe's unavoidable. Maybe you can come over sometime for dinner."

When? "I'd love to."

"Good! Well, Philip. I must get back to my roast."

A roast. Pearl's entire being, his heart and soul, hungered for this roast. "Thank you, Mrs. Raffi," he said.

"Helen. Thank you for what?"

Pearl began to blush again. "I don't know."

"Usually between seven thirty and eight is a good time to reach Chesca."

"O.K."

"That you can thank me for."

"Thank you, Helen."

"Good night, Philip."

A man answered (next night; seven forty-five precisely): his hello was a gaily sung spondee, two notes descending.

"Mr. Raffi?"

"Yes?"

Pearl told his tale once more, in abbreviated form; this time, however, there was the all-important addendum: "I called last night?"

"Oh, that's right. You're the fella from the English department." Francesca was at an evening class. Walter Wunsch's: Did Philip know him? She'd be back about ten.

"Could I call then?"

"Sure! Why not?"

At 10:05 Pearl held the receiver once more, his palms sweating. What was left of his nerve was fading fast. This was not only absurd but idiotic. A female voice answered: similar to Helen's, but—?

"Hello," Pearl said, "I—"

"Hi, Philip, it's Helen. Francesca's gone out with some friends."

"Oh." She had friends.

"Why don't I have her call you back?"

"That's all right."

"Don't you want her to?"

"I—um."

"Tonight'll probably be too late. How about tomorrow?"

Pearl gazed miserably at the wall. "Sure," he said.

"Hey!"

Pearl was walking around Camelot early the next morning, trying, in the clear, reasonable light of morning, to sort all this out, when he heard someone calling. He squinted across the street. He needed a new eyeglass prescription. It was a woman— tall, with long, reddish curly hair. Not bad-looking. For a moment he had the fantasy that this was someone from his past, from the city—an old lover? Someone just on the edge of his memory, here to mock him for this place.

"Hey! How you doin'?"

Pearl crossed the street. She looked better closer up—across a street you didn't see the fineness of her skin or the humor in her large brown eyes. She was wearing jeans and high boots, a fringed buckskin jacket, a purple blouse with sparkly stuff on it.

"You don't remember me, do you," she said, smiling.

"Sure I do. I, uh—"

"Bullshitter."

Pearl smiled. "I remember that I remember you."

She put out her hand. "Jewel," she said.

Something in his head turned and zoomed. He had the powerful impression of having done all this before. "You're the Jewel who—?" He stopped, dizzy.

She batted her eyelashes humorously.

He shook her hand. It was largish, dry, firm. "Phil Pearl."

"Hezekiah's," she said.

"The waitress," Pearl said.

"In one incarnation, yeah. What do you do around here?"

"I teach." Pearl pointed in the direction of school. "Composition, literature, poetry."

"Oh yeah? You a poet?"

"In one incarnation."

She nodded approvingly, not unhumorously. She seemed to be taking him with a grain of salt. "So, Pearl. You finding Pickett inspirational?"

"Very."

"Now I *know* you're a bullshitter."

"It's not too bad."

"Just wait a while."

"Why? How long have you been here?"

"Oh, 'bout twenty years too long."

She seemed slightly "on," theatrical. Around such types, Pearl tended to clam up, get confused. He nodded. "You live in the apartment over the pool?" he said.

"Why, Pearl! That might be taken as a personal question."

He blushed. "I meant it—your friend Tammy said—"

"Tammy? Tammy Spraggs? Girl that was vaccinated with a phonograph needle?"

Pearl smiled.

"What *has* that girl been doing? Puttin' me on the guided tour?"

"I was just looking for a place to live."

"Well? What'd you find?"

"I'm right here."

"Well, I'll be. Camelot?"

"C 14."

She reached out her hand once more. "Meet A 19," she said. "Poolside."

VII

He was sitting in his office with a boy who was doing his best to explain why it was necessary for him to drop World Masterpieces, when Wunsch appeared in the doorway, beaming.

"You realize you'll just have to take this course again later?" Pearl said. The boy, who wore a baseball cap with the word CAT printed inexplicably on the peak, slumped in the plastic chair next to Pearl's desk.

"Yessir."

"It's not going to be any easier then."

"Nosir."

"All right, I'll sign the form. Here, give it to me."

"Yessir."

"Go and be well."

"Yessir. Thank you, sir."

"Jesus, is it me?" Pearl asked Wunsch when the boy had gone. "And what is it with the 'sir's? Does it mean he hates my guts? What are you grinning about, Walter?"

"Oh, Philly."

"What?"

"Oh, Philly. *My,* my."

"My my what? What is it?"

"Someone's been makin' a *lot* of telephone calls around here, has he not?" Wunsch's teeth, Pearl noticed, were exceptionally white and even.

"What?"

"Thass all right, Philly. Perf'ly O.K."

"Walter, I—"

"You just keep it up. You seem to be doin' fine." Wunsch turned, laughing his barrel-bottom laugh, and walked across to his door. "My, my," he kept saying to himself, as he turned the key in the lock. "*My,* my."

Pearl had finished his meal of stir-fry frozen vegetables. He was sitting at his Formica counter, chin in hand, *World Master-pieces 1* open in front of him (Elpenor sliding off Circe's roof; Juniper somehow mixed in), when the phone rang.

The phone was an alarmingly bright red to begin with, and the bell, even turned all the way down, had, in Pearl's space-capsule of an apartment, the force of a gong.

Elpenor had just hit the ground, the nape nerve shattered.

"Is this Phil Pearl?" the familiar female voice asked.

"Helen. What's—"

"Hi, Phil. This is Francesca."

Her voice was almost exactly her mother's, identical in timbre, equally cool and delicious, but slightly higher in pitch. The result was a different quality: a clinginess, Pearl thought, as in certain kinds of wet air. Francesca, moreover, had a trace of a Southern accent.

"I feel kind of silly," Pearl confessed. "I mean, I don't know exactly how to explain why I called."

"Oh, that's all right. Why don't you tell me 'bout the English department. How you like teaching. All that stuff."

Also like her mother, and her father, she spoke in a kind of recitatif. Something about this family music put Pearl at ease: he felt, in a strange way, as if he knew them already—had known them for years.

"The English department?" Pearl said. "You really want to know?"

"Sure!"

"It's ridiculous," Pearl blurted. "I mean, teaching's ridiculous." Was this the right thing to say? Was it even what he wanted to say? He had made them cough in Masterpieces this morning; after lunch, in Composition, he'd gotten flustered, had lost his train of thought, and had stood there blushing and opening and closing his mouth like a fish while the freshmen laughed at him. Then the boy had come in to drop his course. All this was unpleasant enough, but was it teaching's fault? Or was it, perhaps, hers?

Or Wunsch's?

"I mean, I—I shouldn't be telling you this," he said.

"You think it's news to me? I been goin' here three years."

"I mean," Pearl said, his resolve slackening at the sound of her voice, "they sit and *stare* at me."

She laughed, a little tune. "They do do that, don't they?"

After a while, as if it were the most natural thing in the world, Pearl took the phone receiver and lay down on his brown carpet with it. Their conversation went freely, lightly, touching on this and that—nothing personal, of course (it was almost as if all this were known, and accepted, already), but nothing trivial, either. They discussed the town, the campus, department personalities—Wunsch conspicuously excepted. It seemed a sort of orientation, at last, into the reality of the place. There were no silences. When the first pause came, over an hour had passed. Was there any reason, thought Pearl, cozy with the phone in the thickness of his shag carpet, that they shouldn't be married at once?

"I'd like to meet you," he said. "Would that be all right?"
Polite Pearl!

A hesitation. "Sure."

What was wrong? He hastened to solidify his position.
"How about Culpepper? Tomorrow?"

No reply.

"Tomorrow's no good?"

Silence again. Pearl repeated the question.

"No, tomorrow's all right," she said. "How 'bout outside
somewhere?"

"The front entrance? One o'clock?"

She didn't answer. It was almost as if the connection had
gone bad.

"Is anything wrong?" he asked. But if anything were, would
she tell him?

There was another pause. "Why don't we make it the side,"
she said.

Twelve oh five. Darla glanced up, big-eyed. "Mester
Wunsch was lookin' for you," she said, and Pearl saw that
Wunsch's door, like a coquette's fan, was wide open. What were
the chances, Pearl wondered, of getting across the office, to his
own shuttable door, unnoticed? He had made it halfway when
he heard the single syllable of his first name rumble out of
Wunsch's doorway.

"Hello, Walter."

Wunsch was sitting with his cowboy boots propped up on
his desk. "What ho, young Lochinvar. How goes it."

"Pretty well, I guess."

"Stop in. Be neighborly."

"I've got office hours."

"Darla'll tell 'em where you are. Won't you, Darla?" he
called.

"Yes sir."

"Set yourself down, Philly. Make yourself comfortable."

"I really shouldn't stay long."

"Sit *down*, Phil. Relax. Tell ol' Uncle Walt how everything's goin'."

"Fine."

Wunsch smiled broadly. "I bet it is. Oh, Phil. You a devil, you know that?"

"How exactly do you mean, Walter?"

"Love it. *Love* it. So tell me. When we gone play some tennis?"

"Tennis?"

"Sure. Bat the ball around. Get a suntan." He lit a cigarette, shook the match out.

"I didn't know you played, Walter."

He looked injured. "Me?"

"I'm sorry. I just meant—I don't know."

"You didn't think I was the athletic type."

"I didn't say that."

"You thought it, though, Phil. Thought it. I could see the brain waves, comin' out of your head." He made little wavy motions with his hands. " 'Walter not athletic. Would look funny in shorts.' 'M I right?"

Pearl bit his lip.

"Aw, come on, Phil. Now, how do you know I couldn't whip the pants off you in tennis? I used to play, you know. Nearly every day—four, five hours. Look at that surprised look on his face."

"It's not surprised, Walter."

"It's—?"

"Thoughtful."

"Ah. Well." A quick smile. "Things going swimmingly for you in the academic department?"

"Pretty well. It's all—new."

"I see what you mean. See perfectly what you're driving at." Wunsch rested his cigarette hand on the desk, next to a black plastic ashtray, and stared at Pearl through smoke for what seemed like a full minute. Finally Pearl averted his eyes. The walls of Wunsch's office were completely bare, he noticed, except for a piece of paper, some kind of form, taped to the wall in back of him. Pearl squinted, trying to read it. It seemed to say MISSISSIPPI DEATH CERTIFICATE.

Wunsch blew smoke toward the window. He raised his eyebrows, looking over Pearl's head. "Student, Phil."

Tommy Havens was standing in the doorway, pipe in hand. "Very funny, Wunsch," he said. "I can bother you later, Philip."

"No no. That's all right," Pearl said, standing. "I'd better get back to my office, anyway. I'll see you, Walter?"

Wunsch tapped his cigarette on the rim of the ashtray, once, twice. He glanced at Pearl. "Uh-huh."

"How well do we know each other, Philip?" Tommy closed Pearl's door behind him.

"Pretty well, Tommy. I guess." Pearl smiled at Tommy's serious expression, but then saw that a slight tremor was playing around his lips. "Is everything O.K.?"

"Well enough for me to ask you a favor?"

"What is it, Tommy?"

"Do you think you could find it in yourself—" He seemed to search for the words.

"To?"

"To read something I've written," he said, all but inaudibly.

"You're kidding."

He looked surprised. "Why?"

"I mean—sure. Why not?"

"It's a poem."

"Fine. Just give it to me anytime."

"I've already shown it to everyone else in the department. Last year. No one liked it. Wunsch laughed."

"No."

"Please don't tell him you've read it."

Pearl peered once more at Tommy to see if he was serious. He was entirely serious. "I won't," Pearl promised.

Tommy cleared his throat. "I uh. Happen to have it on me."

"Great."

He produced several folded sheets of paper from his jacket pocket, cleared his throat again, and handed them to Pearl. "It's about my bloodhound, Oscar," Tommy said.

"Huh."

"I bought him in Fayette," Tommy explained. "Hence the title." He had relaxed a little; he took his pipe, which he had put in his pocket, out again and began searching for matches.

"It's a ballad," Tommy said. "Iambic tetrameter. A little bit after Alfred, Lord Tennyson, but most think it's closer to Robert Service."

"It sounds like fun, Tommy." Pearl glanced at the poem, which was titled "The Fayette Fyce." It began,

> On winter nights of snow and ice,
> When storm clouds cross the hunter's moon,
> And Boreas shakes the house, I dream
> About the Fayette Fyce . . .

"I know it's not serious poetry," Tommy said, "but I think it's kind of rhythmic and enjoyable, and I thought you might be able to tell me if you think any place you know of might be interested in publishing it. Not *The New Yorker*, of course."

"Great. I'll read it and let you know."

"There's absolutely no hurry."

"I'll read it tonight."

"Thank you, Philip. I appreciate this."

"Sure, Tommy."

"The other people in this department can be such assholes. It's refreshing to find somebody nice for a change." He nodded to emphasize his words, and scratched a wooden match on the cinder block. Holding the flame poised over the bowl of his pipe, he stared meaningfully at Pearl.

"Knock knock."

Five of one. The man in Pearl's doorway—thin and smooth-faced, his jaws working a piece of gum—looked in coolly, with long-lashed, almond-shaped eyes behind small round gold-rimmed glasses. He held his trim body lazily, cockily: like a dancer, Pearl thought. The impression was reinforced by his outfit—tight jeans and a collarless shirt.

"That's all right," the man said. "Don't get up." But Pearl had already begun, with the result that he shook hands from a kind of crouch.

"Nat Wadkin," the man said, squeezing Pearl's hand hard.

"Good to meet you, Nat."

"Knight. Like the chess piece." He smiled quickly, letting Pearl see, for an instant, the piece of green gum in his mouth. It seemed Pearl's turn to say something—but what? He indicated, deprecatingly, the pile of papers before him. "Pop quizzes," he said.

Wadkin shook his head sympathetically. "You're on the treadmill already," he said. "Welcome aboard." His voice was soft and rich, with a trace of an accent that sounded Southern and yet seemed different from the local variety. He slouched in the doorway—so small was Pearl's office that Wadkin had been able to shake hands without entering—and scanned the walls and bookshelves, nodding slightly (approvingly?), as if to the beat of some inner song. His gum-chewing became more pronounced as he nodded: Pearl could see the double-banded contours of his jaw muscles as they flexed and relaxed, flexed and relaxed. Wadkin's thin cheeks were astonishingly smooth, as if he never had to shave; yet there was a haze of whiskers above his lip and around his chin.

"This was Wunsch's office, wasn't it," Wadkin said, his eyes on the far wall.

"Last year."

Wadkin nodded. "I'm over on the other side," he said, indicating, with a motion of his head, the identical wing of offices around the corner. Such was the force of Pearl's habit that he had never been there. "Don't get over here much," Wadkin said. He smiled whitely, once more showing Pearl the green gum. "So," he said. "How's it goin'?"

"Oh, not bad." More of an answer seemed to be called for. Pearl riffled the pile of papers in front of him. "I give them a lot of these."

Wadkin winked. "That's the way," he said. The gum chewing had become, if possible, even more vehement. Wadkin stared at Pearl until Pearl had to avert his eyes. When he looked back, Wadkin had resumed his survey of the cubicle.

Some sort of commotion was going on out in the office. Pearl could hear Darla's voice: "Mester *Wunsch*," she was saying, exasperatedly. Pearl craned his neck to see, but Wadkin was standing directly in the way.

"Walter, Darla," said Wunsch's voice. "Walter. When you gawn learn?"

"Mester Wunsch, ah *need* that book."

Wadkin smiled at Pearl. "Gettin' any?" he asked.

"Excuse me?"

"Gettin' any more used to this place? I heard you were a little"— he shrugged—"homesick." His glance just grazed Pearl's before moving off again.

Heard? From whom? Pearl hadn't spoken of this to a soul. The man had cut it from whole cloth. "I'm fine," he said.

"Long way from home, though, huh?"

"I guess so."

"Me, too," Wadkin said. "I'm from North Carolina. That's as good as New York when you're down here." He smiled brilliantly.

Wunsch's voice rolled in from outside. "What's my name," he said.

"Mester *Wunsch*."

"What's my name."

"Wolter," said Darla's reluctant voice.

"I can't *hear* youuu," Wunsch sang.

Pearl tried once more to see, but Wadkin was leaning cozily into the doorjamb, as if he were quite prepared to stay all day. "You just need to make some friends, is all," he said to Pearl. He lowered his voice. "There are a number of fine young women on this campus, Phil."

Pearl stared at him.

"Then again, not everyone likes young women."

"I like young women."

"So I've heard."

Pearl finally said, "I don't understand."

"How's that?"

"What have you heard?"

"Oh, that." Wadkin pointed, as if at something in the air. "That's just a figure of speech." He smiled ingratiatingly. "Healthy, good-looking young man arrives on campus—creates a certain amount of interest. Bound to happen."

"I see."

"Watch out, though."

"Excuse me?"

"Watch out you don't break any hearts," Wadkin said.

"Down here they tell their daddies." He pulled an imaginary trigger and clicked his gum.

Now he stood up straight and stretched luxuriously. "Hey, you ought to come over for dinner sometime," he said. "Deanna's a hell of a cook."

Pearl winced a smile.

Wadkin pointed his finger at Pearl and pulled the trigger once more. "We'll get you later," he said. And left.

VIII

The side door of Culpepper let out beneath a little breezeway that connected to the next building. To the left was a huge air-conditioning unit, roaring like a jet in takeoff; to the right was a small dusty courtyard with, oddly enough in this land of live oaks, an actual deciduous one, *quercus alba*—a transplant?—shading a small concrete bench. Pearl sat down. A squirrel flitted around in the dust, almost at his feet, ignoring him.

Outside the courtyard, beyond the shade of the tree and the building, the sun-struck quadrangle was too bright to look at. It was, Pearl realized with a small shock, the first of September. This made no sense. The September he knew had to do with change and urgency, with Vivaldi's "Autumn." But Vivaldi bore no relation to this hot flat place, to the unbearable sunlight or the fantastic heat or the persistent dull boom of the air conditioner. His heart was booming, too—pounding quite uncontrollably. Let it, Pearl thought.

At his feet, the squirrel flicked through dust the same color as himself. Shadow-tail. Its movements were quick, jerky, almost insectlike—movement of a different order from our own ponderous and smooth animation. Smooth, at least, was what Pearl hoped for. He prayed no one he knew would pass by: he was in no shape for small talk. But this was the midst of lunch hour; most classes had let out at noon. He had seen Wunsch amble off to the Pantheteria. And this was the side, less-used, entrance to Culpepper. Which she had specified for a reason.

The glass doors beneath the breezeway, half-obscured from his perspective by a hedge, opened, quite interrupting Pearl's pulse. *But no one emerged.* The door stayed open for a moment, then swung shut. A wheelchair, its motor emitting a small electric whine, came around the edge of the bush. The occupant (the driver?) of the chair, a pretty blond girl with a longish sharp nose and pale eyelashes, looked at Pearl and smiled. From a stick on the back of her chair fluttered a small Confederate flag. Pearl started to wave, but she had already turned her chair and begun to descend the ramp on the other side of the breezeway.

He sat for a moment, looked at his watch. Nearly one fifteen.

Then the door opened again, and Francesca, in all her amazingness, was walking toward him. Pearl stood, shakily.

"Hi," she said.

"Hi," Pearl said back, opening his mouth but stopping there, for he could think of nothing further. He had actually had something planned, but the reality of her appearance had knocked it out of his head. Her expression, too, gave him pause: she looked not distracted but Distracted. Was this the facial equivalent of her telephone voice, a kind of projection to an imaginary audience? Or was it something more serious?

"What's wrong?" Pearl asked her.

Her eyes were huge and light blue under black brows.

"Where should we go?" she said.

Anywhere. "Why don't we go to the Union and have some lunch? Have you had lunch?"

"How 'bout somewhere off campus?"

Pearl blinked. The only place he knew was Hezekiah's,

where he had eaten with Wunsch the day of his interview. He
mentally counted his cash. If only he had a credit card—

"We could go to my house," she said.

"We could?"

They walked out into the overpowering sunlight. As they
crossed the quadrangle, Pearl looked around to see if anyone he
knew might be witnessing this. *He wanted someone to see them
together.* Foolish, he knew; yet, why not? Wouldn't she be his?
He made sure to keep such thoughts slightly satirical. There was
something more than a little studied about this girl. Also quite
young. He worried about the way her body made his heart thump.
She was wearing tight jeans, high heels, a sleeveless gauzy pale-
blue blouse. Her front was neither too small nor too big. Her
upper arms were thin and milky, dotted with tiny moles. Could
such a body be subsumed into the system of intellectual and
spiritual betterment Pearl had in mind for himself? He had a
brief, uneasy fantasy: a party on West End Avenue, writers clus-
tering around her like bees. He shuddered.

"Are we going to your car?" she asked abruptly.

"My car?"

She stared at him.

"I walked to school," he said. "My car's back at my
apartment."

"You *walked* to school?"

"It's only a mile. I like to walk."

She sized him up for a moment: interested? appalled? "That's
O.K.," she said. "Mine's right across the street." And she smiled.

Where was the seat of the emotions? Which organ? The
Greeks, waffling perhaps, had used various words for it. In any
event, at that moment something inside Pearl turned over, profoundly, and was gone, forever.

They crossed Jackson Street in ferocious sunlight, passed

into the parking lot of an orange-and-blue building shaped like a giant pup tent.

"Do you always keep your car at International House of Pancakes?" he asked.

She took out her keys. It was a Buick Electra: a huge, late-sixties sedan, four-doored and square, with a peeling black vinyl top and a flaking paint job. The car had once been silver.

"Cheaper than a permit," she said.

Pearl glanced at the license plate. "Who's from Connecticut?"

"Oh. No one. It's just one of Giuseppe's cars." He looked at her for clarification. "You can get in," she said. "It's not locked."

The interior of the car was like a sauna. The seats, moreover, were covered with a pebbled clear plastic, too hot to touch. Pearl settled in gingerly.

"Don't the police ever stop you, with Connecticut plates?" He was trying to maintain eye contact, but his gaze kept moving instead to her midsection, the juxtaposition of filmy blouse and stiff jeans, her rump fitting neatly into the interstice of the car seat. Wasn't it hot wearing jeans in such weather? he wondered.

"Uh-uh," she said. "They got their hands full with all the wrecks and hot-rodders. This state has the worst drivers in the country. You'll see." She turned the key, and the engine roared. "Don't open the window," she said. "I'll turn on the air conditioner." She clicked the fan on high. It squealed urgently.

"You must get terrific gas mileage in this thing," he said.

They pulled out into Jackson Street, like a parade float. A moment later they came to a red light at the crossing of the interstate. They sat silent as the air coming from the vents began to cool. The traffic on the highway was steady, riverine—the majority of it, Pearl noticed, headed south, toward the Gulf. The white sun dazzled off windshields hurtling past. Homesick, he watched license plates, looking for something familiar: Mississippi, Alabama, Louisiana, Mississippi. Michigan—a white-on-black plate on a sparkling black Mercedes. Inside sat two black men in dark jackets and ties, grinning with white teeth. South Carolina . . . Maine! A potato truck. Pearl craned his neck to watch this exotic vision recede. He could, he had calculated, drive up to this light anytime, take a left, and be in Times Square in twenty-five hours. Yet suddenly the thought seemed hollow, the mere echo of an idea: why leave? He glanced at the girl next to him.

Now a flatbed truck was going by, loaded with pigs. They were huge, engorged animals, patently on their way to slaughter. Their skin, pink-white, was uncomfortably similar to human flesh. They did not look happy. Why should they? Pearl thought. What did they have to be happy about? He, on the other hand, was going to lunch with a beautiful girl.

"Hi-i," Francesca sang as she opened the screen door, which squeaked an echoing double note. Pearl stood on the stoop, behind and below. He held the door open and stepped up into a dark room, his eyes all but useless at first. A screen shone in the darkness, its colors garish: a doctor in white, his face purple, was speaking to a green woman in a mink stole. Across from the television, on a couch, a cigarette tip glowed orange: behind it, Pearl now saw, a woman reclined.

The orange tip moved forward and to the left. "My midday dose of idiocy," the woman said.

"Phil Pearl, this is Helen Raffi," Francesca said.

"Mother to you." She reached up to shake hands. "So this is the famous Philip." Her eyes, Pearl could see, were small and dark and amused. Her left hand, its plump white wrist bent, was poised just beneath her mouth, not quite hiding what it seemed to half-want to hide: a creamy roll of flesh below her chin. Her eyes at once acknowledged and dismissed all questions.

"You don't look like your voice, Philip," she said.

"How am I different?"

"You look younger. God, you look young. How old *are* you, Philip? They're really letting you teach here?"

"*Mo*ther! Don't give the poor man a hard time. My God! It's bad enough he had to come here from New York."

"I was just teasing, Philip knows that. It's nice to be young." She smiled wanly.

"Uh-oh," Francesca said. "I wouldn't touch that one with a ten-foot pole." She plopped her books down. "Mother, have you seen my Borges?"

"There's a pile of your stuff on the counter." Helen puffed on the cigarette and nodded away the smoke. "Have you had lunch, Philip?"

"I—uh, not yet, no."

"I invited him over for a sandwich," Francesca said, distractedly, as she went through the pile of books. "Oh shit, everything's here but the one I want."

"Watch your language, young lady." Helen looked at the TV and sighed. "I've *got* to turn this junk off." She picked up the remote control and, cigarette jutting from the side of her mouth, right eye squinting, aimed the little box at the screen. With a sharp metallic *click*, the picture collapsed and shrank to a tricolored ghost-y dot, like a genie going back into a bottle. Helen turned to Pearl and smiled crinklingly, conveying something that was lost on him.

Then, disconcertingly, she was looking beyond him. "There you are," she said.

A little girl, a ravishing child of five or six, with huge blue eyes and dimpled cheeks, was standing in the doorway.

"Cristina, say hi to Mr. Pearl," Helen said.

"Phil," said Pearl.

Grinning, the child stared at him with her moon eyes.

"Cristina!" Francesca scolded. "Be polite."

"Hi," Cristina said, all but inaudibly.

"Hi, Cristina. What grade are you in?"

She spread tiny fingers over her eyes.

"Ooh, now she's bein' obnoxious," said Francesca.

"I think she has a little cee are you ess aitch on Philip," Helen said. "Careful, Philip. Her attachments are very strong."

"I think I've got one on her, too."

"Well, that's one taken care of," Helen said. "Now what about you, princess?"

Francesca made a cartoon throat-clearing sound. "What would you like for lunch, Phil?" she asked.

"I'm making tuna," Helen said, standing and stubbing out her cigarette.

"Tuna sounds great," said Pearl.

"I think I'll have ham and cheese," Francesca said, opening the refrigerator.

Pearl sat on a tall stool by the counter, across from Helen, who had begun to open cans of tuna. Suddenly Cristina was kneeling on a stool immediately to his right, her elbows on the counter and her cheeks resting on her hands. "What's a cee you are ess aitch?" she asked her mother.

"Chesca, you want to take that one?"

"You're the mommy."

"I'll tell you in just a couple of years, honey. How do you want your tuna? Mayonnaisey or very mayonnaisey?"

"Very mayonnaisey," Cristina said.

"Philip, I can make yours separately if you'd like."

"No, very mayonnaisey's fine."

"Is he Fresca's boyfriend?" Cristina asked.

Francesca, putting packages and jars on the counter, rolled her eyes. "*Oh* boy," she said.

"Is who?" Helen said, elaborately disingenuous.

"Him." Cristina's index finger was an inch from Pearl's nose.

"Baby, don't point," Helen said. "What's his name?"

She shrugged, her lower lip sticking out.

"*Phil,*" Pearl whispered.

"*Phil,*" whispered Cristina.

"Here you go, sweetheart." Helen slid her a plate. "Crusts off, just the way you like it. Philip, crusts on or off?"

"On's fine," Pearl said, unable to stop staring at Francesca, who was walking back and forth between refrigerator and counter. Here, within her own house, the effect of the high heels and tight jeans was almost comic—as if she were a little girl dressing up. Almost comic. For the sight of her nearly made Pearl's eyes moist. Hadn't her mother spoken to her about this outfit? Pearl glanced at Helen—her expression, as she sliced his sandwich, was significant but enigmatic—and then back at her older daughter, who was swinging her ass in the most blatant way as she moved about the kitchen. She must be aware of his gaze—still, he thought, how else could anyone walk, in those pants, on those shoes? But what was her point? He tried, in his mind's eye, to clothe her in something neutral—khaki pants and sandals, say. The image wouldn't come. Pearl's imagination, lately, had somehow stripped its gears. Or been outstripped.

Francesca sat down at the end of the counter and began to eat.

"Mildred's been trying to get you on the phone," Helen said. "She must've called here twelve times. What's this Jewel business?"

"Her *name,*" Francesca said, through sandwich.

Pearl blinked.

"Her name's not Jewel, it's Mildred, for G— for heaven's sake. It's been Mildred as long as I've—"

"Well, she changed it."

"Legally?"

"Oh, Mother, you're so narrow-minded. What does it matter if it's legal or not? She just doesn't want to be Mildred anymore."

"I guess I can understand that. But Jewel?"

"It's numerological."

"Oh God." Helen looked at the ceiling. "I love the South!"

Pearl stole a peek at Cristina, who caught him and grinned with tiny mayonnaisey teeth. He waved at her. She waved back.

"Did she leave a message?" Francesca asked.

"Who?"

"*Jewel.*"

"Only to call her. What's she up to these days? Has she finished school yet?"

Francesca shook her head. "Waitressing at Hezekiah's."

"What?"

"She dropped out."

"No."

"What's wrong with that?"

"You know, that girl used to have a good mind? What is her problem?"

"Man troubles."

"Oh, she's had man troubles since she was twelve. That isn't any excuse. Sorry, Philip."

"What's man troubles?" Cristina said.

"Where *has* this child been hanging around?" Francesca asked.

"Ah ain't been hangin' 'round nowheah," Cristina announced triumphantly.

"There," Helen said. "There. You hear? I told your father," she said to Francesca. "I'm going to pull her right out of that— school."

"And do what?" Francesca asked. "Hire a tutor?" Her glance suddenly fell on Pearl: she seemed surprised he was there.

"What's a tutor," Cristina giggled.

"All right, young lady," Helen said. "That's it for you. Naptime." And with one miraculous movement she rose, swept the child off her stool, and carried her out of the kitchen. Even as Helen started around the corner, however, Cristina turned her head and kept her amazing eyes, wide, blue, and knowing, fixed on Pearl.

Pearl and Francesca sat on the swing on the Raffis' front porch—the very swing he had seen two weeks earlier from Wunsch's car. The past, from this viewpoint, seemed nothing if not premonitory: Pearl wondered if Wunsch had, that afternoon, somehow visualized the two of them exactly this way. Now he had won. Would win. It was silly, giddy, to think this, but here in the sun, on her porch, it actually seemed possible. Past and future slid back and forth, making Pearl dizzy. He could squint out at Sparks Street and almost see the black Alfa Romeo sitting there, the spectral face of Wunsch staring envious through the dark glass.

It was strange: you came to an unthought-of place, yourself unthought of there; then it belonged to you, as did everyone in it. It made him almost smug. Where had she been two weeks ago? What had she been? Where else in the universe was she now but here with him? (Where, indeed?) He glanced sideways and inhaled deeply. He wasn't used to her yet—would he ever be?—and each sight of her was freshly jarring. He amused himself awhile this way, glancing over, being jarred.

Pearl was not without experience with women (sometime back), but after a time it occurred to him that he simply had no idea in the world how to proceed. Here he was on a swing on a porch, alone with this unbelievable girl. But still a girl. The sun was shining. A certain acquaintance had been established. Yet something besides mere caution told him to watch his step. Helen was inside; they were in full view of the street. More important, he had no idea what this girl wanted. She simply sat, giving off no signals. What did her silence mean? When she wasn't transparent, she was maddeningly opaque. For the moment, she seemed to want simply to sit and swing. So they did, wordlessly.

A train whistle, a mournful chromatic chord, blew just a few blocks off, and Pearl could feel the slow insistent concussion of the wheels vibrating up through the ground. The whistle wailed again. He looked at her. She was gazing out at the street, squinting in the sun, a few loose strands of her pulled-back hair floating in the breeze. The train wheels boomed; the earth shuddered. It seemed to him, that moment, that he not only wanted her but loved her—loved her passionately, meltingly, with all his soul. Just then, however, a disturbing idea struck him, with all the force of truth: she was completely conscious of being looked at. She was posing. And this was all she really wanted from him. Could it be?

The screen door squeaked. They both flinched.

"Hello hello." The man who had emerged was short, dark, curly-haired, his thick sideburns just beginning to go gray. His face was boyish, puckish, and his eyes gave Pearl a start: big and bright blue, they were his daughters' eyes. Exactly. "I hope I'm not interrupting anything," he said, smiling.

Pearl stood—to prove he could? "No, no."

"Hi, Daddy," Francesca said. "This is Philip Pearl, from the English department."

"Joe Raffi," the man said, smiling with his mouth, not his eyes. "Somehow I'd pictured you as being older, Philip. Older and balder and a little portly."

"*Daddy.*"

Joe shrugged and grinned. As with his daughter, there was a kind of projection of expression, as if he were playing to the back rows. "Sorry," he said. "I must've been thinking of someone else. Good to meet you—is it Philip or Phil?"

"Phil's fine."

"You two have lunch yet?"

"Didn't Mother tell you? We just ate."

This was distinctly peevish. Joe looked at his daughter questioningly, then put up his hands in mock surrender. "O.K., O.K. Sue me. I was just trying to scare up a little company." He opened the screen door partway and stood with his hands poised on the door edge. "So how's teaching?" he asked Pearl, nodding his chin upward.

"All right, I guess."

"Aha," he said to Francesca. "He knows."

She smiled quickly, grudgingly. Joe raised his eyebrows at her, posing another question altogether. Pearl glanced back and forth from father to daughter. "Knows?"

Francesca stood. "I should be getting back," she said.

Pearl looked at her.

"Actually," she said, "you can stick around if you want, Phil. You're driving back to school after you eat, aren't you, Daddy?"

"Sure."

Pearl looked at her again. "I'd better get back too," he said quickly.

She shrugged. " 'Kay."

"See you later, babe," Joe said. Then he turned to Pearl, his eyes merry. He wrinkled his nose. "We'll talk," he said. And closed the door.

Downtown Pickett, which for some reason Wunsch had not included in his tour, was a little grid of low, bleached sunstruck buildings from another time—jewelers, five and tens, pawn-shops, haberdashers. Pearl stared out the Electra's window. Francesca had agreed to stop by the post office on the way back to school, ostensibly so he could see if a missing carton of books could be traced, actually so he could prolong the somehow endangered time he was spending with her.

He looked out at a small, square Southern burg that, even in its day, had probably had little enough character. Barber poles turned, here and there a glass door opened and closed, the traffic signals on the carless streets went from red to green, green to red. Business was clearly not booming. The only people he saw on the sidewalks were black, middle-aged or old, walking slowly. Downtown was a museum piece, the husk of a Mississippi that Pearl had once heard and read about. In this courthouse, in that movie theater, there had once been segregated water fountains. Not long ago. Pickett, he now remembered with a start, had once made the national news. There had been Trouble. Where had it all gone? The malls uptown had somehow left it far behind. Pearl almost longed for it, or at least for a taste of it—the sight of fat white men in white short-sleeved shirts and skinny ties and stingy-brimmed straw hats, the Mississippi of old Paul Newman movies. Where had it gone?

Francesca parked at a yellow curb on a one-way street in front of the post office. "Want to come in?" Pearl asked.

"I'll wait," she said.

He scanned her face for a sign of irritation, of friendliness—but her eyes were unreadable behind her sunglasses. The glasses were big and round, with clear frames and smoky lenses. Pearl thought of her standing in a store and modeling them in a mirror, seeing how good they looked on her. Her vanity touched him: it was in perfect proportion to her beauty, not a fraction too great or small. The life-force of a healthy organism. Healthy; but friendly? She smiled. It was a social smile, he realized, willed not won, a smile of mere compliance. She meant no harm by it—her only desire, no doubt, was to get back to school and be rid of him.

"I'll just be two minutes," he said, leaning into the window. He heard the anxiety in his voice, and detested himself for it.

Would she drive away and leave him? As if she were his mommy. But then another interior voice spoke to him, from a grade-school book: *Faint heart ne'er won fair maid.* Words to live by.

As he opened the building's heavy glass-and-iron door, he turned back and saw a remarkable thing, a vision: the sun was glaring blindingly off the Electra's windshield, but just visible through the glass was Francesca, waiting obediently, her hair pulled back, her sunglasses propped model-style on her head, palpably wife-to-be, a photograph for eternity. He imagined the two of them on vacation—on Cape Cod—and felt the thrilling regularity of their days together, buying postcards, doing laundry, going to the beach. He saw this in great detail—saw the triangle of the crotch of her bathing suit, emerald green over her thin sandspecked loins. He could smell the suntan lotion. Surely all that life was meant to be was contained in the odor of suntan lotion. She had opened the car windows and turned on the car radio. Now the music drifted across the sidewalk to him:

Hurry don't be late
I can hardly wait

—a song, too, for eternity. Tears sprang to Pearl's eyes as he imagined a Francesca of Babylonia, under this same fierce sun, whispering the words in her lover's ear.

The interior of the post office was dark and cold, the air like delicious water. Up on the main wall, near the ceiling, was an old mural, WPA no doubt, in faded blue-gray colors: an allegory of progress, 1930s-style, full of people and machines, all with oddly rounded contours. Round farmers, cowboys, Indians, hardhats, women, children; round cars and aerodynamic trains. Even the landscape was fat and fruitful-looking. Pearl could remember this vision of the world. Its tendrils had extended twenty-five years from the Depression into his childhood. It was a hearty, melioristic vision, devoid of irony, almost Communistic in its purity. A black-and-white world, where sleek ships and planes crisscrossed the seas and skies at brave, hopeful angles. Men slicked their hair; women wore makeup and hats and heels. Pearl thought, too, of the Manhattan of his youth. It had all vanished forever—poof—about 1965.

He made the necessary inquiries about his carton—to no avail—and was given forms to fill out. He began to write at the desk, but then a very small old woman with an enormous package tied in twine appeared behind him, and Pearl went over to a brown linoleum-topped counter (it smelled exactly the same as his second-grade classroom) to continue.

The window in front of him faced the street. The Electra sat directly outside, Francesca's pale elbow on the sill of the driver's door. She was tapping her fingers on the sill—whether to music or from impatience it was impossible to tell. He watched her for a moment. Suddenly she turned from the window, to the passenger's side of the car. Pearl squinted into the hard white light. Now she was leaning toward the passenger's window—he could see, beneath her blouse, the sinuous curve of her spine—apparently in conversation with someone on that side of the car.

Pearl could see no one at first; then, over the Electra's roof, he discerned a black, shiny knob: what appeared to be the top of a helmet. Inside the car, Francesca was moving her shoulders, shrugging, talking animatedly. The helmet was highly polished plastic, mirrorlike, a white reflection of the sun shining on its crown. It moved forward and then back a few times, as if the wearer were undecided about staying or going. Francesca leaned even farther forward for a moment—*why?*—and Pearl saw a white crescent of flesh, shocking as a brand-new moon, open between her jeans and the blouse. Then the helmet moved forward decisively and out from behind the car. Its owner sat on a huge motorcycle, whose chromed pipes and spokes gleamed blindingly in the sun. He wore jeans and black boots and a cut-off black T-shirt. His thin arms were almost dead-white. His face was not visible—the visor, too, was polished black—but from the rear of the helmet, extending down the back of the T-shirt and making the head in the helmet look exactly, disquietingly, like one of the dead armadillos Pearl had seen lying out on the shoulder of Route 83, protruded a long ponytail, coppery red.

BOOK II

IX

"All right," Pearl said to Joe. "I give up. How do you open it?"

"Push that button."

They were standing in the driveway at Sparks Street; Pearl, holding a plastic bag with a swimsuit and towel inside, towered over the sleek silver car. He looked at his reflection, wide and squashed, in the window.

"This button?"

"You got it."

Pearl pushed the button and the door swung up and open. He sat down inside. His legs were straight out in front of him, and his rear end seemed to be just inches above the ground. Joe climbed in. The car's two doors closed simultaneously. "You like?" he said.

"I think."

Joe turned the key, and there was a rumble. They backed out the driveway in one quick motion, then slid up to the stop sign at the corner.

"The short way or the long way?" Joe said.

"What's the difference?"

"The long way we can go fast."

"Let's try the long way," Pearl heard himself say. His palms, however, were prickling.

"That a boy."

They tooled down the street, but instead of going straight, they took a left Pearl had never noticed before. Soon the large old houses gave way to smaller ones, and suddenly they were in a kind of shantytown of tarpaper shacks. Black children were playing in mud puddles by the side of the road; they gaped as the strange apparition went past. Pearl gaped back.

"The *shvotzehs* never saw one like this before," Joe giggled.

Now the shacks thinned out, and the trees filled in. Giuseppe and Pearl were out in the country, on two-lane blacktop that curved and curved through pine and scrub. Joe accelerated, and the flatulent sound of the engine crescendoed, crescendo meaning only one thing to Pearl, whether car engine or dentist's drill: danger. The trees slanted backwards. Pearl's body pressed back into the seat.

"What's the fastest you've ever gone in this thing?" he asked, trying to make his voice nonchalant. Due to the tilt of the instrument cluster, the speedometer was just out of sight.

"Oh, not that fast. Maybe a hundred, hundred ten. She'll do one sixty, but these country roads aren't built for it." Now they went into a sharp curve. Pearl grasped the sides of his seat, expecting to veer out sideways, as if he were on a bobsled; but something about the car's engineering defied physics, and he remained upright. He cleared his throat, which was dry.

"How about on the highway?" he asked.

"Strictly double nickel."

"Pardon?"

"Never over fifty-five."

"You're kidding."

"You kidding *me*? You know what the cops think when

they see one of these go by? Besides," Joe said, "I have a certain percentage in not getting stopped in this particular car."

Pearl looked at him, but now they had come to a straight-away, a long tunnel through the woods, and Joe floored it. The engine whined like an angry hornet; Pearl closed his eyes.

"Some fun, huh!" Giuseppe shouted.

"Yeah." Pearl felt his chin spreading across his neck.

"And it stops on a dime!"

"Really."

"A hundred to zero in three seconds flat! Watch!" And the car slowed and halted, the trees unbent—just like that, no screech of brakes or tires, just a smooth unwavering deceleration, and they were standing still on the silent road, in the middle of nowhere, the engine clicking, Pearl's ears ringing.

"You're looking green around the gills," Joe said.

"I guess I'd like it just a little better if we could go a little slower."

"Sure."

"It's not very adventurous of me."

"Hey—no problem. Speed isn't everyone's thing."

They continued along the straightaway at normal speed. "It's kind of nice out here," Pearl said. "I didn't know it got so rural this close to town."

"Brrr," Joe said. "Woods give me the creeps. You want nice? I'll show you nice."

Caesar's Spa, a couple of hundred yards from U.S. 59 on the outskirts of Pickett, was a mock-stone building without windows. Niches on either side of the front door contained purple-lit plaster statues—Venus on one side and a muscular, partially clothed centurion on the other. There was a fountain in the lobby, with orange and blue lights and trickling water playing over a statue of Diana the Huntress.

"*This* is nice," Joe said, turning to Pearl for agreement.

They entered a locker room. Like the lobby, it was pile-carpeted, yet at the first unmistakable acrid hint of chlorine in the air, something caught in Pearl's chest, and something in him was back in the primal locker room of high school, a terror-filled jumble of cold cement, clanging metal, zoo smells. And the whiff of chlorine presaging an even worse horror, just beyond: a blurred—for Pearl had had to leave his precious glasses behind—shimmering reeking trapezoid of aquamarine, the color of pure fear.

(The years had dulled but not dismissed the fear. He thought of the night at the Holiday Inn. Fear hadn't entered his mind. Why had he leaped before looking? *He had been leaping to change his life.*)

Joe, oddly enough, was not a convivial undresser: he had chosen a locker five doors away from Pearl's, and was disrobing silently, his eyes downcast. Pearl was just as glad—there was rarely anything completely natural or easy in the way naked men addressed each other. And the tacit ancient ritual of checking out would in this case bear the extra weight, for Joe, of ascertaining what might be pending for his daughter. But the question was begged. Giuseppe looked down primly as he put on his bathing suit, his garrulity laid aside for the moment. The locker room was empty but for the two of them: maybe this accounted for the awkwardness. A bald man, bright red, nude, and quite fat, bobbled in from the steam room or shower. Pearl started to nod, but the man ignored him and opened a locker. Maybe restraint was the house etiquette.

"Ready?" Joe called, in his chipper boy's voice. He looked boyish, too, in his suit, despite the hair on his chest: it had to do with his narrow shoulders and thin neck, and the owl eyes.

They sat silently in the steam room for a while—the steam was eucalyptus-scented and not particularly hot—then went through a pair of glass doors into a room that contained the strangest swimming pool Pearl had ever seen: it was perhaps forty feet long and no more than ten feet wide, a tank, a Band-Aid of a pool. Joe got in and began to crawl back and forth. A man was in the water already, stroking industriously and spouting like a whale as he went lap after lap. Pearl lowered himself into the water (it was tepid), swam a few strokes, and almost immediately bumped into the first man. He stood up and got out of the pool. He had no patience for exercise swimming—after a while, his nearsightedness made him feel as if he couldn't breathe. He sat on the tile ledge and watched Giuseppe and the other man go back and forth. There was an image here, Pearl felt: something poignant about the measured motion of middle-aged men in the water; life as laps. The sleek striving racing of youth giving way to getting by.

Joe climbed out of the pool and sat on the ledge near Pearl. They watched the man swim for a few moments. Joe was breathing hard. "So," he said. "How do you like my daughter?"

"What?"

"I said, how do you like the water? It's a little too warm, dontcha think?"

"I guess I'm not really much of a swimmer."

"So!" Joe play-punched him on the shoulder. "What do you think of this burg?"

"Oh, it has its points."

"Oh yeah? Name two." He wrinkled his nose. "I said to Helen when we first got here: if you stick with me through this, you must really love me."

"I guess it is pretty bad."

"Bad? Listen, I've been in just about every town in this country, and Pickett's right up there with Worcester, Mass., and Fargo, North Dakota. You don't have to be diplomatic with me, man. What do you think I'm gonna do, turn you in to Marshak?"

"How come you've been so many places, Giuseppe?"

"Gigs."

"Gigs?"

"Piano. Jazz piano."

"I didn't know you did that."

"Only for about fifteen years."

"You're kidding. You played alone?"

"Nah, mostly trios, small combos, like that."

"So who'd you play with? Anybody famous?"

"Famous? Sure, famous. Coltrane, Billy Eckstine, Sarah, Max Roach, everybody. *Tutti gli famosi.*"

"Really?"

"Sure."

"Why'd you stop?"

"Oh, I met this classy violinist in Minneapolis, then we had this classy kid."

Pearl's heart took a little hop. "You needed more money?"

"Nah, the money was all right. Helen just figured she and the kid might get a little confused if I didn't come home every night."

"So what'd you do?"

"You really want to hear the depressing part? I got a job teaching theory at a little community college up in St. Paul, then I got a job at the University, then I got a job at another university, then another university, then somehow, God knows how, I ended up at this university. And that's all she wrote."

"Oh."

"So the moral is, young Philip, Enjoy your freedom while young, etcetera. Hunt dragons. Court fair maidens. Run off and teach in Mississippi. Think you'll be here next year?"

"I don't know. Maybe."

"Ah, always the diplomat. Know what your problem is, Phil? You're too fuckin' polite. You know what'll happen if you're here again next year?"

"What?"

"You'll be here again the year after that."

"You think so?"

"I'd bet money on it. And then you'll end up looking like what's-his-face, Havens. Or that sad sack Marshak. Or Wunsch. He publish anything lately?"

"Walter?"

"Yeah, Walter. When was the last time he had a book out? Or even a recipe?"

"I think I saw something a couple of years ago—"

"That's the whole point, Philip. This isn't Princeton. Or even Purdue. It's not even Podunk, for Christ's sake. All you have to do down here is be a good boy, smile at the dean and the president, teach your freshmen, and stick around. Publish or languish. They'll get used to you. They'll be so grateful you stayed that they'll give you tenure, then you can stay till you die. Like that poor bird, you know, Juniper-bush."

"Ted."

"Poor bastard. I hear he's really a basket case since his wife ditched him. Not that he was such a prize before. Did you know they had him up in front of the academic board for twanging his guitar in some local beer joint?"

"I heard something about it."

"He said he was playing his own songs, it was part of his art. He was also getting paid for it. They let him off with a warning."

The swimmer got out of the pool, shook himself, and slapped across the tiles to the door.

"On the other hand," Giuseppe said, "you may be interested in an academic career."

Pearl stared at him. He was smiling quite impenetrably.

"Maybe you'd like to freshen up before dinner, Philip?" Helen said.

Pearl didn't precisely need to, but he had just drunk the

better part of a large glass of red wine rather quickly, and he was open to suggestion. He closed the bathroom door behind him and smiled at himself—as if at a surprise guest—in the mirror. His bluish alter ego looked intensely self-satisfied. And why not? He felt like a safecracker in a bank vault. He was freshly showered, and ravenous, and he was in the Raffis' house.

Just outside the door, the four Raffi voices, like an operatic quartet, were raised in argument, or mock argument. Joe's voice was as expressive and insistent, and almost as high, as his wife's and daughters'. Around this boomed the sound of the television. Even so, Pearl took care to turn on the faucet and make the appropriate sounds. The faucet handles were grooved bronze— Romanesque—and the sink was shell-shaped, like something out of Botticelli. Pearl smiled as he thought of Francesca standing in the sink like Venus, smiling down at him. He stopped smiling. For the imagining was incomplete: he could see only her head, neck, and shoulders, perhaps part of the legs; the rest was hazily filled in. Something was stopping him. What? Was it the precise size and shape of the breasts, the diameter and color of the nipples, the extent of the pubic hair? Pearl had seen a number of women naked, not just lovers (he had drawn for two years at the Art Students' League). He had, he felt, no illusions about female perfection; yet he was also willing to believe that Francesca, in the bloom of her twenty-first year, was more perfect—picture-perfect—than he could hope to imagine. *She had defeated his imagination.* This was her secret, the source of all her smugness: she was absolutely in the right. Other women looked beautiful from certain angles, in certain lights, in the context of love; Francesca was clinical beauty, the *Ding-an-sich*, carving space, bending light. Now he had a flickering vision, for an instant, of her on all fours above him, white, laughing. He shuddered.

The room was paneled in dark wood, and carpeted—a slightly kinky but also nice touch: most bathrooms were too echoey. The toilet was discreetly hidden behind a partition. It was light blue, modern, compact—like a Princess phone. Above it hung a wicker basket full of scented soaps. Like something in *House Beautiful*—all was in place, nothing idiosyncratic. The medicine chests, with their portentous contents, and the wet towels and hanging underwear were all upstairs. Nothing for Pearl to get a handle on: the room was all flirtation and no substance. Aha? Even the rim of the john was scrupulously clean. No stray pubic hairs to wonder about.

The seat up, he availed himself. *Pissing in my lady's toilet.* He zipped himself and flushed, wiping himself and then the toilet rim with a square of paper: careful. He was wearing khaki pants. The water swirled down in utter silence—this had probably been a big selling point. He suddenly remembered the toilets in his grandmother's apartment on 79th and Amsterdam. It had been one of those big old brown buildings: citadels of the Upper West Side. The toilets had had no tanks, were flushed by pressure from the roof, probably. You pressed the handle—a sculpted tapered chrome cylinder, mounted on a raised pipe in back, like a well head—and, *Whoosh!* all gone, with impressive force. The water in these prewar bathrooms had a sweet smell, like a woodland spring. Pearl remembered it precisely. They said you weren't supposed to be able to do this, olfactory memory was supposedly the weakest, but he could do it anyway. Perhaps his one absolute gift. Hard to make a name from this. Billions of odors, each a universe; all gone.

Chicken cacciatore was the olfactory present. Helen stood at the stove by a steaming skillet, spatula in hand, looking back over her shoulder at Francesca and Cristina, who were playing tug of war with a plastic bead necklace. Joe sat on the couch, his hair still slick from the spa, smiling on benignly, *il signore*. Cristina was perched on a kitchen stool, her shoulders hunched with the effort of pulling; Francesca leaned against another stool, the object of all Pearl's faith and hope resting lightly on the wooden seat. She smiled teasingly at her sister as she held her end of the necklace, barely straining.

"Phil! We were just talking about you," Joe said, wrinkling his nose.

"Chesca," Helen said, "now you *know* that thing is going to break."

"It's mine," Francesca said to Cristina.

"*Mine*," said Cristina. Catching sight of Pearl, she stuck out her under-teeth sideways and smiled, her concentration evenly divided.

The necklace snapped, beads flying around the den.

"Aww," Francesca said. "See what you've *done?*" Cristina shrugged.

Helen, her broad forehead wrinkling, pointed with the spatula. "Clean it up," she commanded. "Now." She looked accusingly at Francesca. "You, too."

"I'll help," Pearl said.

"Philip, don't you dare," Helen said. She blinked. "Joe, why don't you give Phil a refill?"

"Certainly."

"Thanks, I'm fine," Pearl said.

"Come on, it'll put hair on your chest," Joe said.

Pearl stared. Joe's smile was nothing but friendly. "Give Phil a refill," Cristina began to sing.

"Cristina," Helen warned.

"Give Phil a re-fill," the baby chanted, grinning at Pearl, who now had to struggle not to smile back.

"Young lady, you are going to bed without supper if I hear one more word out of you." Helen's hands were on her hips; her eyes gave off lights Pearl had never seen in Francesca's. He understood, as if for the first time, that age brought more than decay.

"Filaree fill, filaree fill."

The baby's eyes were wild, her cheeks flushed. Down went the spatula. Cristina beat Helen to the doorway, but—this could be heard but not seen—lost the race halfway up the stairs. The three left in the room looked out the doorway.

"Phil, I do believe you are a bad influence on that child," Francesca said.

By candlelight they sat around the linen-covered table in the dining room, Joe and Helen at the ends, Pearl and Francesca across from each other. The baby's banishment had stuck, although Helen had softened halfway through the meal and taken her a plate. Cristina had refused to touch the food. Helen had come back to the table angry, but now she emptied her wine glass and covered a smile with her hand.

"Our mid-life child," Joe said, shaking his head.

"Our love child," Helen said.

"Well, thanks!" said Francesca.

"Oh, you know what I mean," Helen told her.

"Yeah, I was on purpose."

"She does get right to the heart of things, doesn't she?" Joe said to Pearl.

"Huh-um." Helen pretended to clear her throat. She smiled and regarded them all serenely. "Well," she said—but she said nothing further. She was holding her chin, covering the soft roll of flesh beneath. The light in her eyes had softened; she was tipsy.

Pearl, who had been watching Francesca whenever she turned away, was suddenly caught. She returned his look boldly until he could hear his blood. Against all odds, he held on, and then he lowered his brows in inquiry.

"So how's your car holding up, Phil?" Joe said.

"Excuse me?"

"That old lunch pail of yours. How's it running?"

"Oh, all right."

"It's not your first one, is it?"

Pearl nodded.

"Ah, that's the one you always remember. Right, Hel?"

Helen smiled dreamily.

"How many miles on it?" Joe asked.

"Almost ninety thousand."

Joe stuck out his lower lip, raised his eyebrows. Mock-impressed? "What would you take for it?"

Pearl shook his head. "Oh, I don't know. I really—"

"Come on, you must have some idea."

"I really think I'd like to hold on to it for a while. I mean, as long as it's working."

"Uh-oh. Do I sense an emotional attachment here?"

"I'm gonna start to clear," Francesca said.

I'll help, Pearl wanted to say; but Joe's eyes were on him, holding the question. "Maybe," Pearl replied, smiling.

"Wrong, Phil. Wrong. There's your first mistake." Joe's face was animated; a tiny pool of sweat gleamed in the cleft above his lip.

"But you love your car, don't you?"

"I'd trade it like that if I could get something better. Listen," he said, raising an index finger. "A car's nothing but a hunk of machinery. There ain't one that won't disappoint you in the end. The whole game is to unload it on some sucker before you're stuck. Right?"

"I guess."

"You gotta convince the poor *shmegegeh* you're selling to that he's getting the greatest deal of his life. I once had this '64 Lincoln—"

Francesca, who was picking up Pearl's plate, groaned directly behind his right ear, raising the hair on the left side of his neck. "Bondo," she sighed.

"Quiet, I'll tell it," Joe said to her with a quick smile, excited. "Anyway. '64 Lincoln. *Terrific* engine, rebuilt, car went like a bat out of hell, but there's a rust hole maybe two feet wide in the passenger door. I see this great little MG I know I can get for a steal, but my cash flow is just a shade precarious at the moment—"

"So he put an ad in the paper," Francesca recited, from the doorway.

"So I put an ad in the paper for the Lincoln."

Helen sighed. "Beautiful car," she said, to no one in particular. She smiled hazily.

Joe blocked out the words in the air with his hand: " ' '64 Lincoln, low mileage. Like new. Must sell. Must see. Collector's item.' " Now he was actually wiggling in his chair. "Right?" he said to Pearl.

Pearl nodded agreeably. If he played the game, would he win the prize?

"So I immediately get a call, the first night of the ad, from this poor joker, I can tell he's on the hook from the word go. I tell him a little more, just to whet his appetite. Then we make an appointment for that Saturday." He looked eagerly at Pearl.

"What happened?"

"Have you ever heard of Bondo?"

"Bondo?"

"Bondo," Francesca sighed, as she picked up Joe's plate.

"Bondo." Helen smiled.

"It's a fiberglass caulking compound," Joe said. "Quick-dry. For plastic swimming pools, boats, stuff like that."

"Can you use it on metal?" Pearl asked, puzzled.

Joe beamed. A straight man. "First I pack in steel wool," he said. "Then I apply the Bondo. Sand it, paint it, and voilà!"

"The guy bought the car?" Pearl said.

"Like that." Joe snapped his fingers.

Francesca, standing behind her father, snapped her fingers also, looking at Pearl, who took the opportunity to requestion her with his eyes.

"Dessert, Phil?" she asked.

He sat by himself at the table, staring drunkenly into the guttering flame of the candle nearest him. Joe had excused himself; Helen and Francesca had taken away the rest of the supper dishes, not allowing Pearl to help. He gazed into the flame. His life, over the past two years, had been spiraling outward like a nebula, vacuous and chaotic; now it had imploded, with terrific force, into a single house in a strange corner of the world. Pearl felt like one of those compacted stars that weigh tons per cubic inch—could the floor hold him? He wanted nothing more, at the moment, than to sit here, forever, with the sounds of female voices and clattering china and running water, and the smell of coffee, coming in from the kitchen; with everything in the world about to happen. He heard a squeak of furniture in the next room, then the sound of a piano being played expertly. A song, American, popular. The song ascended airily, descended, then rose once more and landed on a strange, multicolored chord. Pearl had heard this song before, something in him knew it deeply. The music circled the room, flickered with the candle's light on the ceiling. Helen came in, carrying a sponge cake and a glass bowl full of whipped cream. She paused for a moment and listened to the music, her eyes just slits: she looked, Pearl thought, like a cat being stroked.

"What *is* that?" Pearl asked, nodding toward the music room.

" 'Stardust,' " Helen said.

* * *

Joe smiled over his shoulder as they walked into the room; he winked broadly at Helen.

"You two," Francesca said.

"Any requests?" Joe asked.

" 'I Concentrate on You'?" Pearl blurted. Vino. Veritas. His forehead began to prickle.

"Ah, Porter," Joe said. "Great." And then to Helen, "Baby, you care to sit in?"

"Oh, Joe. My chops are in pitiful shape."

"Don't be coy."

"It's true."

"*Mother.*"

"Oh, all right," Helen said, reaching down behind a chair, uncasing a violin, then slinging the instrument to her shoulder with a quick, professional movement. She tuned the violin, then, with a sly glance at Pearl down the instrument's neck, bowed into the melody.

Pearl, his blush growing deeper, sat down on the carpet. Francesca was sitting across from him, leaning against some bookcases, but Pearl didn't dare look at her: instead he turned artificially toward Helen and Joe. His head felt exposed and very red. He had not only tipped his hand; he had laid his cards on the table and pointed at them. But did it matter? Must he go on with this game as though nothing had happened, continuing to bluff and raise?

Chops or no chops, Helen played, to Pearl's ear, every bit as well as Joe. He was the trellis, she the vine; the sinuous, oddly masculine wail of the violin wound around the piano's quick chords and runs. Helen and Joe did a medley of Porter, then they played a number of songs Pearl didn't know; then they moved into sacred territory—Gershwin.

As Joe and Helen began "Someone to Watch over Me," Pearl finally relaxed. The music was old, but it was great—it was his, somehow; he was speaking to her with it. He finally stole a look across the room.

But it wasn't Francesca that he saw. The girl who sat across from him—her arms on her knees, her head turned down so that the lines in her face were deepened by the angle of the lamplight—was grotesquely ugly. She was scowling, and Pearl realized that the music was indeed speaking to her, and that the look on her face was one of misery.

X

"Hi, Francesca?" Pearl was on the pay phone downstairs in Culpepper. Composition was over; the rest of the day was wide open.

"No, Philip, it's Helen. I think she's working this afternoon."

"Working?"

"Out at Goldblum's, at the mall."

"I didn't know she did that."

"Oh, she's been doing it for a couple of years now. She goes one or two afternoons a week. I think she's in men's shoes these days."

"That must be uncomfortable for her."

"No, I don't think she minds it very much."

"I meant—you think she's over there now?"

"I think so-oh."

Pearl traced a rapid figure eight with his index finger on the wooden enclosure. "So—how are you, Helen?"

"Oh, *I'm* fine."

"And Cristina?"

"Also fine. She asks for you about every twenty minutes.

'Is Phil coming over for lunch today?' she wants to know. I had to tell her lunchtime was three hours ago."

"That's nice."

"Oh, they're all wild for you, Philip."

His heart tripped a step. "That's not true."

"He wants me to argue with him. Look, Philip, I have laundry in. Plus, I'm sure you didn't call to make conversation with me."

"Helen, what could be more wrong?"

"Ah, flattery will get you everywhere. I do have to go, though. Try Chesca at Goldblum's."

The afternoon, like every other in recent weeks, was bright and clear, the sky a soulless blue. A thousand miniature suns glared off the windshields in the parking lot of the Big Mall: America was shopping.

Pearl locked the Volvo and strode across the asphalt toward the entrance of Goldblum's, but a spasm of shyness headed him off at the last moment. He was suddenly acutely conscious of its being exactly three ten, precisely twenty minutes after his last class. How could he mask this beelining? He turned past the glass doors of Goldblum's and headed up toward the next entrance. He would buy something first. What did he need? What could he afford? Then it struck him, like poetic inspiration: shower sandals. He slowed his pace. He would act the *flâneur*. Amble into Woolworth's, look around for a while, pick up his sandals, check out the bookstore, browse through the record store, wander into Goldblum's. An afterthought.

All this seemed to go very quickly. He was soon walking through the indoor portal of Goldblum's, brown Woolworth's bag in hand, senses on edge, his ears literally pricked. Even through his heightened readiness, however, something struck him as he entered the store: the miraculous sameness of department stores everywhere. He had traveled to the underside of the earth, yet here were the taupe carpeting, the brass fixtures, the sedate Muzak, the mysterious bells, the combined perfumes of dozens of women. He had grown up, practically, in such stores, dragged along by his mother or grandmother. It had never been entirely unpleasant. These were, after all, temples, of and to women. Surely Pearl's early concept of eros had been formed in Saks and Altman's. He looked around. It would change; he didn't want it to. Some ancient Pearl, he thought, must have harbored hopes of immortality for the marketplace in Ecbatan. The world would end, slowly or fast—and this world, of beveled brass-framed glass cases and chimes and mannequins in lingerie, would scatter its minky vapors out among the stars.

Glancing around at the Southern women and children, Pearl felt a sudden sharp anguish—a kind of time-panic or nostalgia in advance. Nothing must change; everything would! Where would he be a year from today? Where would *she?* And all at once he felt an urgent need to see Francesca, that instant—to declare to her. Why not? Man was free. She might be his in a moment. *Wild for you.* What, exactly, had Helen meant by this? Through Pearl's head flashed a silent scene: he at the wheel of the Volvo, she beside him, as they turned left on-to 83 from Jackson Street and headed north. They could leave without luggage, without notice: right from the mall parking lot.

Why not?

Wild for you.

Dreamy Pearl was drifting through the aisles, sidestepping shoppers, when he was jarred awake. She stood by a wall rack of moccasins and loafers, talking to a man in a dark suit. The hair on the back of Pearl's neck rose. *Who?* Francesca's hair was in a ponytail, which bobbed as she talked. She was wearing jeans, of course, and a strange, ugly blouse, iridescent, grayish-green. Her right side was to Pearl, and he looked at her, almost superstitiously, for any sign of imperfection, an awkwardness caught unawares, revealed from a new angle. Hopeless. As he hovered, unseen and undecided, he caught the dark-suited man's eye, and, at the same moment, Francesca turned around.

"Hi!" Pearl said, with all the inadvertence he could muster.

"Hey, Phil!" she sang, her accent strongly Southern—modified, Pearl guessed, for this guy. "Whatchew doin' around here?"

He held up the Woolworth's bag. "Just a little shopping."

"Lookin' for some shoes?"

"Shoes?"

"Better watch out, she's some little saleswoman," the man said. He was short, thick, prosperous-looking: the dark suit hugged him expensively. His shirt collar cradled his neck lovingly. His hair, too, was thick, and ridiculously lush, swept up in a tremendous pompadour. His eyes were long, blue, hooded—Southern eyes. On his wrist was a huge gold watch: it must have been an inch thick. Pearl tried to imagine the two of them together. Crazy. Wasn't it?

"Phil, this is Boyd," Francesca said. "Phil teaches over at State, Boyd."

"Zat so? What you teach, Phil?"

"English."

"Uh-oh, I better watch out," Boyd said. "English never was my subjeck."

"Phil's a poet," Francesca said brightly. He could have throttled her. "He's published a book."

Boyd raised an eyebrow. "Zat so?"

"Yes." Pearl glared at her.

"Huh," Boyd said.

But she won the staring contest. "We were just talking about Boyd's watch," Francesca said.

"That is quite a watch," Pearl said.

"Idn it?" said Boyd.

"I was tryin' to get him to tell me how much it cost."

Francesca was suppressing a smile, her wide eyes even wider than usual, as if she were riding a bicycle fast downhill.

Boyd was grinning. "Let me tell you," he said. "You don't even want to know about it."

"You must have a lot of money stashed away someplace, Boyd," Francesca said.

"Hail no. I just got lucky." He winked at her. "Maybe I'll get lucky again."

"I think I would like to see some shoes," Pearl said.

"You would?"

"I would."

"Well, looks like you got you a customer." Boyd was all smiles. "Bah bah." He backed down the aisle.

"That was neatly done," Francesca said, after he was gone.

"Who *is* that guy?"

"Assistant manager of Reed's. The men's store across the hall. Boy," she said, shaking her ponytail. "I thought he'd never shut *up* about that watch."

"It looked to me like you were enjoying yourself."

"God, Phil. You must think a lot of me. It looked like something you'd see on a pimp." Her accent, he noticed, had shifted ever so subtly back north.

"So. What about Wallabees?"

"You were serious?"

"Aren't I always?" He looked hard at her, but she didn't rise to the bait.

"Wallabees, huh? Very professorial."

"If the shoe fits, wear it." He mentally calculated his checking balance. He had about thirteen dollars. Minus service charges. Before the Wallabees.

"What size is the shoe?"

He told her. She disappeared into the back room, and for a moment, Pearl was nothing, nowhere—merely standing, merely breathing. Her reappearance took care of that. She handed him the box: beige-cream tending to taupe, with bog-green print on the white end label. A beautiful box. "You're not going to put them on for me?"

"Uh-*uh*."

It was easy enough to provoke a petulant response from her—the one button he could push with any regularity. What about the rest? He sat down and took out the shoes. The smell and feel of the creamy new suede were intoxicating. He tied the shoes and stood up. A man could fly in such shoes. He wiggled his left, larger, foot and felt a slight pinch. "This one's a little tight," he said.

"Walk around a little."

"Boy, you've really got the routine down, haven't you. All except for putting on the customer's shoes." She gave him a look. He walked. "It's still tight."

"The leather's going to stretch out some," she said. "It's a soft shoe."

"Even the patter. I'm impressed."

"They look good on you."

"Now you're playing dirty."

"What makes you say that?" She gave him a poker look, very bold, daring him to speak his mind. He shook his head. The words wouldn't move from his brain to his mouth.

"O.K.," he said, after a moment. "Wrap 'em up." Remembering his mission, and the long afternoon in front of him, he suddenly felt short of breath, as if he were ascending rapidly in a plane or elevator. Time. He was running out of time.

"Why don't you just wear them?" she said.

Or as if he had just sprinted a hundred yards. What had happened to his lungs? "Perfectly right," he said, feigning normality. "Very good point. I think I will wear them." He pointed to his old shoes, dirty bucks gone beyond repair. "Will you take these in exchange?"

"If you give me money, too."

"You drive a hard bargain." His voice was croaky. "How about a check?"

"Will it bounce?"

"Of course. When are you off?" The two consecutive statements of truth made him feel as if he himself had bounced, once, on the high board, then leapt out into space. He felt his chin quiver, as if he'd been slapped, or reproached; he hoped, nonsensically, that she hadn't noticed. He put his checkbook on the counter and began filling out the register, not daring to watch her reaction.

"Oh, I can leave whenever I want. It's real slow today." Now he glanced meaningfully at her. She shrugged. Pearl nodded, noticed he had written October 78, 1919 on the check.

"Sherry isn't doin' anything back there except stackin' boxes. Are you, Sherry?"

"Huhh?" drawled a voice from the stockroom.

"Would it be all right if I left now?" Francesca said.

A short round-faced girl—face like a peony, Pearl thought—appeared in the doorway. She had a Belle Starr hairdo and wore a steel-green dress. She wiped her forehead with the back of her hand, then, seeing Pearl, followed through and stroked the hair on one side of her face, smiling. Here, in the wrong place, was flattery. "Sure, hawun," Sherry said. "You go rat ahead."

Francesca raised her thick eyebrows. "We're off."

"You don't have to punch out or anything?"

"Nah, I just write my hours down."

"They trust you?"

"Well, thanks!"

Pearl had meant this in a comradely way, worker to worker—yet had he really? He didn't trust her for a second.

They walked out into the arcade. From the organ store at the corner came the sound of "Tie a Yellow Ribbon 'Round the Old Oak Tree," played with a chuffa-chuffa beat. As they passed a mirrored column, Pearl caught their reflections: his, self-conscious, yearning, asymmetrical, glasses slightly awry; hers, perfect sideways, ponytail bobbing perkily to the music.

She turned to him. "Where are we going?"

It was a crucial question. He looked at her with some alarm and said the first thing that came into his head—a terrible mistake. "I have no idea," Pearl said.

He was blushing. He had somehow assumed she was leading him. All at once he saw his entire problem with awful clarity: he was pushing a string. The case against him compounded in his brain. He found himself thinking of their tennis game two weekends before. She had invited him!

"Hello, Philip! Don't you look sporty!"

Pearl, in tennis clothes, stood inside the Raffis' screen door. Helen was opening the refrigerator. "Chesca's getting ready," she said. "I'm having some orange juice. Care to join me?"

He closed the door behind him. "No, thanks."

"Lemonade? Vodka martini?"

He shook his head. "Thanks."

"So"—her voice began in an upper register, where it was nearly identical to Francesca's, and descended into a smokier range—"what's new with you, Philip? How are you enjoying Pickett? Have you joined a church?"

"Oh, Helen, it's the pits."

She poured herself a glass of juice. "Isn't it just awful?" she said gaily.

"Hii," Francesca sang. She was wearing short short yellow shorts—Pearl couldn't quite bear to look—and a dark-blue T-shirt; her glossy hair was tied back in a ponytail. "Whatchyall talkin' about?" she said.

"Ohh, to be able to wear shorts again," Helen said.

"There she goes again," said Francesca. "Mother, you look *fine* in shorts."

"I do not."

"Ready, Phil?" Francesca asked. "I'll be back in a couple hours," she said, and, without waiting for an answer, walked out, letting the screen door slam behind her.

"Have a nice game," Helen said, raising her juice glass and her eyebrows.

They walked through the garage and out to his car. Francesca, her racket resting on her shoulder, clicked the handle of the Volvo's passenger door. Click. Click. "This is locked," she said.

Pearl looked at her over the car's roof. "You O.K.?"

She tapped the metal with her nails.

"O.K., O.K." He got in and unlocked her door. She sat down, staring straight ahead.

"I didn't mean to be nosy," he said. "I just—"

She gave him a sharp look with one blue eye. "Aren't you *bored?*" she asked. She circled a finger in the air. "In this place?"

Quick—the right answer? Too quick for anything but the truth. He shook his head. "Too new."

"I can't believe I spent my formative years in this town," she said. "It'll probably stunt me for life."

"Johnson says you should just study till you're twenty-five, then you can travel."

"Who?"

"Samuel Johnson."

"Oh God. Don't mention Samuel Johnson. We had to read him in high school. I was never so bored in my entire life."

Bored, boring: Pearl believed she was speaking in a kind of code. *He* was boring *her.* How to unbore?

"Johnson also said he'd like nothing better than to spend all his time riding in a fast coach with a pretty woman."

She looked at him. Here was a start.

"He did not."

"He did." If the woman understood him, Johnson had said. "He was a sucker for pretty women."

"God, that's pretty cool. I guess we didn't get that far."

"Or you fell asleep."

"Now you're bein' mean."

Smiling, Pearl started the car. So he had his answer. How mean could he be?

They headed back over the railroad tracks. She was silent, but it felt sufficient, for the moment, that she was with him in this enclosed space. They drove uptown, toward school, the highway, the malls, the present. Francesca seemed to breathe a little easier here: the air in the car seemed to depressurize.

They stopped at a light at 15th Avenue. Outside a discount liquor store on the right was a mobile sign, a plastic marquee mounted on a trailer. Colored bulbs around the sign's perimeter flashed in sequence toward the store, and on the sign the message read, in black plastic movable type:

KNOW YE NOT THAT THEY WHICH RUN IN A RACE
RUN ALL BUT ONE RECEIVETH THE PRIZE? SO RUN
THAT YE MAY OBTAIN **   I CORINTHIANS 9

One receiveth? All but one receiveth? The light changed before Pearl could reread the sign. Surely one receiveth, he hoped. As if hoping had anything to do with it.

The Bundy Park courts were in a piney clearing just off Jackson, behind the Little Mall. The school courts were better and more numerous, but Francesca had pointedly wanted to play here. Why? Here, Pearl guessed, they were less likely to be seen. But by whom? Pearl was not unwilling to be conspiratorial—if he could gain by the conspiracy. There was a tacit agreement between them. This was nice. He wondered, though: to what, exactly, was he agreeing? In whatever game it was they were playing, he was obviously far behind. Logically, he seemed to have two choices—to play catch-up or to throw in the towel. He was not about to concede, but how did he start to play? Or was he playing already? As they walked toward the courts, Pearl made a pretense of nonchalance, feigning a carefree stride, racket swinging—but Francesca was walking ahead of him, quite oblivious of his show. And staging, of course, a far superior show herself.

They took the last open court, on the end, next to two women in Bermuda shorts with piled-up hair. The game the women were playing, with their old wooden rackets, resembled badminton. The women held their rackets face up, like carpet beaters. They conversed as they played. The birds in the trees around the courts also conversed loudly. Someone was in the hospital, someone was getting divorced, someone was running around. Back and forth went the ball. Pearl knelt to take off his racket cover. The surface of the court was green-coated tar, cracked and bubbled. Francesca stood beside him, as if awaiting instructions. He glanced up—he meant to be companionable—but his eyes went no further than her legs. They were thin, curiously childlike; their skin was milky white and, like her face, dotted with tiny moles. One in particular shone, like an early star—a wishing star—at the top inside of her right thigh. Pearl searched for a hint of coarseness, for the inevitable network of follicles on her shins—but all he could see at the moment was white, blinding white.

She looked down at him, big-eyed. Content to be assessed. Suddenly she turned mischievous. "Ready?" she asked. And skipped, actually skipped, to her end of the court.

Pearl walked to his baseline and hit her a ball. She jumped and swung with an exaggerated motion and hit the ball high into the air. It arced up through the tree shadows and out into the orange sunlight—climbing, climbing; it poised for a millisecond, then dropped, landing directly between the two women (who continued their conversation without missing a beat), and bounced over the chain-link fence into the trees.

"Oh shit!" Francesca yelled, then clapped her hand over her mouth.

Pearl hit her another. She bounded around the court, he thought, like a young goat—like Alison in "The Miller's Tale" (coming up in Masterpieces next week). Or like Nausicaä, playing ball with her maids on the shore while filthy Odysseus dragged himself, naked and barely alive, through the leaves. The sun shone, the birds sang, the heart ached with October, and Pearl was reasonably happy, hitting Francesca balls—although, at a distance of seventy-eight feet, and engaged in an activity for which she seemed neither particularly suited nor particularly minded, she lost a certain part of her magnetism. Pearl's mind began to wander a bit. Maybe she was aware of this. For she began to let the wider balls go. Pearl hit her a backhand that she simply let pass. A forehand to the corner. She watched it sail by.

"Hit it *to* me," she commanded, across the length of the court.

"God, you're lazy," he said.

"Are you sayin' something?" she called.

"No."

"Yes, you are!"

He hit a shot hard, straight at her. Shielding herself with her racket, she managed to sidestep the ball. "Phil!" she said.

"What?"

"If you—"

"—"

A sound, gigantic and incredible, split the air.

"—you don't have to," Francesca continued.

"*What?*" Pearl said.

The sound came again.

And again.

And again.

Someone, plainly, was setting a phonograph needle down

haphazardly on a record of a football crowd, the result being amplified at top volume over a powerful public address system a few feet away. Pearl looked for the speaker. He saw none. He shook his head in disbelief. The women on the next court continued to rally as if nothing at all were happening; across the net, Francesca stood with her hand on her hip.

"What *is* that?" Pearl shouted. She cupped her hand to her ear. He motioned her to the net.

"What *is* that?" he repeated. As suddenly as it had begun, the sound now stopped.

She wrinkled her forehead. "What?"

"You're kidding?"

"Oh, that," she said. "That's the—"

"—"

The sound started again, louder, if possible, and more urgent. He looked at her as the air concussed for what felt like a full minute. Then there was silence once more.

"—*lion*," she said.

"*Lion?*"

"In the *zoo.*"

"The zoo."

"Over there, through the trees. The Bundy Park Zoo. You didn't know about it?"

"No."

"He's probably just hungry or horny or something." She looked around impatiently.

"Why don't we call it a day."

"We haven't even been here an hour!"

"You're tired."

"I am not," she said indignantly. But she was panting lightly, and sweat had gathered in the cleft above her upper lip, picking out the tiny black hairs there. Pearl noticed for the first time that she hadn't much in the way of chin. The more he looked at her, in fact, the stranger her face seemed—like a word repeated to absurdity. The proportions were wrong: the eyes too big, the moles too numerous. He savored the moment.

"You're sure?" he asked.

"Phil, I need to get some *exercise*."

"You'd get a lot more if you ran for a few balls."

"You're hittin 'em where I can't get them."

They looked at each other, at an impasse. On the next court, the two ladies, still in conversation, were zipping up their racket covers. The lion roared again, then, as if bored or dispirited, stopped, leaving only the sound of the birds. A light wind blew through the pines. The sun had slipped a couple of degrees, crossing the fine boundary between mid and late afternoon. The air—Pearl registered the strangeness of this—actually felt cool.

"Francesca—" he began.

"What?"

He stopped. *Who is it? Who who who?*

"I guess maybe I am gettin' kinda bored," she said. Then, to temper this: "Tennis isn't really my game."

What is?

He followed her in silence to his car. Pearl looked down at the carpet of pine needles. That was it then—*bored*. The word thudded down like a coffin lid. What was he to do? Throw her down in the bushes? Lost, lost. All he could think of was the waning light and his solitary supper; winter was coming and he was eating alone.

"Francesca—"

She turned brightly, her racket over her shoulder. "What?"

"Nothing."

"Didn't you say you needed clothes?" she said. They were walking down the mall's main hallway.

He recalled having mentioned this in passing on the first day they'd met. Her act of memory struck him as oddly childlike, oddly winning—as if she had suddenly asked if he didn't like marshmallows in his cocoa.

"Why don't we go into McKee's and see what they have," she said briskly.

So he was being led. It was fine with him. Francesca walked a half step ahead as they passed under the McKee's portal. He shuddered, pleasantly. Buying clothes—what would they be doing together next?

They went to men's trousers. He found a pair of corduroy pants, in a splendid sandy tan, to go with the shoes. He would be splendid for her. (Later, out of the fluorescent light of the trousers department, the pants would prove to be an odd, up-setting shade of brown.) She sat and waited as he tried on the pants: it was titillating to be undressing for her. But when he came out of the dressing room, full of fresh wonder at this divine joke—shopping for his clothes! as if they were a married cou-ple!—he immediately saw the distraction in her eyes. She was as unsubtle about it as a child. The suction was breaking. *She wanted entertainment.* But what could he do to entertain her? (And why did he have to?) He wrote another check for the pants: payday was next Friday. He might make it.

Now they entered the main, giant room of McKee's, a space with the dimensions of an old-fashioned big-city train station waiting room. They were standing in a region of shirts in bins when Pearl got an idea. Not an inspiration, but an idea. "Why don't we go have some coffee?" he said.

"How 'bout shirts?" she said. She was wandering among the bins—they would proceed, he saw, according to her agenda.

"Shirts?"

"Shirts." Her eyes were wide again—maybe she was crazed with boredom, he thought.

He thought of his checking account. "Shirts I have plenty of."

"Yeah, and they're all the same. Now, what about one of

these?" She held up a short-sleeved acetate number with palm trees and leaping fish.

"I don't think so." She was starting to get on his nerves.

"Come on, Phil—lighten up! Didn't you know I was kiddin'?"

"Sure I did."

"Now, here. I think these are real nice." She held up a pin-striped shirt with no collar.

Pearl blinked. "You're serious?" he said, after a moment.

"Sure!"

"I don't think it's exactly me."

"Oh—" She shook her head, still wide-eyed. She was deep into performing territory; he couldn't locate her. "That's the whole problem!" she said.

"What?"

"*You're* too exactly you."

It seemed a stunning indictment. "You think so?" he asked.

"You need to change your act a little."

"My act?"

"All those cute little freshman chicks are just gonna think you're a big square."

He took the shirt. "Is that what you think?"

"I think they're real handsome shirts."

If I wear one, will you sleep with me?

"I don't know," Pearl said. "Don't you think there's something kind of—"

"What?"

"I don't know. Kind of vaguely faggy about them."

She quickly turned serious. "I don't think that's true."

He rushed to apologize. Why? What was he apologizing for? "I just meant," Pearl said, "you know—kind of male-modelish. A little too cute."

She was shuffling absently through the bin of shirts.

"I just meant—" Pearl began. He sighed. "How about coffee?"

Go-cups in hand, they sat in wrought-iron chairs by the shallow end of the pool in the courtyard of Camelot. The late afternoon had begun to turn chilly. Francesca hunched her shoulders. A chill wind rippled the water's surface; an empty Styrofoam cup rode the waves. They sipped their coffee awhile, saying nothing. Pearl felt what he must say bubbling up like indigestion through his chest and into the base of his throat. He looked over at her. Her forehead, like the water, was rippled.

"What are you thinking about?" he asked. The lover's question, cruel parody—yet what did he have to lose?

"You," she amazingly said.

"Me?"

"I like you, Phil. I—like you." She sipped, inconclusively. The black windows of the apartments around the pool stared blankly down.

"Francesca." Here it came. *Ready or not.*

She didn't look at him.

Pearl took a breath. "I'm crazy about you, you know," he said.

One. Two. Three. "I know."

"And I really don't know what to do about it." He put his hand on top of hers. It was the first time he had ever touched her. Her hand felt cold. It lay on the arm of the chair, not turning, not moving. The windows stared.

"Phil."

"Yes?"

"I don't think this is a good idea."

"You don't."

"I don't."

"You mean, being here? Or—"

"Any of it."

Now the wind blew, hard, pushing the empty cup across the pool. She pushed her chin down into her sweater.

"You're cold," he said. "Do you want to go inside?"

She took her hand out from under his and put it in her lap. "I think I'd better go home," she said.

XI

Pearl drifted through the health and beauty aids section of Winn Dixie, lonely as a cloud, though not entirely unhappy—no, now that he thought of it, not really unhappy at all, the sheer weightlessness of Friday evening buoying him, however irrationally, as he pushed his cart through wide, slick, empty aisles. His mind was playing "Water Music"—an intricate, trilly, frilly horn passage, note for note (how extraordinary the brain was!)—even though the store's p.a. was broadcasting a xylophony version of some Burt Bacharach thing or other. He came to the end of the aisle, glanced through the floor-to-ceiling plate-glass window. Outside, in the gigantic parking lot (Winn Dixie was part of the Little Big Mall), the gray Volvo sat almost alone under an immense Pickett sunset sky, perfectly cloudless, unmarked by jet vapor trails, flawlessly blending from electric blue at the dome to orange at the rim, with Venus poised in the middle, like a beauty mark. The mercury parking-lot lamps had just come on: the cold green-white chips of light, dotted across the ten acres of asphalt, flickered sharply, matter-of-factly, against the old-fashioned romantic glow in the west. It was seven o'clock, and everyone in Pickett had gone home.

Friday had set in with peculiar portent. Was something going on that he didn't know about? The campus had begun clearing out at one o'clock—did people need time to dress? to pray?—and by three, when Pearl had finished his poetry class, Culpepper was like a morgue. Even Wunsch had gone somewhere: his door, at three thirty, was conspicuously closed, its curtain pulled across its pane of glass. Darla sat at her desk with nothing to do, sitting out her hours, her big eyes rolling in boredom. Only Marshak remained when Pearl finally left—Pearl caught a glimpse of him, through his partially opened door, the big pale moon-face staring grimly down at the papers full of department facts and figures on his desk: he hated being chairman, he was a teacher at heart.

Pearl lingered in the frozen-foods section of the market, looking incredulously at several bags of bagels lying between the pie shells and waffles. This was the New South with a vengeance. He picked up a bag and saw that the bagels had been baked in Queens. His heart hopped. Should he buy them? A wavelet of nostalgia passed over him, but he shook it off. Be *here*. Then, from some depth in himself, he heard another voice: *why* be here, only? He flipped the bag into his basket. He would take communion at breakfast.

This thought brought, with a thump, the thought of the hours between then and now. He felt a cold current of fear, but somehow the sweet odor of Friday possibility (not unrelated to the fragrance that hovered in the aisles of the supermarket) refused to desert him. He was an optimist. Something of a fool, too— but an optimist, nonetheless. It occurred to him that this Friday magic might be in some way related to the Sabbath. He had certainly never been observant—had been the opposite, in fact. And at once it struck him that the High Holy Days had recently come and gone, in this strange desert of a land, without his being even slightly aware of them. Usually he felt something, if only a vibration of guilt. What, tonight, had made him think of the Sabbath? Perhaps the past stirred the blood. Regardless of what he sometimes liked to believe, he hadn't sprung from nothing. He was composed of others—thousands, incalculable powers of two.

"Mr. Pearl?"

He jumped, guiltily, as if he had been caught shoplifting. Here were a girl and a boy, with a cart chock full of groceries. Was it only themselves they were shopping for, or a whole houseful of people? The boy he had never seen, but the girl's face was achingly familiar. She was blond, plump, healthy, not bad-looking. Where did he know her from? College? Graduate school? How had she come here?

"I'm Pam Brown?" she said. "Masterpieces? Halfway back on the left?" She had a teasing expression, her tongue actually stuck in her cheek.

"Of course," said Pearl, trying to visualize the seating chart. "It's halfway back on the right for me. How are you, Pam?"

"That's O.K., I know you don't know me from Adam. No reason you should. I never was much good at school." She wrinkled up her pug nose. Flirtatiously? "Oh," she said. "This here's Rollie."

Pearl started to put out his hand, but Rollie kept both of his in the back pocket of his jeans. He nodded curtly at Pearl.

"Let's see what a teacher eats," Pam said impulsively, peering into Pearl's basket. "Yuk," she said. She picked up the bag of bagels. "What are *these?*" she said, wrinkling her nose again. It was less endearing the second time. Rollie looked on impassively.

"Bagels," Pearl said, only something stuck momentarily in his windpipe, and the sound didn't quite come out. He cleared his throat and repeated himself, waiting, stiff, for the slight, or the whiff of one.

But Pam, incurious as ever, merely dropped the bag back into the cart. "Oh," she said. Her flirtiness had abruptly evaporated. Pearl's novelty had been exhausted. "Oh well, bah," she said. "Come on, Rollie."

They went on ahead of him and turned left at the end of the aisle. Pearl doubled back in the direction he had come from. He would have to be circumspect if he didn't want to encounter them again. His cheeks still hurt from grinning. At least Rollie had had the dignity not to smile. Why, Pearl wondered, did he feel such a need to ingratiate? What was he making up for? He rolled his cart, at top speed, toward square one, the produce section. By the time he got back to where he had left off, surely Pam and Rollie would have checked out.

Pearl wheeled down an aisle that contained nothing but candy, shelf after shelf of it. For some reason it made him think of Marvell: sweetness in one ball, etcetera. Thank God Marvell had never seen a supermarket. How could you ever write again after seeing a supermarket? Jarrell had tried. He had tried to write about the supermarket. The effort, or the sadness overflowing, perhaps, had killed him. Pearl had not even tried. Anything. In how long now? Best not to think about it. He took a sharp right turn, at the rear of the store, along Winn Dixie's amazing meat section. Red filled the entire right side of his vision: the sight of these meats was somehow more than he could bear. He took another sharp right, and came face to face with Ted Juniper and Leon.

"Philly boy!"

"Ted. Leon."

"Will you look at that, Lee? We found us a carpetbagger in the supermarket."

"A sorry sight, Ted."

"How are you two doing?" Pearl asked.

"Come south to burn our crops and steal our women. Or vice versa."

"And assimilate our precious folkways."

"Damn! Go at it, Leon!"

"I think you two are the only ones who've been burning crops around here," Pearl said.

"Uh-oh," Ted said, smiling. "Boy's got a tongue in his head."

"Not to mention a accurate apprehension of the situation," Leon said.

"Shh, now I *told* you not to mention it," said Ted.

"Stoned again!" Leon crowed. A supermarket man in a white apron, stacking tomatoes at the end of the aisle, turned to look at them.

"What Leon lacks in vivacity, he makes up for in subtlety," Ted said.

Leon, seeing the man in the apron, called down the aisle: "*Sto*-oned again!" The man looked down at his tomatoes.

"I don't think he heard you, Leon," said Pearl.

"St—" Leon began, but Ted clapped a hand over his mouth. Leon rolled his eyes and flapped his hands.

"Whatchew doin' in Winn Dixie on a Friday night, boy?" Ted asked. "How come you ain't out paintin' the town?" He took his hand off Leon's mouth and shook it.

"—oned again," Leon crooned softly.

"You and that eye-talian gal have a spat?" Ted asked.

"I—"

"Ain't none of my goddamn bidness anyway." Ted turned to Leon. "Right, son?"

"Right, dad."

"Leon here's my illegitimate offspring, by Robbie Sue Lynette." Leon feigned gagging. "It's a well-kept secret around the campus."

Pearl was laughing.

"Only question is," Ted said, "how'd he get so fuckin' *big?*"

"Just clean air and good livin'," Leon said. "Plus judicious doses of poon-tang."

"You gonna go home and eat them bagels alone, Pearl?" Ted asked.

"I, uh—"

"Well, damn! Why don't you throw it all in the fridge and come out alleycattin' with us?"

They stared at him.

"I don't know if I'm the alleycatting type," Pearl said.

"You don't know—Leon, is that the sorriest answer you ever heard?"

"Sorriest one, Ted."

"Phil, we ain't askin' now—we're tellin'. Where is that goddamn Swedish car of yours? Right outside?"

Pearl nodded.

"Well you get your Northeastern intellectual butt into it and follow me over to my house. First we gone whip up some chili'll fry your Yankee eyes out. Then we gone get your ass *wrecked.*"

Pearl had not smoked pot in a long time, and this, according to Juniper and Leon, accounted for either the extreme ease or extreme difficulty of getting him stoned—they couldn't agree on which. In any case, by the time they all left Juniper's house later in the evening, Pearl felt as if he had been breathing nothing else all day: his eyes burned, and, for some reason, he couldn't stop sneezing.

"I think I'm allergic," he said, as they went out into the yard. The stars looked large and close; the pines swished in a cool wind that brought the smell of wood smoke from somewhere. For a moment Pearl felt intensely sad without knowing why. Then he sneezed again.

"Allergic my ass," Ted said. "You're just out of the habit, is all." They were standing next to his pickup truck. "Hop in, boy."

"We could all go in my car," Pearl offered. In his present condition, he felt it might be best if he were belted in.

But Leon was already holding the pickup's door for him, looming in the dark. "In you go, Perfesser," he said, and Pearl obediently climbed in and sat in the middle of the bench seat.

Leon's huge bulk pressed, bearlike, against Pearl, pushing him into Juniper's hip; but Juniper, looking preposterously phlegmatic with his meerschaum in his mouth, seemed not to notice. Pearl was pressed so tightly between the two men that he could smell them both, Leon's acrid musk (why did large men so often give off a sharp odor?) and Juniper's neat, pipey scent. Ted hummed what sounded like a hymn as he drove them through Pickett's gridded dark back streets, slowing down carefully at each crossing, though no one else was around. His Rebel sharpshooter look was especially strong tonight, the pipe in his mouth somehow emphasizing his high flat cheekbones and the stubborn set of his jaw, his right eye squinting as if he were drawing a bead on a Yankee instead of just trying to see into the dim path of the old truck's flickering headlights.

Then they were out in Jackson Street, the spine of the town. Pearl tried to imagine the main drag as it had been fifty years ago: out this far, a mile from what had been downtown, it would have been narrow and dark, flanked by little white houses, each with its yellow-lit radio playing, among thick groves of pine and live oak. The world outside gigantic and far away. *Distance is romance; romance is gone.* Pearl stared out at the passing gauntlet of Western Sizzlin' and Wendy's and Sambo's and Long John Silver's and the Little Mall and the Drive-In Beer Barn and Burgerama and the trailer sign with its movable type, tonight reading FORGIVE THEM LORD FOR THEY KNOW NOT WHAT THEY

DO. Then the pickup bumped down off the pavement and into the gravel driveway of the Armadillo Bar and Grill.

Leon alit from the cab with a yell before the truck had stopped moving. Pearl took the opportunity to lie down to the right, across the seat, his head in the corner by the door. Things were turning.

Juniper took the pipe from his mouth. "Wrong with you, boy?" he said.

"I suddenly don't feel so hot, Ted." Pearl sneezed and belched simultaneously. "Maybe I'll just lie down awhile."

Juniper stared down at him with some concern.

"I'll be O.K.," Pearl said. "Why don't you just go in? I'll be along in a little bit."

And then skepticism.

"Really. I'll be fine, Ted. Just go ahead in."

"Just don't freeze your butt, boy. It's *cold* out here." He closed the door and was gone.

The small thing that was whirling in Pearl's head, just above the eyes, continued while he slept, and was still whirling when he awoke some time later, shivering and sore. He lay in the same position, slumped in the corner between the seat and the door, looking up at the cab's forest-green metal ceiling. From where he lay he could see nothing out the truck's windows except cold floodlit mist against the dark sky, but he could hear muted pounding music and voices and car doors slamming and the crackle of gravel in the lot. He remembered riding home late at night from his grandparents' house when he was a child, lying like this in the back seat of the car, trying to guess where on the well-known route he was, gazing at the pale lights fanning across the headliner, feeling the car turn right and left, slow down, speed up, seeing nothing out the dark glass but lampposts passing, and knowing he would never die.

He wished whatever it was that was whirring in his head

would stop. He sat up quickly and got down out of the truck. Surely Juniper would drive him home. The night air was even colder than the inside of the cab, cold and clinging. Pearl heard a noise like cloth tearing: by the side of the building, in the shadows, someone in a cowboy hat was doubled over, throwing up.

The noise inside was a substance: Pearl could feel the molecules of disturbed air brushing his face. The light was the light of a photographer's darkroom. Pearl pushed through the crowd, not quite knowing where he was going, excusing himself at the top of his lungs, inaudibly. Then he caught a glimpse of Leon, sitting at a table near the stage with a girl, raising his bottle in salute.

Pearl started toward them, but the sound drove him back. The musicians on the tiny stage wore cowboy hats (a specific type of hat: not the stiff felt Lone Ranger style that Pearl had worn as a boy, but battered straw, the brim pushed down at either end so that the overall shape resembled a croissant), Smith Brothers beards, stringy hair to the shoulder. Pearl moved to the bar, not away from but at least not toward the buffeting sound. He leaned against the rail and scanned the room for Juniper. Nothing. Maybe he was relieving himself. Pearl felt woozy. He closed his eyes for a second. He would collect himself and then search the place.

A hand descended on Pearl's shoulder: he turned and saw the bartender—in the same type of hat as the band—miming pouring from a bottle. Pearl smiled wanly and shook his head. The bartender repeated the gesture. Pearl shook his head again, trying to appear as friendly as possible. The bartender frowned and turned away. Just then, the music stopped, with a clash of cymbals and a squeal of feedback, and Pearl saw Juniper climbing onto the stage.

Ted made his way through the tangle of equipment and bent over solicitously to speak to the drummer, who still sat at his kit, his face in shadow. Was Juniper requesting a song? Pearl wondered. Then the drummer lifted his head. He had pale skin and red hair tied into a long red ponytail.

Pearl felt another tap on his shoulder. It was a stocky person with a wispy beard, wearing the same cowboy hat—Armadillo standard issue?—and a friendly smile. A heartwarming smile, really. Pearl smiled back.

"Sir, it's just a house policy," the man said, quite apologetically, through the ringing in Pearl's ears. "We got a two-drank minimum? Have to pay the band," he added, as if this pesky detail were just between the two of them.

Ted was still in conversation with the drummer, whose cowboy hat moved from side to side as he shook his head vigorously.

Pearl, also willing to be conciliatory, said, "I really just came in to find a friend. There he is right there—" Pearl nodded toward the stage. "I'll be leaving in two minutes."

"Sir. You don't seem to understand, sir?" The smile became, if anything, even warmer. "If you walk in the door, you bah two dranks." He spoke slowly and elementarily. "There's a sign right out front?"

"Right. I'm sure there is. I promise you—"

"Perfesser! How the hell you doin'?" Leon was grabbing Pearl's hand—engulfing it—and pumping it.

"Leon, what is Ted doing up there?" Juniper was now jabbing the drummer's chest with his index finger. The drummer raised his open hands as if in surrender. One of the other band members was watching Juniper closely.

"Just talkin'," Leon said. "This dude givin' you any trouble?"

"There's no trouble, friend," the stocky man said to Leon. "I was just tellin' this boy the house policy."

"This *boy* happens to be a professor of English at the university, you asshole."

"Leon, Leon," Pearl said.

"There's no need to get ugly about it, son," the stocky man said. "Now—"

"Only ugly thing around here is your goddamn face, you little pimp." And suddenly Leon had the man's shirt collar in both hands. The odd thing, Pearl noticed in the next moment— it seemed to go extremely slowly—was that the man made absolutely no move to defend himself. As Leon grabbed him, he merely threw both hands out to the side. But it hardly mattered. There was a terrible sound, a deadened crack, and Leon's grip went loose. Pearl swiveled to see the bartender crouching atop the bar, a baseball bat in his hand.

"Oh my God," Pearl said. The place had gone dead silent, the red-tinted faces around him were gaping.

"That's all right, folks," the stocky man said, with truly amazing equanimity. "Y'all go back to your fun. Just a little misunderstanding." And the jukebox cut on, loud.

> *Still the same*
> *Baby, you're*
> *still the same*

Pearl looked to the stage, but Juniper and the drummer had vanished.

The stocky man and the bartender took hold of Leon underneath his arms, turning him over on his back in the process. He was alive, at least—his mouth opened as he breathed, and his brow was wrinkled, as if he were contemplating the difficult problem of coming to. Under the crashing music, the bartender mouthed something to Pearl.

"What?" Pearl shouted.

The bartender put his mouth to Pearl's ear. "I said it would hep if you'd take his feet," he yelled. And so the three of them dragged and carried Leon through a dividing sea of gaping customers to the front door and then outside. They sat him on the gravel against the wall of the building. It was quiet and cold in the parking lot. As Leon's back touched the cold cement, he started. "What?" he said.

"I'd appreciate it if you'd tell your friend that he might be best off stayin' away from here for a couple weeks," the bartender said, almost apologetically, to Pearl. "Probably be best for you, too."

"Thanks."

"I ain't meanin' no harm by it, friend," he said. "All right?"

"Sure."

The bartender put out a hand for Pearl to shake, but Pearl kept his hands in his pockets. The bartender shrugged, and he and the stocky man went inside.

Pearl bent down and shook Leon's arm. "Leon! Are you all right?"

Leon opened his eyes painfully, and winked. "Hey, Perfesser," he said.

"Leon, where the hell has Ted gone? His truck isn't here."

"It isn't?"

"You don't have any idea where he went?"

"Perfesser, I don't have any idea about *nothin'* right now." He touched his temple and groaned. "Fucker must've blindsided me. Shit, that hurts."

"A baseball bat, Leon. He hit you with a Louisville Slugger."

"Ohh, Christ. It feels like it."

"Listen. I should get you to a hospital."

"Who was it? That little bartender?"

Pearl nodded.

"Goddamn it. If I had me a gun, I'd go in there and shoot his pecker off, you know that?"

There was a crunch of gravel, a disturbance of light. Pearl

squinted up into the glare and saw sparkling rhinestones on the front of a black dress.

"Well, well. The two outcasts. Ain't you a pretty-looking pair."

"Hey, Jewel," Leon said.

Pearl glanced from one to the other. "You know each other?" he said.

"This isn't New York, Pearl," Jewel said.

"Jewel's a ol' barfly, just like me," Leon said. "We meet in all the wrong places, don't we, hon?"

"Quit trying to sound like a goddamn country song, Leon."

Leon winked at Pearl. "Her bark's worse than her bite." He wiped at his face with his sleeve. "Aw, shit," he said. "My goddamn nose is bleedin' like a son of a bitch."

Jewel knelt down by him. Her long, black dress inhibited the movement of her knees, so that she had to shift sideways to get into place. What, Pearl wondered, was she doing dressed so formally on a Friday night in Pickett? "Lean your head back, you dumb cowboy," she said. She felt behind his hair. "You concussed?"

"I really think we should get him to a hospital right away," Pearl said. Jewel gave him a no-kidding look.

"Can you walk?" she asked Leon.

"Dunno."

"Let's get his arms, Pearl."

They hoisted him up—she was surprisingly strong—and walked him a few feet. "Owww," Leon said.

"You can't be hurt too bad if you're squawkin' so damn much," Jewel said. She turned to Pearl. "I can understand this happening to him," she said. "What's your excuse?"

Pearl suddenly found himself trying not to smile. "I don't know."

"Quit looking so damn pleased with yourself, Pearl," she said. "You're not the one who got beaned." They had stopped by a big blue dented Dodge; now Jewel opened the back door, and they helped Leon in. She squinted skeptically at Pearl for a second. "Come on," she said. "You can tell me all about it on the way downtown."

"Your friend has a head like concrete," Dr. Gupta said. They were standing in the emergency room at Pickett General. Dr. Gupta was tiny and round-faced and hopeful-looking. He stared up at both Pearl and Jewel as if he were trying to memorize them. "He is very fortunate," Dr. Gupta said. "You said he was hit with a what?"

"A baseball bat," Pearl said.

"I think it is wonderful how sports-minded the Americans are," Dr. Gupta said, writing something on a clipboard. "A wonderful country and a wonderful city. Pickett, Missippissi. Such euphony. Such intelligent natives." He smiled brightly at them.

Jewel smiled wanly back. "Intelligent enough to pronounce the name of the state right, anyway," she said.

"I have mispronounced?"

"You said Missy Pissy. It's Mississippi."

"Did I not say this?"

"You did not."

"I apologize completely. You are a native?" he asked Jewel.

"Boom biddy boom boom," Jewel said. "Uh-huh."

"Ah. And you, sir?"

"I'm from New York," Pearl said.

"Ahh, New York! You are here voluntarily?"

"More or less." Jewel narrowed her eyes at him. "Why?" Pearl said to Dr. Gupta. "Aren't you?"

"Oh, completely. That is—I came of my own free will. Sight unseen, of course. Pickett, Missi"—he smiled—"ssippi. It had such an exotic sound." He sighed. "Perhaps, when my residency is over, I will see the rest of your charming country."

"You won't find anywhere better than here," Jewel said. "Or worse."

"An admirable attitude," Dr. Gupta said. "But I long to visit your New York," he said to Pearl. "I myself am from Bombay. Very different to here." He sighed. "Very much indeed. But—" He smiled again, apologetically. "No matter. At least your friend was not in a smashup. I think I have never seen so many smashups as I have seen in this town. My heart is in my mouth every time I take the wheel. I—"

"*I* think we'd better get going," Jewel said.

"Ah. Yes," Dr. Gupta said. "Well. As I said, we will give Mr. Battle an EEG in the morning. But all my experience leads me to believe that he has sustained nothing worse than a lump." He smiled beseechingly at Pearl. "Very fortunate. Perhaps when you come back to visit, you can tell me more of New York."

"Let's go, Pearl," Jewel said.

"Bye-bye," Dr. Gupta said. "Y'all come back now."

"Not if I can help it," Jewel said, as they pushed through the doors to the parking lot. "Christ!" she yelled to the dim stars. "He gave me a *pain?*"

"I kind of liked him."

"You would."

"He was just lonely."

"He was just a pain in the goddamn—*butt!*" She shouted the last word, but the sound died in the dark trees. The street was quiet. It was after three. In back of them, beyond the hospital, the interstate was nearly empty. A half-moon—it looked oddly upside-down—had just risen over the Wagon Wheel, and the sky was bright. Pearl yawned.

"Poor Pearl," Jewel said. "You're not used to honky-tonkin',
are you."

"What's with this 'Pearl' stuff? I have a first name."

" 'Philip' is queer-bait," she said. "I'm gonna call you Pearl.
Doesn't anyone else?"

"No."

"Good. It's kind of cute, don't you think? Sounds like a
girl. Pearl the girl."

"Yeah, yeah. Jewel the—"

"Don't say it." She took a pack of Vantages out of her bag,
shook one out, offered the pack to Pearl, and, when he put up
his hand, stuck the cigarette in her mouth and lit it. "Anyway,
I changed my name. Thank God."

Pearl felt he ought to tread carefully here. "You're not Jewel
anymore?"

She rolled her eyes. "I'm not Mildred anymore."

He stifled a smile. "Mildred?"

She pointed at him. "Watch it." She inhaled deeply and
let the smoke out through her nose and mouth. "My mother
was *in*sane," she said. "She named me after a goddamn
movie."

"A movie?"

"*Mildred Pierce?*"

Pearl made no show of comprehension.

"You know—with Joan Crawford? You don't? My God,
what rock have you been under, Pearl?"

"A big one."

"Well, I guess so." She let out another cloud of smoke. It
shivered away on the chill night air. "What in hell ever made
you come down here, anyway?" she asked.

"Don't ask that. Everybody asks that."

"Oh yeah? What do you tell 'em?"

"That I'm a Northern spy."

She began to laugh, started to cough, then settled on a mixture of both.

"What's so funny?"

She held her hand at the base of her throat. "That's an *apple*."

"How'd you know that?"

"I just had this mental picture of this cute little curly-haired Jewish apple runnin' around." She began to laugh and cough again. "Sorry," she gasped.

"You sound terrific, you know that? You ought to try smoking a little more."

She coughed again, and took another drag from the cigarette, eyes closed. "Oh, Pearl. *You* sound like somebody's mother."

"Do I?"

"Uh-oh, now he's gettin' sensitive on me. Do me a favor, Pearl. Let me be the sensitive one around here. You be the man."

"Now, that's a sensitive thing to say."

She looked annoyed. "What time is it getting to be?" she asked.

"Three thirty-five."

"Goodness gracious, I had better get you home before you turn into a pumpkin."

"A Jewish pumpkin?"

She laughed sharply. "All right, Pearl," she said. "You're all right."

"Well, Pearl." They were getting out of her car. "I'd ask you up for a drink, but I know you want your beauty sleep."

He felt a sudden dizzy tightness between and behind his

brows that could only translate as a question mark. "How do you know that?" he said.

"Come on up, then." She fished her keys out of her pocketbook. Pearl was touched by this small gesture: she owned things. She did things. "I tried beauty sleep for a while," she said, "but all I got was the sleep."

They were entering Camelot's courtyard. The pool lights were on—so no one would fall in? The water was perfectly still, perfectly transparent: at the bottom of the deep end sat a single Budweiser can, upright. The windows around the courtyard were all dark. Pearl glanced straight up and saw Orion in its Tinkertoy splendor, circumscribed by the apartment roofs. Somewhere he had read that if you stood at the bottom of a well, you could see the stars overhead in broad daylight. What would anyone be doing standing at the bottom of a well?

Jewel was climbing the concrete steps to the second-floor balcony. From behind and below she had a large, practical, resigned look: it was something about the black dress and the keys in her hand. She was a large woman. Not fat, but tall and big-boned. Her self-deprecation to the contrary, not at all unattractive. Particularly nice were her large, dark, liquid eyes, so soft when they might have been hard. She had been through much, or she liked to give this impression. Pearl watched her face in the yellow porch light as she put the key in the lock. No trace of disingenuousness, of hope or coquetry, flickered on her features. It was the face of a tired woman opening a door. Pearl was glad.

"My God," Pearl said. "It's my place."

He looked around at Jewel's apartment. Except for the orange-and-brown plaid furniture and the beige wall phone, he could have been home. But this place also had a different bouquet—a spicy, beauty-counter smell. He liked this smell.

Jewel was bending over, a little awkward in her tight-kneed dress, and taking off her shoes. "Oh yeah?" she said. She grunted as she pried off the second shoe. "Pardon my informality," she said. "These things have been murdering me since seven o'clock. Christ," she said, picking up and rubbing her left foot. "You're from New York. Tell me—who designs women's shoes? It has to be gay guys, right? Someone with hate in his heart for the whole gender?"

"You don't have to wear them."

"You are a little too goddamned logical for a supposed poet, anyone ever tell you that?"

Pearl laughed. "You're absolutely right," he said.

"O.K. I got beer and cheap cognac. I recommend the beer."

"I'll go with the cognac."

"I'm impressed with your lack of logic there, Pearl." She shuffled around behind her counter, the same counter on which he read his Cervantes and Jonathan Swift—the same color Formica, even. Jewel's version of the counter, however, was scattered with record jackets: the Eagles, the Doobie Brothers, Dan Fogelberg. Pearl recognized these names; they floated vaguely in his cultural consciousness; but he wasn't sure which name went with which of the whining sounds he had occasionally heard coming from someone else's radio. He picked up one of the album covers.

"Do you know what a Steely Dan *is?*" he asked her, alarmed.

"No, what?" She handed him a Flintstones jelly jar half filled with cognac, and drank the head off the beer she had poured herself.

"Thanks." Pearl sipped his cognac and looked around the room. "I can't get over this," he said. "Imagine everyone living in exactly the same place." He shook his head. "It's weird. Kind of nice, in a way."

Jewel sat down in an orange-and-brown-plaid easy chair. "Take a load off," she said. "You can have the couch."

He leaned back into the soft cushions. They smelled like a furniture store. It suddenly occurred to him that the chair and couch were large objects of great weight in a second-floor apartment. "Is this stuff yours?" he asked, patting the arm of the couch.

"Uh-uh. Came with the place. Twenty-five extra a month. Otherwise it was sleep on the floor. Why? Didn't what's-his-face offer you that deal?"

"No," Pearl lied. Stubbs had offered, and Pearl had imagined what the furniture would look like (he had been right). He had supplemented his mattress with some yellow deck chairs he had found at K&B. Now, as he reclined on the couch, he wondered if he had made a mistake. There was something about a big couch that pleased the soul, whether the couch was brown-and-orange plaid or not. He leaned back, pleased, and stared at the crusty white ceiling. If you squinted, it resembled the Alps seen from the air.

Jewel jumped up. "Do you mind if I put on a record?" she asked. "My nerves are kind of jangled." She was telling more than asking. "I'll play it soft," she said. The stereo sat on the carpet, against the wall. She took an album from the counter and deftly put the record on the turntable. Pearl was pleased to see that she had none of the awkwardness around machines he had often seen in women. The music came on softly—horns, unidentifiable instruments. Not at all what he had expected, not something he would have heard at Juniper's house. This wasn't half bad. The chord changes were surprising: usually he made a joke of rock music by humming, the instant before it happened, the too-obvious base note for each too-obvious phrase. But this song kept fooling him. He stopped trying, and closed his eyes, smiling. He was slightly high from the perfumey cognac: not dizzy the way he had been on Juniper's dope, but relaxed.

"You know," Pearl said, "I was wondering—"

"Shh, this is my favorite part," Jewel said.

*This is the night
of the expanding man . . .*

The horn played a descending figure, jaded but urgent, reminding Pearl of something he seemed to have experienced, an exact light and weather and odor in the hills above Hollywood; a time, a desire—but he had never been to Hollywood. What was he thinking of? It all went away.

"I'm sorry," Jewel said. "You were saying?"

"I forgot." He opened his eyes, trying to remember. Then he remembered, and he was ashamed. *You know Francesca Raffi.* He had been preparing to bring this up as a matter of casual interest. But there was nothing casual about it, and he was constitutionally unable to lie.

She peered at him humorously. "Come on. What was it?"

"Nothing, really." Even this small an untruth was more than he could handle.

Jewel smiled oddly. "Poor Pearl," she said. "Got it bad, huh?"

"Excuse me?"

"Chesca."

"What?"

"I saw you, Pearl. I didn't mean to, but I just—saw you." She shrugged.

"Saw—?"

"You and Chesca. At the pool. You were right outside my window, for God's sake."

Pearl's mouth opened. Nothing came out.

"I kind of guessed things weren't going so terrifically."

"I—"

"It's all right, Pearl. Why don't we drop it." She sighed, lay back in the chair, looked up at the ceiling. "Everybody's burnin' up, I guess. For some jerk somewhere."

"Who's yours?"

"Some jerk somewhere."

They got a name for the winners in the world,
I—I want a name when I lose

the singer sang.

"Maybe I should get going," Pearl said.

She glanced at him, blinked. "Suit yourself."

He stood stiffly, stretched. "God, it's been a long day," he said. Jewel didn't answer. Pearl took his glass to the sink exactly as if he were at home—it was odd: as he walked across the room, he *was* at home. But—strange detail—her faucet handle was different from his, a single stick shift instead of individual hot and cold controls. He turned on the water.

The music stopped. "That's all right," Jewel said, yawning. "I'll wash 'em later." She was putting the record back in its jacket. The world was the world again. Pearl put on his Brooks Brothers windbreaker and went to the door. She had been squatting down, rearranging records, and now she rose with a rustle, distracted, as if she were surprised he wasn't gone already.

Pearl opened the door a crack. The night air was chill; the pool glowed below, bright near the edges. Some compressor or pool machine was running, a mindless night noise, frightening somehow. "O.K.," he said.

"O.K." Even without her shoes, she was as tall as he. She faced him directly, not smiling, not frowning, her eyes focused somewhere just to the side of his: perhaps she was abstracted, perhaps just exhausted. He suddenly wanted her attention back. He reached out a hand. "Good night," he said.

She smiled, took his hand. "Good night, Pearl."

He leaned forward to kiss her on the cheek. But Jewel, in mild surprise, or feigning surprise, turned her head—to watch what he was doing?—and his lips ended up awkwardly on hers.

"Now, *what*," she said—softly, for he was closer to her now—"did you do that for?"

"I don't know," he said, actually puzzled. He kissed her again.

"Pearl," she said, with a trace of annoyance, and some hint of warning.

"What?" His arms were around her, and she was solid and warm. He was conscious of the crisp material of her dress, of her underclothing beneath, in a way he hadn't been conscious of such things since the sixth grade, the first time he had danced with a girl.

"What are you *doing?*" she said, the annoyance gone, nothing but wondering in her voice.

"All night I've just been doing what I've been doing," he said. It sounded idiotic. Her forehead wrinkled. "I mean," he said, "things have just been *happening*. Usually it doesn't work that way with me. I think more."

Still in his arms, she screwed her mouth to one side and shook her head at him. "Oh Pearl," she said. "What is to be done with you?"

He kissed her again. She cocked her head inquisitively and began to kiss back. He pushed the door shut behind them with his heel.

He fell from some distance and awoke with a thud. The thud was his heart. An alarm? The phone was ringing. *What had happened?* He reached over—and bumped into Jewel. She picked up her phone.

"Yeah," she said. She listened for a moment.

"No," she said. "*No.*" She hung up.

"Wrong number?" Pearl said. The light in the room was blue—Jewel's bedroom, on the corner of the building, had one more window than his, along the side wall—but he could see her face, scrubbed and startled-looking without makeup. Her breasts, blue-white and large, seemed to look at him, too. He reached for her, smiling.

But she blocked him gently with her arm. "No, Pearl," she said. "Uh-uh." He persisted, thinking she was teasing.

"*Pearl.*" She pulled the covers around herself and sat up.

"Morning," Pearl said. Then, glancing at the window, "What *time* is it?"

"Time for you to go." She avoided his eyes. "Don't look at me that way, I'm serious," she said. She reached over to the night table and shook herself out a cigarette.

"You really are, aren't you."

She lit the cigarette and inhaled, the tip casting a faint orange glow on her face and chest. She nodded.

"Why?"

"Because I don't want to be making you coffee four hours from now, and trying to think what to say—that's why. I don't want to have to think about how to spend Saturday with you, and then worry about whether you're going to stay again tonight. Easiest time to decide is now. And the decision is, out you go, Pearl."

He yawned.

She laughed. "God, it's good to see you're taking me seriously." She pushed his shoulder. "Go *on.*"

"Did I do anything wrong?"

"No, damn it, you didn't do anything wrong. You did everything just fine." She wouldn't look at him.

"Then I don't see—"

"Don't see. Just put on your pants and leave."

His clothes, on the floor, led in a backwards trail out the bedroom door. He located everything but one sock. Why wouldn't it be next to the other? He got down on his hands and knees and searched the carpet, squinting in the half-light. "I seem to be missing a sock," he said. There was no response from the next room. He tied his Wallabee on over his bare right foot and went to the bedroom doorway. "I'm going," he said. She was still sitting up in bed in the shadows, the glowing orange dot hovering in front of her face.

" 'Bye," Pearl said.

"Pearl."

"What?"

"Come here."

"What?" He stood by the side of the bed, looking down at her. She took his wrist and pulled him down. Her tongue, nicotine-coated, tasted electric. He put his arm around her, but she pushed it back.

"Now, get," she said.

He went back to his room and slept for three hours. He awoke after nine, ferociously hungry—and remembered that he had left his entire bag of groceries (the frozen bagels!) at Juniper's. Leon was in the hospital. Where had Ted gone? Pearl would find out later. Breakfast first. The prospect of another supermarket did not enchant. Then he thought of the convenience store out on Jackson, just around the corner.

Pearl recalled as he walked down the echoing steps that he hadn't picked up his mail in a few days. He had more or less given up on the mail. It had happened at about the same time he had given up on the mailman.

He had made the man's acquaintance in the first few weeks of school: during a bout of homesickness, he had actually engineered the encounter, as if propitiating the bearer might somehow stimulate the flow of letters from the few scattered friends he had left. His friends didn't write. (Enmeshed in mooning stratagems, Pearl hadn't written them.) Even after all hope should have been gone, he continued to imagine he would find a letter from Francesca in the box, on purple paper, her strange handwriting (had he ever seen it?) in ink as black as her eyebrows. Girls in his day had written such letters. No letter came. But the mailman, increasingly puzzled and homesick himself, remained constant, as did the talk of fishing.

The man had surprised Pearl at first. He had originally, unimaginatively, expected a lean old Southern civil servant, courtly and laconic, or perhaps a tobacco-chewing redneck; but in actual fact the mailman was plump and sandy-haired and wistful, and came from California. "I don't know what I'm doing here," the mailman would say to Pearl, shaking his head. "One day the wife and I just left Modesto, and here's where we ended up." Then he would hand Pearl his coupons and bills and say the same thing, every time: "No news from home today. Fishin's good, though." The mailman lived to fish, and assumed that, naturally, as a fellow expatriate, Pearl did too. Pearl had never gone fishing in his life. The thought of fishing made his eyelids heavy. Soon Pearl began to avoid the mailman.

He turned the corner of the building and saw that the mailboxes were all open, in preparation for filling, and that the mailman was at the other end of the arcade. What to do? Breakfast first, he decided. He doubled back around the corner and walked out to Jackson.

At the Stop 'N Save Pearl bought eggs, orange juice, bread, milk, raisins, peanut butter, a Dura-Beam flashlight, and a burgundy polyester baseball cap with a picture of a leaping stag on the crown. He bought a Pickett *Post*. He was a citizen! Making important purchases. The sweet-smelling air of the convenience store seemed full of mystery and promise. The man at the cash register smiled and nodded to Pearl when he paid, and Pearl smiled and nodded right back.

He put on the baseball cap and whistled as he carried his sack of provisions down the street. He sang to himself as he rounded Camelot's first brown-brick corner and saw that the boxes were closed and the mailman was gone.

Pearl fished for his key and opened his box—as always, with a rising heart, however foolishly. But the only item inside today was a single white card, leaning leisurely in the back corner. Some sort of ad, Pearl told himself, for luck: a circular for a lawn-care company. The card was plain white, prestamped, standard post-office issue. The stamp was not canceled. Curious detail. Also, Pearl's name and address were printed, in black, crisp, modern type. He turned the card over and immediately smiled. Someone had sent him a cartoon. He looked at it for a moment and stopped smiling. The drawing, slightly shaky but not at all badly done, was of a double-barreled shotgun, with pellets and smoke flying from its muzzle. The caption beneath, in the same neat black type as on the front of the card, read:

KAROOOM!!!

XII

"All right—so what *about* this red wheelbarrow?"

Pearl surveyed his circle of poetry students for a flicker, a twitch, anything. Zilch. They sat and stared at him. He suddenly felt like one of those *National Geographic* reporters surrounded by New Guinea tribesmen daubed in clay. He thought he detected a certain incredulity in the room at the idea of such a thing as Pearl, sitting and hectoring them about a red wheelbarrow, glazed with rainwater, among white chickens. A red wheelbarrow, for God's sake! White chickens! Five lines! They had now sat for two solid periods—ten pairs of opaque eyes, ten mouth-breathers—while Pearl ranted on about Williams's poem.

"What is it about this red wheelbarrow?" Pearl said once more. "I mean"—he shifted his chair, scraping the floor with a sound like a low note on a cello—"I want you to under*stand*—maybe just to get a glimmer—before you try your own experiments."

Silence, thick and palpable. Hostile? Maybe it was his accent? Was he too much an alien, too much the fast-talking New York yid? True, if rushed, if passionate, he tended to lapse into

Manhattanese: dropped final *r*'s; dentalizations; giveaway vowel sounds like the *o* in *dog*. He tried to watch this in himself. Why? This kind of thing, thought the part of Pearl descended from three generations who had shopped at Brooks, was for cabdrivers and yeshiva boys. Wasn't it?

"Joey, what did you think of the poem?"

Joey—moon-faced, nearly albino—pressed together his white brows for several suspenseful seconds. "I liked it," he finally admitted.

"You liked it. *Why* did you like it?"

Joey grinned, blushed, ducked his head.

"Any idea at all?"

"I don't know. I just did."

"Fair enough. Fair enough. Dot, what about you?"

Dot, fortyish, a Baptist minister's wife, her hair scrolled back from her wide white forehead and flipped up at the sides, looked pained. "I didn't like it," she said.

"Good! Why not?"

"I don't know."

"Dot. Please. Just tell me what's on your mind."

"I guess I just didn't get what he was trying to get across."

"To get across. To get across. I see. Well, what's *in* the poem?"

Dot shrugged. "Just some chickens and a wheelbarrow."

"Great! Now—what does that tell you?"

She screwed up her mouth, shook her head. In the left corner of Pearl's purview, he detected a stirring, an impatience. Wise pedagogue, veteran of eight weeks, he ignored it. Maybe it—whatever it was—would catch. He scanned the eyes to his right.

" 'Just some chickens and a wheelbarrow.' All right. What does that *tell* you?"

Nothing.

"Anybody?"

Nobody.

Pearl sighed. "All right, Errol."

Errol Nightingale, whose barely bottled enthusiasm Pearl had just bypassed, sat directly on Pearl's left, his handsome dark face tilted at an aw-shucks angle, his long-lashed liquid eyes embarrassingly open, seeming to pose an entirely different question from the one at hand.

"Errol?"

"I don't know. I *had* an idea a minute ago, but now it just seems too crazy."

"Come on, Errol. Be crazy. What is it?"

Errol shook his head, squinching one side of his mouth into his cheek.

"What does Williams mean by 'So much depends upon'? I mean, why does anything *depend* on this wheelbarrow?"

Outside, the smoky autumn sun on the gravel of the flat roof, *quercus virginiana* quivering.

"I don't know," Errol said. "I just thought—like, what if it's just *about* this wheelbarrow? I mean, that's *all* it's about? That's stupid, right?"

The twenty eyes were wide on Pearl.

"That's it, Errol! You win!" Pearl hopped up and, chalk shattering, scrawled in gigantic letters across all three panels of the blackboard: NO IDEAS BUT IN THINGS. "What does this mean?" he asked. Rhetorically, as it turned out.

A vengeful corollary quickly came to mind. No ideas, period. Not in these things.

"It means," Pearl went on, drawing out the words until all hope of a response was gone, "it means exactly what Errol said it means. It means it's just *about* the wheelbarrow. It's just *about* the chickens. Just *about* the color red."

He looked at them. They at him. From somewhere down the hall came a secret migratory signal: the sounds of many voices, footsteps. They began to shift in their seats. Pearl glanced at his watch and, in that instant, lost them. Amid a concerto of scraping chairs, defeated, he stared at the floor.

"Mr. Pearl?"

Dot. Pearl brightened. "Please," he said. "Phil." A liberty he allowed his poetry students.

She closed her eyes, making a conscious effort. "Phil. I'm sorry, but I guess I still just don't understand the poem." She was short and delightfully prim in her bronze-colored dress. Her mouth was wide and thin-lipped, her nose tiny and upturned; her eyes were long and narrow, hooded, cool. She had a certain presence, a quiet, undogmatic ardor—the look of a believer.

"Maybe you're trying too hard, Dot." Errol was standing behind her, looking off to the side with an embarrassed half-smile, rocking from foot to foot, as if he were going to ask permission to go to the men's room.

"Too hard?"

"I mean, maybe there's less here than meets the eye."

A double furrow appeared between her brows. "I don't understand."

"Maybe you shouldn't worry so much about understanding."

She smiled indulgently at him. "I guess I'll just wait till next time," she said. And left, her hair bobbing, the shape of its upswept curves unchanging as they moved through the air.

"Errol?"

Errol snapped out of a reverie. "Yeah?"

"You had a question?"

"Uh, yeah. I wanted to ask you—I'm going to have to miss class Thursday." He said this as if he had just thought of it.

"Any special reason?"

"Er, yeah. I got some personal business to attend to." You look like you don't believe it yourself, Pearl thought. How do you expect me to?

"You can't take care of it any other time?"

"Uh-uh."

"You know that ordinarily I prefer you not to miss class unless it's unavoidable." It struck him, even as he said it, how particularly *teacherly* this was. Then it hit him, for the first time, that he actually was a teacher. Strange. He had been a poet once.

Errol blinked. "Yeah." He was gazing out at the wall again. Pearl studied his face. His skin was shiny, dark, nearly eggplant-colored. Yet his features were distinctly European. He glanced out the door, then quickly resumed eye contact with Pearl. "Look," he said, with a pained smile. "I got a problem."

"Poetry?"

"I lent this girl some *money*."

"Girl? What girl?"

"I mean. She comes to my room the other night and says she needs some money. So I give it to her." Still smiling, he shook his head incredulously.

"Do you *know* her?"

"A little, uh-huh. But not too good."

"How much did you lend her?"

"Oh, man." He averted his eyes again.

"How much, Errol?"

"I don't even want to talk about it."

"How much?"

"Mr. Pearl—"

"Errol."

"Two hundred dollars."

"Jesus Christ, Errol. What did she need it for?"

"I don't know. Somethin' about her family."

"Wait a second. Errol. Did you knock this girl up?"

"What?"

"You heard me."

"I don't think it was me, uh-uh."

"You don't *think*?"

"Listen. I *know* it wasn't me."

"What makes you so sure?"

A knowing look.

"But you gave her the two hundred dollars."

An amazed smile. "Yeah."

Pearl sighed. "Oh, Errol."

His eyes grazed Pearl's, adding to the question they had posed before. Then he turned away. "I just felt like you might, you know, understand," he said, to the wall.

"Understand?"

The liquid brown eyes, signifying what surely must be understood by both of them, blinked. "I mean. About woman troubles and all."

"I'm not sure what you mean."

"I gotta go."

"I'm not sure what you mean," Pearl repeated.

But Errol only smiled helplessly as he backed into the hallway.

"Come on in, Philip, my boy, what can we do for you?" Edwin Marshak said. The department chairman sat with his linebacker's arms folded on his desk, his big pale face thrust forward.

"It's just a quick question, Ed, but it's an important one."

"Sit down, sit down. Make yourself at home. Important question, huh? Better shut the door so Darla don't listen to us. Ha! Testing, testing. Hear anything, Darla baby?"

"No sir," Darla said.

"Close the door," he said to Pearl, more quietly. "Now. What is it."

"It's just that I have this student—I don't know what to do about her." Pearl shook his head. "I'm not making myself very clear. She's in my Masterpieces class—she *was* in it. She hasn't shown up for about the last ten times. She's missed two important tests and three pop quizzes."

"Flunk her." Marshak smiled. "Next question?"

"That's just the thing. I was about to just cross her off when she showed up this morning and asked if she could make up what she's missed."

"Flunk her."

"She says her husband's in the V.A. hospital in Jackson. He's a paraplegic. Vietnam. She says the reason she's been missing class is that he's been very sick and she's had to be in Jackson the whole time."

"Has she made any attempt to get the assignments? Do the reading outside?"

"I guess not," Pearl said. "She's morbidly shy—she hardly talks above a whisper. I don't think she even knows anybody else in class. I mean to get the assignments from."

"She black or white?"

"White."

" 'Cause some of these country blacks, they'll tell you the damnedest stories. Break your heart, and not a single word of it true."

"I'm pretty sure she's telling the truth. She was a pretty good student, actually. She had a B average before she disappeared."

"Philip, I think you know what you have to do. The drop deadline is long gone. Student doesn't do the work, doesn't take the tests, doesn't show up for class, doesn't make any effort to get the homework—there's only one choice in the matter. 'Course, it's the teacher's choice. Strictly a matter of your discretion."

"It is?"

"Absolutely. I'm not gonna tell you what to do. *I'd* flunk her, but that's me."

"All right."

"I confuse you properly?"

"Sort of."

"All part of a chairman's job. Now—anything else I can help you with?"

"No, I guess not."

"You happy?"

Pearl looked at Marshak for a second. This was a serious question. Of course the truth wouldn't do. "I'm all right," he said.

"I hear you're not lacking for feminine companionship."

Pearl felt his voice rise a note. "Where'd you hear that, Ed?"

"Oh, word gets around. I'd watch myself, though, if I were you, Phil."

"What do you mean?"

"Why don't you take out some of these nice local girls? Huh? You prejudiced against Southern women?"

"No."

"Not much brains, but there sure are some good-looking ones. Goddamn. I have a sweet little thing baby-sits for me—you want to meet her? I can arrange an introduction."

"Sure."

"Goddamn. If I was your age, I'd be balling my brains out. Good-looking young guy like you. I shouldn't be saying anything, you probably are already. So. What do you think of this fine institution here?"

"It's great."

"Why don't you just tell the truth and say it's a dump. Did I say that? Department chairman shouldn't be talking like that. Ever been up to the Northwest, Phil?"

"Northwest Mississippi?"

"No, damn it. Oregon. Washington. Ever been up there?"

"No."

"That's God's country, Philip. I say it without fear of ridicule. God's country."

"Is that where you're from?"

"Yup. Born, bred, and well-fed. Even got to teach there for a few years. Don't ask what you're about to ask."

"I was just going to ask how you got to Pickett."

"Told you not to ask."

"Come on, Ed. Why'd you come?"

"Money, my boy, money. The warp of the universe. Or was it the woof? Southwest Washington State was becoming limited in its munificence."

Pearl found himself unable to say a word. *Why didn't you just stay*, was all he could think of. Poor lumberjack Marshak among the live oaks and magnolias. How much money could it have been? Then he thought of himself. He had been dead broke and they had offered him fourteen thousand per. He had half-wondered, at the time, what he would do with all that money. Somehow, now, he was broke again.

"I'd better get going, Ed," said Pearl. "I've got a class."

"Can't keep your public waiting—right, Phil?"

"Thanks for the help."

"What help?"

"I mean the advice."

"What advice? A little equivocation, a little circumlocution. A little periphrasis. God, I thought I'd forgotten that word. Thought I'd completely lost my vocabulary in this pesthole. Nice to know it's still in there. Somewhere. Want my advice, Philip?"

"Sure, Ed."

"Flunk the cracker out."

Wunsch, a cigarette hanging from his mouth, was putting books and papers into his fancy leather satchel. Pearl walked into the office without knocking.

"Do you have *any* idea what this is?" he said, holding out the postcard.

Wunsch looked sideways across the desk, squinting one eye and raising the brow of the other. "Phil!" he said. "Unexpected pleasure."

Pearl held the card in Wunsch's face. "I'm asking you a question, Walter. Do you have any idea what the hell this is?"

Wunsch took the card and examined the front. "Pres-type," he said. "Helvetica bold."

"The other side."

He turned the card over, and his eyes widened. "Yikes," he said.

"It gets the message across, wouldn't you say?"

"I'd say."

"You always know so much about what's going on around here," Pearl said. "Do you know anything about this, Walter?"

"You're not asking me if I sent it, Phil?" Wunsch showed his teeth on the *t* of *sent*.

"No. No, I'm not. I wouldn't suspect you of such—unsubtlety."

"Flunk anyone out?"

"I don't think it's one of my students."

"Sure?"

"It's too good a job."

"Alienate anybody? Make any enemies?"

"Everyone."

"Come on, Phil."

"I may have nettled a few people, but I don't think enough to make anyone do this."

"Steal anyone's gal?"

"What?"

Wunsch's eyes were wide again, actually questioning. "It's actionable, you know," he said. "Legally, if not otherwise."

"Legally—?"

"Alienation of affections."

"Oh, come on, Walter. That's only if they're married."

"It's the South, Phil," Wunsch said, with the barest brief hint of a smile. "Passions run high."

They looked at each other for a moment.

"You don't like me very much, do you, Philly?" Wunsch said. He leaned back in his chair, cigarette between his teeth. The backlighting from the pale-blue cinder-block walls was reflecting onto his face, bleaching the irises of his eyes almost white.

Pearl stared out the window. The trees swayed slightly; cars entered and left parking spaces.

"Come on, Philly. Talk to Uncle Walt."

"I wouldn't say that's true, Walter."

"Come on, Phil. Ain't no one else around, just you and me. Tell the truth, now."

"Walter, I am."

"I don't mean about me."

"What?"

"You know what."

"No, I don't. What are you talking about?"

"Philly, Philly. You're such a smart boy. Stop actin' like you're not."

"Walter, I—"

"You know what I'm talkin' about. Francesca. Prin-*ches*-a. Did you fuck her?" He seemed almost to smile as he said this, with a flash of white teeth. He took his cowboy boots off the desk and sat up. His eyes were glowing blue—not a color, really, but a deep light, somewhere out at the end of the spectrum.

"Walter, I—"

"I don't even care. Don't you see? This is not the point."

"What is the point?"

"Point is, Phil, you're treadin' on dangerous soil."

"What are you talking about?"

"My God, do I have to spell it out for you? She's a student, man. Her daddy's a professor. Big shot. Friends with the president."

"She's not my student," Pearl said. Knowing as soon as it was out that it was a mistake.

"That don't matter doodlysquat, Philly. I'm not even talkin' ab—"

"Forget I said that," Pearl said. "Forget it. It was a mistake. Listen, Walter. This is all nonsense. It doesn't apply. I like Francesca, she likes me. We talk every once in a while. We're *friends*." He said the word the way she had said it.

"Not what I hear, Phil."

"What do you hear? What the hell do you hear? Who are you hearing all this from? My God, I can't believe this bullshit!"

"I got eyes in the back of my head, Philly. Long ears. I hear, I see."

"Well, you're hearing and seeing cockeyed, O.K.? I mean you're just completely, totally—"

"O.K., Philly. Cool down, now."

Pearl glared out the window. The same things—trees, cars—were out there, but transformed somehow, distorted.

"You cool, Philly?"

"Sure. I'm cool."

"Forget I said any of this, all right? I just want you to be *care*ful, Phil. Ol' Uncle Walt's only lookin' after your best interests."

"Careful of *what*?"

"Come on, Phil. Cool down. Just be a little more discreet. News travels real fast around here. Get my drift?"

"No. I don't."

Wunsch laughed. "O.K., Philly. End of lecture. You can go. Just remember," he said, taking the cigarette from his mouth and squinting through the smoke, "you have been warned."

* * *

Pearl heard laughter as he approached Culpepper 203. This was the lecture room where he taught World Masterpieces first thing on Monday, Wednesday, and Friday mornings. It was his habit to close the front and rear doors as soon as all his students were seated; now, however, both doors were thrown wide open. As he drew even with the back of the room, he glanced in and saw students facing alertly, eagerly ahead, eyes alive. When he came to the next door, he saw Knight Wadkin, leaning against the front desk as if he were waiting for a bus. Wadkin, a full professor, held his trim body lazily, confidently: like a dancer, Pearl thought. The impression was reinforced by his outfit—tight jeans and a white collarless shirt.

Pearl stopped just past the doorway and listened. "What, then," the man was saying, in honeyed, soothing tones, "can we say about the Elizabethans?"

"They're daid," suggested a voice from the rear. More laughter. The man was so relaxed that he joined in too. "What else?" he asked.

Silence. Two beats, three. "Well," Wadkin said, "one thing we're *sure* about is that it was an age of discovery." A cough from somewhere in the room, as chalk began to squeak on board. One person, at least, was not charmed.

Pearl heard footsteps, echoing clacks on the linoleum, coming down the hall behind him. Quickly he pretended to rearrange his books, and continued on his way.

How did the man do it? he wondered as he walked. Pearl's own lectures, conducted behind closed doors, had an air of secret struggle. The effort of holding the class's attention and keeping the string of his thought playing out at the same time, at the right speed—when his audience wasn't grabbed, it was more than Pearl could handle. It made him speak in a tortured syntax, certainly nothing he'd want passersby to hear. For this guy, on the other hand, the whole business was a breeze. The clacking footsteps, echoing on the tile walls, grew louder behind Pearl.

He had, a few times, heard some of his students muttering in clusters as he walked by. Had it been about him? When teaching went well, it went well, but when it didn't, which was most of the time, it was like pulling teeth. And the harder he tried, the worse it got. He told jokes and got stares. He made local references and mispronounced the names. He was trying too hard, he knew. Yet in his imaginings about teaching (how much he had imagined! how little he had got right!) Pearl had hoped that, because of his own youth, some unprecedented communion might occur. He would change the rules, speak to them in their own goose language—and doors would open; he would be loved. No such luck. Even at teaching's best, a teacher was a teacher. Unless, apparently, he was a Wadkin.

Still, there had been moments—

Now the footsteps were closing in. Pearl sped up. He was a fast walker, a Manhattan walker, but whoever this was was clearly bent on overtaking him. As he neared the stairway, he half considered making a run for it. But how would that look?

He turned to face his follower.

A girl, tall, dark-haired, stunningly familiar-looking. Thin-lipped, white-skinned. Slightly goofy. She smiled, wide-mouthed.

"Oh, ha?" she said, breathily.

Pearl, ordinarily good at faces, was stumped. He knew this person, but from where? He was thinking, for some reason, of Broadway and 79th, an afternoon in March—

"You must be Dr. Wadkin?" she said.

"Dr. Wadkin?"

"You're not Dr. Wadkin?"

"No."

She put her hand to her mouth—it was a largish hand—and Pearl remembered. The girl from the drive-in bank. Ages ago. Here?

"They said—" she said.

"Who said?"

"The girl in the English department? They—she. I mean. Oh." Reddening, she spread the hand over her face.

"I'm Phil Pearl."

She peeked through her fingers. "I know?" she said.

"You know?"

Her eyes were wide. She touched his arm lightly. "Phil, I am so *sorry*? I mean, I *asked* that girl at the desk—you know, the real pretty one?—and she said you wore glasses, and I—" She shook her head. Her blush grew deeper. "I—" she began.

"You're—Terry. Tammy."

She nodded.

"So—how've you been? How's the bank?"

Another shake of the head.

"You, uh"—Pearl pointed to the walls—"came to see somebody?"

She nodded quickly.

"Well. It's none of my business. Good to see you, Tammy." He put out his hand. Hers was long, thin, limp, and very moist.

"I just feel so *stupid*?" she said.

"Stupid?"

"Bumpin' into you this way?"

"Well. But there's no need to feel st—"

"But I had to see what you were *like*?"

Pearl looked down at himself, then shrugged, in a way that suddenly struck him as being oddly, exaggeratedly Jewish. "Just like this," he said.

He was at the wheel of the Volvo, Tammy in the passenger's seat. They were driving down a curving back-country road, in the biblical light of a Mississippi autumn late afternoon. The

road was newly paved—no lines had been painted on it yet—
and moving over it felt more like gliding on air than riding in
a car. The world looked freshly made, and strange. Now they
were passing amid thick, jungly vegetation, vines and hanging
mosses: through a break in the trees, a small waterfall appeared.
Tammy, in a stiff-looking lime-green dress, hunched forward a
little in her seat.

"Well I *know*, but"—she clicked her tongue—"see now?
You're not like I thought you'd be at all?"

"How did you think I'd be?"

"Oh, kind of stuck-up and unfriendly, I guess?" She clapped
her hand over her mouth, then let it drop into her lap. "Don't
pay me any mind, I cannot keep my mouth shut to save my
life."

"But I'm curious. Why'd you think that?"

"Oh, just a lot of things people say, you know how people
talk, most of it's so silly?"

"People? Which people?"

She clicked her tongue again. "Well," she said. "But you
said you came from New *York*?"

"Guilty."

"*God*," she said. "I mean—I don't know."

"Where are you from, Tammy?"

"Hairkin?"

"Pardon?"

"Oh, just a little itty bitty town way up in the north of
the state, it's spelled Hurricane, you know, like the storm? Only
we don't say hurricane, we say Hairkin?"

"Really?"

"Uh-huh."

"Hurricane, Mississippi."

"Hairkin."

"Ah. Right."

"A lot of people down here make fun of me, you know, for comin' from such a small town and all? But like I always say, how big is Pickett, to be makin' fun of Hairkin?"

"I can see your point."

"They act like all we got to do up there is chase wild wooves or somethin'," she said. "I mean—there *might* not be *much* to do, but there's more than *that?*"

"Chase wild what?"

"Wooves—you know, like they howl?"

"Wolves."

"Uh-huh. Everyone keeps tryin' to make it into this big thing that w—"

"You have *wolves* in Hurricane?"

"Hairkin. Yes, uh-huh, we do."

"Yeah, but—Tammy. You don't *chase* them."

"It was just a couple that was gettin' in my mother's garden?" she said. "But now everyone's tryin' to make it out like I'm Annie Oakley or somethin'. It is so unfair. I mean, they're no different from dogs, except they *never* bite."

"You didn't catch them."

"Oh *no*, I just threw a couple of rocks, but now everyone down at the bank is goin' around sayin' I grabbed them by the tail and all?"

Pearl glanced away from the road and over at her. She was smiling indulgently. "I mean," she said, "it is *way* too ridiculous."

Pearl smiled back.

"I'm sorry I talk so much. It's a nervous habit?"

"Not at all."

"My mother always tells me—she says, 'My my, Tammy, how you do go on and on.' My grandmother on my father's side says—oh."

"Oh?"

"I think we might should've turned back there?"

Pearl braked, and they came to a stop. "Where?"

She pointed. "Into the woods?"

Through a clearing and down across a meadow Pearl saw, in the dusky light, a small wooden building with a screen porch and yellow bug lights under the eaves. Several cars were parked around the door.

"That's it?" Pearl said. "It looks like someone's house."

"Uh-uh, that's Jack's."

"Where's the driveway?"

"I think you just drive across the grass?"

He looked at her, sitting in her green dress in the waning light, all eyes. Could he possibly be as strange to her as she was to him? Tammy shrugged. She was a Mississippi girl in a lime-green dress in the blue-orange light, and all the sense had gone out of the world. The car idled. Pearl heard crickets chirping. In Delbertsville, the first frost had come; the crickets were all gone. Where in God's name was he?

"I could never understand why they call it a fish *camp*," Tammy said. "I get the fish part fine, but camp? Now, that sounds like a whole lot of tents to me, doesn't it to you?"

They were sitting at an oilcloth-covered picnic table on a screen porch in Jack's Fish Camp. Moths batted against the screen, frantic to get in out of the useless yellow light. Pearl looked at his menu. The entrees were fried shrimp, fried oysters, and fried catfish. Tammy thrust out her lower lip, raised her eyebrows.

"Isn't that strange?" she said. "I mean, me bein' from Mississippi and all?"

A very young girl was standing at the head of the table

with a doubtful expression. She had braces on her teeth and a T-shirt that showed a leaping sailfish and read, "VISIT Beautiful Tarpon Springs." "We're out of the shramps," she said.

"What about the fried oysters?" Pearl asked.

"We're out of them, too."

"I guess I'll have the catfish, then." He smiled at her, but her expression didn't change.

"And hush puppies," Tammy said brightly. "Don't forget hush puppies and cole slaw and tea with plenty of sugar."

"Y'all can have Coke or tea."

"Could I just get a glass of water?" Pearl asked.

"All we got's Coke or tea."

"You're kidding." The waitress stared at him. "Nothing for me," Pearl told her.

"Phil, you better have something," Tammy said. She lowered her voice. "Sometimes it's kind of dry?"

"All right. Tea. Please."

"I'll have a Coke?" Tammy said.

The waitress took their menus.

"I guess you don't have fish camps in New York?" Tammy said. "That's a dumb question, right?"

"No, no. It's funny—"

"Tammy?" said a deep voice.

Pearl looked up at a short man with a blond mustache and thick-lensed, square-rimmed glasses. He wore a blue nylon windbreaker. Next to him, in an identical windbreaker, stood a tall, dark-haired woman.

Tammy turned around. "Chuck! June! Hey!"

"Mind if we join you?" Chuck said.

"Uh-uh!" Tammy said. Pearl slid down the picnic bench as Chuck pulled in next to him. June sat next to Tammy. "Chuck, June, this is Phil Pearl?" Tammy said.

"Pleased," Chuck said, taking Pearl's hand in a viselike grip. June smiled. Her face, which at first had appeared smooth and young, was in fact networked with fine wrinkles. She seemed much older than Chuck.

"Phil teaches at State?" Tammy said.

Chuck leaned back from Pearl to get a better look at him. "Is that so?" he said.

The waitress gave Pearl and Tammy each a brown plastic bowl of cole slaw and a huge yellow plastic tumbler full of ice and brown liquid.

"We'll just have a rerun," Chuck said to the waitress. "We were here last night," he explained.

"Oh!" Tammy said.

"Chuck's a catfish nut," June said.

"Whiskers are my favorite part," Chuck said, with a wink.

Pearl took a bite of the cole slaw: he could feel the grains of sugar between his teeth. He took a drink of the tea, which was, if possible, even sweeter.

"What do you teach, Phil?" Chuck asked.

"English."

"And poetry?" Tammy said.

Pearl looked at her. "And poetry."

Chuck leaned back. "Is that so?"

"That's right."

"I write a little poetry myself," Chuck said. "Strictly on Christian subjects, though."

"Chuck and June are missionaries?" Tammy said.

"Missionaries?"

"They've been just everywhere in the world?"

Chuck pushed up his glasses with an index finger. "Well. Not quite *every*where."

"Where are you from, Phil?" June asked.

"Phil's from New York?" Tammy said. "Y'all've been to New York, right?"

"New York?" Chuck said.

"We've been to New Guinea," June said, smiling.

"But not New York," Chuck said. "Yet." He raised his eyebrows.

"Are you a Christian, Phil?" June asked.

"Me?"

"Didn't you say you were Jewish, Phil?" Tammy said. "I could've sworn you told me that?"

Chuck regarded Pearl with heightened interest. "Is that so?"

"By birth, yes."

"But not by practice?" June asked.

"I'm sort of out of practice right at the moment," Pearl said.

June smiled sweetly at him.

"Uh-oh, y'all aren't fixin' to try and convert Phil, are you?" Tammy said.

"Not unless he wants to be," June said, still smiling, but with a searching stare.

"We respect a person's wishes," Chuck said. "Phil'll come to Christ when he's ready."

The waitress put down four brown plastic plates filled with crusty strips and pellets.

"Well!" June said. "Rub a dub dub, I see some grub."

Chuck closed his eyes. "Oh Lord, let us be grateful for these thy fruits."

June and Tammy closed their eyes. "Amen," they said.

Chuck cut a piece of strip and put it in his mouth. "Mm," he said. "Good batch."

"Mm!" Tammy said, looking at Pearl. He tasted the fish. It was salty and rubbery. Now they were all looking at him. He nodded. "Fish," he said.

"I thought last night was much drier, didn't you?" June asked Chuck.

He swallowed and shook his head. "No comparison."

"Have you two known each other a while?" June asked.

Tammy put her hand on her clavicle and rolled her eyes to the ceiling. "Oh my, no!" she said. "No no *no*. Uh-uh."

"I, uh—" Pearl began.

"Phil drove up to my drive-in window, lookin' for a place to live?" Tammy said.

Chuck's eyes widened.

Tammy's chest and cheeks began to turn a mottled scarlet. "No! No! That didn't come out right? I mean—" She swallowed air and closed her eyes. "I mean"—she took a breath—"in Pickett?"

"Huh," Chuck said.

"Did you find a place?" June asked.

"That same day, yes."

"Ah!"

"Then we ran into each other in the hall today at State?" Tammy continued. "It was the *strangest* thing. I was havin' my teeth cleaned? You know—at Dr. Waters'? Over across the street? Anyway, I decided I'd see if Phil was havin' any luck—you know, with findin' a house and all? But I didn't know his *name*."

June looked puzzled. "Phil's name?"

"Uh-huh. 'Cause we'd had this big conversation and all, at the drive-in window? But he didn't say his *name*?"

"But I told you my name," Pearl said, confused.

"Uh-uh, no you didn't," Tammy said. "So I had to *describe* him? To the English secretary? You know, like 'Cute little short guy, with curly hair and glasses?' Like that. And *she* says, 'Oh, *you* must mean Dr. *Watkins.*' "

Pearl put his fork down. The yellow bug bulb under the porch eave shone with the light of revelation. "Wadkin," he said.

"And then I *met* Phil, but I thought *he* was Dr. Watkins? My face was *red*?"

"That is a *riot*," June said.

"Funny story," Chuck said, through fish. "Got it all straightened out, didja?"

"Phil, are you O.K.?" Tammy said. " 'Cause you have not touched a *bite* of your food?"

Pearl sat silent, fingering the collar of his shirt.

XIII

The same moon that shone over Manhattan shone over Pickett, and Pearl walked, moony. The stars, he had noticed, were never very visible here. One would have suspected the opposite. Proof he had lost his way? It was the combined effect, he guessed, of the miasmal air and the lights of shopping centers. In Delbertsville, in upstate New York, the stars had been frightening in their numerousness and clarity. This had been—he shook his head in disbelief—just three months before, in a summer that even then was rapidly becoming autumn. Now he was in an autumn that couldn't shake off summer.

Driving late at night back down the dirt road to the farm, Pearl had been terrified every time—not only of the solitude, but of the myriad stars that awaited him. He suffered from a kind of open-air agoraphobia, a fear of the sky itself. Something seemed bound to fall down and strike him. He remembered being taken as a child to Hayden Planetarium: things had begun pleasantly enough, the pink dome dimming, the classical music swelling; but then many stars appeared, and were made to move rapidly. Outsized pictures of planets whirled across the vault.

White arrows darted from constellation to constellation as an amplified narrator spoke solemn sense. Young Pearl sank in his seat, too scared to close his eyes. Ever since, he had cringed under a clear night sky, ready and unready for it all to start into motion.

In Delbertsville, by way of defense, he had bought a sky chart and learned as many of the stars as he could. Just as a reforming acrophobe might force himself to the edge of an observation deck, Pearl would stand knee-deep in a wet field at eleven p.m., chart in hand, knees bent with fear, trying to pick Aldebaran and Regulus out of an enormous overpopulated sky.

In Pickett, the few stars that were to be seen seemed to have been rearranged. Here, Pearl thought with wicked pleasure, constellations would be named after television personalities. But this, he knew, was petty. He would have to choose a larger target than Pickett. The present was definitely spreading. In Manhattan it was possible to burrow into a prewar apartment with great books and classical music and pretend the whole mess out there had never happened. Once you left town, it was another story. And there was no getting around the fact that Pearl had left town.

He found himself standing in front of Culpepper Hall. Pearl remembered that he had, accidentally on purpose, left his Masterpieces book in his office that morning. He did this from time to time: it gave him a reason to walk.

Beneath the breezeway, to the side of the building, the huge air conditioner was booming. Pearl had been puzzled by this on his earlier nocturnal walks; then he'd discovered that the building was cleaned at night, by what seemed to be entire families of black people—men, women, children. Such, anyway, was Pearl's inference. For the maintenance people were as shy as deer. Twice he had seen a man. Once he had seen a woman. Once he had heard a child. These sightings were always momentary and a hall's length away. Pearl regretted this: he longed to make contact, even though he had expected at first to be challenged, however mildly, for being in the building so late. Black people especially always thought he was nineteen. (Why? Because they looked nineteen at twelve?) But he was thinking of Northern blacks. No one here ever said a word to him. No one got close enough to say a word. He would let himself in at the front doors (he had a set of keys to Culpepper—this, somehow, was worth almost as much to him as the money he was being paid), and would immediately hear the echo of a conversation coming from, say, the second-floor landing. As he paused to listen, the conversation would cease. When he got to the second floor, of course, no one was in sight.

This was the case again tonight. Turning from the top of the stairs onto the second-floor hallway, he heard a clattering of buckets from a broom closet, but when he approached the closet, it was empty—although the door was ajar and the light burning. The bulb, hanging from the ceiling on a wire, was of a type that seemed to be standard issue for janitor's closets: the glass transparent instead of frosted, the filament glowing with all the ardor of the history of electricity, glowing like something out of Blake. A sweet-sharp reek of ammonia and chalk dust emanated from the closet. Pearl stared at the mops and cans of cleanser and recalled something keenly, he wasn't sure what. Something to do with elementary school: with janitors' closets and Janus, the two-faced door god, and the concrete gargoyles in the archway of the entrance to the school. And, no doubt, with his own two faces, looking to the past and future.

He opened the department door and flipped the wall switch. The fluorescents came on with a one-two-three jerky flash. Why did he always expect, in this most licit of places, to catch someone fucking? His mind's eye saw a flash of flesh, a sudden scurrying. Who? Vaguely he imagined Wadkin, with some sophomore. Or—?

No. Just as with Pearl's imaginings about the department

at night, it was more often the case that nothing was happening. People's lives—even beautiful girls' lives—were vacuous to an alarming degree. Now, as Pearl stood in the middle of the department, by Darla's desk, he witnessed a nothing of the purest order. The second hand on the big electric clock glided around, the lights hummed faintly, the louvered office doors were all closed. Such nothingness intrigued Pearl and disturbed him. It was the opposite of, say, noon in Manhattan, or even of midnight in Delbertsville. It was the opposite of anything. Had such nothing ever existed before modern man? Pearl doubted it. Medieval monks would contemplate a skull to think about death; Pearl now considered Darla's salmon-colored Selectric, *memento nulli*. Where would this contemplation lead him? Only as far as an IBM repairman, in black polyester pants and a pale-blue short-sleeved shirt, a beeper on his hip. Or Darla, home watching "Hee-Haw" with her parents.

Pearl crossed the room, opened his own door, flicked on the light, and regarded his office with dismay. Where else but on submarines were there rooms without windows? The office had previously belonged to Wunsch—in fact, Wunsch had brought Pearl here the day of his interview, had propped his boots up on the desk and tried to put the prospective assistant professor at ease. Wunsch's desk had been smack in the middle of the tiny room, facing the door. This was surely Wunsch's idea of a joke: facing the doorway, the windowless wall behind him—like a Minor Functionary, someone out of Kafka. Nowadays, Pearl kept the desk flush against the right-hand wall, so he could at least pretend to be absorbed in something while—as was the case during his office hours—he was on display to the outer room at large. Now Pearl glanced at his Motherwell poster: a bit of countermagic intended, originally, to draw his mind out of Culpepper and even out of Mississippi as he sat grading papers. But, with time, the poster had grown a kind of carapace—it was recognizable but no longer visible. Sitting in his office these days, Pearl was *here*. Alarmed, he picked up his book, turned off the light, and shut the door.

As Pearl walked past Darla's desk and rounded the corner, he glanced into the other wing of the department, a mirror image of the one that housed his and Wunsch's offices. He had never been over here before; there had never been a reason. Wadkin's office, someone had once told him, was the first on the left. This door was ajar. Pearl listened at the crack for a second, then—palms sweating—pushed the door open. He switched on the light. The office was windowless like his, but considerably larger, and the walls were lined with books on the Elizabethans. Above the desk was a photograph of Wadkin in running shorts and a tank top crossing a finish line, his wiry arms raised, his mouth open, his almond eyes closed.

Then Pearl turned and saw her.

The picture, black-and-white and glossy, had been taken at a party: the camera had caught people in loose attitudes, mouths open, eyes eager. Pearl saw Perry in one corner of the frame, and, cut off at the edge, what looked like Wunsch's back. Wadkin, in jeans, stood in partial profile in the left foreground, the flash gleaming from his glasses. His back was to Francesca, who faced the photographer, smiling, her pupils replaced by white blazes of reflected light. She looked younger than now by at least two years: the face was slightly fuller, the eyebrows heavier, shagginess of late adolescence. But she was no less astonishing. She smiled mockingly, challengingly into the lens, and Pearl was haunted by this smile—by the picture itself. It seemed, somehow, to contain his death.

And for whom had she smiled this smile?

As he turned his key in the lock of the outer door, Pearl heard a pail clank down the hall. He froze. There was deep silence—then a second, lesser clank. The sound was coming from the janitor's closet. He stood watching the open door—the doorway was beyond it, and hidden—but no one emerged. Now the silence seemed permanent. It annoyed Pearl: shyness was shyness, but this was too much. People were isolated enough to start with.

"Hello?" he called.

Silence.

He walked down the hall toward the closet, listening between his steps. He called again. There was no response. He came to the door and put his hand on it, pulling it slowly to the side.

The closet was empty.

Suddenly, from the stairway at the end of the hall, there was an echoing clatter of footsteps, followed by a metallic crash. Then silence again. Pearl ran to the top of the staircase, and heard a groan from below.

He ran down, turned at the landing, and saw Errol Nightingale sitting on the floor at the foot of the steps in a pool of sudsy water, a mop and an overturned bucket beside him.

"Errol."

"How you doin', Mr. Pearl."

Pearl extended a hand. "Here, let me help."

Errol stood with a grimace. "The steps weren't so slick, but these *shoes* sure were," he said.

"I didn't know you worked here, Errol."

Errol shook water off his hands. "Got to pay the bills," he said. He flapped the back of his pants, which were soaked. "*Shoot,*" he said.

"Errol, why were you hiding from me?"

He blinked long lashes, utterly innocent. "Hiding?"

"Come on, Errol. You didn't want me to see you. You ran down the stairs to get away from me. How come?"

Errol shrugged. "I don't know."

"*Errol.*"

"Listen, Mr. Pearl—"

"Phil. Phil! I *told* you in class—"

"What you do with your time's your own business, I guess."

"What?"

"Ain't none of my business."

"*What's* none of your business?"

"Whatever. You know."

"No, I don't know."

Errol smiled wincingly and gazed off to his right. "Aw, Mr. Pearl—"

"Errol, *what*, for God's sake?"

"You know, if you got a lady. Or whatever."

"Lady?"

Still looking aside, Errol blinked the long lashes once, twice. His pants were dripping.

"What lady, Errol?"

Errol stared down at the puddle on the floor. "I guess I better get some rags."

"Errol, *what lady*?"

"*I* never seen it," he said, to the wall.

"It? What?"

"You and that girl. Up here."

"What girl?"

"Dark-haired girl with the nice butt," Errol said, all but inaudibly.

"Wait a moment, Phil. Have a seat."

Pearl, his afternoon office hours over (not a single student had shown up), was eager for fresh air. "Listen, Walter. I have—"

"Official business, Phil."

"What is it?"

Wunsch motioned to the chair in front of his desk. Pearl sat.

"I'd like you to pick up W. S. Mountjoy Friday afternoon," Wunsch said.

Pearl blinked. *"Mount*joy?" he finally said.

"Uh-huh."

"Here?"

"Uh-huh."

"You're kidding."

"Dead serious, Phil."

"I can't believe it. What would he want to come here for?"

"About twenty-five hundred, plus expenses. Anyway, Philly, point is not why he's coming, but that he's coming" (Wunsch gave the most subtle, subitalic emphases to *why* and *that*, as if lacking the strength or desire for more) "and the more immediate point is that he has to be picked up at the airport Friday, two oh five p.m."

"You want *me* to pick him up?"

"That's about the idea."

"What would I say to him? Anyway, I have Composition class."

Wunsch rolled his eyes. "Philly, you can cut the class short. You can cut it, period. This is W. S. Mountjoy."

"God. I know."

"Fine and dandy, Phil. Our interview is ended."

Pearl stood. "Walter?"

Wunsch looked up from his desk, surprised Pearl was still there. Suddenly the desk seemed part of him—his lower half. As if he were some strange kind of centaur.

"Just one thing. Why aren't you picking him up?" Pearl was thinking of his own interview, Wunsch's red-carpet treatment. This was not a potential assistant professor but a world-famous writer.

"Don't want to."

"Oh, you know him?"

"Nope."

"Don't you like his work?"

"Nope."

"Whose idea was it to invite him?"

"Mine."

Pearl plucked a copy of *The Panther Paw* from the box by the door. W. S. MOUNTJOY, FAMED AUTHOR, TO SPEAK AT PSU, the headline read. The publicity photograph showed Mountjoy holding a cigarette, smiling ruefully, gazing off somewhere to the side of the photographer. He was a handsome man, in a ravaged way: his face had more lines than Pearl had ever seen on a face. It was precisely the way he hoped, one day, to look.

Pearl had read all of Mountjoy—the poems, the novels, the stories, the essays—in his sixteenth summer, in the first blaze of certainty about his vocation; he had composed a long letter, stunning in its precocity, to the author, who was said to answer all his mail (the letter went through three drafts, and finally never left Pearl's house). He had looked up every biographical reference he could find. All this came back to Pearl as he stood with the student newspaper in his hand. He shook his head. Who could believe it? He was an assistant professor of English, and he was soon to meet Mountjoy. Six months ago it would have seemed impossible. Six months ago, in Delbertsville, almost everything seemed impossible—especially writing. Now certain things were beginning to happen.

That evening Pearl found a postcard at his feet when he opened his apartment door. As he knelt to pick the card up, he thought for a sinking second of the menus for Szechuan home delivery that appeared under one's door in Manhattan. Pearl was hungry, he was tired, and the precise taste and texture of thirteen-hundred-mile-distant Moo Shu Pork tingled mockingly on his tongue. This was no menu. The card was similar to the first, except that the shotgun was not quite as well drawn: there was something more urgent and less creative in the rendering. Pearl put the card with the first, in the middle of his collected Stevens—what else could he do?—and took a chicken pot pie out of his freezer and made his dinner.

The next morning, he caught the flu. Caught or came up with, somehow. The medievals had believed in spontaneous generation: maggots sprang from meat, mice grew out of straw. Nothing was going around, but Pearl woke up to find that the arrangement of objects on his dresser looked rather unpleasant to him. He was unable, however, to get up and do anything about it. He finally dragged himself out of bed, went to the bathroom, looked at himself in the mirror, said "I'm sick," called Darla, and threw himself back down on his mattress and slept for twenty-four hours.

It was a strange sleep. The sins of his past and those of the present visited him both one at a time and in illogical concert. He was in Manhattan, Delbertsville, and Pickett simultaneously. Jewel, naked, reproached him and cast him out. Francesca figured prominently—Francesca large and small, narrow and wide, taken and free. Her black, black, handlebar eyebrows seemed preternaturally clear and preternaturally unpleasant: as with the objects on the dresser, Pearl was unable to blur the focus.

He awoke once—it was dark out—to the sound of a girl laughing hysterically in the parking lot. It must have been very late: there was no other sound but her laughter. She laughed humorlessly, endlessly. It was as if she were being tickled to within an inch of her life. Pearl heard a male voice, then another.

The girl was pleading with them, all the while unable to stop laughing.

It occurred to Pearl the next morning that he was well, and that there was no longer any reason to stay in bed. He washed his face, put on some clothes, got his gradebooks, and went to school. The air seemed as fresh-scrubbed as his face. Suddenly the whole outdoors was new: the sky was bluer than it had ever been; the wind had a snap to it. The end of October, and fall had finally come.

Everything—the angle of shadows, the vegetation, people's faces in the street—seemed mysterious and infinitely interesting. Pearl flared his nostrils and sniffed the unaccustomed air. It was sweet, humid, sharp, loamy. Just ahead of him on the sidewalk a boy coming the opposite way had stopped and was looking down an alley between two small one-story houses. For some reason—its absolute normality? the new air and light?—the sight was arresting. The boy resembled every other boy at PSU: jeans and a blue nylon jacket, books under his arm, a Cat hat pushed back on his head. His genitals boxy and just so. Neither too large nor too small—the Greeks had said that a man was good in inverse proportion to the size of his dick. If this were so, this boy was neither very good nor very bad, just a Mississippi boy looking down an alleyway and sniffing the holy air. The word *fyce* came unbidden into Pearl's head. Strange word. A kind of dog, Pearl remembered from Tommy's poem. Not inappropriate. That was what this boy was, for the moment—in contact with a higher order of things. The boy spat, and, having made his decision, walked down the alley.

That was the way to decide! Pearl thought. Sniff the wind, read the signs. The day in Delbertsville he had found the ad in the Sunday *Times* (or had the ad found him?), Pearl had driven to town to get groceries, and, on his way home, had suddenly seen, on a church he always passed, a sign he'd never noticed before. A painted wooden sign, with incised gold letters.

GO AND TEACH, it had said.

He walked through the noontime crowd, books and papers under his arm. The weather was sunny, as was Pearl. He had taught a good class that morning—World Masterpieces 101, section one, was now up to *Don Quixote* in its chronological trudge through the thick, thin-paged text, and his students had taken to the story in the most basic way, clucking about the Don and his scrapes as if he were a charming old miscreant of an uncle. Pearl smiled to himself as he thought of their pleased exasperation. Literature in action! Occasionally. Dante had lost them. Cervantes had grabbed them. Simple as that. And Pearl—he was only, after all (in a way), along for the ride—had reaped the spillover. They smiled at the Don; they were still smiling when they looked up at Pearl. Ol' Mr. P.—there was something about him.

Pearl looked forward to lunch, thinking not of where or with whom he would eat it, but simply of what he would have. The air's autumnal edge had not only sharpened Pearl's appetites in general but had finally made real the fact that he was in school again, for the first time in three years. There was something profoundly nostalgic and satisfying about simply holding books and breathing crisp air—as if the mind, ruled by the body for the summer, now at last regained its proper place.

Pearl was walking by the library, an oblong white structure, "modern" in the fifties sense, faced with waffle concrete. On its best days it was hideous. Today it was marvelous. The light on the white surfaces had gained in poignancy, the shadows in the waffle indentations had gained in blueness. Pearl squinted and pretended, for a moment, that he was on a campus in New England. But he wasn't in New England. The thought gave him a little pang. He remembered that he hadn't seen a *Times* in more than two months. There was only the Pickett *Post*, and, for word of the outside world, an occasional *Times-Picayune*, with in-depth coverage of New Orleans society and miles of ads, all for a dime. And there was always Walter Cronkite, who was beginning, these days, to seem a little overvehement.

Pearl looked around at the people going to lunch. Where was a slouch, a wrinkled forehead? All he saw anywhere were straight backs, cheery smiles. The world was real good! The girls in their dresses, the boys in their T-shirts and designer jeans and baseball caps, even the wheelchair students—all seemed on their way to a perpetual pep rally. They greeted each other in the most congratulatory way: the Panthers, after all, had come within a hair, last Saturday, of taking one from LSU.

And here was Pearl. Jew, mooner, fugitive from a farm. Walking among them: *passing?* A tall, pretty, dark-haired girl in a plum silk dress, her books clasped to her chest, looked him straight in the face and smiled. Could it be?

It seemed entirely possible. He was wearing the wine-colored Lacoste shirt and khaki pants (he smiled as he thought of his tie and jacket the first day of school), an outfit that had long since become embarrassingly banal where he had come from, but which so far had failed to gain currency here. Here he just looked, well, sort of casual, which was exactly right. Perhaps a little rich, like a member of one of the fancier frats. Incredible. Pearl came to the crossing of one of the little campus streets and instinctively stopped, but the car that was there courteously stopped first. It was a low white fastback; inside sat a blond boy with silky sculpted hair, and his girl, a brunette. *They* had never seen *The Battle of Algiers*. And something inside Pearl had, over the past two months, unclenched to the extent that he felt he had never seen it either. To the extent that, at this moment, he wanted this, wanted the package: the car, the girl, the life of postgame parties and rounds of golf.

Really?

His meditation was shattered by the clip-clop of high-heeled shoes.

She was perhaps ten paces in front of him, unmistakable: the bell of silky black hair, the boy's shirt, and the salient feature, denimed, moving with its strange, independent-minded syncopation. He tried to imagine an engineering diagram of such a movement through space. Could a cam be designed to reproduce it? And was the motion innate, or cultivated? He pictured Francesca practicing in front of a mirror. He wouldn't put it past her. He pictured, also, medical charts of his bodily functions, now thrown all out of kilter. There was a way in which he detested her for doing this to him. Resigned to his fate, he walked up on her left.

"Hi," he said.

"Phil! How ya doin'?" Here, among the rednecks (now converging, in roughly fan or delta form, toward the breezeway of Culpepper), she talked like a redneck. She looked flushed, excited: as if she had just been on a fast horseback ride.

"Fine."

His only remaining strategy, he had quickly decided, could be Distance. Thus had she reduced him to high-schoolhood.

She laughed. "*What*'re you doing?"

"Just going to lunch."

"Oh yeah? You got plans? Hot date?"

Think. Think. "Uh-huh."

She laughed again. "Boy! You're a live wire today!"

She looked at him, smiling. *She was happy*. Something or someone had made her happy. They were standing under the breezeway, the crowd moving around them. The glass doors opened and closed with lunchtime traffic. He stared at her, his heart turning over and over in space. Didn't the force of his desire itself give him a kind of claim on her? If he were to take her and kiss her here, in the shade of the breezeway, among the crowd, what would happen? He saw it vividly. Scattered applause from the students. She would recoil, pull away. *Phil*. I told you, *friends*. Friends? Surely she had more imagination! How could she have remotely interested him otherwise?

"So—maybe I'll see you at the reception?" she said.

"The—?"

The glass doors were opening, held by two boys. The girl in the wheelchair emerged, the girl Pearl had seen here several times before: she was twisted, slightly stunted, her back grievously curved, her neck too short, her head bent backward as if she were standing at attention. Her face was quite lovely. Exotic, even. She was blond, pale-eyed, attractively pointy-nosed. Pearl looked at her, and she returned his look directly, questioningly, for an astonishing full second. Then her chair hummed past. He watched the fluttering Confederate flag mounted on the back of the chair recede down the ramp.

Francesca was snapping her fingers in his face. "Phil?"

The English department directly after lunch was quiet and full of white midday light. Ordinarily it was one of Pearl's favorite times: he could sit in his office and read and think, be alone but not quite alone—things would start up again shortly, not quite at their morning pace, but with the pleasant sense of winding down toward three o'clock. Everyone in the world, he had always thought, should be liberated at three o'clock. Even now, with the odd taste of lunch still in his mouth and a slight sickness in the pit of his stomach—*she was happy*—and no idea at all what he would do at three, Pearl looked forward to this twenty minutes alone, to putting his feet on his steel desk and thinking about everything or nothing. There was no mail in his box (thank God); he had (more or less) prepared his class; in short, there was nothing to distract him as he gratefully unlocked the door that he would soon quickly close behind him.

"Phil?"

He jumped, most undignifiedly, the sole of his shoe actually clacking on the linoleum.

It was Wadkin.

"How you doin'?" he asked Pearl. He was chewing gum, very fast, and blinking nervously. He looked as though he hadn't been sleeping.

"Fine," Pearl said.

Wadkin spread his arms and rested his hands on the door frame. He smiled, almost apologetically. "Deanna and I would like to have you over for dinner," he said. Blink.

Pearl looked beyond Wadkin's arms to assess his chances for escape. Distraction would be the key. But there was no one in the outer office.

"Great," Pearl said. "Any time."

"How 'bout tonight."

"Tonight?" Pearl said. "Tonight's—not really too good."

Wadkin chewed furiously. "Other plans, huh."

It was like being stared at by a snake. "Other plans?"

Blink. Blink blink.

"Well—it's just, I've been feeling a little run down lately," Pearl said. "I had the flu, I think." He cursed himself. Why couldn't he lie? Other plans? Yes. Dinner in Paris.

"Nothin'll pick you up like a home-cooked meal."

"I don't think I'd be very good company. I'm really pretty tired."

Fixed smile; fixed gaze. Jaws working. "Hell, you don't have to talk. Just eat." Wink.

Far across the office, Darla walked out of Marshak's door, carrying a sheaf of papers. Darla. Help. She disappeared around the corner.

A door clicked. There was a jingle of keys. Wadkin glanced to his left; Tommy appeared over his shoulder, pipe hanging precariously, comically low. "Hello, Wadkin," he said.

Grin and blink. The side of Wadkin's face, Pearl saw, was even more frighteningly fatless than usual—muscle and sinew and bone seemed almost exposed. "Tommy," Wadkin said.

Tommy gave his key ring a twirl and flipped it into his pocket. "Don't forget, Philip. You call me if you need me." He said this seriously, raising his eyebrows significantly. "Shotguns are no joke where I come from."

Wadkin glanced, eyes wide and inquiring, at Pearl.

Who sat with a form of smile on his face. Tommy. I need you.

"Hear?" Tommy said.

"O.K., Tommy."

He turned and left, his shoulders stooped.

The small eyes were on him again. "What say."

"Could I have a rain check?"

Wadkin was unsmiling now. "Sure," he said.

XIV

The airport—fourteen miles north of town, just off Interstate 83—had a clean, flat, treeless look to it, as if it had been bull-dozed out and sodded the week before. As Pearl pulled into the drive, he remembered being picked up, in the incredible heat of August, and leaving the same day, feeling he would never see the place again. Now, in a sense, the airport was his. It was a single-cell organism: single road, parking lot, terminal building, runway. You drove up, picked up or let off, and left. No one lingered at this airport. No religious groups distributed litera-ture. There were no shady characters, unexplained loiterers, de-serted lovers. Just clean-scrubbed families, students, and servicemen, arriving promptly, embracing or shaking hands, flying or driving off. No one remained but the two Southern Air ticket agents, the lone security man, and the old lady who ran the snack bar. To idle here would be to die of boredom.

There were two commercial flights a day, both on Southern: in the morning came a puddle jumper from Memphis, and in the afternoon a 727 from Atlanta, through Laurel. Both the prop plane and the jet then continued on to New Orleans. Mountjoy was to arrive on the 727. Pearl swung around the road in front of the terminal. It was a pretty afternoon, warm, the sky white-blue: he would wait outside. He angle-parked by a chain-link fence and got out.

Pearl stood at the fence and stared into the milky sky over the runway. He saw nothing, heard nothing. Five of two. The placid sky looked for all the world as if the airplane had never been invented. Yet barring disaster—and surely disaster would never happen if you thought about it first—there was a Mountjoy ten minutes to the north, sitting, probably unrecognized, in the middle of the air, in a red-and-blue seat, a drink most certainly in his hand. Pearl remembered that Mountjoy was a drinker. This was not in the biographical sources, but was frequently hinted at by insinuating *Time* and *Newsweek*. A drunk Mountjoy, his literary idol, wafting down on the promise of money. Shortly to entrust himself to Pearl and his car. Pearl thought of trust and of the five or six dozen souls, each feeling unclouded and immortal, encased in the approaching jet, a tube of sheet metal and rivets held aloft by roaring rockets and steered by a square-jawed forty-eight-year-old man with hair in his ears. What held it all together? Surely it was the sheer force of the mundane, as much as jet fuel or money or the laws of physics. The passengers knew in their hearts and guts that the wing would not suddenly crack off—because of the sunlight in the cabin, the voice of the stewardess, the merry design of the seat covers. The inertia of the status quo. The check would be there when we arrived; the boy who picked us up at the airport would be courteous and reliable, his car would not veer off the highway and hit a tree. The infarction would not suddenly clench the chest. Then it struck Pearl that if anyone could see through all this, it would be Mountjoy, and that this probably explained the plastic cup in his right hand. Still, he was coming—there was something touching about it. The sky remained silent.

Pearl walked through the (sliding, not turning) automatic

doors into the terminal building. A surprising number of people—fifteen or twenty—were waiting for the plane. He tried to read their faces for anticipation, dread, anything. As usual, these faces made difficult reading. Pearl remembered Giuseppe's catch-all explanation of Pickett: *sono protestanti*. Was that it? No, it was facile. Mountjoy was a Protestant. And Sam Johnson. The true answer was cultural, sociological, historical. Pearl wandered into the back hall of the terminal, past the men's and ladies' rooms, where photo blowup facsimiles of great American documents hung on the walls. He was reading the Japanese surrender agreement of 1945 when he heard the roar, the screech of tires.

The crowd had begun to move forward, their faces animated: something was happening. Some were already on line behind a brown velvet cordon, where a brown-suited marshal was supervising the removal of metal objects. Wristwatches and rings and key chains were placed on a salver, like offerings, only to be re-collected on the other side of the detector booth. There was no questioning the solemn procedure; a sign on a tripod warned against even joking about hijacking.

Pearl moved with the rest of the people toward the glass doors. The jet was taxiing directly at them, at what seemed a high rate of speed. Then it turned, turned again, and stopped. One of the ticket agents, now doubling as a runway attendant, wheeled a staircase to the jet. The silver door popped open. The same process was going on simultaneously in a hundred places in the world; yet at the edge of this banality was something thrilling and profound. The crowd at the glass doors parted as if for celebrities; the passengers, faintly triumphant, filed through; Pearl anxiously craned his neck. And there, on the staircase, in the white sunshine, stood an unexpectedly small, unexpectedly gray, and even more than expectedly wizened W. S. Mountjoy, with a black eye.

It was really closer to plum-colored than black. It looked fresh. With an admirably deft motion (he held a leather satchel in his right hand), Mountjoy had lit a cigarette by the time he reached the glass doors, and he walked through squinting in his smoke—voluntarily with one eye, involuntarily with the other. Walking in front of him, emphasizing his shortness, was a huge young businessman with a blue three-piece suit and a shiny helmet of hair. Pearl noted approvingly that Mountjoy's hair was unfashionably crew-cut, and that he wore an expensive-looking tweed jacket and chestnut-colored loafers with tassels. Then, as if in a bad dream, Mountjoy walked right past Pearl.

Who had absurdly expected to be recognized. Moving quickly, Pearl tapped the author on the shoulder, feeling for a split second, with great acuteness, the texture of the fabric of his sports jacket.

"Mr. Mountjoy?"

"Yes? Oh, yes. Thank God. I thought I'd forgotten to tell them when I was coming in."

"I'm Philip Pearl. I'm honored to meet you." Pearl had rehearsed and rejected several opening lines, had finally settled on this, the simplest.

"Yes. Thank you." Mountjoy smiled as if something hurt and shook Pearl's offered hand. His hand was small and soft. "You have a car?"

"Right outside."

"Right. I'd like to try and get some ice for this," he drawled, pointing at his eye. "Is there someplace nearby?"

"God, we're ten miles from town. Wait. There's a snack bar here. Just let me go ask." Pearl glanced nervously at Mountjoy, making sure he was in no immediate danger, then went across the room to the counter. A tiny white-haired lady in an ocher smock and harlequin glasses stood behind it, filling the coffee machine. "Excuse me," Pearl said. "Would you possibly have any ice?"

She peered at him with pale magnified eyes. "Yessir, we got iced dranks."

"All I need is some ice in a cup."

She looked at him as if he might have a gun in his pocket. "I cain't give you no ice without you buy a drank."

"No no, you don't have to give. I'll pay."

She was staring around him—for a policeman?

"I'll give you a dollar for a cup full of ice," Pearl said.

"You don't have to give me no dollar. Just fifty cents for the drank. Plus tax."

"Fine." Pearl put three quarters on the glass.

"I'll be with you just as soon as I finish fillin' the machine."

"Ma'am. Please. I'm in a hurry."

She finished filling the machine. Then she slowly wiped her hands with a towel, gave Pearl a flat look, and scooped a cupful of ice. She broke open a roll of nickels to make change. Mountjoy stood alone in the middle of the shiny tan terminal floor, smoking an inch of cigarette as if his life depended on it.

"I'm sorry it took so long." Pearl handed him the cup.

"Perfectly all right," the author said, putting the cigarette in one side of his mouth. Then, "I'm afraid this isn't going to do me much good, old boy."

"Why not?"

"Well, it's crushed ice, you see."

"Oh, God. I'm so sorry. Maybe if I can get a plastic bag—"

"Quite all right, quite all right. Why don't we just get to your car. You said it's right outside?"

"Yes. God. I'm sorry."

"Think nothing of it, old man. Now. Is there a motel or something around here? Somewhere I can park my weary carcass and freshen up a bit?"

Pearl stared at him. "Yes. I mean, of course. You're reserved at the Holiday Inn."

"Marvelous. Marvelous. I see an ice machine in my future." He laughed hoarsely. "Hahahaha."

Pearl smiled. "Do you, uh, have any luggage checked?"

Mountjoy raised the satchel and shook it. "All I've got in the world," he said merrily, and crinkled up his entire face.

And, just like that, Mountjoy—*Mountjoy*—was in the passenger's seat of Pearl's Volvo. Pearl tried to think whom he could tell about this. Part of the shock of meeting celebrities, it occurred to him as he fastened his seat belt (Mountjoy let his lie), was finding that they were not ubiquitous ideals but limited, locatable entities. W. S. Mountjoy was now nowhere else in America but here. It reduced him somehow. The author was further reduced by his shrunken physical presence, also by the way he sat with his bag held on his lap like a child's lunch box. All this reducing, however, only went toward making him a manageable phenomenon. He was still a figure to be reckoned with. Pearl turned the ignition key. The starter raced, but the engine didn't catch. Pearl closed his eyes. He counted mentally to five, then tried again.

Nothing. "It's hot," Pearl said. "It gets a little funny when it's hot."

A forced smile. "Yes."

Pearl tried again. The engine caught this time, but stalled almost at once.

"You do have gas?" Mountjoy asked.

Pearl had put his hand to his forehead. "Yes," he said.

The engine ticked for a moment.

"Well, if it's hot, I guess it'll have to cool down," Mountjoy drawled.

"Yes," Pearl said.

The only thing to do when the car got this way, Pearl knew, was to sit and wait—so sit they did, while the airport emptied, while the good big solid new American cars, cars that started every time you turned the key, bore away the other new arrivals. It couldn't have been more than five minutes in all, but it felt like a week to Pearl. Mountjoy said nothing; the only sounds were the wind and the clanking of the chain-link fence and the ticking of the Volvo's clock, which was running six hours slow. The right side of Pearl's face burned. Finally he held his breath and tried again, and, miracle, the car started right up.

"It's a little temperamental," Pearl said, as they headed out the drive. Mountjoy did not reply.

They drove the fourteen miles south in complete silence. Pearl was scared to turn on the radio. "We just have to stop by the English department for a couple of minutes," Pearl said, as they exited onto Jackson Street.

"Look here, old man—do you suppose you could take me to my room first? I really am in dire need of a brief nap."

What to do? Wunsch had told Pearl, quite pointedly, to make sure and bring the Great Man around to the department first. The captured elephant must be displayed. "It'll really just be literally five minutes," Pearl said. "We have to check up on some things about tonight," he added, not even convincing himself. Tonight Mountjoy was scheduled to read in front of as much of the student body as could be mustered.

"Yes, well, couldn't they be checked on by phone?"

"I don't think so."

Silence to Pearl's right: he didn't dare look. Somewhere in Pearl's plans had been a pithy sentence or two that would elevate him above mere driver status, establish him as fellow author. As he thought of this now, Pearl blushed. He had been certain they would be on a first-name basis by the time they walked into the department. Wunsch and Marshak would die of jealousy.

They pulled into the Culpepper lot. Mobs of incurious students bustled by in the milky sunshine, heartrendingly unaware of Pearl's fabulous cargo.

"Just five minutes," Pearl repeated.

"So you said," said Mountjoy, jabbing a fresh cigarette into his mouth.

WELCOME W. S. MOUNTJOY read the large hand-lettered

pennant draped across the wall inside the department door. If the students outside were oblivious, the English faculty were making up for it; they milled expectantly inside the door and made a glad noise as soon as they saw Pearl. (So hard had the last forty-five minutes been that Pearl, however nonsensically, appropriated part of this acclaim for himself.)

Everybody was there: Wunsch and Marshak and Juniper and Darla and Wadkin and Perry and Tommy and Carlotta Fry and Joe Baker and many others, faculty to whom Pearl had never been introduced, and some he had never even seen; people to whom he nodded every day in false camaraderie; graduate students; even some people from other departments. All surged forward as Pearl and Mountjoy entered, and extended hands. Mountjoy crinkled up his face and nodded, following as Pearl cleared a path to Marshak.

"Signed, sealed, and delivered," Pearl muttered to Marshak—but there was too much noise for mutters to be heard, and Marshak smiled right through him, putting out his huge hand and enfolding Mountjoy's.

"Ed Marshak, Mr. Mountjoy, very honored, great admirer. I'm the chairman of our little department here."

"Yes," nodded Mountjoy, with a semblance of smile.

"If there's anything at all we can do to make your stay more comfortable, please let me know."

"Yes, well, I would like some ice for my shiner."

Nervous laughter from the encircling crowd.

Marshak raised his chin to Darla, who made a helpless gesture with her hands, then left the room. "I noticed that, Mr. Mountjoy," Marshak said. "Nothing serious, I hope?"

Mountjoy, with every eye in the room anxiously on him, suddenly resembled a wrinkled, indulged child. He seemed to ponder something. "I had been afraid it was a detached retina," he said, in his plummiest drawl, "but my doctor assured me that that was not the case." The crowd looked at him as though he might be about to levitate. "Shiner, pure and simple," Mountjoy said, with a smile like a wince. More tentative laughter. Mountjoy appeared puzzled by it. He glanced around the imprisoning circle as if noticing it for the first time. "An angry woman hit me with her purse," he said, in profound deadpan.

The laughter was more certain now: the celebrity was more than fulfilling his promised purpose—he had not only shown up; he was playing the room. Still, Mountjoy continued to look slightly surprised at the response he was provoking. "I *would* like very much to lie down," he said.

More laughter, tentative once more: what new line was the man's wit taking?

"And unless you want me to do it *right here*, perhaps I could retire to my motel room for a couple of hours."

More laughter. Marshak, looking his most benign, said, "No, no, Mr. Mountjoy, that won't be necessary. Young Philip here will take you straight to the Holiday Inn."

The author blinked. "Weren't there—things we had to check on?"

"No, no. Everything's been taken care of."

Mountjoy's face turned reproachful, but as he glanced at the people around him, it became apparent to Pearl that the author had forgotten what he looked like. Now there was a bustling back toward the door, and all at once Perry Armbruster and Tommy Havens were wedged apart by a small figure who advanced on the alarmed Mountjoy and seized both his hands.

"Mr. Mountjoy," the woman said, "my name is Robbie Sue Lynette."

Pearl had seen her, though not often, around the department, and he remembered her vividly: she was not one to forget. She tended to loud colors and high boots—to offset her face, which was not pretty. Her thick, downturned lips and the deep gutters running from her nostrils to the corners of her mouth gave the impression of a permanent frown or sneer. Still, there was something compelling about her—she exuded a strong odor, and heat. Pearl thought of Eliot's Grishkin, compelling the scampering marmoset.

"I just want you to know," Robbie said, "that if there is anything, *any*thing, you should want or desire while you are here at PSU, I am at your absolute *beck* and call."

She held on to his hands and stared up at him with an unsettling intensity. An apology was beginning to form on Marshak's lips; Wunsch was shaking his head.

Robbie gave Mountjoy's hands a little extra shake, as if they were reins. "*Any*thing," she repeated.

"Mr. Mountjoy, I—" Marshak began, but then he, like everyone else, saw that the author's thin lips were stretching into what was probably his first genuine smile of the day.

"My dear woman," Mountjoy said, shaking her hands back. "My dear, dear woman. What an absolutely charming offer."

Even Robbie looked surprised.

"I shall take you up on it immediately," he said. He spoke to her as if they were the only two people in the room. "As a woman of unmistakable sensitivity, you must realize, as no one else here seems to, that my most overwhelming need is, and has been for the last seven hours, simply to lay my weary carcass on a hard Holiday Inn bed and *ice my mouse*." He spoke the last words with a harsh hushed fervor that silenced the room.

"My car," Robbie said, "awaits."

Mountjoy picked up his satchel. "Done and done," he said, extending Robbie his elbow.

Marshak cleared his throat. "Mr. Mountjoy, hah um. I'm afraid I must insist that Mr. Pearl take you to your motel," he said. "Miz Lynette's—departmental responsibilities, er, unfortunately interfere."

"What thee *hail* you talkin' about, Marshak?" Robbie said.

"Mr. Pearl will drop you off, and then pick you up at about six thirty for your reading." Marshak put his huge hand in the small of Pearl's back and pushed forward. "And then, of course, we will all see you at the reception at Dr. Armbruster's home afterward."

Mountjoy was standing frozen, his mouth compressed to a dot.

"May I take your briefcase, Mr. Mountjoy?" Pearl asked him.

The author tucked the case up under his arm tightly. "No," he said.

Mountjoy swam in a sea of admirers, his lined face elated, his hooded eyes deeply sad. He had read, and he had read successfully—eliciting, with a long sex scene from his novel in progress (told from the point of view of a single spermatozoon), laughs and cheers from his (largely coerced) audience. What new conquests could he make? Soon he would be back in a room alone.

The reception was at Perry Armbruster's house; Perry, apple cheeks aglow, could scarcely have been prouder if his dear dead Faulkner had dropped down from heaven for a bourbon. Like Faulkner, too, Mountjoy was short. Nearly everyone in the room was taller than the author, including most of the women.

Pearl was standing with Tommy Havens, a plastic glass in his right hand, a tuna salad canape in his left, his elbows crooked awkwardly. Pearl and Tommy had worn out their small talk, and a definitive silence had fallen on them, the kind of silence that more skilled partygoers than either of them knew how to avoid: you simply smiled and excused yourself as though something urgent had come up, then went off to someone else, or at least to a neutral corner. Pearl was staring off to the left of Tommy's head, staring as if at something, but really only trying desperately to think of how to escape, or what to say next. Tommy sipped his jug wine and glanced over at Mountjoy.

"It must be nice to be famous," he said. "Nah, I take it back. It must be shit. Look at the poor little bastard."

Pearl looked. The writer was standing with two women and a man, nodding and smiling politely—the wrinkles by his eyes branching out in a fan shape—as one of the women gestured extravagantly with her glass. Pearl noticed that Mountjoy was drinking what appeared to be diet cola. Maybe this accounted for his sour smile. Perhaps it was social smiling, Pearl thought, that had etched the author's face so deeply.

"Still," Tommy said. "I'd take it for a week. Just to see what fools it turns people into."

The two women and the man were laughing uproariously. Mountjoy had on his mock-puzzled look.

"You think he's queer?" Tommy suddenly asked.

Pearl, startled, turned and spilled some of his wine on the rug. "I don't know," he said. "What makes you think so?"

"They say he switch-hits."

"They do? I never heard that before." This came out of the blue to Pearl. Why was he always so slow to hear about such things? And why did they hit him with such force? (That was the point, he guessed. Rumors like this caught fire on the dryness of people's lives and spread like crazy.) The last Pearl had heard, Mountjoy was married, with five children. And what if what Tommy said were true? What difference did it make? Except to liven up a party?

"That's what they say," Tommy said. "Not that I care any. He definitely is a lush, though, isn't he."

"Is he?"

"I don't know, Philip. That mouse on his eye looks to me like it was acquired in alcoholic action."

Oh Tommy, Pearl longed to say. *So what?*

"Wait a minute," Tommy said. "Wait a minute. We may be witnessing a historic moment here, Philip."

The woman with the glass was gesturing again, and

Mountjoy, every crease in his face in sharp relief, was bending over and filling his special large author's glass with wine.

"It might be for someone else," Pearl said.

Mountjoy, still pouring, his head averted from the woman, nodded three, four, five times, then picked up the tall glass and drained all the wine away.

"No such luck," Tommy said. "I hear he's a mean drunk."

"Maybe I'd better go stop him."

"What are you going to do, Philip? Appeal to his better instincts?"

"I have to do something," Pearl said. Still nodding—more and more vehemently, as if it might help exorcise the gesturing woman—Mountjoy started to pour another glass. "Excuse me," Pearl said to Tommy.

Now he began to excuse himself across the room. It was slow work—he ducked, bumped, apologized, smiled. Moving sideways, he thought, was the most efficient. He held up his glass as he went, as if he were delivering a walking toast.

Suddenly a large hand fell out of nowhere onto Pearl's shoulder. "Philip, me lad," Marshak said, in a kind of brogue. "Philip, me boy. Are you enjoyin' yourself?" His face stretched into a wide grin, the department chairman resembled a jolly Man in the Moon.

"Very much, thanks, Ed."

"You know my wife Theresa, don't you, Phil?"

Theresa, a pretty woman with a long-suffering expression, nodded to Pearl. "We met at the president's reception," she said. The woman had a phenomenal memory.

"Of course," Pearl said.

"Ah, we only meet at parties." Marshak sighed. Pearl and Theresa smiled reluctantly at each other. "Philip, Philip," Marshak said. His hand still rested heavily on Pearl's shoulder.

"Yes, Ed?" Mountjoy was pouring a third glass.

"This is a fine moment for our department," Marshak said.

Then, breaking out of the brogue and lowering his voice: "It'll make it a hell of a lot easier for us to get others of his ilk to come along, too. The money is there, Philip. It's only Mississippi that keeps 'em away."

"That's great."

"Ahh, you poets." Marshak smiled slyly. "No real allegiance, right? Only to your art." He slapped Pearl on the back.

"Edwin tells me you've published in *The New Yorker*," Theresa said. Marshak now patted Pearl on the shoulder.

"Just a poem or two, really," Pearl said. "Not my best work." He suddenly realized that he had said this, and thought it, so often that it had lost all meaning. What *was* his best work? What was his work, period? He hadn't written a line since he'd arrived in Pickett.

"Well, I'm very impressed," Theresa said.

Pearl thanked her, his eyes on the wine table. But Mountjoy had vanished. Pearl glanced frantically around the room until he heard familiar hoarse laughter and saw the author in the kitchen doorway, Robbie Lynette clinging to his suede-patched elbow.

"Tell Theresa who reviewed your first book," Marshak said.

"My only book."

"Ah, Philip," the chairman said. "Modesty will get you nowhere."

Theresa was all eyes. "Who?" she said.

"None other than the man standing over there," Marshak said. Mountjoy was demonstrating what looked like some sort of Greek dance, as Robbie clapped along.

"*Mountjoy?*" Theresa said, in a small voice.

Pearl sighed. "He doesn't seem to remember, actually."

"That's wonderful, Philip," Theresa said.

"Pretty damn good review, too," Marshak said.

"It was really just a third of a review," Pearl explained to Theresa. "There were two other poets."

"Pish tush," Marshak said. "A review in the *Times* is a

review in the *Times*, and a review by Mountjoy—a *good* review by Mountjoy—is something special. He can be a nasty S.O.B. I can tell you in all honesty, Philip, that it was that, as much as your publications, that—"

There was a crash of breaking glass, and the room went silent. Pearl craned his neck and saw Mountjoy merrily holding up a reassuring hand.

"No harm done," the author said, in his carrying voice. "Very good luck, I'm told." There was appreciative laughter, and the party noise began again.

Pearl tried to edge out from under Marshak's hand. "I really should—" He stopped.

Entering the room from the foyer, in all her amazingness, was Francesca: smiling, cheeks flushed. She hadn't yet forgotten her fast horseback ride. When her eyes finally met Pearl's, he was included in—engulfed in—this look. He tried to smile at her, but couldn't make his face perform. As if in a dream, she moved through the crowd directly toward him.

"Hi, Dr. Marshak, Mrs. Marshak," she said. "Phil." She was wearing a dark patterned silk skirt and a white ruffled blouse; part of her smiling, flushed expression seemed to be in acknowledgment of the impression she was making. It was the first time, Pearl realized, that he'd seen her in anything but jeans.

"My, Francesca, don't you look pretty?" Theresa said.

"Lovely." Marshak smiled. "Just lovely. Don't she, Phil?"

Pearl nodded, unable to speak. He wondered what being shot or stabbed in the stomach felt like.

"Why thank you," Francesca said. "Isn't this exciting?" She nodded in the general direction of Mountjoy, and she and the Marshaks went on talking for a moment—but Pearl heard nothing except a kind of humming buzz as he watched Francesca speaking and nodding and smiling. Twice, when she glanced at him, she frowned slightly with her black eyebrows, in inquiry. With what gesture could Pearl answer such a question?

"Edwin," Theresa was saying. "Why don't we let the two young people talk together?"

"Haven't I heard that someplace before?" Marshak said. "On TV or someplace?"

She took his sleeve. "Edwin," she said.

"Yes, dear." Marshak rolled his eyes. "Don't ever get married," he said—to them both? Marshak lumbered off, Theresa at his side.

"Well," Francesca said. "This must be a big day for you."

"Big day?"

She smiled as if he were trying to put something over on her.

"Oh, you mean Mountjoy."

She shook her head at him cartoon-style. "Uh-huh."

"I guess so."

"You guess so." She was still smiling, and watching him closely—as if he knew a secret. Did he?

"So—what've you been up to?" he asked.

"Oh, this and that." She watched him. "Where've *you* been?"

The emphasis was just enough to cause a physical reaction in Pearl. He stared at her. "Where've *I* been?"

She blinked her owl eyes: once, twice.

"I called you," she said.

"You called me," he answered dully. What detestable place had he been when his phone had rung this amazing ring?

She wouldn't stop staring at him. "You keep repeating what I say."

"I do?"

"*Phil.*"

"You called me," he said. "Why?"

"Aren't I allowed to call you? I wanted to talk with you about something."

"What?"

"I w——"

"Excuse me. I don't mean to interrupt." They both swiveled around and saw a small bespectacled man with slicked-down black hair and long sideburns. He wore a gray short-sleeved shirt and an indescribably ugly necktie, a tie whose complex loops and whorls so suggested the depths of a bad dream that Pearl had to avert his eyes. The man's look suggested that Pearl ought to remember him.

"Dave Untershrecker," the man said, nodding to Francesca and extending his hand to Pearl. As he nodded, several strands of his oily hair fell onto his forehead, and he brushed them back. "I'm the office two doors away," he said. "I guess that almost makes us neighbors." His eyes, behind the lenses of his glasses, were eager, even aggressive.

"If y'all'll excuse me, I'm going to get a glass of something," Francesca said, with a look at Pearl.

"Sure," Untershrecker said.

"I——" Pearl watched Francesca edge away, her eyes on his.

"I wanted to try and catch you here, because I know our hours don't often coincide at the shop," Untershrecker said.

She was gone. Pearl drank from his wineglass for only the second time since he had picked it up. He watched her cross the room.

"I'll be very direct," Untershrecker said, looking at Pearl as if he had just announced mate in two. "I'm thinking of compiling a book of Shakespearean insults."

Pearl stared at him.

"And since you're the only guy in the department with hands-on New York publishing experience, I thought I'd ask your advice."

"I see."

"You don't sound too enthused about it." Not easily deterred, Untershrecker still wore the same foxy expression.

"No, no. I, uh——" Pearl scanned the room. Francesca was

standing with Wunsch, who must have just arrived. Just like him to come at the end. A wave of jealousy went through Pearl, like a sudden chill or nausea.

"Does it seem marketable to you?"

"Well, I couldn't really—"

"You know, I've done a little market research on this," Untershrecker said. "Were you aware, for instance, that the Shakespeare gift-item industry is enormous?"

"It is?"

Untershrecker wrinkled his nose. "Immense," he said.

Wunsch and Francesca were laughing.

"So I guess my question to you, Phil, would be, what do you think my plan of attack should be?"

"Attack?"

"I mean, do I prepare a manuscript first, or just a couple of chapters? Or do I just hit 'em with a letter?"

"Oh. Well—"

"I've already contacted a couple of the textbook publishers. They were pleasant enough, but they really don't seem terribly interested. I talked to friend Mountjoy, but I think he operates on a higher plane than the rest of us."

Mountjoy. Where was Mountjoy?

"But I don't really see it as a textbook anyway," Untershrecker said.

The crowd seemed to be thinning out slightly, and the author was nowhere in sight. Maybe, Pearl thought, he was simply in the den or kitchen, listening to Robbie.

But what if he wasn't?

"Do you?" Untershrecker asked.

"Do I—?"

"See it as a textbook?"

"I—no."

"I thought you might feel that way. So, I guess we go the

trade route. Just off the top of your head, Phil, can you tick off a couple of publishers I ought to try first?"

"I'm sorry," Pearl said. "Could you excuse me a second?"

Patty Armbruster was clearing the white-covered table of plastic wineglasses; she held a teetering stack in each hand.

"I always hate to throw these things out," she said to Pearl. "It seems such a waste, doesn't it?" Her round brown eyes, identical to Perry's, were dancing, flirty—wide with the success of her party.

"Patty, have you seen Mountjoy?" Pearl asked.

"Why Phil, you look alarmed. Is anything wrong?" She was teasing him, restraining a smile.

"I just—" He stopped. Francesca was coming through the kitchen door, her coat in her hand. She had just been laughing, and Pearl caught the tail end of an expression directed at someone else. She saw him, and her grin changed into a softer smile.

"Excuse me," Patty said, and went into the kitchen.

"You going?" Pearl said to Francesca.

She nodded. "I have to."

"I'm looking for Mountjoy. You haven't seen him?"

She shook her head. "Why don't you walk me to my car," she said.

The Electra was parked down the block, under pines, just beyond the glow of a streetlamp. The night was completely silent except for one cricket, very close at hand, chirping quite loudly. Pearl and Francesca said nothing as they walked to the car. They both leaned against the driver's door. Pearl looked at her in profile for a moment. Her eyes were cast down: she seemed, for the first time, to be not posing but thinking.

Finally she said, "I have to leave."

"Is that what you wanted to tell me?"

And then, for an astonishing moment, she was kissing him. It was like eating a fruit he had never imagined but which he had suddenly discovered an endless hunger for. He began to kiss back, but she pushed away. She shook her head. "Good-bye, Phil."

"Francesca—"

She pushed by him and opened the car door. "Good-*bye*," she said, and closed the door behind her. He tapped on the glass. She waved once, without looking, and, as he stood back, pulled out of the space and drove down the street. The Electra's left taillight, he noticed absurdly, was out.

The kitchen, fluorescent-white, was full of people who seemed reluctant to leave. Perry, looking serious, appeared to be explaining something to Wunsch, who stood listening with an indulgent smile.

Wunsch suddenly saw Pearl, and threw an arm around his shoulder. "Philly. My man. My yong Amairican fren."

"You all right, Phil?" Perry asked, his brow wrinkled. "You don't look very well."

"You haven't seen Mountjoy, have you?"

"I thought he was in the den," Perry said.

Tommy Havens walked up, munching a chip as if he had just arrived. "I hear someone mention Mountjoy?" he said, licking his fingertips.

"Phil here," Wunsch said, "has misplaced a major American writer."

"I'm sort of supposed to be responsible for him," Pearl said.

"You picked a bad night to be responsible, Philip," Tommy said.

"Why?"

"He and Robbie Lynette walked out together about a half hour ago."

"Lord have mercy," Perry said.

"Uh-oh," Wunsch said. "Love comes to town."

"This is serious, Walter," said Perry. "There's no telling what that little woman'll do once she gets tanked up. And that car of hers—a deathtrap."

"Oh my God," Pearl said.

"Easy, Phil," Wunsch said. "Cobra Woman probably just took him back to his motel."

"There to have her way with him," Tommy said. "I just hope they waited till they got there. Those moving violations are the most dangerous kind."

"Oh my God," Pearl said.

Late on a Friday night, Jackson Street was even deader than usual. Pearl crawled along at fifteen miles an hour, looking right and left for either a yellowish-green or a greenish-yellow Toyota with a wired-on front bumper. (Or an Electra with a broken left taillight.) He saw nothing but blank plate glass, empty parking lots, flickering crime lights. He had checked the motel, the bars, the restaurants, even the malls. No Toyota. He looked up Robbie's address in a phone-booth phone book and drove by her house. (He drove by Francesca's house, too.) Nothing. Had they gone parking, like teenagers? Had they driven down to the Gulf? Were they in a ditch somewhere? Pearl could see the *Times* headline:

W. S. MOUNTJOY, AUTHOR,
KILLED IN MISSISSIPPI

It would be a two-column square in the lower right corner of the front page, with the famous picture of Mountjoy, his mouth open as if in speech, his eyes wide with a deer-in-the-headlights stare, his boyish cowlick standing straight up. The account of the accident would be deadpan and mysterious, somehow managing to obscure more than it revealed. Robbie would be identified as R. S. Lynette, Associate Professor of English; the paper would bend over backwards to avoid any hint of carnality. Not a whiff of the persistent rumor about an attempted acrobatic feat just before the accident, not a word about the disposition of the bodies. Pearl, of course, would be fired: writers, always quick to pick up on rumors, would henceforth avoid Pickett like the plague. Poor Marshak.

The night was cold and misty, the resident creosote stench particularly strong. This miasma seemed appropriate: Pearl shivered. It had been believed until relatively recently that night air was poisonous. Science had disproved that. (Now it was known that all air was poisonous.) Science had killed all the old gods off one by one, replacing them with itself, a blank-faced idol. Pearl looked with revulsion at the black-windowed malls, the appliance stores and insurance agencies.

Ain't any best place. Ain't even any good place.

We created a blankness to reflect our own blankness. But— and here was where he differed from Wunsch—it wasn't as if something had been lost, only as if it was being neglected. Who was to say that the old gods, tutelaries, and sprites didn't still exist just beyond our benighted purview? In the bushes behind the Beer Barn, for example? Pearl passed the portable Bible sign, whose letters were jumbled up into gibberish—imps at work here, surely. Coming up on the left was the Armadillo. Pearl wondered if Juniper was all right.

One thirty. Though no car was outside Mountjoy's cubicle at the Holiday Inn, the room lights were on. Pearl tapped at the door. No answer. He tried to peer through the window, but could make out, through a slit in the drapes, only a small section of wallpaper and the edge of an unused bed. Pearl knocked harder, and suddenly the door clicked open.

Mountjoy lay on the farther bed. He had a glass in his left hand, his tie was loosened, his eyes open but unseeing. Barely able to breathe himself, Pearl looked for movement in the writer's chest.

"Why don't you come in," Mountjoy said, in his high-class drawl.

Pearl put his hand to his heart. "Christ," he said. "I thought—"

Mountjoy looked him up and down. "Oh, it's you," he said. "Hello."

"Are you all right?" Pearl asked.

The author smiled faintly. "Wonderful," he said. "I'm wonderful." His eyes, unfocused, stared at a point over Pearl's left shoulder.

"You're sure?" Pearl asked.

"Oh, quite sure, yes."

"I guess I'll go, then."

"Don't be silly," Mountjoy said. "Why don't you sit down and have a drink." He made a vague, backhand gesture at the dresser. "I've got a bottle somewhere."

"I really think I'd better get going."

"Come on," Mountjoy said. "Don't be a goose. Have a shot. Get you to sleep better than anything."

When, again, would he have a chance to drink with W. S. Mountjoy? "Well," Pearl said. "Maybe one."

"There's the man." He handed Pearl his bathroom tumbler and indicated another one on the night table. "Here, why don't you pour me one, too." Pearl uncapped the bottle of Jack Daniel's and gave himself and Mountjoy each about a third of a glass. He handed Mountjoy his and sat on a brown vinyl armchair by the dresser. He lifted the glass to his mouth and immediately remembered his dislike of hard liquor: the sweet sharp reek of it climbed into his nostrils and stung the tip of his tongue.

"Ah." Mountjoy smacked his lips. "Now. You must tell me about yourself. You want to be a writer?"

Pearl looked up from his glass. "I already am one."

"You've published?"

"Some poems and a collection."

"Very good, very good. Who brought out the book?"

Pearl told him.

"What was it called?"

"*Oedipus at Secaucus.*"

Mountjoy frowned. "Why does that have a familiar ring to me?"

Pearl sighed. "You reviewed it. In the *Times*. Along with *A Gladness at Actium*, by Dennis McReedy, and *Bringing in the Sheaves*, by Ann Sloan."

Mountjoy looked concerned. "Yes," he said. "They weren't very good, were they."

"But you did say some nice things about my book."

"I seem to recall, yes."

" 'Pearl has a lyrical voice that can be nearly riverine, and a gift for making images that are as startling as they are inevitable.' "

The author wagged a finger. "No fair quoting one to oneself." He lifted his glass to his lips and winced.

"But I appreciated it. A lot. It got me through some bad times."

Mountjoy rolled his eyes. "Oh, the power we hacks wield. And all for a lousy buck."

"You're hardly what I'd call a hack, Mr. Mountjoy."

"Please. Call me Bill."

Pearl drank a stinging mouthful of whiskey and smiled to himself. Bill.

"I can well remember," the author said, "when a holy terror

named Montgomery Sweet nearly stopped my writing career, such as it was at the time, dead in its tracks." He shook his head, his eyes moist. "All with a single unkind word."

"Montgomery Sweet?"

Mountjoy raised his glass. "My point. Precisely. Here's to his blessed oblivion."

They were silent for a while. Pearl took another gum-stinging mouthful of whiskey and swished it around his mouth.

"The thing, of course," Mountjoy said to himself, "is to simply outlive the bastards. *'D'abord il faut durer,'* as Hemingway said."

"There's something I've been wanting to ask you?" Pearl said.

"Be a good fellow and pour us another," Mountjoy said.

Pearl stood and poured an inch of whiskey into the proffered glass.

"Come on," Mountjoy said. "Don't be stingy."

"Are you sure?" Pearl said.

"My dear lad," Mountjoy said, peevishly. "One is sure of so few things; this is one of the few things one is sure *of.*"

Pearl decanted another inch.

"There's the fellow. You?"

Pearl held up his glass to show he still had half of his original shot.

"Oh, nurse?" Mountjoy called in an effeminate voice, raising the pinky of his glass-holding hand. He crinkled up his eyes. "Ha ha," he said hoarsely, more speech than laughter. "Ha ha. You've got to do better than that to keep up with me, Mr.—ah . . ."

"Pearl."

"Pardon?"

"Philip Pearl is my name."

"Yes." He lifted his glass. "Well. Happy trails." Thirstily, he drained half the whiskey away.

"What I wanted to ask you—"

"Did you think I read well?"

"Very well, yes."

"They seemed to laugh in the wrong places. I didn't think it was one of my better shows, actually." He pointed at Pearl. "Should've seen me at Harvard, though. Had 'em in the palm of my hand."

"They can be a pretty tough audience here. I think they liked you, though."

"I never went to college. Did you know that?"

"Yes, I've read."

"Thoroughgoing autodidact. A lonely road, Mr. Pearlman."

"Just P—"

"Of course I've always had a horror of the so-called educational institutions. Still, they do *pay* well."

Mountjoy closed his eyes for a moment. He shook his head and stared at Pearl. "There you are," he said. "Why don't you pour us another drink?"

"Isn't there still some in your glass?"

He held the tumbler up and squinted one eye at it. "Right you are," he said. "Soon remedy that." He drank off the rest of the whiskey. "There," he said, holding out the glass.

"Mr. Mountjoy—"

"Bill." He crinkled his eyes at Pearl.

"Bill. In your essay on Stevens—"

"Oh, bother Stevens. A snotty tub of lard." He wiggled the glass. "Why don't we go for broke."

Pearl emptied the bottle into the tumbler, just filling it. "Excellent," Mountjoy said. "Excellent. Don't you need a refill, too?"

"I'll just finish this."

"Brave lad." He drank, wincing. "Now, tell me all about yourself. Do you have somebody special?"

"Excuse me?"

"You know, a little friend. You're not married, are you? Not that it has to matter."

"No."

"Excellent. Perfect. You do have a good nose, you know."

Pearl involuntarily put his hand to his nose. He took it away.

"You are *shy*." Mountjoy's eyelids drooped, then closed. Pearl began to count to himself: two, three, four, five. He stood up. The writer started awake.

"Ah, you've returned," he said, drowsily. "Won't you stay?"

"I really should get going."

"Don't be a silly billy."

"No, I have some—things to do first thing in the morning. Even before I pick you up." Pearl was backing toward the door. "I can't even think if I don't get seven hours of sleep."

Mountjoy smiled slyly, his eyelids slitted. "Nonsense." He patted the bed. "Come sit down."

"No," Pearl said. "Thanks. Really." But before he had spoken the second word, Mountjoy's head had fallen forward, and Pearl didn't wait to count this time.

Pearl heard his phone ringing as he climbed the stairs. It was after two in the morning, and there was no other sound in the neighborhood. He ran down the balcony to his door, inserted his key with a shaking hand. Who but her? Regretting her terrible mistake. He threw open the door and lunged for the phone. It had rung five times, at least.

"Hello," he gasped.

No one answered.

"Hello," he said again. He listened for a moment, feeling strongly the presence of someone on the other end. "Francesca?" he said.

There was a sound of cloth shifting. A click and a dial tone.

Pearl hung up, his lips pressed tightly together. He was blushing to the roots of his hair. He stood staring reproachfully at the phone, still breathing hard.

It rang again. He grabbed the receiver. "Listen—" he said. "Pearl."

Why did he know this voice, yet not know it? "I—" he began.

"*Jewel.*" She sounded annoyed.

"Oh. Hi. Listen, did you j—"

"Where in hell have you *been?*"

"Reception. For Mountjoy?" He exhaled. "It's *late*," he said. "Are you all right?"

"Not exactly, no. What are you doing?"

"I was about to go to sleep."

"Can you come over?" Her voice was thick—as though she'd been crying? "I've got a situation," she said.

"I'll be right there."

Jewel opened her door a crack. "Hi," she said.

"Can I come in?"

"Are you alone?"

Pearl rolled his eyes. "*Jesus*, Jewel," he said.

She opened the door wide; she tried a smile. "As long as He's with you, you're never alone," she said. "Come on in."

Pearl sat down on the orange-and-brown couch. She was wearing jeans for a change, and a beige chamois shirt, untucked, with the sleeves rolled up, and scuffed brown cowboy boots. She was holding a lit cigarette in her left hand. There were circles under her eyes, which looked larger and browner than usual.

"Do you want something to drink?" she asked.

"God, no. I've been drinking with Mountjoy."

"With—?"

"W. S. Mountjoy, the writer?"

"He's here?" She was walking through the questions, her eyes flitting toward the front door.

"What is it, Jewel?"

"Oh, goddamn," she said, and sat on the other end of the couch. She put the cigarette between her lips and sucked on it as if she were trying to get oxygen. "It's fuckin' Charlie Phelps, that's what it is," she said.

"Who's he?"

"I *suppose* you could call him my ex, though he doesn't seem to realize he's been exed. He, uh—well, there's no decent way to say this, Pearl."

"To say what?"

"I told Charles I was involved with you."

He looked at her for a moment. Exhausted as he was, he savored the moment, savored even her discomfiture, the roundness of her eyes. He suddenly remembered what her nipples had looked like. "Why?" he said—not with heat but with interest.

She averted her eyes and flicked her ash onto the carpet. " 'Cause I wanted to get rid of him, that's why." She sounded annoyed.

"The postcards," Pearl said.

"Postcards?"

"I got a couple of postcards from somebody. With a picture of a shotgun."

"Oh, shit. See, now—would Charles do that? I don't know. I just don't know."

"Who else would've done it?"

"I don't know. Somebody who was jealous of you and Chesca, maybe? Jealous of what they thought."

He remembered the kiss and remembered she was gone.

"I'm sorry," Jewel said.

"What—"

The phone rang. Jewel jumped. She went and got it.

"Charles," she said, first thing. No hello. She listened a

second. *"Charles,"* she said again. She listened a second more, then hung up.

"You better go," Jewel said.

"Why?"

"He's on his way over, that's why. He called from the parking lot at Sambo's."

"That's right around the corner."

"That's why you'd better go."

"I—is he going to hurt you?"

"I can take care of myself, Pearl."

"Maybe I should stay."

"And do what? Duke it out?" Her eyes were wide.

"I don't know."

"Go, Pearl. I'll call," she said. "I'll be fine."

He got up and left.

Pearl sat back in one of the wrought-iron chairs by the pool, in the shadows, and watched Jewel's balcony. A car door closed, its sound the essence of car-door-ness in the silent night. The man who climbed the outdoor stairs surprised Pearl by the elegance of his bearing, the refinement of his figure. His hair was blond, his nose and chin were long. His face looked noble and aesthetic. He wore a light-tan suede jacket, a yellow button-down shirt, black slacks. Pearl could even see the tassels on his loafers. He tapped just once on Jewel's door.

The door opened—Pearl couldn't see Jewel from this angle—and the man went in. Period. There was no gunshot, there were no raised voices; not even any silhouettes on the shade. Pearl's heart was racing. He sat and watched a long time, and he began to shiver. He could feel the wrought iron through his chinos, and he had worn no jacket for the short walk from his apartment to Jewel's. The late-night air was cold and devoid of movement or hope. Nightmare time. Pearl thought of his bed and shook with desire. The light stayed on in Jewel's apartment, and nothing continued to happen. After a few minutes he stood up and walked home.

It was when he got to the foot of his own outdoor steps that he realized he had left his keys in the apartment. This was a joke. Had he pulled the door closed? He walked down the balcony with rising dread. The door was closed. Furious, Pearl jiggled the door violently, turned the knob as hard as he could. To no effect.

He tried to think. Where could he sleep? His car? His car was locked. The key had been on the ring with his other keys. There was a spare car key—locked in the apartment. He felt like crying. If he were in Manhattan, he thought—but he wasn't in Manhattan. If he were in Manhattan, he thought anyway, he could call a twenty-four-hour locksmith. Instead, however, he was in Pickett, Mississippi, at three in the morning. He hated this place. He was shaking with rage. Hated it. He walked down the stairs and headed down the street, with no idea in the world where to go.

Sarcastically, Pearl tried the side door of Culpepper, under the breezeway—and the door opened. The cleaning staff must have forgotten to lock it. Pearl thought of Errol and smiled wryly. The louvered door to the English department was locked, but there was a two-cushion orange vinyl couch by the vending machines on the second-floor landing. It was here, by the sputtering white light and hum of the soda machine, that Pearl finally laid himself down for what was left of the night.

XV

Wide awake in the early light, Pearl used the men's room near the English department. He washed his face and dried himself with a brown paper towel. It was five forty-five. He bought a Mr. Pibb from the soda machine, went downstairs, and pushed open the heavy glass door under the breezeway. The birds of Pickett, hundreds of thousands of them, sang like thunder, a great shawl of sound in the air. The sky was blue-gray, and the world was blessed somehow, in a state of prelapsarian innocence.

Not sure what else to do, Pearl walked. He walked and walked, nearly the full length of Pickett, straight down Jackson Street. There were few sidewalks along the way, so Pearl shuffled through wet grass or over worn earth or, sometimes, walked in the street itself. He examined the ground carefully, as if for wonders. The few people he saw up and about seemed dear: the gas-station attendants, the women in brown-and-white uniforms setting up at the Wagon Wheel, even the drivers who sped by without daring to look. None of them, Pearl decided, was responsible for the grossness that was to come as soon as the world was fully awake.

What was different? His internal weather had somehow changed. The homesickness and intense strangeness he had felt in August, the actually physical illness in the hot early mornings, lay like a dim double image behind what he felt now: the place had grown familiar. The thought made him oddly serene. The sheer banality of it—the green-and-white street signs, block after gridded block; the drive-in this and that; the sheer bumptious forthrightness of everything, the curious innocence. A big white Buick went past—the Japanese didn't sell many cars here—and the driver, a blond girl, honked and waved. A student? Pearl couldn't place the face. Likely she had just felt friendly. He waved back at the receding car.

Now he had crossed the highway and was heading east, downtown. The sun was up in front of him, like one of the giant lollipops of his childhood, an all-day sucker. He was approaching Bundy Park, where he had once, in a previous life, played tennis with Francesca Raffi. Where the lion had roared and roared, saying what Pearl hadn't dared say. He sighed. He had been a fool. Still—what else could he have been? His insides had moved, willy-nilly, the first time he'd seen her; it would always happen. He thought of it in tragic, Greek terms: a fatal flaw, a predisposition to be affected by just such a form. Even as he thought of her now, he felt in miniature what he felt when he saw her. She was gone but not gone.

And someone else was here but not here. The thought stopped him in his tracks. What was he to do about this? She had told Charles they were involved. An interesting fiction. Well, they had been, briefly. It wasn't so farfetched. But that look to the side as she'd admitted it to Pearl—what had that look meant?

Pearl walked back along Jackson to the corner of his street and decided to stop in at Sambo's. It would be the first time he had ever set foot in the place. It was a day for firsts. The restaurant was dark and over-air-conditioned. It had the universal overworn early-sixties brushed-steel-and-Formica tonality. The waitresses were listless, the water glasses yellow. Pearl put a dime in the orange metal box in the lobby and took his *Times-Picayune* to the counter and drank bitter coffee from a heavy cup with a thick rounded rim. It all might have been depressing, but he wasn't depressed. He was new. The coffee, the paper's bad tidings, the specks on his water glass, the sore on his waitress's lip—all were simply facts of the world, bumps on the earth's surface.

He paid the check and tipped a hundred percent, not even glancing back for a reaction. He cut through Sambo's parking lot and walked up his street. It was a new street, the asphalt still black, and it was flanked by two apartment complexes, Camelot and Villa Hermosa, across the street. Camelot, of course, was brand-new, but the buildings of Villa Hermosa were a little older and poorer-looking: instead of housey cedar shingles and wrought iron there were cinder blocks and unrelieved flat surfaces of gray-green aluminum. This morning, though, tinged by the peachy light, even Villa Hermosa seemed blessed, and the stumpy palm tree by Camelot's dumpster glowed with the fire of revelation. It was after seven, but the streets were still quiet—Sambo's had been almost empty. Then Pearl remembered: it was Saturday. How strange and pleasant to forget what day it was. Then it struck him as even more strange that a small crowd was standing on the balcony by his door.

They stared at him as he clanged up the stairs—his hitherto mostly unseen neighbors, all students: boys in gym shorts and T-shirts, a couple of girls in housecoats, their arms folded. Their stares were sleepy and annoyed, and Pearl's first reaction was annoyance back: what had he done? Stubbs was among them, in jeans and shirtless, unsmiling for once. He detached himself from the center of the group, shaking his head. "What?" Pearl said, but now he saw what the crowd had gathered around: the splintered remains of his front door, hanging from useless hinges.

"You know anything about this?" Stubbs said.

"No." Pearl stared at the mess. A police car pulled up on the street below, its radio squawking clipped and incomprehensible phrases that nevertheless had a strong Southern accent. Across the street at Villa Hermosa, shades were going up, doors opening. Pearl turned back to Stubbs. "No, I don't," he repeated, as if trying to convince himself.

"You wasn't home when it happened?" Stubbs asked. His wandering eye gazed off over Pearl's shoulder, as if it had already decided on the matter and refused to accept extenuations.

"I just got here," Pearl said, glancing at his neighbors for confirmation that he had in fact just come up the stairs and not stepped out of his apartment. But no one would look him in the eye.

A policeman, tall and plump, his extreme youth masked only slightly by an almost white blond mustache, shouldered through the still-gathering crowd. "What's goin'—ho-ly," he said.

"Shotgun, looks like," Stubbs told the policeman, his thin lips compressed.

"Well, I guess so," the policeman said, fingering the splintered edges of the door. "Damn. Where's the tenant?"

"It's me," Pearl said.

"What time did this happen?" the policeman asked.

"I wasn't home," Pearl said. And then: "I didn't stay here last night." The policeman blinked twice.

"Happened about five thirty," said a tall boy with a blond dome of hair and PSU black-and-gold shorts. "I thought the roof'd fallen in."

"Did you see anyone?" the policeman asked.

The boy shook his head.

"I didn't see anybody," said a girl in a flowered bathrobe.

She was wearing lipstick and eye makeup, Pearl realized. Had she slept in them? "But I did hear someone run down the stairs and drive off real quick," she said.

"Did you see a car?" the policeman asked.

"Huh-uh," the girl said. "I heard it, though. It sounded kind of souped-up—like a sports car or somethin'?"

"I can't have this goin' on in my place," Stubbs said to Pearl, his hands on his skinny hips.

"I'm sorry, I really don't know why this happened," Pearl said. His stomach sank as he thought of the postcards—the silly, melodramatic postcards. Was such a thing actually possible? He looked at the door. Apparently it was.

"I just bet you don't," Stubbs said, his good eye mean.

"You don't have any idea who might've done this?" the policeman asked.

"I really don't."

Below, another police car pulled up next to the first one, its siren giving a quick hiccup.

"You ain't foolin' no one," Stubbs said, in a surprisingly even voice.

"Excuse me?" Pearl said.

"I seen you in and out of that girl's place at all hours of the day and night."

The policeman eyed Pearl curiously.

"Even if that were true," Pearl said, "I don't see what it has—"

"And he ain't the only one, either," Stubbs told the policeman.

"What?" Pearl said.

"It was probably a jealous boyfriend," Stubbs said to the policeman. "That must be it. That explains the whole thing. Just a jealous boyfriend. This dude has a real reputation."

"*What?*" Pearl said.

The policeman folded his arms and pursed his lips.

"I can't have this goin' on in my place," Stubbs said, once more. "I'm just a employee. They'll have me out on my ear."

"I'll pay for the door," Pearl said.

Stubbs twitched. "You damn straight you will. That's a fireproof, double-strength door."

"I'll pay."

"With a wood core, and a fish-eye viewer."

Pearl put up a hand. "I'll pay," he said.

"You're damn straight you'll pay. You'll pay and then you'll get the hell out of here," Stubbs said. "I don't want you in my place no more."

Pearl dialed Jewel's number from a pay phone inside the garage of a Sunoco station on Jackson Street. The number was busy. A mechanic in a blue jumpsuit worked underneath a car on a lift as Pearl tried the number again and again.

"Busy?" the man said, ducking down to look at Pearl. He had a stiff gray crew cut and amused blue eyes.

Pearl nodded.

The man smiled and winked. "She'll get off," he said.

Pearl had been going to phone from his apartment, but Stubbs had kept standing around with his pale arms folded, watching his every move. Now Pearl tried the number four times in rapid succession—or in a succession as rapid as was possible on the greasy dial of the pay phone.

The mechanic wiped his hands with a rag. "Still busy?" he said.

"Yes."

The man clicked his tongue sympathetically. He reached up under the car and began to unscrew something. Pearl thought about his possessions—his stereo, his clothes—sitting unguarded behind the gaping former door. They weren't much but they were all he had. Stubbs had made vague noises about calling a carpenter, but surely that wouldn't be for hours. Pearl had to get back. He also had to find a new place to live. He had tried to talk Stubbs out of his decision, but the superintendent had stood, arms folded, unbudging, refusing to look at Pearl. Where would he go? Maybe Juniper would have him back?

Dialing Jewel, thinking, and staring at the mechanic working had become so automatic that Pearl almost jumped when the number began to ring.

"Hello," a strange female voice said.

"Jewel?"

"Hello."

"It's Ph—Pearl."

"Hi."

"Is everything all right? You sound strange."

"I'm fine."

"I, uh—you sure you're O.K.?"

Silence. In the hissing background there was a faint, deep, scratchy sound, like grunting, or someone talking far away: cross-talk? The mechanic began to hammer, loud.

"Jewel?"

"Yeah."

"A strange thing happened over at my apartment this morning."

"Uh-huh."

"Why do I get the feeling you're not listening to me?"

"That would be fine."

"Someone's there," Pearl said.

"O.K., good. I'll talk to you later."

"Jewel?"

In the movies, Pearl thought, there was always a click and a dial tone, and whoever was left holding the phone said, "Hello? Hello?" Now there was no click, no tone, just a muffled, drawn-out, echoing sound, as if the receiver had fallen a great distance but had hit no certain bottom.

The mechanic came out from under the car. "Bring her a box of candy," he said. "She won't stay mad for long."

A sawhorse stood in front of Pearl's doorway, and a carpenter was at work hanging new hinges. Pearl, in the Volvo, slowed down and watched for a minute, until Stubbs emerged from the apartment, stepped over the sawhorse, and seemed to squint directly down at him. Did Stubbs know his car? Possibly, but probably not. Pearl refrained from accelerating away; sure enough, Stubbs had been staring at something else in the street, or, more likely, at nothing at all. Now he turned to the carpenter, putting one hand on his bare potbelly and scratching his back lazily with the other. The carpenter looked up from his work and laughed. Pearl watched for another minute, then drove off.

His options, at this point, were limited. It was a sunny Saturday; ordinarily Pearl might have slept late, eaten a big breakfast, played tennis with Juniper, gone for a walk. But ordinariness was gone. He had called Marshak an hour before, pleading car problems, to arrange for someone else to drive Mountjoy to the airport.

Now Pearl drove around the block and stopped opposite the interstice between buildings through which it was possible to see one side of the swimming pool, a section of balcony, and Jewel's window. Her curtains were open and her shade was half-way up, leaving a square of black glass as mute as the mouth of the man in the moon.

He drove to Juniper's. The only car in the driveway had Tennessee plates and three tires. The screen porch was unlocked and the front door wide open, but Pearl's calls met with no answer. He was not in the mood for an empty house. He got back in the Volvo and tried to think. He drummed his fingers on the dashboard and pursed his lips. He might phone Wunsch— then the folly of the idea hit him. Wunsch did not like to be disturbed at home. He would talk in riddles and put Pearl in a worse mood. What else was there? Joe and Helen? The thought gave him a pang. He could hang around and wait for Juniper to get back—but that might be Monday. He could—what? He felt a pressure growing in his temples. He drove back out onto Jackson Street.

The street and the stores were busy. Happy people were doing their weekend errands, spending their money. Money. It suddenly hit Pearl that he had been walking around with three dollars in his wallet for the past two days. Whatever he did, he would need cash. He might have to stay in a motel. He would have to buy a toothbrush. And toothpaste.

There was only one car in front of him on the drive-in line at First Mississippi. Pearl took the folded check he kept in his wallet for emergencies, and filled it out except for the amount. How much would he need? How much did he have? His register was with his checkbook, back in the apartment. He could ask the teller for his balance. If there was a balance. Could he be that low? Payday was a week off. Anything was possible. Pearl had never been one to keep careful accounts. The last thing in the world he wanted to see was a pitying smile on a teller's face. Maybe he would just fill in the check for a hundred. Did they call up your balance here before they cashed the check? He forgot. In Delbertsville they had. But this was Mississippi. The Hospitality State. The woman in the car ahead seemed to be having a lively conversation with the teller; she was nodding and gesticulating. Laughing? The world was in a great mood this morning. Pearl's hands moved toward his horn, but then the woman's brake lights went off, she pulled from shade ahead into sun, and Pearl pulled into the shade.

And found himself facing Tammy Spraggs, her face aquarium-green behind her thick pane of glass. "Why, hey!" she said, through the speaker.

"Hi, Tammy," Pearl said. "How are you?"

"Why, I'm just fine!" She shook her head, as if in a daze. "Why, *Phil*! It is good to *see* you?"

"It's good to see you, too, Tammy," Pearl said, surprised to find he actually meant it.

"Where have you *been*?"

"Been? Just here."

"I mean—" She looked down. "I thought maybe you were mad or somethin'?"

"No no. I've just been—things have been really busy."

"Oh well." She was suddenly cheerful again. "Did you want to cash a check?"

The brushed-aluminum drawer popped out of the wall beneath Tammy's window and extended up to Pearl like the exploratory snout of some metal beast. Pearl put his check in the drawer, and it retracted with a bang.

"Phil?"

"Yes?"

"This check—it's blank?"

"Oh." Out banged the drawer again.

"Phil, I *know* it is none of my business—"

Pearl filled out the check for a hundred and put it back in the drawer.

"—but is everything O.K.? I mean, you seem all kind of, I don't know."

"Tammy, I have kind of a funny question."

She leaned toward the green glass, her black eyebrows rising.

"Have you ever heard of a Charles Phelps?"

"Oh my! Oh—*yes*!"

"You have?"

"Oh, yes. Uh-huh? Mr. Charles Phelps? He is just a *real* good customer—and a real real nice man, too. How come? No, no—I shouldn't ask you how come? I mean—" She put her hand over her mouth.

"You wouldn't happen to know what business he's in?" Pearl asked. "Just out of curiosity."

Tammy's eyes were wide. She opened her fingers and spoke through the gap.

"Sells cars?" she said.

Huge sheets of green transparent plastic hung in the showroom windows of Pickett Dodge/Ford/Cadillac—presumably to shield the merchandise from the sun; but the plastic also had the effect of giving the cars, from the sidewalk, a mysterious crystalline aura, as if they were fabulous stones freshly dug from the depths of the earth. Inside the showroom, conversely, the green windows lent the streets of Pickett a bilious, unreal tinge, as if the only real world were here, amid the shining chrome and dizzying smells.

Pearl wandered among the cars, running his fingers carefully along the shiny surfaces. Poor people, he thought, probably walked in here and felt they had died and gone to heaven. A new car, in its own way, was as wondrous as a newborn child—all possibility, decay only a distant nasty rumor. His thoughts turned naturally to his Volvo. Who had seen it new? He was its third owner, had bought it with close to seventy thousand miles on it. What would it be like to have a new car? The American siren song of virgin automobiles was in Pearl's blood, but thus far, it had been a song he had had to ignore. Perhaps someday . . . When? If he published a dozen books of poetry, he still wouldn't have enough for a down payment. Of course there was always the possibility of staying with teaching—but then when would he ever write anything? On the other hand, he thought, fingering the pale exquisite blue-green veneer of a Sedan de Ville, if you could have one of these, why would you need to write? It would be redundant.

He thought of Francesca, then quickly turned his thoughts away.

"Idden it a beauty?"

Startled from his dream, Pearl looked into a plump florid face with small, close-set blue eyes. The man wore a white short-sleeved shirt and a brown tie patterned with the tiny repeated figure of a golfer following through on a drive. He smiled and extended a chubby hand. "Rye Wallace," he said.

Pearl shook hands.

"Well now, Phil, you thinkin' of takin' home one of these lovely machines?"

"Not exactly, no."

Wallace squinted slyly and cocked his head slightly, as if he had caught Pearl trying to play a trick on him. "I seen you around here before, Phil?"

"I don't think so."

He clicked his tongue. "You sure look mighty familiar. Well now. Maybe you'd be more interested in something along the Dodge line."

"Actually—"

"Now, don't price yourself out of anything, Phil, till I've shown you what we can do for you. You work here in Pickett?"

Pearl nodded. "At PSU."

"You a student up there?"

"I teach in the English department."

Wallace gave Pearl a don't-kid-me look. "You foolin'?"

"No. I—"

"Damn! You look young to be a teacher."

Pearl attempted a smile.

"Other people tell you that?"

"Yes, they have. As a matter of fact, though—"

"You from around here, Phil?"

"No."

"Where from?"

Pearl sighed. "Topeka, Kansas."

"No."

"What I wanted, actually, w—"

"You come all the way from *Kansas* to teach in Pickett?"

"Yes, I did. What I really wanted was to talk to Mr. Phelps."

The salesman stopped, suddenly seeming to age ten years. "Charlie?"

"That's right."

"Now, what would you want to see Charlie for? I can hep you just fine."

"It's a personal matter."

Wallace pursed his lips and examined Pearl narrowly for a moment. His salesman's smile had thoroughly disappeared. "Charlie don't work Saturdays," he said, as if explaining the most obvious fact in the world.

"He doesn't."

"Shit, if you owned the place, would you work Saturdays?" Wallace looked Pearl up and down as if he were trying to guess his weight.

"So he'll be back Monday?"

"You know what?" the salesman said, with a small smile. "You don't sound like you're from Kansas at all. You sound like you're from Jew York City."

"He'll be back Monday?"

"Moren likely." The salesman seemed unable to decide between discretion and bragging about his boss. The result was an uneasy combination of the two. "Sometimes he'll stay an extra day," he added.

"Oh? Where's he staying?" So patently feigned was this nonchalance that by the time it was out, Pearl barely expected a reply.

"His country place."

"A farm?"

Wallace now had a sour look, as if he had compromised himself thoroughly, and was hanging in the conversation by the merest thread of social obligation or in hopes of bringing off a last-second reversal.

"Used to be," he said petulantly. "I don't believe he farms it anymore."

"Bad soil?"

"No sir, Delta soil's about as good as you get. I just don't think Charlie's much of a one for farmin'."

"What part of the Delta is it in, exactly?"

"I think you might talk to Lenore on that," Wallace said, looking Pearl in the eye for the first time.

"Lenore, this gennemun's lookin' for Mr. Phelps," Wallace said, leaning in a doorway. With a last, long, purposeful stare at Pearl, he turned and went back down the hall.

The woman Wallace had spoken to sat behind a gray steel desk next to a frosted-glass wall, and she, too, was gray—her hair, her skin, and her dress, everything but a large cameo brooch pinned to her lapel. She was tiny, almost insectlike, and the impression was reinforced by a large pair of iridescent-framed harlequin glasses that resembled nothing so much as dragonfly wings. She peered up at Pearl.

"Yessir?" she said. "Perhaps ah can hep you." Her accent was rich and musical, wavering rapidly between high and low tones, with a strange fluting at the upper end: the accent had nothing to do, Pearl realized, with the sounds he had heard from smiling salesmen and slow-talking, sullen students—it was, perhaps, the true sound of the old South. The woman smiled now, a cold, hard smile.

"Yes, ma'am. I'm trying to get in touch with Mr. Phelps, on a personal matter. It's kind of urgent," Pearl said.

"I'm *so* sorry, but Mr. Phelps is in New Orleans on bidness this weekend."

"He is?"

"That's right."

"But I thought—Mr."—Pearl nodded back down the hall—"Wallace said he was at his farm in the Delta."

"Did he? Now why on oith would he say that."

"He's not there, then."

"Certainly not." *Soytinly*, she said. Yet there was a hauteur, a faint airiness in the diphthong, that distinguished it from the Northern, Bowery Boy variant.

"If I did want to get to his farm, where would I find it?"

"I'm sorry, sir, I couldn't tell you. I never have been there myself." She smiled, quite convincingly—or rather, without the need to convince.

The showroom was empty when Pearl walked back out, and the world outside looked curiously pink as he pushed open the green-tinted glass doors. It was hot out. November, and it was hot. As Pearl went down the sidewalk toward his car, he passed an open garage port, inside of which a black man in a white coverall was washing, lovingly, a low red sportscar which, except for the color, was the exact double of Giuseppe's. Pearl stopped.

"Nice car," he said.

The man smiled—not at Pearl but at the car—and wiped his forehead. "Uh-huh," he said. Now he looked at Pearl oddly. "You drive one of these?" he asked.

"Me?"

"I thought I seen you in one," he said. "You or someone that look like you."

"Not me."

But the man nodded obstinately. "I seen you," he said.

"I'm telling you, it c—" Pearl stopped. Could the man have seen him and Joe? "Oh," he said. *"That's* right."

The man raised his eyebrows.

"It must've been the one Charlie lent me."

"Mr. Phelp?"

"He wanted me to try one out," Pearl explained.

The man didn't seem to like this story either. "I ain't talkin' about *lend*," he said. "I'm talkin' about *own*."

"Oh—well, I own it now."

The garageman put his hands on his hips. "You just said you didn't."

"That wasn't what I meant," Pearl said. "I meant—listen, you wouldn't happen to have any idea of where Mr. Phelps is this weekend, would you?"

"You his friend and you don't know?"

"Well, we were supposed to meet here in town, but then he must've changed his plan without telling me."

The man looked him up and down. "He must have."

"You don't know, then?"

A level look. "I did know, but I must've forgot."

"You forgot?"

There was a longish pause before it sank in on Pearl what he was to do.

"Now I 'bout half remember," the man said, taking the bill from Pearl's hand.

"Jesus," Pearl said. "You're breaking me."

"Well then, you can just drive over to the bank in your brand-new Whoosis and take you out some more."

"You remember now?"

The man smiled and pocketed the crisp bill. "I believe I do."

"Are you going to tell me?"

"Nacoma," he said. He spat. "Damn if I know what he want to go there for. Damn if I know what you want there, either."

XVI

It was just noon when Pearl set out, heading west on Jackson, crossing the interstate and into Woods County, where the road turned into fresh two-lane blacktop, Mississippi Highway Number 88. He had come out this way a couple of times on exploratory drives, but had always turned back after a few miles: the narrow road cut through thick pine forest, nearly unpopulated country, and something about this country spooked Pearl. It was always a relief to make the U-turn and head back, to pass over the interstate once more and see the malls along Jackson Street.

Every mile Pearl now drove was farther west than he had ever driven before. Only two cars came in the other direction in a half hour; he could see nobody ahead of him or in his rearview mirror. So thick and tall were the pines that the sky itself was only a pale-blue band, a faded mirror of the road below. Every few miles Pearl would see a mailbox: every mailbox had its dirt driveway leading into the pines, white crackerbox of a house, yellow dog. Every house, of course, had its TV antenna.

As Pearl rounded a curve exactly twenty odometer miles from Pickett, he saw another of those yellow dogs, a sweet country dog with a kind look on its trusting face—only this dog was horizontal and split almost in two, and a large vulture stood atop it, hard at work.

The forest opened out into alluvial plain, and Pearl began to pass through tiny towns, five miles or so apart. Sometimes there was just a sign at a rise in the road; sometimes there were a few white buildings, a gas station, and a general store; sometimes there was a Montgomery Ward and even a small supermarket. There were few people to be seen. The towns had names like Clyde, Seminary, Enon, Oloh, Kokomo, Summit, Bude. Towns from which the rest of the world must have looked like something seen through the wrong end of a telescope. The air itself seemed to gather Pearl in; the pale November sky seemed silent and full of judgment—the sky of another time. In Roxie he turned north onto Route 33, which connected in Fayette with Highway 61. It was hot out, and Pearl drove with the window down.

The land, which had rolled gently as he traveled from east to west, was now dead flat, with only small stands of trees separating wide brown fields, fields that grew ever drier as Pearl moved north. The road was narrow, and the terrain unlike anything he had ever seen—it looked lunar, or biblical. Brown dust rose in clouds from the fields and swept across the road. Pearl began to feel grit between his teeth, and closed the window. There had been traffic and commerce, modern interchanges, green highway signs, as he had passed through the greater Vicksburg area, but now, once more, there was nothing—he seemed to be the only car on the face of the earth. So straight and level was this north-south highway that for a time Pearl drifted into a state between waking and sleep, where nothing moved except the broken white line in the center of the road: the Volvo seemed to consume these line segments greedily, but, like foods in a fairy-tale banquet, they were never all consumed. Pearl tried counting the segments for a while, but it was too hypnotic. After what seemed a very long time he shook his head to make sure he was awake, and saw a car in the rearview mirror.

It was a big, white, chromey, late-model American car, a Buick or an Olds, perhaps. Pearl tried to see who was at the wheel, but the blinding white disk of the sun glared off the windshield precisely in the place of the driver's head. The reflection hurt Pearl's eyes. The slight curves in the road didn't allow enough change of angle for the blazing disk to shift, so the illusion persisted: he was being followed by the sun, at the wheel of a white car. Tailgated. The white car drew closer and closer to his rear end. Pearl tapped his brakes, without effect. The car was only a yard from his bumper. Pearl floored it, and the Volvo accelerated sluggishly to sixty, sixty-five, seventy: the white line segments were now shooting into the center of the hood. And the big car stayed as firmly on his tail as if it were chained there. Each time Pearl glanced in his mirror, he was dazzled by the reflected sun. Suddenly, at seventy-five miles an hour, the white car pulled out to the left and shot by Pearl as though he were standing still. He blinked and peered through the car's side window as it passed, but could see only the black afterimage of the sun.

Toward four o'clock Pearl stopped at an ancient gas station just north of Clarksdale. The light was thin; the heat had abated somewhat. The station was a white stucco building, with graying black letters on the front that read B. D. SMITH—GASOLINE—BAIT—COLD DRINKS. The tall red gas pumps, with round fluted shoulders and glass disks on top, looked like weird mannequins. Painted on the disks were red flying horses. Smith—if it was Smith—was bent and grizzled and deeply lined, his eyes a watery blue. He glanced at Pearl without curiosity, spat, then stared off into the distance as he filled the Volvo's tank. "Nacoma," he said. "Halfway between Rich and Dubbs, two mile east of the highway." He spat again, and looked at Pearl's Pickett County license plate. "What the *hail* you doin' in Nacoma."

"I'm going to visit a friend."

"Charles Phelps?" the man asked, without interest.

"No," Pearl said.

Going north, he had passed through Rich—a gas station and a feed store—and then had driven through fifteen miles of empty terrain without seeing a turnoff of any sort on the right. Pearl was lost. He was on an old road parallel to the highway, passing through a little grove of willows and live oaks, when he saw an ancient wood building with a tarpaper roof. Outside the building, in a dusty yard, six old black men were sitting and standing around a rickety card table, pondering an array of dominoes. Brown dust devils whirled around the yard in the sunset light.

Pearl rolled down his window. "Excuse me," he called. "Can you tell me how to get to Nacoma?"

"Nacoma," one man repeated solemnly, shifting a toothpick from one side of his mouth to the other. He was wearing a tiny-brimmed hat that looked as if it was made out of black plastic. "Huh."

"What he want?" another man said.

"He want to know how do he get to Nacoma."

"Take the right-hand road," croaked an ancient man in a gray suit and a white shirt buttoned to the neck.

"How do I get to that?" Pearl asked.

"Half mile past the de Palmer place, then you go on a dirt road west," said a man in a brown-and-yellow baseball cap. "That'll take you there."

"How will I know the de Palmer place?"

They all looked at each other. There was a silence.

"They's a big willow tree," said the man in the plastic hat.

"And a skinny old black-and-white dog," said the one in the baseball cap.

"How far is the de Palmer place from here?" Pearl asked.

"Six mile."

"Shit. Ain't no six mile," another said.

"What you say then?"

"More like three and a half."

"Bull*shit*, three and a half."

"Bullshit six. I walks it in one hour."

"Your mother walk it in one hour." Laughter.

"Do the de Palmers have a mailbox?" Pearl asked. "Any type of sign?"

"Do the de Palmers have a mailbox."

"Do they?" another said.

"Uh-huh." said another.

"Uh-huh? Uh-uh. It fell down."

"When it fall down?"

"Windstorm last April."

"What windstorm?"

"What windstorm. Damn. You gettin' *daffy*."

"That's all right," Pearl said, waving. "Thanks."

He headed south again on 61, clocking the distance, seeing nothing at three or four or six miles. There was a house at eight miles, but it appeared to have been boarded up for years. No willow tree, no black-and-white dog, no de Palmers. At ten miles, Pearl saw a willow and a big black dog, but no house. The dog watched him as he drove by.

He clocked a half mile past the willow, then saw a flattening of the dirt on the right shoulder that might be a road. He pulled off the pavement and saw that it was indeed a road, heading west through a field of low, sharp-looking, brown-green stalks. Pearl started down the dirt road at ten miles an hour: even so, the Volvo rocked and bumped furiously, its springs squeaking in violent protest. In the mirror he saw that he was trailing a thick plume of brown dust. Obscuring the past. Where was the past? He was nowhere but here, no time but now. The horizon ahead of him glowed faintly, and for a moment a brown light seemed to hover in the field, but now the light was deep blue, and Pearl turned on his headlights. Dust and stones danced up into the beams. He drove this way for what felt like several miles. Where was he going? What was he doing? He no longer knew.

His stomach growled. He suddenly remembered that he had eaten nothing all day except the cup of coffee at Sambo's and a Coke and some cheese-and-peanut-butter crackers at B. D. Smith's. The road was falling slightly now, the land on either side rising up in banks, and the air smelled cool and clayey. The road curved to the left and came down an incline to a wooden bridge over a ditch that, in other times, may have been a stream. The bridge's planks looked worn and dry but solid, and Pearl drove across and into a grove of willows and cypresses where night had settled in to stay.

As his eyes adjusted, he saw a row of houses raised on stilts of cinder block and wood. There were five buildings in all, twenty yards or so apart, all of them dark but the last, where a yellow bulb glowed over the front door. The road inside the grove was a lane of smooth white sandy earth, gleaming in the darkness.

Pearl crept along in first, barely touching the gas, staring up at the dark houses as he passed. It was impossible to tell if they were occupied, vacant, or deserted. Some of the windows were covered on the inside with aluminum foil. As he approached the last house, he heard, over the sound of his engine, a high, thin, metallic sound. He stopped and squinted up into the light. A man was sitting on the front porch.

The yellow bulb shone directly behind the man, making

him difficult to see. Pearl turned off the ignition and got out of the car, shielding his eyes with his right hand. Now the grove was utterly silent but for the metallic sound he had just heard, which he realized was the tinny whine of a guitar. Underneath this sound, Pearl made out the rhythmic squeak of a rocking chair on wood, and, more faintly, from within the house, the tire squeals and gunfire of a TV show. The rocking and guitar playing continued as Pearl stepped forward.

"Hello?" he said.

The squeaking and the music continued.

"I'm looking for Nacoma?"

"You lost."

"I know," Pearl said. "You wouldn't possibly have any idea of how I could get there, would you?"

No answer.

"I'm—supposed to be meeting a friend there. I'm pretty late."

There was a phlegmy snort—whether laughter or simply throat clearing, Pearl couldn't tell.

"You wouldn't happen to have a phone I could use, would you?" Pearl asked. "I'd pay." He stepped toward the first stair of the porch to get a better look at the man.

The music stopped. "Don't come no nearer," the voice said. "I has a shotgun."

Pearl stepped back, put up his palms. "O.K.," he said. "O.K. Sorry." He opened the car door. "I'll go," he said.

"Go where."

Pearl stopped and reflected on this. It was a good question. He was a hundred miles from nowhere with a quarter tank of gas. There was no need to tell this man about it; yet as usual he felt the urge to explain welling up. "To try and find a gas station first, I guess," he said.

"Ain't no gas station."

"I thought that maybe back in Rich—"

"Closed till day," the man said. "Tomorrow Sunday, too. Be lucky if you get any fo' Monday."

"I see."

The man laughed, a kind of cackle. "Looks like you out of luck tonight."

"You don't have any gas, do you? I could—"

"No car."

"Oh."

"No car, no gas." And he began to rock and play again, humming along in a hoarse voice. A soft wind blew through the branches above, and Pearl could see stars, many of them, all looking very bright and close. Each breeze seemed to blow the stars brighter. The television's faint cacophony crackled from the house. Pearl stood with his hands on his hips, trying to think.

"What you gone do now," the man said, rocking and playing.

"I don't know."

"Come up and sit on this porch."

"Really?"

"Nothin' funny, now. I got you covered."

Pearl climbed the rickety steps. In the shifting yellow light he could see that the man was old and thin, with close-cropped white hair. His skin was nearly black. The corners of his mouth turned down, giving him a look of permanent disgruntlement. His eyes were heavy-lidded and slightly bulging, their whites bloodshot and as yellow as old ivory. White grizzle glazed his muscular cheeks. He wore a white shirt with voluminous short sleeves; his right elbow rested on top of the guitar, which gleamed, through many scuffs and scratches, in the porch light. Also gleaming was one of the fingers of his left hand, encased in what looked like the sawed-off neck of a liquor bottle. One of the other fingers ended at the knuckle. There was no gun in sight.

"Sit there," the man ordered, indicating an upended plastic

soda case. Pearl sat. The case was low, and it rocked whenever he moved. "Where you from," the man said.

"Pickett," Pearl said.

The man sniffed. "You don't sound like no hillbilly."

"I'm really from New York. Originally. I teach at the college there, at Pickett State."

"New York?"

Pearl nodded.

The man frowned and shook his head. "They say it's bad up there," he said. "Say they kill a man for the change in his pocket."

"That's not exactly—"

"Papa?" A small girl in jeans and a red velour shirt stood behind the screen door, staring at Pearl.

The man didn't look at her. "What is it, child."

"Who he?"

"Nobody. Go back in, child."

"But Papa."

"Yes, child."

"The man on TV, he wanted to kill that other man."

"Oh, child. You turn that nonsense off."

"But Papa—"

"Off." He turned to her for the first time. "Hear?"

She pouted at Pearl, then disappeared. The man shook his head and looked at the floor. After a while, he leaned back in the rocker and started to play again. He picked single notes with his right hand, occasionally sliding the bottleneck on his left ring finger across the strings, producing a sound that made the hair on the back of Pearl's neck rise.

"You play very well," Pearl said.

But the man ignored him. He played some more, then began to sing, softly but deeply, almost croaking. Pearl couldn't make out the words.

"—" the man sang.

He jiggled the bottleneck over the frets high on the guitar's neck, and a woman cried. Low, and a train whistle whined. The wind blew. An animal howled.

Pearl smiled. "That's great," he said, but the man gave him a look, and he kept quiet.

Next the old man played a fast run of single notes, and then, abruptly, as if he had become bored with the song, changed keys and started a new tune—slower, more minor, with something menacing about it, a bending and snapping and vibrating of the bass strings.

"How you get here," the man said, over the song.

"Excuse me?"

"You come in from Budd?"

Pearl nodded. "On Highway 61. Then I turned right onto a dirt road about eight miles south of town."

The man frowned. He played for a minute more, then said, "You see anyone?"

"See anyone?"

"By the road."

"I saw some men playing dominoes."

"Who else."

Pearl thought, then shook his head. "Not a soul," he said.

"Nobody?"

"Nobody."

"Man? Woman? Animal?"

"Well—I did see a dog," Pearl said.

"What color."

"Black. I was supposed to see a black-and-white one, but—"

"Oh Lord."

"Excuse me?"

"Sun were goin' down?"

"Right about then, yeah. Why?"

"Lord, Lord." The old man shook his head and played on absentmindedly.

"Was it your dog?" Pearl asked.

"My dog? Uh-uh. Weren't nobody's dog."

"I don't understand. Was it a stray?"

"You didn't *see* no dog."

"Sure I did. I just told you. It was a perfectly ordinary, big, bl—"

"Wasn't no dog."

"Come on. I saw it."

"Wasn't no dog," the man said firmly, and nodded once, to settle the matter. Now he gazed over Pearl's shoulder as if Pearl had suddenly vanished, and played his song.

Up the country, 'bout a mile or so

He twanged the bass string harshly, bending it up into the wood of the neck.

Up the country, 'bout a mile or so

His eyes seemed to be fixed on something behind Pearl. Pearl turned around, but nothing was there except the next house, fifty feet away in the darkness, and the nodding, swishing trees.

Seen a blue light, knocked upon the do'

the old man sang. He shook his head as if in remembrance, and played on awhile without singing. Then all at once he stopped, sat up straight in his chair, and put the instrument down beside him. Pearl could see the muscles in his forearms working, his hands gripping the chair arms, and he realized that the man was trying to stand. He still stared sullenly off to Pearl's side, as if he were alone on the porch.

"Hep me," he commanded, annoyed.

Pearl stood and extended a hand. The old man seized it.

His palm was astonishingly hard, like horn or some substance other than flesh. He stood, with difficulty, then threw off Pearl's hand and moved, bent at the waist and agonizingly slowly, toward the screen door.

"I'll get it," Pearl said, reaching for the door handle.

But the man swatted his hand away and opened the door himself. "Sleep on the porch, if you wants," he said. "Or sleep on the ground. Won't rain on you none tonight." He stared at Pearl. "Just don't get bit by no dog, that's all," he said. He snorted. Then he turned out the porch light, and all was dark.

Pearl locked himself in his car, with the windows all but rolled up, and tried to sleep. Everything was against it, but after a long time he forgot, for just a moment, Francesca and Jewel and his door and the dog and the noises in the night and the discomfort of the seat and the stuffiness of the car, and his body took what it so badly needed. Sometime in the night he heard a scratching on the glass by his head, a snuffling at the crack above the window. He started awake with a cry. Nothing was there. He turned on the headlights for a minute, and saw only the trees bending in the wind and midges swirling in the beams. Fearful of the dark, but even more afraid of running down the battery, he finally turned the lights off and sat wide-eyed in the blackness, his heart a thudding canvasy balloon up near his clavicle. He would forget about sleep; he would keep watch for the rest of the night. He folded his arms and stared out into nothing, his eyes burning with the futility, the necessity, of seeing in the dark.

The stars. Through the windshield he saw thousands upon thousands of them, and they were beautiful. They were moving.

In the western sky, over the river, there flickered a new constellation: an Indian maiden, kneeling.

But, as if he had never been fully able to let go, he knew exactly where he was when he woke up again. Strange, to be in such a place yet not feel lost.

It was an hour or so after dawn, and the wind was still up: the willows bent urgently in the gusts; white sun speckles danced over the beaten earth of the clearing. The row of shacks still looked empty. Pearl realized that he was hungry—he was ravenous—and when he stepped out of the car, he smelled bacon. He climbed the porch steps of the old man's house and knocked on the front door. He would simply say good-bye and ask for directions, he thought; the best way to get bacon was not even to think about it.

But there was no answer. He peered in through a window and saw an iron cot with a white cotton bedspread; a framed portrait of a heroic-looking (white) Jesus, his eyes turned heavenward; a picture of a saintly John Kennedy; a very large plastic doll (black) in a pink dress. Pearl rapped hopelessly on the window screen, producing a small, tinny sound. The doll stared at him. The old man's guitar leaned against a chair in the corner. Pearl thought about last night, about the music and the man's strange talk. He was old and odd and superstitious, Pearl figured; on the other hand, in Delbertsville, Pearl himself had believed in everything—ghosts, elves, woodland demons, what have you. Solitude and silence did wonders for the imagination, were in fact the original breeding ground of the imagination. Cities, television, etc. were the equivalent of beating drums to ward off devils. Devils that in Delbertsville had hovered among the leaves. If only Pearl had been able to enlist these devils in the service of Art. Instead, he'd been immobilized: nights, by fear; days, by writer's block. Meanwhile the woods across the field outside his cottage window had hissed. Yes, hissed. What had caused this hissing? Insects, wind, yes; but it was more. What? His stomach growled. He would go find a diner somewhere. But then, as he put a foot on the porch step, he saw the dog.

The hair on his neck rose. It was the same dog he had seen last night at the crossroads—large and black, the breed undefinable. It sat by the Volvo, regarding Pearl quite intelligently, as if about to speak. Pearl stepped slowly and carefully back onto the porch. The dog followed his movements attentively but (it seemed) with a certain boredom, as though disappointed by Pearl's predictability. Would it attack? Its face was noncommittal—neither friendly nor unfriendly. There was none of the obsequiousness of a domesticated animal, none of the hostility of a vicious one. The dog was merely interested. Perhaps, Pearl thought, with the beginning of tremendous relief, this was simply a normal farm dog, out on morning rounds. The old man had been trying to scare or entertain him. Ghost stories. Yet for some curious reason Pearl's body wouldn't move. And where was there to move to? He could bolt off either end of the porch—to where? Surely the dog could beat him to wherever he had in mind. He reached behind himself, but felt only air. He was, he judged, about a yard from the doorknob. Which, of course, would be locked. Watching the dog carefully—its eyes never once left his— Pearl tried to pick up his right leg. It was heavy, but it moved. He took a backward step, then, slowly, followed with his left foot. He reached again, felt the door frame, then the knob. It turned and clicked. Open.

The dog waited and watched. Was there any chance that it could cover the distance from the front yard to the door before he could get inside? The answer seemed obvious; but logic was the furthest thing from Pearl's mind right now. He began to count to himself, not knowing exactly why; when he got to ten, he pulled the door open, stepped quickly inside, and closed— slammed—the door.

He leaned against it, holding the knob in a death grip. There was no latch, only a keyhole to which he had no key. Surely a dog couldn't turn a doorknob? The interior of the house smelled thickly and sweetly of bacon. It was all one room, with low partitions separating the two narrow iron cots from the stove. The television was an old metal fifties model—shaped aerodynamically, as TVs were then, as if it were a virtue for a TV to move easily through the air. Little flags of aluminum foil were at the tips of the rabbit-ear antennae. Just like Juniper's TV. Pearl wished he were playing tennis, right now, even with Ted.

He looked around the room without letting go of the doorknob. What if the old man came back? Pearl leaned sideways toward the window. The only way to get far enough to see out was to release the doorknob, and this Pearl did, reluctantly.

The dog was gone.

Gone or hiding? Pearl opened the door a crack and peeped up and down the porch. It had appeared to be an intelligent dog, but only a diabolical beast would wait in ambush. Of course, this was exactly what the old man had been hinting at. Could Pearl believe such a thing? He stepped cautiously out onto the porch. The only sound was of wind blowing through willows and cypresses. The dots of sunlight danced back and forth over the beaten soil of the clearing. And somehow it was this sunlight that saved him. This was what Pearl believed in—the laws of nature, the light of reason. A dog was a dog. Not enough to banish fear, perhaps, but sufficient to get Pearl to the Volvo. Toward which—feeling curiously weightless, not daring to look to either side—he ran as fast as his legs would carry him.

There was an open Oklaco station ten miles down the highway. Pearl apparently hadn't seen it the first time he'd passed, but he wasn't asking any questions. It was Sunday, and he had found gas. The attendant, a very fat, nearly albino man in a

T-shirt that read PECANS R 4 LOVERS, filled Pearl's tank, staring philosophically into the distance. Pearl looked on with a double satisfaction: his car was once more becoming a vehicle of potential, instead of a liability on wheels; and his Mississippi plate—or, rather, Pearl in relation to the plate—aroused no suspicion. He had come *up* from Pickett County, not down from New York.

"How can I get to Nacoma?" He spoke quickly, lightly, trying to get away with it.

"Take a right two miles up on old Highway 48," the man said, bored, without a second glance. Had he bought the accent? Pearl was nearly breathless with excitement. Success emboldened him.

"Men's room?" he said.

The attendant gave a quick sideways nod, still unquestioning, one Southern man to another.

Pearl availed himself, then performed his morning ablutions as well as he could in the filthy sink. Only the cold water worked. He splashed his face, cleaned his glasses, brushed his teeth with his finger. He looked at himself in the speckled mirror, expecting, as usual, to be vaguely pleased; but what he saw disturbed and startled him: for the first time in his life, his face looked mortal. It may have been the dirtiness and dimness of the mirror, which somehow made the image he saw resemble a daguerreotype. It occurred to Pearl that someday this very moment, and all that upholstered it, including the freshness of his own face, would simply vanish. There were sixteen-year-old girls far in the future, their grandmothers as yet unthought of, to whom this moment, in all its beauty and horror and mundaneness, in all the immediacy of its sunlight, would be a rumor of a rumor, a whisper not quite heard. The thought made him miss Francesca, his one chance—wasn't it true?—for immortality, blown. Fate pulled strange tricks. They, Pearl and Francesca, had been two jigsaw puzzle pieces—pieces of sky, probably, that heightened unreal postcard blue—which, at first glance, seemed to go together, but which, when actually tried, didn't quite mesh. Pearl needed a counterpart with some horizon in it, some earth.

He opened the metal men's room door and squinted in the sun. The day would be hot. A warm dry wind was blowing in off the parched brown fields. The fat man was wiping the Volvo's windshield. Down here they did it without being asked—amazing. Now, reaching over to the other side of the glass, the attendant leaned his bulk almost lovingly over the car, rocking it gently.

"Thanks," Pearl said, with genuine gratitude.

"Lady in there says she knows you," the man said, breathing hard from his effort. He pointed toward the office.

"Me?" Pearl said. And then saw Jewel standing in the doorway, shielding her eyes with her hand, as if she were giving a salute.

XVII

"Pearl?" she said, walking toward him, her hand over her eyes. "I *thought* it was you."

"Jewel," Pearl said. "Jesus Christ."

"That wreck of yours," she said. "I said to myself, 'Now how many gray 1964 Volvos can there *be* in the state of Mississippi?'"

"Good God," he said. "What happened to you?"

She touched the slightly soiled cast that began just below her left palm and went halfway up her forearm. "Fell."

Pearl looked at her, but her eyes were impenetrable. He scanned the station lot. "Where's your car?" he asked.

"My car?" She waved vaguely. "Oh, that thing. Down the road a piece." She squinted at him. "Pearl."

"What?"

"What in hell are you *doing* here?"

"I was worried about you." It was the solemn, childish, absolute truth.

"Oh, Pearl. You are hopeless."

"I don't get it. You were walking?"

"Tryin' to. These shoes aren't exactly made for it." She smiled. "Those gay guys."

"Where were you going?"

"There's a bus stop about a mile from here that I still might make if you'd shut up and give me a lift."

"Bus? Where to?"

"Is being particularly nosy a particularly Jewish trait?" She searched his eyes for a second. "You know, for a medium-funny guy, Pearl, you have just about the least sense of humor about yourself I've ever seen. I'm going to Memphis, if you have to know. I figure from there maybe I can work my way in stages up to New York."

"New York?"

"Pearl, shut *up*. Now, I am gonna miss my bus unless you get your tail in gear."

"What time is the bus?"

"Oh, I don't know. Ten minutes ago, probably."

"What do I owe you?" Pearl asked the fat man.

"Ten fifty." His tiny pale eyes, in the shade of his baseball cap, flicked back and forth between Pearl and Jewel.

Pearl took out his wallet. "All I've got is two tens," he said.

The man took the money and pulled a wad of bills out of his pocket. He gave Pearl eight dirty dollar bills, then leafed through some tens. "No sangles left," he said, and lumbered toward the office.

"Pearl," Jewel hissed.

An old lady cradling a chihuahua under her arm was sitting in a lawn chair by the bus stop. The bus had left a half hour before. The next one wasn't due till two thirty.

"Why don't we just drive around," Jewel said. "I can show you the neighborhood."

They took Highway 48 west to Nacoma. It was an ancient river town of narrow, hilly streets and bleached, empty-seeming buildings: a boarded-up movie house with a Moorish marquee; a town hall in white stone, with Ionic columns; an old five-story brick hotel. In front of the hotel stood a faded white Civil War obelisk with many names engraved on it. All was silence. At the end of the main street, where the street suddenly fell to the river, the sky stretched vast and white. They drove around the back streets for a while, among tiny houses in dusty pinks and greens and blues, under live oaks and pecan trees. Jewel pointed at a small unpainted wooden shack among the vivid houses.

"This old black woman used to live there when we were kids," she said. "She used to make tamales and sell 'em for fifteen cents." Pearl looked at her.

They drove down to the river. A narrow blacktop in bad condition angled steeply down the bluff to the riverside. Standing on a slight rise above the bank, you could see a couple of miles north and south. The river was unbelievably wide, and red-brown, smooth as glass where it wasn't rippled with currents and eddies. It was moving, slowly, this vast wide sheet of muddy glass—more like a moving territory than like a river. "Wow," Pearl said.

But Jewel seemed bored and restless. "Let's go," she said.

"This is where you grew up?" Pearl asked, as he drove back into town.

"Unfortunately."

"Why do you say that? This seems like a great place to grow up."

"It had its moments. About two of them."

"Why'd you go to Pickett?"

"Oh, lust for adventure, I guess."

He glanced over at her. She was staring straight ahead, squinting in the sun. "Are you all right?" he asked.

"Stop asking me that." She suddenly pointed. "Take this left."

A small street angled off through a neighborhood of tarpaper shacks in high-grassed lots. Broken-down cars sat in the lots; black children chased each other through the dirt. Their parents sat on porches and stared. After a mile or so, Jewel said, "Go right, here."

Pearl turned between two brick gateposts. They were entering a cemetery. The grass was neatly trimmed; the stones stood far apart. They drove on a road that barely seemed wide enough for the Volvo.

"My grandfather used to bring me out here to practice driving," Jewel said. "That way if I had a wreck, worst I could do was tump over someone's gravestone. Go left."

They took a tiny road to the outskirts of the cemetery, near the edge of a stand of pines. Here the graves were even farther apart. "Stop," Jewel said, in a quiet voice, and Pearl stopped, and turned off the car. The wind was blowing lightly. Jewel walked over and sat down on a stone. Pearl sat next to her. In front of them and just to the right stood a stone belonging to Jimmy Ray Steadman, who had died the year before. Pearl subtracted the first year from the second, and got seventeen. An oval photograph of Jimmy Ray Steadman was mounted on the stone. It showed a smiling, handsome, bespectacled boy in a dark tie and jacket. HE IS NOT DEAD, the stone read, HE IS JUST AWAY.

"Charles and I used to come out here," she said, staring out at the cemetery. "At the beginning." She smiled and took out a cigarette. She lit it. "I was just an ignorant little kid," she said. "I thought it was so romantic. I was kind of cute, I guess. Charles was—he was something. His father had this library, with three thousand books? Charles once told me he'd read every one of 'em. Maybe he was lying, I don't know. I was kind of Charles's project. Like Pygmalion—you know. *My Fair*

Lady. Anyway, he was also in the process of getting divorced when we met, so it didn't look too good. And this is a small, small town. I don't suppose you know too much about that."

"Parts of Manhattan can be like a small town."

She exhaled sharply, humorlessly, blowing some smoke out her nose. "Anyway. Business was none too good, and the car business wasn't either. So Charles up and went to Pickett. And I went with him."

She took a long drag of the cigarette and let the smoke out slowly. "I was sixteen," she said. "It got real old real fast, being Charles's little project. I met some people; I didn't always come home on time. Charles would get ugly—he can get real ugly. By the time I started at PSU, we were on again, off again. Then mostly off. I was living in the dorms, anyway. I could make money. The string was cut. I guess I'm just sort of a failed experiment." She smiled. " 'M I boring you, Pearl?"

"No, no."

"When my father died last year, I got a little money. Real little. But enough so I didn't have to borrow from Charles anymore—which also meant I didn't have to listen to him much anymore. I guess I'm gettin' kind of independent in my old age. Which doesn't seem to sit too well with Charles." She tapped her cigarette on the edge of the stone and stared out at the cemetery. She seemed calmer than Pearl had ever seen her. The wind blew among the stones, seeming to bring with it a faint, distant music. Pearl listened hard but couldn't quite make it out.

They left the cemetery and headed in the direction of the bus stop on Highway 48. Jewel sat silent, the hand with the cast shading her eyes.

"Are you all right?" Pearl said.

"Fine."

He looked at her. Her leather handbag was in her lap. "Is that all you have with you?" he asked. "Don't you have any luggage or anything?"

"Oh shit," Jewel said, sinking quickly down in her seat, below window level. She lay there, curled up alongside the door. "Did he see me?"

"See you? Who?"

"In the green sports car that just went by. Charles."

Pearl swiveled his head, and caught a brief flash of dark-green car, a head of blond hair. He glanced in the rearview mirror, but now they had rounded a curve. "I don't think he saw you," he said.

"What time is it?" Jewel asked. She was still hunched down in the seat.

"One forty."

"Oh, Christ. Drive, Pearl, drive."

"O.K." He glanced at her and smiled. "I think you can sit up now," he said. But she stayed where she was.

Pearl looked back at the road, and started: coming up alongside him, not two feet away, was a black Cadillac, attempting to pass. They were on a long curve with a double white line. The Cadillac was completely in the left lane. It was an old car, as dotted with rust spots as if it had been rained on by a corrosive substance. Something on the car, some open body sore or loose part, was catching the wind and producing a high, wavering whistle. Now the car was directly alongside, and Pearl could see clearly through its open window. The driver, a heavy black woman in a black dress and a small black straw hat, sat stiffly, her jaw set, her eyes wide. She held her fat arms straight in front of her, as if she were pushing back from the steering wheel, preparing to abdicate responsibility for controlling the whistling car.

"Oh shit," Pearl said. "Lady."

The Cadillac, its engine thrumming powerfully but ineffectively, was barely managing to overtake the Volvo. Pearl tapped his brakes. The Cadillac was just past now, dark smoke spiraling from its broken tailpipe. Then he saw the truck approaching in the oncoming lane, and the Cadillac swerving in front of him, its rust-dotted door directly in his path. He jerked the steering wheel to the right.

Almost immediately there came a huge, hollow, resounding, metallic bang, like the sound of a titanic, hellish, out-of-tune gong. It kept ringing in Pearl's ears, this amazing noise, over the other sounds that he was later able to pick, like bits of broken glass, from his memory: the Doppler-ing of the truck's double air horn, the urgent screech of brake pads and tires, the double *whunk* of impact with the embankment and of Jewel sliding off the seat and onto the floor. And the sound of someone's voice—his own?—screaming "Shi-i-i-i-it!" Pearl's seat belt seemed almost to cut him in half at the hips as his torso jerked violently forward and snapped back. Then all was quiet.

The Cadillac lay almost on its side about fifty yards ahead, its crumpled passenger door open and pointing at the sky. A bird gave a quick, liquid, throaty call—whether commenting on the spectacle below or just going about its business, it was impossible to tell. Pearl kept expecting someone to pull up, but the road was empty; the truck had simply vanished. Then the woman emerged, crouching, from the Cadillac. Her black dress was of a shiny material that caught the morning sun iridescently. Her small black hat had a crisp veil. She stumbled to the ground a few feet from her car, and clasped her hands together. "Oh Lord," Pearl heard her say. "Oh Lord, oh Lord, oh Lord." In the silence, he could hear her perfectly. The bird gave its quick call again. Jewel was lying on her back in the footwell of the car, beneath the dashboard, staring at Pearl, saying nothing. There was a small, neat, horizontal cut on her forehead. She blinked.

"Are you all right?" Pearl asked her.

"You just asked me that."

"I did?"

"I'm just gonna lie here a minute, if that's all right," Jewel said. "If my back's busted, I don't want to know about it yet."

Pearl's eyes blurred for a second. He shook his head, and they cleared. "I can't believe the truck didn't stop," he said.

Jewel exhaled derisively through her nostrils.

"I can't," he said. "It's against the law, you know. Not to."

"Oh, Pearl."

The black woman was still on her knees, moving her lips soundlessly now. It was a lovely morning. Hot, but cloudless and dry. The birds called, the wind blew, and Pearl simply sat. A long time seemed to pass. He heard a whine, far off. He turned his head. The sound was coming up the road behind them.

"Oh, Christ," Jewel said, and tried to move.

"What?" Pearl said.

"Oh Christ," she said again.

The whine grew husky until, as the green vintage MG rounded the curve, the low belches of combustion grew audible. The car pulled up and stopped on the grass, and the man Pearl had glimpsed two nights before stepped out.

He wore a pressed white button-down shirt with the sleeves carefully rolled halfway up his forearms; cream-colored slacks; and expensive-looking loafers, without socks. He had a long, handsome, country-club face, and Pearl's first feeling, as this man walked up to the Volvo, was one of warmth and relief: *here was a man who knew what to do.*

"You all right?" the man asked Pearl, sounding slightly amazed.

"I think so."

Then the man looked into the car. "Good God," he said.

"Hello, Charles," said Jewel.

"Are you all right?" he asked her.

"Everyone keeps *askin'* me that," Jewel said.

"Don't move," Phelps said. He walked around to the other side of the car. "Don't move," he said again. "Try not to lean against the door, darlin'," he told Jewel. "I'm going to open it."

But before he could do anything, Jewel quickly pulled herself up and onto the seat. Now she leaned forward, hugging herself. Phelps opened the door and knelt down, putting his arms around her shoulders. "Oh, honey," he said.

The black woman was on her knees on the grass, rocking back and forth, her hands clasped.

"Oh honey," Phelps said again.

"Don't honey me," Jewel said.

Phelps's eyes were wet. "I better get y'all to a hospital," he said.

A few minutes later a highway patrol car, its blue lights whirling, pulled up behind the MG, and a trooper emerged. He leaned on Pearl's door. "You all right?" he said.

Pearl nodded. Charles wiped his cheeks and stood up. "Billy," he said, smiling.

The patrolman took off his sunglasses. He looked about seventeen. "Mr. Phelps," he said.

"Billy, these two young people are friends of mine. I'm going to take personal responsibility for getting them to the hospital," Phelps said.

"Can you move?" the patrolman asked Jewel.

"I'm fine," Jewel said.

The patrolman squinted at the cut on her forehead. "Did you hit the dashboard?" he asked.

"No I did not," Jewel said.

"Ma'am?" the patrolman called to the black woman. She was still on her knees, rocking. He walked over to her. "Ma'am? You O.K.?"

She looked heavenward. "Oh Lord," she cried.

"We better get someone to take a look at you," Phelps said to Jewel.

"I don't need to get looked at. I just need to get to a bus stop."

"Not before you go to the emergency room," Phelps said.

"Bull*shit*."

"Honey, now listen to reason," Phelps said.

"Is there any problem?" the patrolman called.

"No problem at all, Billy," Phelps said.

"You have never spoken one word of reason in your entire life," Jewel said to him. "You are nuts."

The patrolman was helping the black woman up, taking her arm.

"Now, either he's going to take you there or I'm going to take you there," Phelps said to her, quietly. "Which'll it be, honey?"

"I don't want to go, period."

With some effort, the patrolman was walking the woman toward them. She was limping, and trying, with large, panicked gulps, to catch her breath.

"Easy go," the trooper said to her. "No hurry, now. Do you want to stop?" The woman nodded, her eyes closed. "Are you going to take the young lady in your car, Mr. Phelps?" the trooper asked. "I can take these other two folks easy."

"Well now. That's an idea," Phelps said, looking at Pearl.

Pearl returned his look. "I'd just as soon stay with Jewel," he said, firmly. "It was my car she was in." As if this made sense. But firmly, to make it make sense.

Long-nosed, brown-eyed Phelps searched Pearl's face for a moment, then gave the briefest of nods. "There's a bench seat in back," he said, to no one in particular. "We'll fit."

And it was there that Pearl sat, his arm thrown across the trunk, the warm, smoky air, cooled by speed, roaring in his ears and the corners of his eyes.

Phelps and Jewel, in the two leather bucket seats, did not converse, but Phelps, his fine sandy hair flowing backward in the wind as smoothly as water, kept turning his head toward her as if she were about to say something. Jewel huddled as far to the right as possible. They were traveling north on 61, the police car (with the black woman in the back seat, as if she were a taxi passenger or an apprehended perpetrator) escorting them up ahead, its dome lights flashing. They entered a small town and approached a traffic light. The light turned yellow as the police car sped through, and Phelps came to a halt. Suddenly, Jewel began to stand up, and just as quickly, Phelps's hand was on her arm. An old man in baggy overalls, slowly crossing the street in front of them, watched curiously.

"Wait," Phelps said to her.

"Goddamn it, Charles. Let go of me."

"Now, just wait," Phelps said. He grasped her shoulder tightly. She began to stand again, but he reached over with the other hand and held her down. The car jerked forward and stalled.

"I'll take you to the bus," Phelps said, as Jewel struggled. "Goddamn it. I will *take* you."

She abruptly sat back down. She was looking at him bitterly, sitting oddly quiet. "You asshole," she said. "You coward."

"There's no need to be abusive," Phelps said. "I said I'd take you."

"Yeah. What's that for, then."

"Just to keep you from jumpin' out and hurtin' yourself, honey," he said.

It was then that Pearl saw, between the seats, what he had taken an instant previously for some part of the car: the blue metal barrel of a pistol, pointed at Jewel's side.

"Why don't you just shoot me and get it over with," she said.

He reached down carefully, not taking his eyes off her, and started the engine. "The next bus isn't till tonight," he said.

"Why don't you come over, have a cold drink, put your feet up." The light changed. The police car was out of sight. Phelps turned in his seat, smiling hospitably. "How's that sound to you, Mr. Pearl?"

Phelps's house was not the pillared antebellum mansion Pearl had expected, but a suburban-style, rambling brick ranch at the head of a long driveway and a surprisingly green lawn. The property was ringed with planted trees and set in the middle of miles of brown fields. Pearl couldn't see another house. Two large cars, pastel yellow and pastel blue, sat side by side in the driveway: Phelps pulled up behind them at an angle, blocking both with a possessive carelessness.

"You got us covered, Charles?" Jewel said. "You gonna march us in with your little phallic symbol poked in our backs?"

Phelps smiled. "Now, now. What would the neighbors think', darlin'?"

"Probably exactly what I think," Jewel said.

"Perhaps you could spare me that, just for the moment," he said. He took a white handkerchief from his hip pocket and patted his forehead, then gave the pistol a little embarrassed wave. "*Could* I put this thing away now?" he asked them both.

"Fine with me," Pearl just managed to say.

"Go ahead and do whatever you want," Jewel told him. "I'm walking anyway. Think you could hit me at forty yards with that thing, Charles?"

Phelps sighed. "All I want is for you to sit down for a bit and talk. I said I'd take you to your bus."

"Thanks. I can get there myself just fine." Jewel began to walk down the driveway. Looking extremely reluctant, Phelps pointed the gun off to the side and pulled the trigger.

Pearl jumped the instant before the report echoed out over

the fields. A large crow flew from the top of one of the live oaks along the driveway and flapped slowly up, a black cross against the white sky. In the distance, Pearl could hear the echo of the shot, and then, oddly, banally, the sound of a tractor.

Jewel stopped and turned. "You missed," she said.

"Come around back, darlin'," Phelps pleaded.

She looked at them both. Pearl was listening to the tractor, off across the fields. He was the man on the tractor, doing his work in the sun, thinking of nothing but the rows of unturned earth ahead. He came back, almost relaxed, and saw the pistol again.

"Jewel," Pearl said. He cleared his throat. "I really wish you would."

She sighed, shook her head. "Oh, Pearl. Why'd you even bother," she said. And walked back toward them.

"What can I fix you, Mr. Pearl?" Phelps asked. They were on a patio behind the house, next to a swimming pool. The pool was empty. Pearl and Jewel sat in deck chairs near the diving board; Phelps stood by a small rolling bar. He had put the pistol in his hip pocket, after carefully clicking the safety, and it rode there, flat and sleek, just creasing his golf trousers.

"Nothing, thanks," Pearl said.

"You're sure? It's been a hot day. No?" He turned to Jewel. "Darlin'?"

She stared at him.

"Come on, honey, you know how I hate to drink alone."

They looked at each other for what seemed to Pearl a solid minute. Finally Phelps raised his brows and averted his eyes, not in defeat but as if in the natural motion of turning toward the bar. "Oh well," he said, and poured himself some whiskey from a cut-glass decanter. When he lifted the glass to his mouth, Pearl saw that his hand was shaking quite violently. Pearl looked out over the dry fields. The midday heat rose from the brown earth. The psychic. Here?

Phelps settled into a deck chair directly across from Jewel. As he leaned back, the pistol slid from his pocket down the canvas of the seat, then clattered onto the concrete, where it lay, as in a weird game of spin-the-bottle, pointing from Phelps to Pearl.

All was silence for a moment, but for the far-off sound of the tractor. The three of them stared at the gun. It may have actually lain there for five seconds. A half second too late, Pearl realized that he could have taken it, that the vehemence of diving and possibly grappling for something on the ground was simply not a part of Phelps's makeup. But then the car dealer bent over slowly and carefully, delicately raising his glass with the other hand, and picked up the pistol, as if it were a stray martini olive. He checked the safety and replaced the gun in his pocket, with an apologetic smile at the two of them.

"I hear that you're a writer, Mr. Pearl," he said.

Pearl nodded.

"Published?"

Pearl cleared his throat. "A couple of things," he all but whispered.

"Ah. Very good. What sort of things?"

"Poems."

Phelps raised his eyebrows and took a drink. He seemed to have calmed a little. "I've done a little in that line myself," he said. "Strictly of an expurgative nature, of course. 'Bout the closest I've come to being published is gettin' my picture in *Southern Living*. Did I tell you, honey?" He turned to Jewel. "They ran a spread on the living room."

"Congratulations," Jewel said.

Phelps laughed, a soundless exhalation through the nostrils and a slight rocking back of the head. "That's a little joke between us," he explained to Pearl. "She picked out all the furniture."

"Ha ha," Jewel said.

"I don't have a lick of taste," Phelps said. "Except, of course, in literature and women." He said *literatoor*.

"What time is it getting to be, Pearl?" Jewel asked.

"Darlin'!" Phelps said. "You never told me how you liked the pool!" He turned to Pearl. "I told her I'd build her a pool if she came back to me," he said. "Didn't I, honey?"

"It's empty," Jewel said.

"Why, that only awaits your part of the bargain, hon."

Pearl looked behind himself, down into the deep end. He moved his chair a little farther from the edge.

"Pearl. Time," Jewel said. She pointed at her wrist.

"Now, there's no hurry," Phelps said anxiously.

"The bus is at six fifteen," Jewel said, "and I want to be five minutes early."

"Well now, there'll be another one tomorrow," Phelps said. She sat up straight. "I am going to be *on* that bus."

Phelps looked into his glass. "Maybe you will and maybe you won't."

"What?" Jewel said.

Phelps raised his eyes almost shyly. "I said, maybe you will and maybe you won't. What you don't seem to understand," he said, "is that I am a dangerous man." He smiled, less easily now, twitching a little around the eyes. "Aren't I, sugar."

Jewel slumped back into her chair and began to bite her thumbnail abstractedly.

"Aren't I?" Phelps said.

"Sure, Charles."

"Did you tell Mr. Pearl how you got your sprained wrist?" he asked. "No?" He looked at Pearl. "I did it," he said. "I hit her and she fell on it. Isn't that terrible?"

Pearl shrugged.

" 'What kind of man would hit a woman?' I believe that's

the stock question, isn't it? What kind of a man do you think would hit a woman, Mr. Pearl? Your opinion as an observer of human nature."

He stared until Pearl had to look aside.

"Mr. Pearl?"

"Don't know," Pearl said.

"A cowardly man?"

"Don't know."

"An unbalanced man?"

Pearl shook his head.

"A desperate man? I would maintain," Phelps said, "that a physical struggle between a man and a woman is most nearly comparable to one between a dog and a cat." He smiled. "Let's say, so as not to offend anyone involved, between a pedigreed dog of limited vigor and a reasonably well-bred cat. While all the odds might seem to be in the dog's favor, in reality the reverse is true. Cat'll scratch a dog's eyes out every time, ain't I right, honey?"

Jewel still bit on her nail.

"I was provoked, Mr. Pearl. I was most cruelly provoked. That's not to excuse my action, of course. Only to explain it."

His eyes were large and brown and moist, and sweat had gathered in the cleft above his lip. Pearl was startled by the realization that Phelps looked like nothing so much as a desperate little boy, standing off the entire world. Phelps took a long drink, closing his eyes almost in gratitude as he tipped the glass back.

"Who are your favorite authors, Mr. Pearl?" he asked, with a half smile.

Pearl shrugged. "There are a lot."

Phelps nodded once, quickly, not letting Pearl off the hook.

Pearl couldn't think. "Well," he said, feeling his voice shake slightly, "there's—Stevens. There's Williams—"

Phelps looked bewildered. "I'm sorry," he said. "Who?"

"Wallace Stevens? William Carlos Williams?"

"Poets?"

"Yes."

"Ah, I see. I'm really more of a prose reader myself. I find modern poetry—abstruse. Unrewarding. Like a riddle I don't care to know the answer to."

"Oh."

He smiled. "A one-word reply? No argument?"

"You have a right to your opinion."

"De gustibus non disputandum est, eh, Mr. Pearl?"

"Especially if one side has a gun."

Phelps threw his head back and laughed—laughed inordinately, laughed till the tears rolled down his face. He wiped his cheeks with the back of his hand, still laughing and shaking his head.

"He's funny!" he said to Jewel.

Jewel smiled quickly, more wince than smile, and glanced at Pearl, who questioned her with his eyes but got no answer.

"Very funny," Phelps continued. "I have to say"—he wiped at his eye—"honey"—he paused to get his breath—"I really almost can't blame you."

"For *what?*" Jewel said, scornfully.

"Why, for runnin' off with the man."

She rolled her eyes. "Charles, the only place I was ever running was away from you."

"Which explains what you were doing in his car."

"Oh God," she said.

"Tell me, honey," Phelps said. "Did circumcision pose such a temptation?"

"Yes, Charles. Yes, it did."

"Did it?" He was staring now.

"It was sublime. It made all the difference."

"Is that right."

"That's right."

The liquor in his glass shook. "I could shoot you right now, you little cunt, did you know that?"

"Why don't you do it and get it over with."

"I could shoot you and not feel the slightest twinge of guilt. I could shoot you and him and no jury in this state would ever convict me."

"Then *do* it," Jewel said, her voice hoarse. She was on her feet now, standing in front of him. "Do it, do it, do it! Why can't you just fuckin' do it, you fuckin' coward!"

Phelps shook his head. "I gan't," he said. He was crying. "I gan't." He took out the pistol and looked at it. "I gan't," he said again, shaking his head. "I gan't."

Pearl closed his eyes and held his breath. Behind his head he sensed, like a blind man, the immense, the yawning space of the deep end of the pool.

"Here," he heard Phelps say, in a thick voice. "Go ahead. I'm no good anyway."

Pearl heard the pistol strike the concrete and skid across the patio; there was a slight skip of silence, then an echoing clatter as it landed on the floor of the pool. He opened his eyes and saw Jewel standing over Phelps, who held his face in his hands.

"Fuck you, Charles," she said quietly. And walked to the edge of the patio, where she stood for a moment, waiting for Pearl. Who now rose and followed her.

BOOK III

XVIII

Someone had put a rocket ship on the lawn outside the windows of Culpepper 201, where Pearl was teaching World Masterpieces 102 this spring. The rocket, nearly ten feet high, was extremely realistic, silvery, quite NASA-ish. It must have been expensive to make, yet its purpose was not clear to Pearl, who had stopped reading the *Panther Paw*. He suspected a rich fraternity—the Bretts and Brads and Rhetts—had erected it in an access of techno-phallic high spirits. Rain had been falling for nearly an entire week, and as Pearl stood and taught, he watched the rocket ship carefully, waiting for it to take off or fall over or somehow announce its purpose. It did nothing, though, but stand in the rain, ingloriously earthbound, getting wet.

Pearl was teaching *The Sun Also Rises*, presenting the Lost Generation to one perhaps even more lost. It was one of his favorite books, but to his distress, he found his enthusiasm almost impossible to convey: the class, consisting of those sufficiently ambitious not to have dropped the course after the first semester (and sufficiently intelligent not to have flunked), was a kind of smoothly running Darwinian machine, rattling through the syllabus with barely a hitch, racking up C's and B's and even A's on the pop quizzes and tests, squinting carefully at Pearl, as he spoke, for Important Names and Significant Terms.

"Does anyone have any idea *why* Brett went off with Cohn?" Pearl asked, almost musingly. Importunate hands shot up.

"Roy?" he asked a sullen blond boy with his arms folded on the desk.

"Is it gonna be on the test?"

Laughter as Pearl smiled and rolled his eyes, his heart breaking. They "understood" him now, or understood what they wanted to understand: he was no longer an X quantity, he was just—Mr. Pearl. Good ol' Mr. Pearl: the Northerner, the Jew, in his alligator shirts and khaki pants. He was funny, both ha-ha and the other. It shocked him, in a way it saddened him, that he had once been (and was no longer) to them as the rocket ship was to him—mysterious, alien, even upsetting. Now there was a certain familiarity, even (within bounds, of course; it was still the South) a polite cheekiness.

"I don't *know* if it's going to be on the *test*."

More polite laughter at Pearl's predictable reaction, and at the Manhattan cadences of his response, the slight dentalization and upturn of tone on the final word; cozy laughter at the quiddity of Mr. Pearl.

"I just want to know, if it's possible, why you *think* she did it. If she didn't even *like* him very much."

Stares: *you tell us.*

So they had lost their virginity. In one semester they had got their bearings. They were in it now for the money: for the grades; for the good job and the house by the golf course. The New South, a dollar sign smack in the center of the Stars and Bars. He could barely blame them. A little, but not much. After all, what did he himself want? A life of scavenging for foundation grants? Intellectual respectability, sunken-in cheeks? If he stayed here—amazing thought—his salary would go up year by year; soon he would have a house (with bookshelves! with air-conditioning!) and—amazing thought—a new car. He could play tennis eleven months a year. There were worse things—pace Wunsch—than the meaninglessness of modern existence. There was poverty; there was winter.

You'll go nuts. You'll turn into a vegetable. There's nothing to do at night.

Who needs to do at night? Night is for sleeping.

With?

"*I* don't know why she went with him," Pearl finally said. "Maybe she really did love him, for a little while." Pens scratched paper. Pearl was lost, openmouthed, thinking of a light, a moment, in fall. Aeons ago. Time passed. They were staring at him. "Sometimes there isn't any answer," Pearl said. Heads shook: this puzzled them. This they didn't like. Pearl blinked back the past, shrugged. Class was through.

Then the week of rain was over, and Pickett was sparkling, hot, full of blossoms. The same song came from every car radio:

Wise man has the power to reason away

Pearl's heart soared—in short, controlled leaps. He couldn't tell why the town looked at once better and worse to him.

The fraternities and sororities seemed to have turned inside out: at almost all hours, smiling girls and boys, healthy if not beautiful, crowded the outdoors, dotting the wide green lawns of the campus. Girls in oversized frat shirts and short shorts and makeup, meticulously informal, stood on the grass median strip of Jackson Street with cardboard signs advertising slave auctions and car washes. Pearl returned their smiles. It was partly the indulgent smile of a teacher, but was also the smile of a fellow citizen.

Pearl walked everywhere, even though the Volvo had long since been towed back to town and fully repaired: insurance had covered all the thousand dollars but two hundred. He'd even got a new paint job out of the deal. His car had been reborn, in British Racing Green.

Camelot had recently been bought out by a real estate venture group and renamed Avalon. Stubbs the superintendent had vanished, replaced by a blue-haired lady who filled Stubbs's beery apartment with knickknacks and watched soap operas all day on a giant-screen color TV. Pearl had been able to move back into his old apartment with no questions asked, as if he were a different person. Perhaps he was. In the long orange late afternoons, amid the dizzyingly redundant vapors of a million white blossoms, he felt he could breathe again, that his life had, in a number of ways, been amplified and simplified.

Marshak was sitting on the edge of Darla's desk, his half-glasses down at the end of his nose, as Pearl came in from Masterpieces and went to his mailbox.

"Yonder comes young Philip, Darla," Marshak said.

"Yessir," said Darla.

"Hello, Ed," Pearl said, as he leafed through his mail: an announcement of a departmental meeting, in pale blue-purple print still reeking sweetly of mimeo fluid; a fifth notice from campus security about a four-dollar fine he still owed for having parked his overladen car in the wrong zone eight months ago; two makeup tests on *The Sun Also Rises*, from Cindy Ellerbee and Mike Stopes ("Brett loved the bull fighter," Mike wrote, "because he was more of a man than Cohn or Jake. But I really could not understand what went on after that . . ."); a folded piece of pink stationery, patently unofficial. Pearl unfolded it and began to read. The handwriting, in red ink, was vivid, loopy, urgently slanted. "Dear Mr. Pearl," it began. "I have been watching you now for four months, not saying anything . . ."

"A word with you, young Philip?" said Marshak.

Pearl quickly refolded the paper. "Sure, Ed. I'll be right there."

"The sooner the better."

Darla was smiling slightly.

"What's up, Ed?"

Marshak got off the edge of the desk and looked down at Pearl through the half-glasses. "A hell of a mannerly fella," he said. "Don't you say hello to our gorgeous department secretary here?"

"Hello, Darla."

"Hey, Mr. Pearl."

"*Phil*," Pearl reminded her.

She closed her eyes, smiled bucktoothily. "Phil," she said.

"That's good. That's nice," said Marshak. "O.K., young Philip," he said, holding open his office door. "In we go."

Inside, Marshak, seated at his desk, his huge hands clasped on the blotter like amorous dolphins, nodded toward the door. Pearl closed it.

"Is anything wrong, Ed?"

"You may sit."

Pearl sat. "Is anything wrong?"

"I'll come right to the point, Philip. How'd you like to stay at this place another year?"

"But my appointment—"

"That's changed. Mullins isn't coming back."

Pearl looked out the window, at the trees that had once seemed so strange. "Wow," he said.

"We can only raise you to fifteen thousand. If you're rehired next year, we can talk more money—maybe even tenure track."

"I thought—" Pearl said, watching the live oaks' lozenge leaves swaying in the white sun.

"What?"

"I thought I wasn't doing such a hot job."

"Who said that?"

"I don't know. There was the disciplinary committee after Mountjoy and Robbie—"

"Never sat."

"Never sat?"

"What else?" Marshak said.

Pearl looked bewildered.

"You were listing your flaws."

"Oh, I don't know. And then that kid, complaining—"

"Kid? Complaining?"

"Walter never told you?"

Marshak shook his head. "Kids always complain, Philip. They're more likely to complain if you're doing your job right than if you're doing it wrong."

"Oh."

"Word has it you're a fine teacher."

"You're kidding."

Marshak stared at him deadpan.

"I had absolutely no idea what I was doing for—I think at least the first three months," Pearl mused.

"Probably all in your favor," Marshak said. "Make you think about what you're saying instead of just reeling it off mechanically."

"I still get nervous."

"Who doesn't?"

"Wadkin?"

Marshak narrowed his eyes, cleared his throat. "Any other complaints?" he asked. "How's your digestion?"

"Fine."

"Your love life?"

"Ed—"

"Philip, Philip. You take me too seriously. Now. You gonna consider this?"

"I guess I need a day or two to think."

"You got it. One day."

"One?"

"If you turn me down, Philip, I have to start looking for someone else. Pronto."

"Oh."

"Got it?"

"Got it."

"Now." Marshak unfolded his hands and slapped the blotter. "Wanna meet my baby-sitter?"

As if he were moving through a fine mist, Pearl walked across the department and unlocked his door, part of him unable to keep from wondering whether, if he stayed, he might get an office with a window.

"Philly!"

Pearl turned and saw, through the open doorway, Wunsch sitting at his desk. Next to the desk stood a tall, dark-haired girl Pearl had never seen before. She was quite pretty; she might even, Pearl now saw, be beautiful.

"Hello, Walter."

" 'M'ere a second. I want you to meet someone."

"Can't right now, Walter."

"Philly?"

The last thing Pearl saw before he closed his door was Wunsch's eyebrows rising, rising. He sat down at his desk and clasped his hands behind his head.

* * *

The mailman called to him as Pearl crossed the street toward Avalon. Pearl tried to think of a way to avoid the encounter, but in a second the man was standing directly in front of him, sweating, smiling, looking good. His face was tanned; he appeared to have lost weight. Even his posture was better.

"You've been scarce," the mailman said.

"How's the fishing?"

The mailman shook his head knowingly. "Oh, I'm off that."

"You are?"

He made a face. "Catfish, catfish, and more catfish. A bass here and there, but not too damn often. I got so's I was seeing those ugly catfish faces in my sleep." He shuddered. "No, my new game's golf."

"Golf?"

"Great game. Ever tried it?"

"No."

"Hell of a game. You ought to give it a try—put some color in your face. Oh"—he reached into his sack—"here's something for you."

Pearl took the postcard, saw GREETINGS FROM LOS ANGELES *printed, in red, above a photo of a palm tree.*

"My old neck of the woods," the mailman said. "Good golf there, too," the mailman said. "Well—we'll catch you later."

Pearl turned the card over. The message was in black ink, the script slightly childish:

> *Dear Phil,*
> *I'm living in L.A. now, with a friend I met out here.*
> *It's a long story. I just wanted you to know I'm*
> *happy. I think of you sometimes. I hope you find*
> *happiness, too.*

The signature, large, almost alarming, taking up the space left by the paltry message, read: FRANCESCA.

There was no return address.

Pearl sighed and unclasped his hands.

* * *

Juniper's screen porch was packed, the crowd divided evenly between those Pearl knew and those he would never have seen anywhere else: department people and cowboys. The music— steel guitars—was cranked up all the way:

> *Others think highly of things I despise,*
> *I like the Christian life*

As if in announcement of the party theme, Leon towered by the front door, dressed in boots, jeans, and cowboy shirt, holding five cans of a Budweiser six-pack in his right hand. With the left hand, he clapped Pearl on the shoulder.

"Perfesser!"

Pearl smiled and nodded, unable to make himself heard.

"Perfesser!"

Leon kept grinning and slapping his shoulder, in endless approval. How to disengage? It was always Pearl's problem at parties: no sooner was he in the door than he was trying to think of ways to get out. His usual method was to explain; but the noise here made this impossible. In desperation, Pearl gave Leon's hand an extra squeeze, and—stroke of genius!—winked. It worked! It was as if Pearl had found the secret panel. Leon instantly understood. Pearl pushed off easily into the packed foyer. Someone touched his arm.

"Mr. Pearl? I mean Phil?"

Pearl turned. It was Darla, standing hand in hand with a pale tall boy dressed all in black. The boy's red hair was tied in a ponytail.

"You," Pearl said involuntarily.

"Phil," Darla said, "I want you to meet Danny?"

"Hey," Danny said, and grinned. One of his upper front teeth, a canine, was missing.

"You two—" Pearl stopped.

"We're engaged?" Darla grinned, ducked, and blushed.

"You are?" Pearl said.

The two of them nodded, in unison, for a second. Darla ducked her head again. "Well," she said.

Pearl stared at them, momentarily unable to speak.

"Well," Danny said. " 'Bye." They moved backward into the crowd.

"Congratulations," Pearl said, too late to be heard.

He caught sight of Wunsch and Margo, half in shadow in the hallway, and began to wade toward them; but something in Wunsch's expression, and in the tentativeness of Margo's smile, warned him off. Then he saw Wadkin, standing in the shadows by the staircase with the two of them, unsmiling. Pearl was carried sideways by the human current. The noise was nearly insupportable. He felt his ears would be damaged. He would find Juniper, give his regrets, explain he didn't feel well . . . No. He would find Ted, squeeze his hand, and wink. Then disappear into the blessed silence of the Pickett night.

Perhaps, he thought with some excitement, he had at last stumbled upon a new way to live: a life without explanations. Perhaps the concept would even seep its way into his work. Perhaps he would work again. Tonight, however, he was like a bubble in water. Never had he felt less need to stay at a party.

But his host was nowhere to be found: not sitting on the stairway, among the cowboys whispering promises to their cowgirls; not dancing in the den, where Juniper's thousand books sat watching on their shelves in the semidarkness; not around the bowls of chips and stacks of six-packs in the dining room, where a red-faced Perry Armbruster, arguing with a bow-tied Tommy Havens, suddenly caught sight of Pearl and began to wave urgently (Pearl waved back, winked, and walked the other way). Not in the back hall or the bathroom or the bedroom, all packed and clamorous. He came to the rear of the house, and the kitchen door, which was closed. He tried the door, but it wouldn't budge: something on the other side was holding it back. He pushed harder, and whatever it was scraped against the floor, allowing the door to open a foot. Pearl saw a pretty blond woman—an astonishingly beautiful blond woman—and a man in a huge Mexican hat, sitting at the kitchen table, their hands joined. The woman looked up at Pearl and smiled, and then the man in the hat turned around. It was Juniper.

"Hey! Amigo!"

"Ted."

" 'Mon in here, boy."

"I don't want to interrupt."

Juniper got up and pulled aside the heavy carton that leaned against the door, and Pearl walked in. Juniper pushed the box back. "Just a precaution," he said. "My lady and me wanted to be alone for a momentito." And he smiled with such brilliance that the crazy thought flashed through Pearl's mind that Ted had undergone some sort of religious conversion.

"Maybe I'd better go?"

"Go? Hell, no. You just set yourself down right here, Jack." He pointed to a chair.

"Ted, I don't think I—"

Juniper pressed his shoulders down. "Don't *think* nothin'," he said. "Just sit."

The woman looked on with amusement. Close up, she was even more astonishing—her skin and her eyes pale; her hair, long, straight, and sand-colored; her head held erect yet relaxed; her long white hands lying calmly on top of one another. She was like a freak, a freak of perfection. Pearl could both barely look at her and barely stop looking.

"Now," Juniper said. "Phil Pearl, I'd like you to meet Dawn."

XIX

Packed once more, and more fully, if possible, than the first time, the Volvo sat in the Avalon parking lot, inches off the asphalt, in the thick May sun. Pearl's possessions seemed to have multiplied and expanded in the rich Southern air, making the load he had traveled down with almost prim by comparison. Pearl stood, like a figure in a cartoon, scratching his head at a puzzle: the pile of things at his feet still had to get in, and he had no place whatever to put them. He tried to think what he had acquired, over the past nine months, that was taking up so much room: true, there was the vacuum cleaner and the TV, but other than that, only a few pots and pans, some plates and utensils, a couple of books. It didn't figure. The vacuum and the TV weren't even in yet. Now he would simply have to throw things out, as if he were in a balloon losing altitude. What would go first? He didn't like this.

"You gone fit all that in?"

Pearl closed his eyes and took a deep breath. It was the third time this precise question, in these precise words, had been put to him that morning. This time the asker was a skinny boy, barefoot, in cut-off jeans and a Pickett Panthers T-shirt, with a cast on his right ankle.

Pearl stared at the cast for a second. "I am," he said.

"I don't thank you're gonna make it."

"Really."

The boy shook his head. "No way."

Defiantly, Pearl stuffed some towels into a crevice in the back seat. "Well," he said. "I think I will."

"Wanna bet?"

"What?"

"Wanna bet that TV set?"

"No," said Pearl. "I don't."

"Wanna sell it?"

"Sell it?"

"I'll give you twunny-five dollars for it."

"Twenty-five—listen," Pearl said. "That TV's almost new. I bought it six months ago at McKee's for a hundred bucks."

"I'll give you forty. But that's it."

"You expect me to take a sixty-dollar beating on this TV set?"

The boy shrugged. "What else you gone do with it."

Pearl shook his head and tugged a suitcase out of the back seat. "I'm going to fit it in." Grunting and sweating, he was able to wedge the TV carton into the suitcase's place. Now, however, the suitcase sat on the pavement. The boy stared at him, expressionless.

"Listen," Pearl said. "I'll sell you the vacuum cleaner."

"I don't want no vacuum cleaner."

"I got it for forty bucks at Sears in January. I'll give it to you for twenty-five."

"I already got a vacuum cleaner."

"Not like this one, you don't. It's got a light, you can see under furniture."

The boy folded his arms.

"Plus about twelve different nozzles and hoses."

No sale.

"All right," Pearl said. "Suit yourself."

"I'll give you fifty for the TV and the vacuum cleaner."

"Oh no. That's highway robbery."

"Way I look at it, I'd be doin' you a favor."

Pearl stood with his hands on his hips, staring at his gathered things but seeing nothing.

"You'd probably just have to leave 'em anyway. This way, at least you'll have fifty bucks," the boy said.

"Sixty."

The boy shook his head, smiling slightly. "Fifty's top dollar."

"Oh, all right."

He took his wallet out and gave Pearl two twenties and a ten. "You did good, buddy," he said.

"You're going to carry them?" Pearl asked.

The boy raised his hand, and a large white convertible moved from its spot across the street. Its steering belt screeching, its cylinders thrumming, it lumbered into the lot and pulled up to where Pearl and the boy stood. The driver was another boy who looked remarkably like the first one. "Hey," he said to Pearl.

The first boy patted Pearl on the shoulder. "Have a good trip," he said, then, quickly, he loaded the vacuum cleaner and its attachments (this seemed cruelest of all; Pearl remembered discovering the uses of each of the nozzles) and the TV into the trunk, and they drove away.

Pearl stood trying to imagine life without his television set. He looked at the plates and bowls and pots sitting out on the hot asphalt, and he thought of the many times he had used them, of the times *in which* he had used them. He thought of how he had felt then—happy, sad, or hopeful (he had been so hopeful) —and all at once it came to him that he would have to leave them, would, in fact, have to leave everything; that the past was already receding at a terrifying rate, like pavement glanced at from a car going sixty.

"You think you can fit all that in?"

This time he had an answer ready. Then he turned and saw Jewel.

"Hey," she said, softly. She was wearing faded jeans and an odd gauzy something of a blouse, puffed at the shoulders. She seemed not exactly at ease in the clothes, and Pearl realized, even as he stared at her, unbelieving, that it was only the second time he had seen her not in a dress. He put his hand to his chest. "My God," he said.

She shrugged. "Couldn't stay away."

"You made it to New York?"

"For a while."

"What happened?"

"Happened? Not much. I got homesick," she said.

"Homesick?"

"Strange, huh?"

They looked at each other for a long time.

"So this is it for Professor Pearl," she finally said.

He nodded.

"I guess maybe you got homesick, too," Jewel said.

"Sort of."

"Pearl, don't you *ever* feel anything all the way?"

He thought about it for a moment.

"Pearl!"

"Come with me," he said.

"What?"

"Come with me."

"Where'll you fit me?"

"I'll throw it all out."

"Uh-huh."

"I'm serious. Come on. What else do you have planned?"

"Pearl—"

"Come on. It'd be great. I could show you everything."

"Statue of Liberty, Empire State Building—"

"You know that's not what I mean."

"Pearl." She held his chin. "Thank you for the very sweet offer. Really. I do appreciate it." He tried to avert his eyes, but she kept catching them. "Really," she said.

"Yeah."

"The nicest one I've ever had. I'll remember it."

"All right." He was staring off at nothing in particular, the pines across the street moving in the white midday light, their outlines starting to fuzz.

"What are you going to do, Pearl?"

"Do?"

"I mean, besides write poems. You're not gonna go live out in the woods again?"

"I guess I haven't given it much thought."

"Oh, Pearl, what is to be done with you?"

"Search me."

"*Pearl.*"

"What."

She put her fingers on his cheek, turned his head back toward her, and kissed him.

As if impressed with its own weight, the Volvo made its stately way down Jackson Street, like a float in a parade. A one-car parade; one-man, too—not at all the sort of thing Pearl would ever have envisioned for his leavetaking. The afternoon had turned close and light gray, opalescent, all the infinitude of Pickett's blue dome gone, the town turned in upon itself, the place exuding its placeness. And nothing else. The creosote smell had vanished. Pearl had noticed this several weeks before, in the first flush of the blossom time; he had wondered at it. Was it a seasonal phenomenon? Was it, had it always been, simply in his head?

The odor's absence disturbed him oddly. Something in him missed his trouble; something in him even missed this stink. He shook his head at himself.

It made leaving hard, this haze over Pickett. Pearl would not be projected out into the clear ether, the difference between there and here so negligible that he would find himself a hundred miles away before he thought about it; he would have to leave this specific place, all the details of its gas stations and fast-food restaurants and trees and bushes and sidewalks underlined and de-universalized by the clinging gray air. It was awful, really.

Unable to get the stuffed car to go very fast, Pearl rode along the main drag, feeling over and over that his heart was being yanked out by the roots: this thing, that thing, gone, gone, never again. And that person: there, ambling down the sidewalk in front of the campus, James DelRee! Formerly of his Composition class. Second semester; Monday, Wednesday, and Friday afternoons at one o'clock. Sluggish, phlegmatic, round-faced, slow-eyed James DelRee. An enigma. Even after a battery of what Pearl had intended as self-revealing essays, all he knew about this one was that he had been born in Gulfport and liked moto-cross, whatever that was. This was to be the last person Pearl saw? So be it. James DelRee, walking C +, farewell!

The only thing to do, Pearl finally decided, was to look at the road straight in front of him and get out of town. As he reached the turn—the turn he had envisioned making, not alone (oh vanity!), so many times—the light obligingly turned green for him, the very moment he reached it, as if the town were now eager to be rid of him. Pearl swung the car through the turn cautiously, weightily, from right lane east to right lane north, and eased the gas pedal to the floor.

The Volvo picked up speed to forty, forty-five, fifty. In twenty-five hours, plus stops, he would be on the Jersey Turnpike. He passed under the footbridge on which he had first seen, as he came into town, WELCOME TO PICKETT – HOME OF THE

PSU PANTHERS. He remembered vividly how the sign had looked that first day, when everything had been unknown, when all was possibility. He glanced up into the mirror to see the sign once more, but all he saw was his piled possessions. He quickly looked at the outside mirror, but the bridge was now too far back. It was all too far back—receding, faster than memory.

With a feeling of panic, Pearl pulled off the highway onto the shoulder. He was sweating; his heart was thudding. He sat for a while, thinking nothing. Then he got out and stood on the gravel of the shoulder, the wind from the northbound cars and trucks blowing in his face. *What's wrong with you?* he thought. He no longer knew or cared. He got back into the car and, craning his neck out the window, looked carefully down the road, making sure the way was clear. Then he pulled out onto the pavement. He accelerated slowly, feeling the engine work. The air shooting in the window was cool and wet. He was going home. He glanced in the mirror, then eased from the right lane to the left. As he approached the turnaround on the grassy median, he slowed down one last time.

A NOTE ON THE TYPE

The text of this book was set in Garamond No. 3, a modern rendering of the type first cut by Claude Garamond (c. 1480–1561). Garamond was a pupil of Geoffroy Tory and is believed to have based his letters on the Venetian models, although he introduced a number of important differences, and it is to him we owe the letter which we know as "old style." He gave to his letters a certain elegance and a feeling of movement that won for their creator an immediate reputation and the patronage of Francis I of France.

Composed by PennSet, Inc., Bloomsburg, Pennsylvania. Printed and bound by Fairfield Graphics, Fairfield, Pennsylvania. Typography by Julie Duquet.